A Merry Little Meet Cute

Julie Murphy is the #1 *New York Times* bestselling author of young adult and middle grade novels such as *Dear Sweet Pea*; *Pumpkin*; *Puddin'*; *Ramona Blue*; *Side Effects May Vary*; *Faith: Taking Flight*; *Faith: Greater Heights*; and *Dumplin'* (now a Netflix original film starring Jennifer Aniston). She is also the author of Disney's reimagining of Cinderella: *If the Shoe Fits*. Her books have been translated into more than fifteen languages.

When she's not writing, she can be found watching made-for-TV movies, hunting for the perfect slice of cheese pizza, reliving her glory days as a librarian, or planning her next great travel adventure. Julie lives in North Texas with her husband, who loves her; her dog, who adores her; and her cats, who tolerate her.

Sierra Simone is the *USA Today* and *Wall Street Journal* bestselling author of contemporary and historical romance, including *Priest*, *American Queen*, and *Misadventures of a Curvy*

Girl. Her work has been featured in BuzzFeed, *Cosmopolitan* magazine, *Entertainment Weekly*, and *Marie Claire*.

Her preromance jobs have included firing ceramics; teaching living history in a one-room schoolhouse in full 1904-approved schoolmarm attire; and working as a librarian for several years—not in that order. She lives in the Kansas City area with her husband, two children, and two giant dogs.

This is Julie and Sierra's first book together. You can find out more at julieandsierra.com.

A Merry Little Meet Cute

JULIE MURPHY and SIERRA SIMONE

HarperCollins*Publishers*

HarperCollins*Publishers* Ltd
1 London Bridge Street,
London SE1 9GF
www.harpercollins.co.uk

HarperCollins*Publishers*
Macken House, 39/40 Mayor Street Upper,
Dublin 1, D01 C9W8, Ireland

First published in the United States by Avon, an imprint of HarperCollins*Publishers* 2022

This edition published by HarperCollins*Publishers* 2022
3

Designed by Diahann Sturge
Map by Diahnn Sturge
Illustrations and art throughout © EVA105, Nikitina Olga, Gabi Wolf, Bonezboyz, Nemanja Cosovic,
unturtle, Lemberg Vector studio, aliaksei kruhlenia, Modvector, GoodStudio, bomg, fourSage, GN.
Studio, MicroOne, Vectorpocket, ibom, In-Finity / Shutterstock

With thanks to Curtis, R. (Director), 2003, *Love Actually*, Universal Pictures, StudioCanal,
Working Title Films, DNA Films, for Sam's line, quoted in the epigraph.

A catalogue record for this book is available from the British Library

ISBN: 978-0-00-858046-9

Set in Garamond 3 LT Std

Printed and bound in the UK using 100% Renewable Electricity by CPI Group (UK) Ltd

To Bob Murphy and Doug Hagen.
You've always been like fathers
to us. (And we love you, but you
probably shouldn't read this one!)

Let's go get the shit kicked out of us by love.

—Sam, *Love Actually*

This year, you're my only wish;
babe, you're on my naughty list.

—INK, "Naughty List," *Merry INKmas*

(Bootcamp Records)

WELCOME TO

Christmas Notch

VERMONT

The Mansion

Holy Night
Chapel

Edelweiss Inn

TINSEL LANE

SUGAR PLUM AVENUE

MAIN STREET

Frosty's Diner

FROSTY'S

BETHLEHEM STREET

CHESTNUT CLOSE

Production
Office

SILVER BELLS BLVD.

Kringle's

Town Hall

Mistletoe
Theater

HOLLY GROVE

BAR

The
Dirty Snowball

TOY SHOP

Toy Shop

NORTH
POLE

A Merry Little Meet Cute

Teddy Ray Fletcher

A tusk?" he repeated, just to make sure he'd heard right.

"A *wooden* tusk," the voice clarified. Teddy heard the whoosh of traffic and the sound of a car door closing. Why was it that managers and agents were always going places when they called? Did they save all their phone calls for their commutes?

"Three broken arms, two broken legs, and five concussions between the four of them," Steph D'Arezzo finished over the hum of an accelerating car.

Teddy looked down at his desk, an acrylic thing his ex-wife had gotten him from IKEA before the divorce.

A very stressful production schedule looked back up at him.

He looked away from it, trying to focus on the picture of his two kids grinning from within his arms, their tiny hands clutching the tiny pumpkins he'd bought for them at the pumpkin patch that day. They used to be so little. And so inexpensive.

"Okay, so you're telling me that my entire costume and hair team went into the desert and stood under a wooden tusk, which then collapsed on top of them. And now they can't work on the movie, which starts *tomorrow*."

"Costume team, hair team, *and* your gaffer, Teddy. And there's no need to sound so judgmental about the wooden tusk. It was on a giant wooden walrus sculpture, after all. Don't you know anything about festivals? Haven't you been to Burning Man?"

Teddy squinted at the far wall in his tiny office, trying to imagine the fast-talking, suit-wearing, phone-addicted Steph D'Arezzo doing drugs in the desert. "Have *you* been to Burning Man?"

"We were all in our twenties once. No, don't take the five right now, are you even looking at your GPS?"

Teddy assumed she was talking to an Uber driver and ignored the last comment. "So they were at Burning Man?"

"No, this was *better* than Burning Man," she said. "It was UnFestival in Terlingua."

"UnFestival? I've never heard of it."

"Of course you haven't," Steph said dismissively. "It's exclusive."

"Ah," he said. "Invite only."

"No, Teddy, it's *un*invite only."

"Okay. Uninvite only to UnFestival. Where a wooden walrus fell on my crew."

"Just the tusk," she clarified. "Will it stop dinging at me if

I put on my seat belt? Oh good. And the walrus was part of the Alice in Wonderland theme, Teddy. It wasn't just a random wooden walrus out on a mesa."

She scoffed as if *that* would be bananas.

"And how do you know all this before I do?" he asked.

"Ah, well, about that," Steph said, and it was in that brisk *I have some bad news* voice that all managers seemed to have.

Teddy's butthole clenched.

"I heard because it came bundled with another thing. I got a call from Winnie's agent, and she's going to call you later tonight when she knows more, but she wanted to put me and your male lead in the know, in case the story broke over social media before then. Winnie's in the hospital right now."

Shit.

Winnie Baker was a wholesome child star turned wholesome made-for-TV-movie actress, and she was going to be one of the leads in his first-ever Christmas movie production. More importantly, she was the star his director had specifically *chosen* to work with to make her directorial debut, and Teddy had to keep his director happy, because she made the Hope Channel happy.

And getting *Duke the Halls* distributed by Hope—and their new streaming platform Hopeflix—was the only thing that could turn Teddy's desperate Christmas movie gamble into real money. God knew his day job making cheap pornography wasn't paying for his son's art school tuition or his daughter's startup making carbon-neutral sex toys.

And Christmas movies couldn't be that hard to make, right? They were *almost* like porn. The scripts were on the flimsy side and the production times were shorter than a community college wintermester.

But now the wooden tusk. Now no Winnie Baker.

But Teddy wasn't a total asshole, so the first question he asked was "Is Winnie okay?"

"She'll be *fiiine*," Steph said, in a voice that clearly conveyed how much she cared. "The word is that it was an ayahuasca ceremony gone wrong—also at UnFestival. Do you know how easy it is to get dehydrated on the mesa? Even before you start shitting yourself? Anyway, she's in the hospital now and hooked up to all sorts of IVs. Her agent thinks another few days and then a discharge with strict instructions to rest."

"So no movie for her," Teddy said numbly.

"No movie for her. By the way, if anyone asks, she's being treated for exhaustion. *Not* for puking in a tent full of vegans and DJs."

Right. No one would want sweet Winnie Baker's reputation tarnished—and Teddy definitely didn't want the movie tarnished by association. No, he needed his new production company to appear five thousand percent aboveboard, so that no one would dig too hard and find out that Teddy Ray Fletcher was the same man who owned Uncle Ray-Ray's, a porn studio specializing in—well, less stuff than it used to, now that his daughter was in her twenties and spent every family meal lecturing him about creating ethical mission statements. Last Thanksgiving, she and his son made him identify Uncle Ray-Ray's core values.

Core. Values.

"So if I were you," Steph went on, "I'd round up your director and get that shit recast ASAP. Sweet baby *Jesus*, did you see that? And on a unicycle! Only in Silver Lake, am I right?"

Assuming that Steph was talking to her Uber driver again, Teddy wisely chose not to answer, already stuffing everything on his desk related to *Duke the Halls* into his briefcase—another present from his ex-wife.

He was going to fix this. He was going to juggle Fletcher Productions and Uncle Ray-Ray's so smoothly that no one from the Christmas movie would ever, ever know about his career making porn. He had not figured out how to make separate IMDb accounts (*and* how to furtively use his great aunt Phyllis's address for a new LLC) for nothing!

I can fix this, he told himself as he forced the briefcase closed and bolted for the door. *I can still make this work.*

After all, how hard could it be to keep his two worlds separate?

THREE HOURS LATER, Teddy was sitting across from his director in an airport Chili's Too glowing with chili pepper string lights and mini Christmas trees at every table. He was trying to pull folders out of his briefcase while also choking down a molten-hot mozzarella stick.

"Are you okay?" she asked. "You're flushed."

Teddy fumbled some folders on the table and then dabbed at his forehead with his napkin, hoping he wasn't sweating too much. His pale complexion showed every degree of flush and every stipple of sweat. It made him self-conscious.

"This is stressful stuff, but nothing we can't handle," he said, trying to sound smooth and in control. He'd dealt with any number of porn catastrophes in his day, but unfortunately, the stakes were a bit higher here than having to recast a performer with hemorrhoids. "Obviously, it's less than ideal having to make this decision in the airport right before your plane leaves for Vermont, but ayahuasca is unpredictable."

"Words to live by." The director sighed. She was already pulling his folders across the table over to her side. Even as she sat in a booth made of vinyl and old crumbs, there was no hiding that indefinable celebrity aura she gave off. Gretchen Young had high cheekbones, flashing eyes, and warm medium brown skin—all of it finished off by long, waist-length twists, a nose piercing, and casual overalls that had probably cost as much as his watch.

"And how hard do you think it will be to get someone else to Vermont in time?" she asked, spreading the headshots across the table. "There were a few other women whom I liked at the audition, but with the shoot happening over the holidays and the short notice . . ."

"We'll make it work," Teddy said with a confidence he absolutely did not have. For one thing, the turnarounds on these Christmas movies were *tight*. Two weeks—three at the most. And with the actual filming set to begin in two days, he'd have to get their new actress out to Vermont by tomorrow, or the day after at the latest. While *Duke the Halls* wasn't exactly written in iambic pentameter, he assumed Winnie's replacement would want a day or so to read over the script and familiarize herself with the story.

And for another, *worse* thing, the little Vermont town where Gretchen wanted to shoot the movie—Christmas Notch—

had only one opening in its little Vermont schedule: during the actual, literal Christmas season. And while they wouldn't be shooting on the twenty-fifth, they'd be right back to work on the twenty-sixth, meaning that whoever took Winnie's role would have to be okay with potentially missing Christmas at home.

Jesus. He needed another mozzarella stick. He shoved the breaded lava into his mouth and tried to remember that thing his son had told him about mindful breathing.

"*Fuck*," Gretchen breathed suddenly. "Who is she? We didn't see her at the audition, did we?"

"Uh," Teddy said through his mouthful of food, racking his brain.

"I don't think I've ever seen a headshot with nipples before," Gretchen added thoughtfully.

The horror slid through him in slow motion, as hot and gooey as the burning mozzarella lodged in his throat. He lowered his eyes to the table and saw what Gretchen was looking at: a picture that had most definitely *not* come from the *Duke the Halls* folder. He mentally rewound to three hours ago, when he had been shoving any and all folder-like objects into his briefcase, flustered and hurrying like hell so he could catch Gretchen before her flight.

And now here he was, looking at a still from Uncle Ray-Ray's latest porn shoot and not a headshot for *Duke the Halls*.

Gretchen traced a long finger over the woman's face. "She definitely wasn't at the audition. I'd remember her. Who is she?"

Teddy tried to put his hand over the rest of the folder—if she kept going through these pictures, she was going to see more than just nipples—and sound completely and totally nonchalant. Like this was no big deal. Like Gretchen didn't have her finger on a picture of one of the hottest alt-porn stars of their time.

"She's very talented," Teddy said, the nonchalance difficult to muster as he coughed down some stubborn mozzarella. "But she normally does edgier stuff. You know"—he cast around for the right nonporn word—"provocative. Artistic risks and stuff. Not really Hopeflix fare."

"She's exactly what I want," Gretchen said, still looking at the photo. "She's perfect for the part of Felicity."

"Uh . . ."

"I want her," Gretchen repeated, looking up at Teddy. "I want her in my movie. What's her name?"

He almost said her stage name and then caught himself at the last moment. "Bee Hobbes. But you haven't even seen her act yet," he protested weakly.

"Do you think she has a reel up on her website?" Gretchen asked. "I'll Google her."

Teddy had a sudden, queasy vision of her Googling Bee Hobbes and somehow landing upon Bianca von Honey. And Uncle Ray-Ray's.

"No need to Google," he said quickly. "I've worked with her before and she's brilliant. But maybe we should have some other backup options, in case she can't . . ."

"No, it needs to be her," Gretchen said, shaking her head, looking down at the picture again. "I want a degree of edginess; I want there to be something dangerous in the way the actors play Pearl's script."

Pearl Purkiss was the screenwriter for *Duke the Halls*—and Gretchen Young's girlfriend—and was in Christmas Notch now, preparing for a movie that didn't currently have a female lead. "We could find another edgy person," Teddy attempted valiantly, "if we just take a quick look at the other folder—"

"I hope," Gretchen said coolly, "that you're not balking because she's plus-size?"

"What? No!" Teddy worked with Bee all the time! She was gorgeous and filthy and great for business! But she couldn't be in a chaste-as-hell Christmas movie. For the flipping *Hope Channel*. What if she was recognized? What if Teddy Ray Fletcher was revealed to be a purveyor of porn and then *poof* went this fledgling Hopeflix partnership and his son the artist had to be a barista two years too early?

"I just think that we should maybe pick some alternates in case she's . . . busy," Teddy finally said.

"If we don't get her, then I don't even know," Gretchen said, closing her eyes in a way that sent alarm bells ringing through him. Alarm bells that shrieked, *Keep Gretchen happy so you can keep Hopeflix interested.* "I already lost Winnie. Another disappointment so soon . . ."

The alarm bells got louder.

Would it really be so bad? Teddy asked himself desperately. Would it really be so dangerous to have Bee in the movie?

She'd been begging him to cast her in something ever since he dreamed up this Christmas studio scheme last year, and she would have just as much to lose if her porn career came back to haunt her. And besides, how much did Hopeflix's audience really overlap with the feminist porn watchers? What tattooed, fair trade coffee drinkers with their body-safe silicone toys were also tuning in to sexless holiday schmaltz?

It might be okay, it really might. And if it was okay, if this *did* work, then perhaps he'd just stumbled upon an easy solution for any future casting problems. It was already giving him ideas for how to fill the holes in his production team created by the rogue wooden tusk.

"I'll reach out to her tonight," Teddy promised. "Why don't you, um, keep this folder here"—he carefully pushed the real *Duke the Halls* folder under her fingertips—"in case she can't."

"I hope she can," said Gretchen. "I get a really good energy from her picture. Very open, you know?"

Teddy stopped himself from making the obvious *very open* joke, stress ate another mozzarella stick, and then gestured for the check.

FINALLY, OUT IN the airport parking lot, he set his briefcase in the passenger seat of his minivan, did some mindful breathing that didn't help, and dialed Bee as he stared at a stray cat licking its paws on top of a Tesla.

"Hello?" answered Bee.

"I hope you're sitting down right now," Teddy said.

I know I am, he thought grimly.

CHAPTER ONE

Bee

"I think six bottles of flavored lube might be overkill," I told Sunny.

She nodded as she plucked two from the bundle clutched to her chest and threw them on my bed. "You're right. Six is overkill. Four is the sweet spot. I'm cutting grape and French toast from the lineup. Honestly, what was I thinking including grape in the first place? No one chooses grape lube when there are other options. It's the Pepsi of flavored lubes. And French toast is really more of an acquired taste."

"S, I don't think I'm going to need any flavored lubes at all on the set of *Duke the Halls*. This is Hopeflix we're talking about. If my grandmother's stack of pioneer romance novels and megachurch energy had a baby, it still wouldn't be as squeaky clean as the Hope Channel."

Sunny plopped down on the floor in a sea of dildos, butt plugs, silk ties, harnesses, Ben Wa balls, pocket rockets, anal beads, paddles, ball gags, and vibrating cock rings. Shortly after I found out I was being shipped off to Vermont to star in my very first nonporn film as part of Teddy's venture into wholesome Christmas movies, I dumped out my suitcases, which just so happened to double as storage for my collection of toys, and started packing. And sure, two full suitcases of sex toys might be a bit much, but these are not only essential tools, they're also a tax write-off in my line of work.

"Bee, what if there's an emergency?" Sunny asked. "And you're lubeless?"

She had a point. "One," I said. "Sugar cookie flavored."

She rolled her eyes and tossed the bottle in with my toiletries. "Did you grab the fuzzy pink sweater out of my closet?"

This was one of the benefits of having a friend I could actually share clothing with for the first time in my life. I thumbed through the stack of leggings, jeans, and shirts I'd set aside. "Not yet. Uh, what time is it?"

She checked her phone as she stood and pulled the towel off her head, her damp black hair cascading over her olive shoulders. Colorful tattoos peeked from between the inky curls as she bounced back on the bed. "We've got forty-five minutes before we have to leave for the airport and I told my dad I'd be there in time to light the menorah, so get to packing, baby!"

Sunny was my best friend, roommate, and self-appointed shepherd through the endless hole-in-the-wall L.A. and surrounding area Mexican joints, and her grandmother was my chocolate chip challah bread pudding dealer. We met on the set of my first scene. Even though she did porn, she also worked as a makeup artist and was part of the crew on set that day. I was excited, but terrified. ClosedDoors had always just been me and my camera. That first day on set was the first time I'd let go of some control. She immediately calmed my nerves when she'd said, "This whole shoot is for you, Bee. You're the star of this show. Own it."

And she hadn't been entirely wrong. After I blew up on ClosedDoors, a paid subscription app that was basically a hybrid of Facebook and Instagram, but much more . . . naked, Teddy Ray Fletcher reached out to me with an offer to sign a deal with his porn production company. I got lucky with Teddy. He was one of the good ones. The offer wasn't exclusive. I could work with other production companies and keep my ClosedDoors account active.

My first scene was the top performing video for Teddy that year and even won me a newcomer of the year nomination at the AVN Awards. (Of course, I didn't actually win. It would be too much to let the fat girl actually win. Sunny wrote a scathing Instagram post about body-size disparity in adult films. It was TED Talk levels of good.)

When Teddy landed the Hope Channel contract, I begged him for months to let me have a crack at one of his Christmas movies. I could play the dowdy sister or the dress shop owner. Hell, even Caroler Number 3 would be something.

But he told me over and over again that there would be no crossing of streams when it came to filthy porn and wholesome

Christmas content, which is why I never expected him to call two and a half weeks before Christmas and tell me he needed me in Vermont in twelve hours to take on the role of Felicity in *Duke the Halls* and replace *the* Winnie Baker.

In fact, I almost didn't answer his call.

Teddy didn't know how to text. Or so he claimed. Sunny said she once saw him respond to a text from his ex-wife with the flame emoji, but that was no better than folklore in the unbelievable history of Teddy Ray Fletcher. Which is why I almost sent him to voicemail when I saw his face (a picture of him sleeping in a director's chair on set while people were literally fucking in front of him) light up my screen.

Teddy called for the kinds of things that could easily be communicated in a text: Because there was an accident on I-10 and he wanted me to take some confusing route through the hills, and he didn't trust my maps app to direct me around traffic. Or because he needed ideas for Astrid's or Angel's birthday. He called because he'd stopped for coffee and couldn't remember if I drank "cow milk or that vegan nut shit." He called because my moms were hounding him about sending DVD copies of my latest scene—not for them to watch, but for them to keep in their Little Bee Hall of Fame.

Teddy definitely did not call because he'd accidentally cast me in a Christmas movie as part of his attempt to diversify his portfolio/go legit. (Porn, by the way, was very legit. Just ask the retirement account I started at the behest of my mothers when I was only twenty years old.)

When he told me I'd be going to Vermont, I had to set

the actual phone down while he continued to stress spiral on the line.

"Teddy," I said, finally picking up the phone again, "give me ten minutes. I need to think."

"Five," he demanded, the defeat in his voice palpable.

I wasted a whole minute trying to call Sunny, but she was on an early morning shoot and not in the . . . position to answer her phone.

Growing up, I'd always loved being onstage. In fact, I've spent a lot of time wondering who I might be today if I hadn't become instantly suburban famous in twelfth grade for posting my tits on Instagram before Tanner Dunn could beat me to it. That asshat. But now that the opportunity to not only be in *Duke the Halls* but to star in it was here, I felt frozen with indecision. What if I couldn't pull this off? What if my costar, Nolan Shaw, just walked right off the set after finding out I'd be replacing Winnie? I was a porn star—an adult film darling! Teddy must have been losing his mind if he'd actually cast me in his Christmas movie. Even if I'd asked—no, begged—him to.

And there it was. I *had* asked him. I wanted this in my gut. And if I'd learned anything since putting my titties on Instagram six years ago, it was that I should trust my instincts.

Exactly four minutes later, I called Teddy back. "I'm in."

"Okay," he said as he smacked on his nicotine gum so loudly I could practically smell the minty flavor through the speaker of my phone. "There's gonna be some rules. And not the kind of rules that you and Sunny break for shits and giggles. I'm talking real rules, Bee. The kind that could actually ruin me and this idiotic venture if they're broken."

"Okay," I told him, feeling my inner teenager rear her angsty head.

"I'm serious."

"I said okay."

"Fuck me," he muttered. "Not literally."

I bit back a smirk. In my business, that was a really important distinction to make.

TRUE LOVE WAS driving someone to LAX, and Sunny had proved her love for me on many occasions, but the traffic today was especially heinous.

"Shit," I whispered as I dug through my backpack. "I forgot my charger."

"Check your side pocket," she said calmly. "And the charger for your laptop should work for Rod too."

"Rod! I can't believe I almost forgot."

She nodded. "Leave no vibrator behind."

With chargers resolved, I slid the backpack down between my legs and leaned my head against the headrest, closing my eyes and taking a breather. Doubt washed over me the moment my brain began to quiet. This was an awful idea. I knew it deep down. My intuition was too good. I always felt the truth in my gut, even when it was the kind of truth I didn't want to face. And this was one of those truths.

I loved my job in the adult industry. It was a big middle finger to everyone who ever told me I had a pretty face or that no one would want a body like mine. But it was more than that.

My job fulfilled me. It made me feel powerful. In control. It gave me community. Family, even. But Teddy's new venture with Hopeflix had reawoken dreams I'd put to bed before I could even verbalize them. I'd wanted to be an actress since first grade when I had my first speaking role in the school's production of *Charlotte's Web*. ("Look at that pig!")

It was a few years, though, before I was faced with the realities of being the fat girl with leading-lady aspirations. Eventually, my dreams faded. When it came to acting, it was easier to leave it entirely than watch from the sidelines. It was one clean heartbreak instead of lots of tiny cracks.

But now as an older, more sure version of myself, I wanted to take back the dreams that were stolen from me simply because some high school theater teacher couldn't imagine someone like me getting the guy or saving the day. And everyone in porn—especially women—had an expiration date. I couldn't help but think this might be good groundwork for future Bee. And yet, I had a hard time imagining how I would even pull this off.

"This is a bad idea," I finally blurted as we saw our first sign for LAX. "I need to call Teddy and tell him he'll have to find someone else. And Nolan Shaw! I haven't even wrapped my head around the fact that I'm supposed to be costarring with Nolan Shaw."

Sunny let out an excited shriek. "Do you think it's best to come clean about the INK shrine above your childhood bed before or after you finish filming?"

"Sunny! This is not something to joke about!"

"You used to jack off to the ex–boy band member you're

about to star in a time-traveling Christmas movie with. Oh, and you're a porn star. That is prime joke material."

I let out a soft whimper as I gripped the center console. We needed to go home. We needed to turn this car around.

"Okay, okay," she said, pulling off on a random exit and into a gas station that had a big sign reading PARKING LOT KARAOKE SATURDAY NIGHT. She slid the car into park and took her seat belt off so she could face me and give me her full attention. "You once did a sex scene on a Jet Ski. With a life jacket on. You can do this, Bee. And I've seen those videos and pictures your moms showed us when you took me home for Thanksgiving that one year. Little Bee was a total theater nerd. Little Bee is liv*ing* for this moment."

"Adult Bee is too," I said softly. "But I'm scared. I'm scared I'll fail. I'm scared I'll meet Nolan and he'll be an asshole, or I'm scared he'll meet me and be one of those awful piece of shit guys who are like 'fat chicks need not apply'—"

"Okay, first off. Fuck that potential version of Nolan Shaw. You are a goddess and there are literal human beings in your inbox who would pay to clean your house for you."

"I know, I know, I know. But it's just . . . God, I loved him back in the day. I still have INK in my playlist rotation. But . . . he's expecting Winnie Baker, Sunny. Not Bee Hobbes, total unknown."

"To him," she muttered, and then in her this-is-all-fine-everything-is-under-control-these-nipple-clamps-aren't-stuck-they're-just-stubborn voice, she said, "Listen, I heard Winnie wasn't the only person taken out by UnFestival. Some crew members were there with her, and you're not the only replace-ment Teddy had to come up with on the fly. So there will be friendly faces too. That'll help. And you'll have me. I'll text so much you'll want to bury your phone in a foot of snow."

"Not possible," I said. "Okay, well, maybe a little possible. But what other porn people? Anyone I know?"

She shrugged as she put her seat belt back on and shifted the car into drive, deeming my crisis averted. "I'm not to-tally sure. I heard he was trying to get ahold of some people, but with Christmas coming up, the pickings were slim. So it sounds like it might be a mix of old- and new-school people."

"Okay, okay. That makes me feel . . . better."

She pulled back onto the highway and took the next exit for LAX.

"Oh no, wait. What are you going to do for Christmas?" I asked. "Fuck. What am I going to tell my moms?"

"Bee. Shut up. You know you're my favorite gentile, and I never even did anything for Christmas before I met you."

"False."

"Okay. I did do one and a half Christmases with Cooper before we broke up, but those don't count. His parents open presents on Christmas Eve. Who does that? Isn't Christmas Day the whole point for you people? And your moms—they'll be fine. Hell, maybe I'll go home to your place for Christmas and live it up as an only child."

"My helicopter moms would actually love that. I assure you."

The ginormous white LAX sign cast a shadow over the road as we pulled into the airport and took the signs for Terminal 4.

My brain began to revisit the remaining list of all the reasons why I should not do this. "What if someone finds out I do porn?"

"Okay. This has two possible outcomes. The first and most likely scenario is that no one finds out. The people who watch those vanilla-ass excuses for movies are definitely not the same people who have *Bianca von Honey underwear for sale* in their search history."

"I don't sell my underwear," I clarified.

"Semantics," she said. "But don't pretend you're above it."

"Fair. Okay, what's the second, scarier, much more awful scenario?" I asked.

"The second scenario is that the people at Hopeflix find out about the job you openly do on the internet."

She said it so simply, but it wasn't quite that uncomplicated. There was Teddy to consider. And Nolan, even. The Hope Channel and what they might do when they found out. They were the kind of company that had morality clauses in their contracts, so I didn't think they'd super love finding out how creative I'd been with ropes and condom-covered cucumbers in the past.

"There's Teddy," Sunny said, pointing to a man waiting outside the terminal wearing cargo shorts and a Hawaiian shirt, with a briefcase wedged between his feet like he was nervous someone might steal all of his very important papers with all the same information he could easily find on his phone if he only knew how to use it.

He began to walk toward us the moment he saw Sunny's baby-blue nine-year-old Toyota Prius covered in unmistakable bumper stickers like MY OTHER RIDE IS A DILDO and DON'T YOU WISH YOUR GIRLFRIEND WAS PAGAN LIKE ME?

Sunny put the car in park, despite the crushing traffic behind us, and got out to help me with my bags, which barely fit in a trunk that was roughly the size of my back pocket.

"You're gonna kill it, Bee," she whispered over the honking horns. "You're a star. Don't forget it. Nolan Shaw won't know what hit him."

"I love you, I love you, I love you," I whispered back. "But you have to let me go before someone kills us with their Tesla."

"Fuck your Tesla," Sunny shouted over my shoulder to no one and everyone, and then to me, she said, "I packed an extra travel-size lube in your backpack. In case of emergency."

CHAPTER TWO

Nolan

Christmas Notch, Vermont, was still technically and legally an actual town, but it was hard to remember that when I was dodging chattering extras, crew members laden with equipment, and one very harried production assistant on my way into the Hope Channel production office.

Nestled against the picturesque backdrop of snowy mountains and pristine forest, the small town was a pretty clutch of brick buildings, glass-fronted shops, and gorgeous Victorian houses. Ornate streetlamps lined the small roads, trees spread snow-covered branches everywhere, and, like a glittering ribbon wrapped around a gift box, a pretty, splashing creek ran along the edge of the town. It looked like a place from a postcard, which was why the Hope Channel set so many movies there—enough movies that the town's entire economy hinged on hosting their productions and had for several years. Which meant even when it wasn't the holidays, Christmas Notch stayed in Christmas mode year-round. There were always garlands strung from the windows and lights strung in the trees. The colossal outdoor Christmas tree never left the town square, and Christmas music played in every store, restaurant, and café no matter the season.

Everything about Christmas Notch was artificial and curated, but that didn't bother me in the least. I was used to artificial and curated—I'd started my career in a reality-show boy band, after all.

What did bother me was the constant, incessant reminder of just how goddamn wholesome this whole venture was, and how very *not* wholesome I was.

Focus, Nolan. It's going to be fine. Everyone makes mistakes and all that.

I mean, not everyone gets caught in a hotel room with the sweetheart of American figure skating, along with two Dutch speed skaters and a minitrampoline. And *definitely* not everyone precedes an international Olympic scandal with weeklong parties featuring fountains of single-malt Scotch and naked mimes. And *oh my god*, this movie was already a giant mistake. All of this was a giant mistake. I should get on a plane back to Kansas City right now and forget this stupid idea of rehabbing Nolan Shaw's tarnished reputation. It was never going to work, *it was never going to work*—

My phone buzzed in my pocket, and my mind instantly dropped every thought that wasn't about my family. I'd spent the night awake on the phone with Mom, but what if today was another hard day? What if she'd needed something, and I hadn't gotten it for her?

I stopped walking and hurried to pull my phone out of my pocket, my chest flooding with hot-cold panic as I fumbled my way to my messages. My sister's latest text glowed up from the screen:

Mads: Mom's sleeping now. Barb is here with Snapple.

Barb was our next-door neighbor, and she was an angel sent from heaven. (Snapple was her dog, and a demon.) Without Barb, I didn't know what we'd do when Mom was having a rough time. I wouldn't be able to go to work, and Maddie wouldn't be able to go to school. I definitely wouldn't be able to travel to Vermont as part of a moonshot scheme to somehow turn me into the kind of *People*-magazine-friendly celebrity who got considered for lucrative gigs judging TV contests and stuff.

I texted Maddie and then put my phone back in my pocket, my acute panic fading into the low-key but constant worry I had whenever I couldn't see her and Mom with my own two eyes. With Maddie, I only had the usual older brother fears that she would repeat all my mistakes, but with Mom . . .

Well, Mom was a different story.

I exhaled and tugged at the beanie covering my hair. I had to make this work. Not because I cared about being on judging panels or starring in a slew of made-for-TV movies, but because the INK money was gone—lost with our skeevy manager when he split town all those years ago—and my job working for my local community theater wasn't enough to cover everything we needed.

And Mom couldn't work, and Maddie was in high school, and I had no degrees, no real skills, nothing except a decent voice and a face people liked, and if that was all I had to work with to make sure Mom and Maddie were comfortable, then so be it. I would make it happen.

Which meant I had to be on time for this meeting with Gretchen if I wanted to make a good impression. If I wanted to show her that she hadn't made a mistake casting a famously irresponsible, washed-up pop star as the hero in her movie.

The production office was on the opposite end of town from the inn where the cast and crew were staying, but as Christmas Notch was only four blocks wide, it wasn't a long walk. And while it was definitely cold—the kind of cold that made me want to dunk my entire body into a vat of hot cocoa, and not in a fun, kinky way—the town's sheltered position in the mountains meant there wasn't much wind, so that was one good thing.

I arrived ten minutes early, which was, like, the first time I'd ever been that early to anything ever in my life, and I let myself inside the large house that had been converted into a production office. It was one of those Victorian mansions that looked like a giant dollhouse, with lacy wooden trim and a big front porch. Even in daylight, I could see electric candles glowing from the tall windows and a Christmas tree winking from the very top window above the door. Ridiculous.

And the minute I walked inside, I collided with a woman in

a long floral dress and snow boots. She had a fair, freckled complexion and a blond messy bun that was genuinely messy, and she wore big, square-framed glasses that dominated her entire face. When I caught her elbow to steady her, she beamed dreamily up at me.

I was pretty sure this was Pearl Purkiss, the screenwriter.

"Gretchen!" she called. "The duke has arrived!"

A LOT OF former teen stars were royal fuckups, like me.

Gretchen Young was not a royal fuckup.

Not only did she have an Oscar under her fashionable vegan leather belt, but after she'd retired from acting, she'd spent her time doing good and worthy things, like meditating and climate activism and also adopting rescue dogs that she didn't even make wear kerchiefs for Instagram pictures.

And now that she was back in the business, it would've been easy for her to have a dismissive attitude toward something as superficial as a Hope Channel movie, but she didn't. She was serious and committed and earnest as hell as we walked through Christmas Notch, and it made me very, very aware that I didn't exactly have a public history of being serious or committed to anything ever.

"Most of where we'll be working is along Main Street," Gretchen said, stopping at the edge of the town square. A crew member was laying down track for a camera trolley on the sidewalk while a woman walked a big, snuffling dog down the shoveled path through the middle. "There will be a few scenes here in the square. The diner is just this way—there will be a scene with the duke and Felicity there—and also, this isn't for the movie, but if you want a good drink with no frills, the Dirty Snowball is just off Sugar Plum Avenue down that way. And two blocks south is the old toy shop. It's not actually a toy shop," she added, seeing the question in my face. "It's where hair and makeup will be. Costuming too."

"I meant to ask about that," I said. "My manager said something about an accident with some of the crew? At the same festival where Winnie got sick?"

Gretchen nodded. "But Teddy Fletcher is sending us replacements for the four injured crew. They should be here by today—including the new costume designer. You'll want to get the duke's costumes squared away with him ASAP. I know the old designer already had some costumes shipped, but she never made it here herself, so who knows where they are inside the costume department."

"I'll check in with the new person once we're done," I assured her, feeling like a student trying to impress a teacher for extra credit. I needed all the extra credit I could get. "Is there anything else you'd like me to do?"

"Actually, yes," Gretchen said—and right then, my phone started ringing. With an old INK song.

Which was a little embarrassing.

"I'm so, so sorry," I said, pulling out my phone to glance at the screen as the opening bars of "2 Wicked 2 Love" played. I hadn't silenced it in case my family needed to get ahold of me. But right now, when I was trying to impress Gretchen Young, and by proxy the rest of the world, its ringing was less than ideal. I probably looked like a douchebag.

"It's fine," Gretchen said evenly. "Take it if you need to."

It was my manager, Steph D'Arezzo, not Maddie or Mom, and I was about to send Steph to voicemail when one of the production assistants jogged up to Gretchen to ask her something.

Taking the opportunity to answer, I accepted the call with a quiet hello.

"Nolan," Steph said, sounding vaguely out of breath. "Is this a good time?"

"Sort of," I said, glancing over at Gretchen, who was now bent over the PA's iPad. "Is now a good time for you? You sound like you're doing something."

"I'm a teensy bit late for this little flight I'm catching," she replied, "so I can't talk long. I just called to say that Winnie's replacement should be arriving on set soon."

"Right," I said, kicking at a nearby snowbank. "Bee something?"

"Bee Hobbes. According to Teddy, she's only ever done indie, student-type things, so she's basically brand new to this. Be nice to her."

I was a little wounded. "Of course I'll be nice. I'm a nice guy, you know."

"Nolan, just days after serenading the world at the Olympics opening ceremony, you lured America's favorite wide-eyed female figure skater into an orgy. An orgy with *Europeans*."

"It wasn't like that," I said, flapping my hand even though she couldn't see me. "I already told you that I didn't *lure* anyone. And the Dutch athletes were speed skaters. Have you seen the thighs speed skaters have? They would have done their own luring, even if I had been involved. Well, involved in more than a Good Samaritan way."

"The press didn't see it like that. *Dominic Diamond* didn't see it like that."

I growled a little at the mention of the blogarazzi asshat who'd built his career on my screwups. The Duluth Olympics had been the jewel in his gossip crown, and after that, he became the *it* celebrity reporter, despite being frequently wrong and, well, an asshat.

"I know you hate him, but like him or not, he's got the power to unfresh this fresh start of yours." I heard the sound of suitcase wheels on a hard floor and then the muffled drone of a boarding announcement coming from somewhere distant as she spoke again. "And I don't have to remind you again to—"

"To keep my nose clean," I cut in. "I know, I know."

"Don't play smart with me," Steph said. "I made my name taking duds like you and giving them real, solid comebacks. I know how to do this. But I don't have time to waste on a client who isn't going to follow the rules. And let's face it, you're not exactly known for following the rules."

Well. That was fair.

"I mean it, Nolan. Until your brand is rehabilitated, you will be as pure as the driven snow they're staging for this movie. You will be so celibate that Benedictine nuns will take notes on how you do it."

I was grateful she couldn't see the flinch I just gave. There had been a very good reason I'd fallen so easily into the bad boy role when I was with INK, and it was because I'd basically been born to play it. Getting into trouble came all too easily to me, and being nun levels of celibate for the next however long was going to suck. A lot.

But if that was what it took to help Mom and Maddie . . .

I fought off a sigh. It sounded like my right hand was going to earn its keep for the foreseeable future. Thank God my favorite ClosedDoors creator updated her feed nearly every day.

Steph kept talking, her suitcase wheels still rolling. "The Hope Channel has contractually locked you down for good behavior until the movie's released. So if I hear even a *whiff* of scandal," she warned, "if I hear even the *puff* of a gnat's whisper that you are fucking somebody on set, I will make hair ribbons out of your arteries. Do you understand me? *Ribbons.* I will wear them to your funeral. I will drape your headstone with them like bunting."

"Bunting. Right." I glanced over at Gretchen again.

"Okay, and be nice to New Winnie, and don't close the door yet, I'm seriously right here. No, it's a carry-on. Oh, I will *make* room in a bin. I know what I'm doing."

Steph clearly had made it to her gate, so I told her goodbye and hung up.

And right on time, my phone buzzed in my hand. I looked down and saw an update from ClosedDoors. Bianca von Honey had posted a new video.

My cock gave an automatic stir at the sight of her name on my screen. When I was exhausted from working in the theater shop, when my life seemed to be nothing but overseeing precalc homework and coordinating doctor appointments and sorting through bills and bills and bills, the only thing that got me through the day was knowing that I would eventually get to shut myself up in my room and have a little alone time with Ms. von Honey.

It wasn't that I didn't hook up in real life—I did—but being former INK star Nolan Shaw mostly made dating really fucking weird. I found that most people either wanted a story to tell their friends after we had sex, *or* they were nervous I was going to somehow make them the story instead.

What could I say? It was hard in these streets for a disgraced former boy band member.

But at least I had my little porn star crush. And maybe one day I'd find someone in real life as exquisitely dirty as Bianca. It hardly mattered at the moment anyway, given my new marching orders—pure as the driven snow and all.

Gretchen was finishing up with the PA, and I came up beside her. "I'm so sorry about that," I said, shoving my phone back into my pocket. "You were saying earlier . . . ?"

"Oh yes," she said, "that's right. Will you make sure you say hi to Bee when she gets in today? I know this is a short shoot, so I want to make sure you're both comfortable jumping right into your scenes together."

"Absolutely—" I was cut off as "2 Wicked 2 Love" came blaring out of my pocket again. Gretchen's eyebrow lifted, and I felt like a total dickhead. "I'm so sorry," I said quickly. "It's probably my manager again. Let me just send this to voicemail, one sec . . ."

But when I pulled the phone out of my pocket, it wasn't my manager.

It was Mom.

"I'm really sorry," I said, wishing I could crawl into a snow-bank and hide forever. "It's my mom. Can I . . . ?"

Gretchen nodded. "Of course."

But her eyebrow didn't go back down, which didn't feel like a good sign.

I stepped away from Gretchen and went a few steps down the salted path through the square before I picked up. "Hey, Mom," I said. "Everything okay?"

"Everything's okay," Mom said. "I just—"

"Maddie's okay? You're okay? Do you need me to move the appointment with Dr. Sam to earlier?"

"Nolan," Mom said. "Everything is fine. I was just calling to wish you good luck on your shoot. Doesn't it start today?"

I blew out a long breath, and then looked back to my director, who was currently standing in the cold looking at her phone and probably thinking about how inconsiderate I was. Yay.

"Tomorrow," I said. "Today is mostly about getting ready."

"That's nice," Mom replied. Her voice was nearly toneless. In the background I could hear the sounds of a television and Barb cooing at Snapple the dog.

"Are you sure you don't want me to see if I can move the appointment?" I asked quietly.

"Everything is fine," she said again, and this time I could hear more of herself in her voice. "I want you to focus on your work there, not worrying about your old mom, who will be totally okay without you here, by the way."

I rolled my eyes. "You're *not* old, and I'm not worried." That was a lie, I was a *lot* worried. "I just want to help is all."

"You are helping," Mom responded, "and it's going to be fine, I promise. Call me tomorrow to tell me how the day went?"

Gretchen was looking up at me from her phone, eyebrow still lifted in a perfect, Academy Award–winning arch.

"Yes," I told Mom, needing to get back to Gretchen and also reluctant to hang up. "And I'll call you tonight too. And Kallum is stopping by again, and you can call anytime, okay? I love you."

"I love you too, hon," she said, and I stared at the phone for a minute after she hung up, my stomach in a tight, dry knot.

"All finished?" Gretchen asked as I put my phone back in my pocket and walked over.

"Yeah," I said. And then added, pointlessly, "I'm sorry."

"It's fine," she said briskly. "Let me point you in the direction of the toy shop, and then you can connect with the costume designer. And on the way, we can talk a little about the duke. Speaking of, do you remember how to smolder?"

AN HOUR LATER, the new costume designer—a tall white man with thick eyebrows and hair that had clearly been fussed over longer than the script—came to stand next to me in the costume department–cum–toy shop. He tucked his chin in his hand and nodded thoughtfully at the assless chaps on the chair in front of us, like he was a visitor to some kind of assless chaps exhibit.

"So what you're saying," the designer said after a minute, "is that you can't wear these for the movie."

Relief pumped through me. "Right."

"And what you need are . . ."

"Fall front breeches."

"Fall front breeches. Which for some reason these can't be, even though they're already frontless." The designer was giving me a look like I needed to rethink this.

I stepped to the side, peering around the folding chair to the empty clothes racks and still-packed plastic tubs of costumes. "Do you mind if I—?" I made a gesture toward the plastic tubs.

The designer rolled his eyes up toward the ceiling and let out a deep sigh. "Fine."

I hauled a tub to the ground and popped the lid open, hoping whoever had packed these totes had at least separated the contemporary clothes from the historical ones. But what greeted me under the lid was neither the usual Hope Channel uniform of sweaters and scarves, nor the Victorian-era garb I was hunting for. I held up a tank top and squinted at the dressing table that I could see through the shirt's neon-green mesh.

"When Mr. Fletcher called me, I wasn't really sure what this movie was or what was going on with it," the designer said, "so I brought my essentials with me in case there was nothing else here yet."

I pulled out a leather thong—with a pouchy bit at the front that was definitely made for holding penises—and then dropped it back into the tub. The origin of the assless chaps was starting to make more sense, except . . .

"Wait. *Essentials?*"

The designer shrugged when I looked back at him, as if to say, *I said what I said.*

The next tub was filled with more of the same—plus a few outfits that looked like they came from the section of a Hallow-

een store that was all sexed-up versions of regular costumes—
and a leash. I could think of a lot more things to do with a
leash than make a Hopeflix film with it, but that wasn't help-
ful right now.

"Okay," the designer said. "So, like, those tubs in front are
all mine. There's probably not going to be fallopian breeches
or whatever in there. But all of those in the back were here when
I got in, so I think the last designer had them ordered in."

I dug the heel of my palm into my eye. "You couldn't tell
me this earlier?"

"You were just so determined," he said. "You had a flow. I
didn't want to get in the way of the flow."

"Right," I said, closing the tub with the leash and then going over to the wall of totes he'd indicated. The very first one
I opened revealed a bounty of waistcoats and ruffles.

Historical jackpot.

The designer joined me, peering down at the tub's contents
as I searched underneath the layers of shirts and stockings to
find what I needed. Triumphantly, I pulled a pair of breeches
free and held them up to gauge their size.

"That's them?" the designer asked doubtfully.

"Yes," I said, already toeing off my sneakers. There wasn't
really any time to waste because filming started tomorrow and
the pace would be brisk, even by my standards (and I'd been
on three global arena tours). We had less than three weeks on
set to film the entirety of *Duke the Halls*, and then this twee,
perma-holiday town would be summarily turned over to the
next movie crew after New Year's Day.

"I guess I just don't see what was wrong with the pants I showed you," the designer said after a moment. "You wanted..."

"Fall front breeches," I said for the millionth time as I shoved my sneakers under a chair.

"Right, and see, on the pants I showed you, the front has already fallen. There is no front left to fall. Doesn't that save everyone some time?"

I looked at him. "For *what*?"

"What is this movie about again?"

"A would-be bride who doesn't believe in the spirit of Christmas gets sent back in time by the Christmas Witch? And then she meets a duke and learns the real meaning of Christmas?"

The designer shook his head as I stepped behind the waist-high wall of tubs and started kicking off my jeans. "So there's no sex in this?"

I stared at him, my jeans tangled around my ankles. "Uh. No."

"Huh."

Huh indeed.

Right as I pulled on my breeches and saw that they fit, there was a knock at the door. An assistant poked her head into the room. "Sorry to interrupt, Mr. Shaw," she chirped, "but Gretchen asked me to tell you when Ms. Hobbes arrived."

"Awesome, thank you," I said. I'd just nip out to say hi to New Winnie and then come back to figure out which jacket and waistcoat I wanted to pair with the breeches.

After shoving my feet back into my shoes and finding my coat, I stepped outside the fake toy shop storefront. I scanned the snow-frosted main street until I saw some people clumped on the bridge leading to the steepled church, and I trotted over, pulling off my beanie and ruffling my dark brown hair as I went. Of all the lessons I'd learned in my thirty-one years of life, perhaps the most important one was that my hair was usually a solid fifty percent of what people liked about me. The remaining fifty percent was split among my voice, my eyes, and my general air of *barely giving a shit*, which people found charming for some reason. Or they used to, before the Olympics happened.

But now the *barely giving a shit* had to take a back seat to *blandly appealing* and *safely earnest*, so it was up to the hair to carry my good impressions these days.

Beanie in hand, I approached the group and caught the musical strains of Pearl Purkiss's voice saying, ". . . and this creek is fed by water straight from the mountains, if you'd like to recharge your crystals in running water while you're here."

"Thanks for the tip," came the sultry-voiced response, and as I stepped into the circle of people, I saw the voice's source immediately. Shock ripped through me at the sight of her, and then my entire body flushed with an avid, hungry heat.

Dark hair tumbling everywhere.

Fair skin that had been sun-kissed into a pale golden hue.

Olive-green eyes, pouty lips, and a septum piercing that winked in the weak winter light. And a lush body perfectly and flirtily revealed by a short skirt and a sinfully clingy sweater.

Fuck.

Need made my skin tight all over, and I realized too late that fall front breeches were *not* meant for concealing boners as my stiffening length pressed against the fabric.

I moved the hand holding my beanie instinctively over my

groin as I locked eyes with the woman I'd jerked off to more times than I could count. The woman who'd fingered herself to a chest-flushing, leg-shaking orgasm late last night, live for her fans only.

The woman who'd starred in my dirtiest dreams for the past six years.

Bee Hobbes was none other than Bianca von Honey.

CHAPTER THREE

Bee

When I got to the airport, Teddy handed me a Chili's kids' menu, on the back of which he had thoughtfully hand-written his rules. He had also completed the word search and the maze, and muttered something about keeping his brain sharp when he realized that I had been looking at his work. During the whole flight and the car ride to Christmas Notch, I recited the rules over and over again to myself.

1. No fucking. On camera or for fun.

2. You are Bee Hobbes. You've never heard of Bianca. You've never even watched porn. You use parental controls on your Netflix, because you are that fucking

wholesome. You might as well be a virgin. (Yes, I know. Virginity is a construct. Blah, blah, blah.)

3. Come up with a backstory and stick to it. You were plucked from student-film obscurity and are so thankful for your big break.

4.

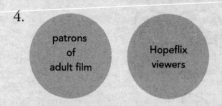

See that giant gaping hole between the two bubbles? That's our only shot at getting away with this. MIND THE GAP.

    4b. Keep the jokes about gaping holes to yourself.

5. No. Fucking.

6. I'm serious.

When I had landed from my red-eye, I was going on nearly twenty-four hours without any sleep. But now I was finally here in this quiet Christmas village that was like the Target knockoff of *White Christmas* come to life with Pearl Purkiss escorting me around and Nolan Shaw standing mere feet from me. Nolan. Fucking. Shaw.

"And if you need any extra crystals," Pearl said, "I keep some loaners at the ready. I like to think of them as, like, energy insurance." She turned away from the dreamy landscape to see Nolan staring uncertainly at me, his blue eyes even icier than they were on every poster in my teenage bedroom. A muscle jumped in the pale slice of his jaw.

My knees suddenly felt weak.

"Oh." Pearl's voice dropped an octave. "This is good. I can already sense the energy between you two is rich with tension." She took my hand. "Bee, we just knew you were the right choice."

"Bee, is it?" Nolan asked, his voice raspy and indifferent. "I guess that makes you New Winnie?"

"No," I said, the word sharp as I forgot for a moment who I was speaking to. "I'm not New Anyone. Just Bee."

"Just Bee," he repeated as he twisted his beanie in his white-knuckled fists.

He gave me that look. The one that I was pretty sure said no one told him his new costar would be fat. I learned really early on in my career to set expectations. The porn industry wasn't exactly known for its communication, so it took only a few failed scene partners suddenly backing out of a job once they got to set before I realized that for better or worse, it was always best to be very clear about exactly who I was.

Pearl shrieked with excitement before reclaiming her serene energy and motioning to the script clutched to my chest. "So what'd you think of Felicity?"

"She's . . . great," I said. "So intriguing . . . and—and compelling. I really am excited to dig into her motivation and discover exactly why she wants to escape the modern world and all of its conveniences for corsets and bedpans."

Thankfully Pearl's blond lashes fluttered under the weight of my compliments, because there was not a whole lot to say about *Duke the Halls* other than: "Actually, I was reading on the plane," I continued, "and I noticed that I'm missing the last page?"

Pearl looked at me, blinking over and over again, like if she did it enough times my question might vanish into thin air. Finally, she took a deep, centering breath and said, "You'll get it when it's time."

And then, even though the only sound was the rushing creek just days away from freezing over beneath the picturesque wood-and-iron bridge we stood on, Pearl perked up and said, "Oh! I just heard my name. I'll leave you two to get better acquainted."

Nolan and I watched as she floated off toward the square, which was half functioning town and half movie set. The steeple of the white clapboard church, where I assumed I would soon leave my fictional husband at the altar to travel back in time and fall hard for the Duke of Frostmere, cast a shadow over us.

I looked back to him with my head still tilted in Pearl's direction. "Was that . . . weird?"

He scratched the base of his throat, his Adam's apple moving under the stubble on his neck. "She's been pretty cagey about the ending."

I opened up my script to the last page, which cut off mid-dialogue. "It literally says 'And all along, the meaning of Christmas was right there in front of me. The meaning of Christmas was—'"

He bit back a smirk, the kind of smirk someone gives when they're just a little too delighted by a whiff of chaos. "I heard the director of photography talking to someone on the phone about how Pearl keeps rewriting the last page. She can't decide what the meaning of Christmas is."

I snorted out a laugh and immediately clapped my hand over my mouth. "What? Are you serious? How are we supposed to film a whole movie if we don't know the ending?"

He thought for a moment, and his pause was just long enough for my brain to remember that *Oh my God, this is Nolan Shaw*. He was somehow taller and a little broader than I expected. Every inch of him was slender muscle, with a strong, firm frame. He wasn't some bulked-out beefhead, like so many I'd met on set after set, and I was so used to seeing guys like Nolan and feeling like I could snap them if I sat on them with all my weight. But something about him felt tested and sturdy. It made me think thoughts I couldn't unthink. I clenched my thighs together, begging my body to remember every one of Teddy's very serious rules. Worst of all, Nolan had the kind of face—the kind of smirk—that helped him get away with just about anything.

"I guess it'll be a surprise," he finally said. "I better get back to my fitting, but it was nice to meet you, Bee-*ee*." The way he said my name was drawn out and abrupt at the same time, like he was sounding it out even though it was only one syllable. "Maybe we could run lines at some point once you get settled?"

"Sure. Yeah, of course. Lines. I'd love that." My insides tingled, even though this was a totally routine thing that people who were in legit movies did. In porn, there were lines . . . sometimes, but it was more about the blocking and the boundaries and the ad-libbing. I hadn't had actual lines to memorize since I played Yente, the meddling matchmaker in my high school theater's production of *Fiddler on the Roof*. (Truth be told, I auditioned for Tevye *and* Golde and was robbed of both. Suburban high school theater programs in Texas weren't too kind to fat girls.)

Nolan turned to walk back toward the costume department at the center of the village and I watched for as long as I could before anyone noticed that I was eyeball stalking one of my adolescent idols.

The first time someone broke my heart I was fourteen years old. I had waited three hours in a Texas downpour for a chance to meet Isaac, Nolan, and Kallum after INK's *Fresh Ink* tour stop in Dallas while my moms protected me from the crowd of relentless fans, the three of us outfitted in matching ponchos that Mama Pam kept in the center console of her Honda Odyssey just in case. In the end, the boys had fled in an unmarked car just moments after their encore, leaving their tour bus parked outside the American Airlines Center, along with an army of drenched, disappointed fans.

If I'm being honest, that first heartbreak still stings.

EVEN THOUGH I should have taken a power nap, I was a little wired from my flight and from meeting Nolan, so I headed back to the Edelweiss Inn, where I was initially dropped off but wasn't able to check in then because I'd been too early. (Despite the fact that the only people staying in the hotel were cast and crew.) The inn, with its timber-frame-cottage feel, was fashioned like something straight out of *The Sound of Music*.

Stella, the stout, older woman who seemed to do everything from checking in guests to whipping up cocktails (at her own pace, of course), handed me a manila envelope with *Bee Hobbes* scribbled across the front.

She walked my luggage around the front desk, which I'd left here earlier. "Something in one of these bags keeps buzzin'."

I bit back a smile. "Thanks." I opened the envelope to find a photocopied, hand-drawn map of Christmas Notch, along with some chamber of commerce pamphlets and my call sheet for tomorrow morning, complete with a Post-it that read *Subject to Change* stuck to the schedule.

I shook out the rest of the envelope's contents, which included a key on a hand-carved wooden key chain labeled MISTLETOE SUITE. After studying the rest of my reading materials—including some information about where to find craft services and a cast and crew phone number directory—I waited at the elevator for a few minutes before Stella finally walked to the doors and taped an Out of Order sign over the buttons.

"Right," I said as she walked away without a word. Summoning whatever energy I had left, I dragged my bags up to the third floor. I always said sex was my cardio, but this worked too.

Once I'd finally made it to the Mistletoe Suite, I was met with a king-size bed adorned with a velvet-tufted headboard in the shape of a heart and a Jacuzzi tub—also in the shape of a heart—looking out over the snow-covered mountains dotting the horizon. It was beautiful enough to make me forget that the entire room save the bathroom was covered in forest-green carpet and red-plaid wallpaper.

The day had been full of so many firsts already that I was

just now realizing this was my first time seeing real snow. Back home in Texas, we'd get snow every few years, but it usually melted before it could stick or was more of a sleet-ice mixture. Still, we'd cancel school and hibernate for a day or two just in case the roads were patchy with ice. Moving from Arlington, Texas, to L.A. straight out of high school meant I'd never had a snow-covered Christmas and—oh shit. I still had to call home and break it to my parents that there had been a change of plans. They knew I was here in Vermont, but I had been light on details. That wouldn't stop them from responding to my text with a nonstop stream of questions.

When I got dressed before my flight, I had a snow-bunny image of myself showing up in this sleepy Vermont village in my fluffy cropped baby-pink sweater and plaid schoolgirl skirt that I would have drooled over in high school but never had the guts to wear. But now that I was actually here, my legs were feeling the chill, so I ditched the skirt for fleece-lined leggings I managed to score at Target last night. I bundled up in my faux-fur vintage jacket, which was a coat only in the symbolic sense, because as a proud CalTexan, cold weather gear was more about aesthetic than function.

Just as I was wrestling with my key to lock the door to my room, my phone vibrated in my pocket.

Four unread messages and two notifications.

Sunny Dee: Call me tonight! I want all the deets. ☺

Mom: You need to call your mothers.

Mama Pam: Honey Bee, Mom is worried about you. She knows you get pukey during landings. Did you ask the flight attendant for a paper bag? You shouldn't be embarrassed. They deal with that sort of thing all the time. Give us a ring.

Teddy: Best. Behavior.

ClosedDoors: 20,440 likes on your video

ClosedDoors: 3,262 comments on your video

It was hard not to buy into the immediate gratification of an app like ClosedDoors. I also liked that it catered to everyone from porn stars to even socialites and influencers with a naughty streak. And it paid my bills and then some. Every person who subscribed to my page paid a monthly fee. It was enough of an income that I got to choose exactly what porn I wanted to do, which also meant other performers did as well. Body positivity might have been having a moment (more than that, I hoped), but there were still plenty of performers who didn't want to scene with me because I didn't fit their brand. Message received loud and clear.

I shot off a quick text to both my moms, promising them that I was okay and that we'd FaceTime soon. Sometimes they'd text me like someone else had my phone and I was being held hostage and the only way to prove to them that I was okay and alive was to show them my face. This was one of those times.

I took the stairs back down and took my time strolling to

my costume fitting. The whole little village reminded me of an Old West town I visited in middle school when we took a family vacation to the Grand Canyon. I couldn't seem to tell who actually lived here and who was in town working on the movie. From what Teddy told me, they had yet to announce Winnie's UnFestival-related absence to the whole cast and crew, but since she wasn't the only one he'd have to replace, I couldn't imagine that secret lasting for long.

It was also a little hard to tell which businesses were real and which were part of the set. Finally, though, I found a coffee shop with a line and safely assumed that the people in it were real.

After getting actual sustenance at the real coffee shop, I walked with my caramel latte and chocolate croissant to the end of the square, where I'd been told I would find the fake toy shop storefront that would also double as the costuming department.

"Hello?" I called as the bell chimed overhead. "Is anyone here?"

"Oh my gah," a voice moaned from the back. "For the last time, this is not an actual toy store. And if it were, these are not the kinds of toys I would—" The voice fizzled out as a tall person in a wool kilt with leather pants underneath and a black knit sweater with simply the word *NO* on it turned the corner.

I gasped.

He shrieked.

"Luca!"

"Bee!"

I dropped my bag and raced behind the counter to hug him. "What are you doing here?" I asked in a whisper, like Teddy might have somehow found out that one of his porn crew members had cropped up on the set of his wholesome Christmas movie.

"Uncle Ray-Ray flew me out," he said.

I rolled my eyes. "Teddy. His name is Teddy." The name of Teddy's studio was a poor-taste decision made when Teddy was in his twenties, and now he was too cheap to bother changing it, despite the way his whole body cringed when he heard it spoken out loud.

"Whatever," Luca said. "I demanded business class but had to settle for extended legroom."

I kneaded my fingers into my hips. "I could have definitely used business class. My whole body feels like it was vacuum sealed."

He scoffed. "Bee, don't pretend like you can't swing an upgrade. Honestly, though, that shouldn't even matter. If Teddy wants your goodies in Vermont"—he motioned to my ample ass—"then he should know that you require premium shipping."

Luca was often high maintenance and sometimes difficult to work with, but I had to admit he had a point. "Well, there's always the return flight . . . which may come sooner than I hope if I can't keep the whole sex-work thing on the down low, if you know what I mean."

He nodded vigorously. "Oh, Uncle Ray—Teddy—has already been very clear that if I am to do costuming for *Duke the Balls* that I have to be, like, as vanilla as an insurance adjuster."

I giggled as his forehead tightened with confusion. "Oh. I thought that—you do know it's called *Duke the Halls* and not *Duke the Balls*, right?"

Realization dawned on him as his lips parted slightly. "That does seem to be more on brand for Hopeflix." He nodded to himself, and I couldn't help but imagine that he'd had a very confusing twenty-four hours preparing for a family-friendly soft-core porn to premiere on Hopeflix. "Have you ever heard of . . . what did Nolan call them? Fall out breeches?"

I patted his shoulder. "I think Google might be your best friend over the next few weeks. Isn't it so weird to actually see Nolan Shaw in the flesh?"

He made a *psh* sound. "Nolan Shaw is dead to me."

I touched a hand to his shoulder. "Oh my God. What did he say to you? I was so nervous he would be an asshole."

"Um, he only ruined a gold medal opportunity for Emily Albright, the American ice princess we needed but never truly deserved!"

"Oh," I said. "That."

He led me to the back room, which was stocked full of tubs that needed to be unpacked.

"Are these all the costumes?" I asked.

He pointed to four bins that each had a piece of duct tape with *Luca* written in marker stuck on them. "All except those. I brought some emergency options. Teddy couldn't tell me what I'd be working with, so I wanted to be prepared."

I glanced into an open bin. "With ball gags and crotchless panties?"

"Don't pretend like I haven't saved your ass on set before," he countered playfully.

And it was true. Luca started working costumes two years ago when Teddy's daughter, Astrid, referred him after he'd dropped out of fashion school and was in desperate need of a gig so he wouldn't have to pack up and leave L.A. for his backward-ass Oregon hometown where he was still known as Jeffrey. Say what you want about Teddy, but he's got a soft spot for people just trying to make it in Los Angeles, and he's not a predator, which can't be said about plenty of people in the industry.

Luca opened an unmarked bin. "Okay, this I can work with," he said, holding up a deep navy corset with a delicate brocade pattern.

I sized up the aforementioned garment. In the rush of re-placing Winnie with me, I didn't think anyone had taken the time to consider that she was Hollywood thin and I was real-world fat. "Luca, you can sew, right?"

He turned from me dramatically, like he couldn't bear to look me in the eyes. "My God, Bee. Are you trying to insult me?"

"Is there another one of those corsets in there? Because I think it's going to take at least two of those things sewn to-gether to keep us out of the *Duke the Balls* zone."

CHAPTER FOUR

Nolan

God, the beautiful, horrible irony. My dirty dream girl showing up in *Christmas Notch, Vermont*, of all places, ready to spend the next two weeks wearing corsets in front of me (!!!), and instead of taking her out for drinks and then proposing marriage, I had to keep everything zipped up tight. And not even zipped up in a sexy *Let's pretend we're in high school and do it over the pants* kind of way, but in a *My manager will fire me and I'll have no money to take care of my family* kind of way.

So I had to keep things professional and chaste.

I had to keep things so platonic that Plato himself would raise a kylix to my efforts.

Goddammit.

I tried to rationalize with my libido as I ate my sad carryout dinner alone in the Edelweiss Inn's dining room. Because even if Steph hadn't threatened to make bunting out of my intestines, or whatever it had been, I'd still try to keep my distance from Bee. I'd touched enough outstretched hands belonging to screaming teenagers to know how one-sided these kinds of parasocial fantasies were. And I was sure it was the same for her . . . except probably with an exponentially higher creep factor. I'd seen enough weird comments on her pictures and videos to know that an uncomfortable number of subscribers felt entitled to her body and to her attention. I didn't want to be the real-life version of that.

But God, why did it have to be *her*?

Cutesy Winnie Baker in all her dimpled, virtuous glory wouldn't have been a problem. Some other equally anodyne actress wouldn't have been a problem. But no, it had to be Bianca von Honey, with all that dark silky hair and all those velvet curves. The kind of curves that begged for fingertips and teeth . . .

Luckily, my phone chimed on the table, distracting me from that completely unhelpful line of thought, and I picked it up to see a text reminder for Mom's upcoming psychiatric appointment. Barb was proving herself an angel again and driving Mom there, since Maddie had school. I forwarded the info on to Mom and Barb, then shot off another quick I love you, call if you need anything text to Mom, even though we'd spoken on the phone again and I knew she was doing fine for the moment.

It was all going to be okay, even though I wasn't there. I had to believe that. Between Barb, Maddie, and Kallum stopping by in the evenings, it would be okay.

I just had to do my part here in Christmas Notch and make sure everything would be okay in the future too.

BEFORE GOING TO bed, I stopped by the costume department, needing to find the designer, whose name I'd learned was Luca. ("Luca what?" "Just Luca. Like Jesus. Or Kesha.")

I'd found a waistcoat and jacket that would work with the breeches, but the jacket needed to be taken in at the waist. And given that the Duke of Frostmere was making his grand declaration *tomorrow*, I needed the alterations done in the hastiest of posthastes.

Except when I found Luca, he seemed even less inclined to help me than he had earlier today. He was sitting at a table with a sewing machine, his high-top sneakers propped up on the table while he carefully picked open the stitches of a corset. A podcast about Tonya Harding played from his phone while he worked.

"Hey," I said, approaching the table. "I was wondering if you could take in a jacket for me? I need it by tomorrow. The shoulders and sleeves are good, it's just the waist, really—"

Luca gave his corset a long blink and then slowly slid his eyes over to me. "I'm busy," he said finally. "With another costume. It will take me all night."

"I—okay." I couldn't shove someone else's costume needs to the side, obviously, but this was a problem.

"So," Luca said.

But he never added on to the *so*; he merely turned his attention back to the corset—after turning up the volume on his podcast.

Six-years-ago Nolan would have had a *real* bad attitude about this, but present-day Nolan literally couldn't afford to have any attitude other than *whatever it takes*. "Okay, so can I borrow your sewing machine, then?" I asked over the narrator describing Jeff Gillooly's childhood.

Luca heaved a giant sigh over the corset.

I squinted at him. "Do you not like me or something?"

He pressed his fingertips to his forehead, like I was giving him a splitting headache. "Let me ask you this, Nolan Shaw: Does everything have to be all about *you* all the time? Do you ever stop to think that other people have lives and careers that need to survive your floppy-haired chaos?"

I was floored by his little rant. Like, yes, the floppy-haired chaos had been real, but it was also *six years ago*. I'd been an upstanding bisexual citizen since then! I went on very normal, disappointing dates! I had health insurance, and I hadn't been in a single other circus-train orgy!

How long did someone have to be quiet and boring before all their floppy-haired sins were forgiven?

"I *guess*," Luca said, with an air of intense martyrdom, "you can hang out here and use my sewing machine when I'm not actively using it. But I'm *not* changing the podcast."

He reached over and slid a pincushion shaped like a character from *Yuri!!! On Ice* across the sewing table. And then he added a spool of thread, setting it down like a bartender setting down a shot glass.

"There," he said, waving a hand at the pincushion and the thread. His tone was—marginally—more inviting. "So you can get started."

Whatever it takes, Nolan, I reminded myself. And to the sounds of Tonya Harding and Jeff Gillooly's burgeoning courtship, I sat down and started working.

I WOKE UP just after dawn, my eyes gritty from too little sleep and my fingers sore with needle pricks from altering the Duke of Frostmere's jacket. I also had an outrageous erection, which refused to abate while I fumbled my way into the bathroom and brushed my teeth, and then throbbed angrily in the tepid spray of the shower. I'd been trying not to jerk off since I met Bee, because it didn't feel right. And also because I thought maybe I could train my erection Monks of New Skete style with lots of tough love and discipline.

But it had been less than a day, and already I couldn't take it anymore. If I didn't relieve the pressure, the Duke of Frostmere was going to be more blue-balled than blue-blooded, and I didn't think I could risk that on set. Not after yesterday's incident with the breeches alerted me to how little they concealed.

So with the help of some lotion courtesy of the Edelweiss Inn guest basket—thematically scented like gingerbread, no less—I gave myself a rough, quick release. I even did my level best not to think of Bianca von Honey as I did . . . although I eventually failed at that particular endeavor. (It was the memory of her nipples poking through a swimsuit on a Closed-Doors post that sent me plunging over the edge.)

After I finished, I pressed my forehead to the tiled shower wall and dragged in a miserable, gingerbread-scented breath. I barely felt any better. In fact, my erection was already valiantly trying to rebound, probably hoping for a lengthier jam session. Preferably with my phone in my left hand and the ClosedDoors app open to Bianca's latest post, which featured some very see-through lingerie and a bright pink vibrator.

Clearly, I was going to have to figure out how to cope with this during the shoot. Starving my cock for attention had already proven a bust—literally—and because of Steph's edicts, seeking out pleasure with a non-costar person wouldn't fly either. *And* I wouldn't do that anyway because I already knew it wouldn't truly scratch the itch. It would be like eating store-brand cookies instead of Oreos or watching *Enterprise* instead of *Discovery*. It would only make me crave the real thing even more.

But I didn't have time to figure it out now. My gingerbread-scented dick and I were supposed to be in the toy shop in twenty minutes for hair and makeup and then in a van to fake Frostmere Manor after that. I was going to have to make a Bee Strategy while I was being coiffed and scolded for trying to eat a croissant at the same time.

I turned off the shower and finished getting ready, making sure to grab my newly tailored jacket on the way out. I was hoping my patient podcast listening had endeared me to Luca last night, so maybe he'd help me more with costumes, although I kind of doubted it.

Maybe he'd been a One Direction fan back in the day.

Hair and makeup went easily enough—I managed to house a Danish before Maya got started on my face—although Denise the hair person had to Google *Victorian hairstyles* before she started working on me.

"Sorry," Denise said, snapping some gum as she set her

phone down and turned back to me. "Just got here last night. Teddy flew me out to replace one of the tusk people."

"No problem," I assured her. She was rummaging through the kits that had been shipped out by the original team, emerging victorious with two hairpieces that would be trimmed down to be my old-timey sideburns.

"Normally, I'm getting rid of hair, not adding more on!" she explained. And then she added, "But at least I don't have to watch someone cover up butt acne today. Or ball acne!" She chuckled to herself as she started trimming the sideburns.

Uh. Okay.

After I'd finished with hair and makeup and pulled on my newly tailored costume, the production assistant put me in a van headed to fake Frostmere Manor. I had to admit, as the van drove up the pass in the mountains that Christmas Notch was named for, that it was a gorgeous location. If I'd been a Gilded Age steel tycoon, I would have built my vacation mansion here too.

And the house itself was as stunning as the snowy views around it. Built from a pale, silvery marble and faced with columns and huge arched windows, the mansion looked like it belonged in Enlightenment-era France rather than tucked away in the Vermont hinterlands. But the tycoon's eccentric architectural vision was Christmas Notch's gain—the city had a pretend English manor house all ready to rent out for movies like ours.

"Hi, hello, hi!" said the production assistant, Cammy, as I opened the van door. She hovered as I stepped out, my boots crunching in the snow as she pranced in place. Red bloomed on her light bronze cheeks, either from the cold or from agitation, and she was currently trying to hand me a hundred different things at once.

Okay, it was only two things—a fresh set of script pages and a coffee—but I was trying to hold on to my top hat, cane, and phone, so it *felt* like a hundred things.

"Thank you," I said, after we'd managed to get everything passed off.

"You're wel—" She broke off as the watch on her wrist buzzed and she read the text message that came through. Whatever it was must have been important because she touched my shoulder to indicate that we needed to move. Quickly.

"Gretchen is in the front hall," Cammy said as we walked. I could see her wrist flickering with texts as she gestured toward the house; a volley of staticky chatter issued from a walkie-talkie hidden somewhere in her coat. Cammy was clearly the woman of the hour—which made sense, I supposed. The Hope Channel made approximately twelve hundred of these movies a year, and that kind of quantity didn't come without pinching some pennies. Pennies like running an entire movie with only one or two production assistants.

"Nothing's changed from the call sheet you received last night. Your first four scenes today are here at the mansion, and then there's one more scene back in the town at six P.M.," Cammy was saying as we trudged around the back of the house to the servants' entrance so we wouldn't track snow into the front of the mansion. "Your first three scenes are inside, two with Felicity and one with your orphaned nephew, and then you'll be out in the garden alone near sunset. Tonight's town square scene will also be with Felicity, down in Christmas

Notch proper. Lunch is at one, here at the mansion, and you're on your own for dinner."

Three scenes with Bee today. Three scenes where I'd have to remember not to think about her gorgeous face or her sexy body or the perfect mouth I was scripted to kiss . . .

I could do this. I could do this.

Easy peasy, lemon squeezy.

"Awesome, thank you," I said, "and thanks again for the coffee."

"It keeps people happy," Cammy said in a confidential tone. "Well, some people. I had to find turmeric tea for Pearl."

We walked inside, and Cammy directed me down a narrow corridor to an ornate door that led to the large central hall of the house. Wreaths, poinsettias, and garlands were everywhere. A marble staircase dominated the room, greenery hanging from its gilded banisters and a massive Christmas tree set nearby. The tall windows looked out onto the snowy valley below and the tree-covered mountains just beyond it.

The morning sun—barely risen—filled the space with a soft light, hued in a pale pink-gold.

It looked so pretty and so impossibly *Christmas* that even I was impressed, and I was basically the Gordon Ramsay of judging Christmas things.

"Ms. Hobbes should be here at any minute," Cammy finished as she walked me over to where Gretchen Young was talking to the gaffer about lighting the scene. "Just let me know if you need anything," she added, and I turned to thank her again, but she'd already jogged off, her walkie-talkie out and her eyes on her watch.

"I just don't want any shadows under their faces," Gretchen was saying.

The gaffer, a skinny guy with even skinnier jeans and light brown skin, was nodding as she talked, like she wasn't saying anything he didn't already know. "Right. Right. No shadows on the boobs."

Gretchen opened her mouth, like she wasn't sure how to respond to that, but then just shook her head. "I guess that's as good a way as any to think about it. Are we ready to go?"

"One final lighting check and then we'll be good," he assured her. "Do you think they'll turn up the heat in here? It's *freezing*."

My phone buzzed as they finished up their conversation. I managed to put my top hat on my head and transfer my cane to my coffee hand so I could free my other hand to use my phone.

> **Kallum with a K:** Snapple bit me.

> **Kallum with a K:** Do you think it's infected?

I swiped my screen open and saw a very gross picture of a finger that was definitely infected.

> **Me:** Yes, you fucking weirdo. I do think it's infected. GO TO THE DOCTOR.

> **Me:** Why did you have your hand near Snapple's mouth anyway???? You know she bites.

> **Kallum with a K:** I made her a special puppy pizza! I wanted to feed it to her!

Like me, Kallum had lost almost all his INK money when our manager fled the country, but he'd had enough left to start a (very) small business, which, instead of being something adjacent to any of his life experience as a Grammy-nominated pop phenomenon, was a pizza parlor called Slice, Slice, Baby. I'd initially thought this was a terrible idea, but since he'd opened the first Slice, Slice, Baby location, he'd seen nothing but success. He'd expanded all over the Kansas City metro area and was thinking about branching out even farther—Iowa, Arkansas. Maybe even Texas.

And because he was a good guy, he'd brought over some SSB pizza to the house last night. He was checking in on Maddie and Mom while I was here, and between him and Barb, I felt like there was a good safety net if Mom's rough patch continued on longer than the rough patches usually did. I was grateful for the help, even if it didn't lessen the giant ball of worry I carried around with me everywhere.

> **Me:** Thank you for donating a finger to the cause.

> **Kallum with a K:** Anything for Mrs. K!!!

(Mrs. K was my mom, April Kowalczk. He'd called her that since the first day he'd knocked on our door in preschool, asking if I could be his best friend and also if he could have some fruit snacks for the road.)

Kallum with a K: Do you still think you'll miss Christmas?

Misery coiled like a clammy worm in my chest as I tapped out a reluctant reply.

Me: Yeah.

When Dad had been alive, Christmas had been the Kowalczk *thing*. We were the house that had ten trillion inflatable things on the lawn; he was the dad who spent days and days cheerfully fucking with Christmas lights; Mom was the mom who turned an entire room of the house into a hyper-organized wrapping depot with ribbons and bows and hand-lettered tags. (Joanna Gaines could never.)

But then things had changed. Dad had died of a heart attack a month after the Duluth cluster-eff, and since I'd been off living up to my bad boy reputation, it wasn't until the funeral that I realized how much he'd done behind the scenes. Mom was brilliant and smart and funny and compassionate beyond all belief, but with her bipolar disorder, our family needed a little more ballast than most families, and Dad had been that for us. So after I came home, I decided to give up on the career I'd ruined anyway and be the family ballast instead. I moved in and got a respectable job (as Nolan Kowalczk, not as Nolan Shaw), and kept all the family traditions alive, including making every Christmas a balls-to-the-wall Kowalczk Christmas.

Except now we needed more money, and the only way I could make it was by being away over the holidays. God, the irony of missing Christmas to make Christmas joy for other people. It burned like hell.

> **Kallum with a K:** Have you seen Winnie Baker yet?

Oh, right. I hadn't told him about the UnFestival disaster yet.

> **Me:** she got sick (long story) and had to be recast at the last moment (even longer story).

> **Kallum with a K:** oh

> **Kallum with a K:** okay

> **Me:** why?

Three dots appeared and then disappeared, like he'd started typing and then changed his mind and decided not to respond.

I shook my head. He'd been weird about Winnie ever since a disastrous Teen Choice Awards ceremony several years back, when he'd sort of injured her with the surfboard-shaped trophy and also sort of caused a giant scandal about her at the after-after-party. Good times.

"Okay, so, Nolan," Gretchen said, and I turned to face her, tucking my phone away in my jacket and trying to look like I was here to be a Serious Actor and not like half my brain was back in Kansas City with my family and a pizza-parlor-owning friend. "I wanted to check in with you. See how you were feeling about the duke since we talked yesterday."

"I'm feeling excellent," I said. Although Gretchen's vision might have been deep, Pearl's writing . . . wasn't. As much. And that was okay, because the pace of the shoot didn't allow for much depth anyway. So I felt pretty confident that I could pull off the brand of grumpy smolder Gretchen seemed to want. I'd pouted and scowled my way into thousands of adolescent hearts once upon a time, after all.

"Good, good," she said, stepping behind the nearby camera to squint into the lens. "And you had a chance to acquaint yourself with Bee?"

Be cool, Nolan. No one needs to know that you've jerked off to your castmate before.

I cleared my throat. "Uh. Yeah. I think she'll work out fine."

Well, that sounded lackluster.

So I added a hearty, "I'm really excited about working with her!" to make up for it.

"Good," Gretchen said firmly, finally looking at me again. "She's new, so I want to make sure everyone's around to lend a hand and show her the ropes."

"I'm new too," I joked, but Gretchen cocked an eyebrow at me.

"Your kind of new doesn't count, Mr. Boy Band—"

She was interrupted by a fresh commotion from the corridor, the chatter of new voices and laughter.

And then suddenly, like something out of a Hope Channel movie, Bee Hobbes stepped into the golden glow of the marble hall, looking like a Christmas princess come to life.

CHAPTER FIVE

Nolan

The light gleamed off the dark red silk of her dress, and her hair was piled artfully on top of her head, where it then tumbled down to spill over her shoulders. Glimpses of pearl and gold hairpins gleamed from the dark tresses. Fake rubies and diamonds glittered from around her neck, but they were no match for her sparkling eyes as she walked across the century-old floor.

Yes, it was official.

Bianca von Honey was just as stunning in yards and yards of silk as she was wearing nothing at all.

And the way her curves looked in that corset . . .

I should have used that gingerbread lotion at least three more times before leaving my room.

She saw me and Gretchen and waved, coming over with the hair and makeup artists in tow. Along with Luca, who was wearing sunglasses inside for some reason.

"Bee, you're beautiful," Gretchen said warmly, and Bee gave her a dimpled grin and did a twirl for us, which was so fucking adorable, I couldn't stand it.

"You look incredible," I told Bee, and she rewarded me with a smile.

"I know," she said, a little smugly. "*And* my boobs look fantastic."

"*And* there won't be any shadows on them," said the gaffer, coming out of nowhere.

"Angel!" Bee exclaimed. "I didn't know you were here!" She pulled the gaffer into a tight hug, and jealousy tore through me, quick as wildfire.

I wanted a hug like that. With the corset and the fantastic boobs and that happy look on her face.

"Daddy called me in after the tusk happened," Angel said. "I wouldn't normally help out, but the semester was over anyway, and besides, I wanted to see you get all fancy. Spread your wings."

"Like you haven't seen her spread her wings before," the hair stylist said.

Bee, Angel, and Luca all laughed really hard at that, while Gretchen, Maya the makeup artist, and I chuckled the chuckles of people who had no idea what the joke was about.

"Angel is Teddy the producer's son," Bee explained to me. "He's a brilliant animator, but he spent two years studying film before he switched majors."

"Which means I can swing some lights around whenever Dad needs me to," Angel added. "And I've lit Bee a few times." He waggled his eyebrows.

"For, um, student stuff," Bee interjected quickly.

"Right," said Angel. "I definitely remember some rulers being involved."

"Well, I'm glad you could help us out," Gretchen said. And then she touched Bee's shoulder. "And I'm exceptionally grateful you agreed to join us with such short notice. Now, does anyone mind if I steal Nolan and Bee really quick? No? I didn't think so."

She led the two of us into a corner of the hall that wasn't packed with either equipment or Christmas decorations, and then turned to face us. "I want to be transparent about the fact that we don't have the budget for an intimacy coordinator on this shoot. There are only two kisses in the script, but I want to make sure that we have them choreographed in a way that feels right."

When I looked over at Bee's face, I found she was already looking at me. She quickly dropped her eyes, but it was too late. My heart had already sped up.

"So today's kiss is the final kiss of the movie," Gretchen said, "and I really want everything these characters are—their bodies, minds, souls—present in the kiss. The Hope Channel isn't big on the bodies part, per se, so I want to make sure that we're still conveying a huge amount of want even with a more restrained physicality."

Want.

Looking at Bee now, all silk and corset and big green eyes,

I didn't think want was going to be a problem. Rather the opposite in fact.

"So let's walk through it here before we start," Gretchen went on. "We have the first two lines, and then I think that if you reached for each other's hands . . ."

I knew we'd have to touch eventually; of course we would. It was our job to be Felicity and the duke and they were in love and so of course they would touch in the safe, Hope Channel way that Hope Channel characters touched. But as Bee looked up at me and held out her hands, I felt a nervousness I hadn't experienced since ninth grade when Jake Casebolt asked if I wanted to hang out with him under the bleachers after dark. Like there was nothing I wanted more in the entire world, and also I was scared to death of getting it at the same time.

I bit the inside of my lower lip to keep my face from doing any stupid face things and extended my hands too. At Gretchen's nod, I wrapped my fingers around Bee's, and so for the first time since we'd met, we touched.

Over the course of my life, I'd touched probably thousands of people—and I'd had sex with a not-insignificant percentage of that number—and yet nothing could have prepared me for what it felt like to hold Bee's hands. *Bianca von Honey*'s hands. Because for the last six years, I'd fantasized nonstop about the very fingers I was clutching right now. I'd watched her use them on herself, on costars, on friends; I'd watched these fingers tease and stroke and rub. I'd worked myself raw thinking of them in my mouth, and around my cock, of them twisting in my hair as I sank deep inside her, and now they were wrapped firmly in my grasp, and—

"Okay, and then Felicity says her line," Gretchen said, breaking me out of my hand-induced trance.

I looked over at our director to see her squinting at us, like we were a pile of IKEA pieces waiting to be assembled.

"Hmm," she said, lifting her hand, and then tilting her head. "What if you tried touching her waist, Nolan? Are we comfortable with that?"

A small smile curled Bee's mouth. "It's fine by me," she said, and I had to wonder what it was like for her to work through intimacy on this scale when normally she was negotiating things like whether or not there would be a condom covering the Hitachi Magic Wand.

I nearly smiled too—moving from porn to the Hope Channel had to be pretty fucking hilarious—but at the last minute, I remembered that she didn't know that *I* knew that she was Bianca von Honey. And I didn't think Gretchen knew either.

So instead of smiling, I chewed on my lip. And then at Gretchen's murmur, I took Bee's waist with my hand.

Bee sucked in a breath as I touched her, and I couldn't tell if it was a pleased breath or an impatient one, but for my own part, I was struggling to breathe at all. Just feeling the corset move with her inhales and exhales . . . feeling the boned stays under the silk . . .

Imagining the lacework on the back and the way her breasts would need lots of petting and kissing after being cooped up in the corset all day . . .

I had to tighten all the muscles in my arm so that she wouldn't feel my hand trembling against her. And my dick was *not* cooperating with me right now, but who could blame it? Because *corset.*

CORSET.

"And then it's the line about Felicity staying in your time," Gretchen said, flipping a script page. "Then it's the kiss—maybe if she touched you first before you lean in to kiss her? That'll warm it up a little."

"I could touch his jaw?" Bee volunteered. "Press my hand against his face and then look into his eyes?"

"That sounds good," I heard myself saying. Gruffly. I cleared my throat. "I mean, to warm up the kiss and all."

And then without any other warning, Bee did it. She pressed her palm against my jaw and peered up at me. Like I was the only person in the entire world. Her fingertips ever so gently stroked my cheek, rasping over the stubble and curling into where my hair waved over my ear.

I couldn't help but close my eyes.

"Nolan, that's *perfect*," Gretchen said, sounding happy. "I love that with you closing your eyes. Okay and then you'll lean in—count one, two, three, and Nolan says his line—and then kiss! Shit, okay, the light is already changing," she said before we could actually get to the kiss. "Do we want to do another quick run-through? Do we have anything we want to change to make it feel better? Or do you feel good?"

Bee shook her head, dropping her hand from my face so fast you'd think my jaw was made of exploding phone batteries.

"No," she said. "I'm ready."

I nodded in agreement. Even though I definitely wasn't

ready to have Bee's corseted waist under my palm again, and I definitely *definitely* wasn't ready to feel her lips on mine.

I could barely handle rehearsing the prekiss blocking. What the hell was I going to do when we actually kissed? Even a stage kiss would have her mouth under mine, her breath mingling with my own, her scent and her warmth all around me.

Pure as the driven snow, Nolan.

Pure as the driven snow.

I couldn't fuck this up.

As Bee was looked over one final time by the hair and makeup artists—and Pearl reemerged from a centering meditation somewhere—I popped a breath mint and tried to imagine I was the duke. A Hope Channel duke who'd never had sex and who never thought about sex and who'd never even seen two horses doing it in a field or whatever.

The duke of no boners. The softest duke who'd ever softed. That was me.

Soon it was time to start, and Bee and I found our marks. This moment happened right after Felicity came rushing back from the present day—her glam Victorian makeover courtesy of the Christmas Witch—to declare her feelings. The duke of no boners had admitted he returned them, and so then . . . the kiss.

Bee's eyes met my own. She looked as nervous as I felt— although it was probably for less horny reasons and more for *first real movie* reasons. I gave her a quick smile, and she returned it, her dimple flashing in her cheek.

"Action!" Gretchen called, and we began.

"So it's true? You do love me?" Bee said, stepping toward me. The rustle of her dress was my cue; I stepped forward too.

"My dear Felicity," I said, in an English accent, "I have loved you since you came crashing into my ballroom wearing your strange clothes. I have loved you since you brought me back to your time and made me try chili cheese fries."

She reached for my hands, just as we'd rehearsed, her wide green eyes pinned to mine. "I want to stay here. With you." The words were breathless, ardent, and when she looked up at me like this, I nearly forgot that she was Felicity and I was the Duke of Softpants. I nearly forgot that all of this was fake, and that I wasn't in a magical Christmas sex dream with Bianca von Honey.

I took her waist in my hand, feeling my cock give a quick kick in my breeches as I did, as if to remind me that we were skating real close to the limit of its endurance right now. "Do you mean it, my love?" I said as the duke, looking down to her high-cheekboned face. I could see the small dent—covered with makeup—where her septum piercing had been taken out. "Do you really want to stay? Even though it would mean leaving everything behind?"

She pressed her hand to my jaw, and my eyelids fluttered closed. I could stay like this forever.

"I mean it, Hugh," she breathed. Hugh was the duke's Christian name. "I mean it with all my heart."

I wasn't acting when I allowed my stare to drop to Bee's mouth. And I wasn't acting when my lips parted in instinctive response. "Felicity," I said hoarsely. "With you, I understand the real meaning of Christmas. With you, it all makes sense."

And with that, I dipped my mouth to hers and kissed her.

It was the seminal kiss of the movie, and so it was meant to be a few beats long. Because #hopechannel, there wouldn't be any pulling her into me, any cupping the back of her neck to keep her mouth fitted to mine as I explored it, hardly any passion at all, but that was all for the best, as I was barely hanging on anyway. The softness of her lips molding to mine, the way she gave in to my gentle demands . . . it was too much.

Even if it was only a stage kiss. Even if it was something I'd done countless times for music videos. Even if it was something that should be simple, it wasn't simple at all because it was *Bee*, and she smelled so sweet, like a warm sugar cookie, and the corseted dip of her waist under my hand felt like sin itself . . .

A flicker of wet heat drew my attention from her waist back to our kiss. A soft graze of her tongue was followed by another one, and then another one after that—little tastes that had me groaning quietly against her mouth. I couldn't help it, not in the least, because she was kissing me *for real*, her tongue seeking mine, stroking it expertly, and I didn't think I'd ever been kissed like this, kissed with such delicate skill. I'd never been kissed like I was already in bed with my pants unzipped. Because that's what this felt like. A kiss made for fucking.

And then, there it was: the collapse of all my gingerbread-infused effort. With a single kiss from Bee, all my control burned away, and my body stirred for her. I was going to have a problem hiding my response after this, but that didn't stop me from deepening the kiss, from holding her tight as she explored my mouth with a soft, sweet greed.

I'd figure out what was going on later.

But then she broke the kiss, gently. And as she pulled back

to look at me with a clear, focused gaze, I realized that she was still Felicity. She was still in the scene. Which meant that the kiss wasn't real and I still had to be the fucking duke, even though my erection was currently siphoning off all the blood from my brain.

Shit. What was my next line?

Oh, right. "Come, my love," I said, taking her hand. I was supposed to lead her off toward the ballroom now, but if she moved even a single inch, my hard-on would be visible to the crew and probably to everyone within a five-mile radius. So instead, I kissed the back of her hand and smiled at her. "Let's find the others and let them know what we learned about the real meaning of Christmas."

She smiled back at me. There was a hint of a flush on her cheeks, as if the kiss had affected her too, but maybe that was just the makeup or the lights.

"Cut!" Gretchen called. "Okay, fantastic take, you two. Let's do a few more takes to make sure we've got all the angles covered, and then we'll break and move to the declaration moment."

A few more takes?

I swallowed, not releasing Bee's hand until I was able to subtly adjust myself in the breeches, and then I decided I definitely wasn't going to survive today. Not if she kissed me like that on every take. My Bee Strategy was going to need some major adjustments, or Steph was going to end up with more tasteful arterial bunting than she knew what to do with.

CHAPTER SIX

Bee

It turned out that fucking on camera wasn't that different from doing other things on camera. Pausing in the midst of a love declaration for lighting adjustments was somehow just as awkward as pausing mid climax for an overhead plane to pass. In some weird turn of events, I was surrounded by more familiar faces than I'd expected, which gave me the boost of confidence I needed to dive into my first scene with Nolan, which was perhaps one of the most intimate moments in the whole script. I found myself actually feeling like maybe I really could forge a career as a mainstream actress. Maybe this wasn't so out of the realm of possibility. I forced my brain to gloss over the morality clause in my Hope Channel contract that could basically cause this whole move to self-detonate if my secret ever got out. Since Bee was my nickname—and since even *Bianca* Hobbes wasn't anywhere except on my lease—I knew any *Bee Hobbes* Google searches would come up empty. So hopefully, if there were any Hope Channel viewers who also watched porn—doubtful—they'd think I just had *one of those faces* and move on.

Potential morality-clause implosion aside, with Angel and Luca on set, Christmas Notch was feeling more and more like home.

The two of them walked a few steps ahead of me while I scrolled through messages on my ClosedDoors account— mostly very specific requests for my next video. Fruit or vegetables as dildos were always popular. They seemed to fulfill some kind of high school sex ed fetish. Foot videos were simple enough to accommodate and in a practical sense were always very period friendly. But every once in a while there was a message that crossed a line. Sometimes it was something innocent but creepy, like someone who'd seen me out in public and wanted to know if I lived in the neighborhood. And sometimes it was downright violent and grotesque—a stark reminder that to some people my body was nothing more than a vending machine for their needs. Immediate and disposable.

I always reported and blocked both. You could never be too careful in my line of work.

Angel turned back to me over his shoulder. "What do you think, Bee?"

"Hmm?" My attention was still buried in my inbox.

"A nightcap!" Luca called as he twirled, basking in the quietness of the dark velvet sky against the fluffy snow dusting absolutely everything.

The magic of this place was very real.

"Supposedly there's a strip club just outside of town called the North Pole," Angel said.

I slid my phone into the pocket of my coat and skipped to catch up to them. "Any other night, I would totally be there, but I'm beat."

Angel threw his arm around my shoulders. "There will be plenty of other nights to lubricate the local sex worker economy," he promised.

Luca bit back a smile. He'd never admit it, because Luca would never dare admit to any vulnerability, but he'd long carried a torch for Angel. I was happy to head back to my room and crash early if it meant giving the two of them a little uninterrupted time together in this winter wonderland.

As we approached the entrance of the inn, Angel opened his phone to search his rideshare apps.

"I don't know if you're going to find a Lyft or Uber out here," I said gently so as not to dash their Christmas-themed stripper dreams.

And as if on cue, the trolley bus parked under the inn's carport opened its door with a creaky wheeze. "You gentle folks look like you could use a ride," the man behind the wheel said. His wiry gray beard was so long it covered the bib of his overalls.

Luca shook his head, his whole body going into L.A. stranger-danger mode. "Uh, we're okay—"

"The North Pole!" I yelled over his hesitation.

The man in the driver's seat let out a knowing chuckle. "Well, hop on in. I'll swing back by fifteen after midnight. If your business isn't done by then, you're on your own till morning."

Angel took Luca's hand and charged forward. "Perfect." He waved to me. "See you in the A.M., Bee!"

Luca glanced back, panic stricken.

I gave him a thumbs-up, and every ounce of anxiety vanished as he rolled his eyes at my overbearing, mother hen levels of enthusiasm.

I laughed as the trolley—dripping in multicolor Christmas lights and garland—sped off toward what I assumed was the only strip club in a fifty-mile radius.

Inside the inn, the blast of heat was so immediate I had to take my jacket off before my trek upstairs. I was beginning to wonder if the elevator in this place had ever worked and if Stella's Out of Order sign was more permanent than she'd led me to believe.

"Oh, Bee!" a lyrical voice called.

Sitting in front of the crackling fire in the lobby were Pearl and Gretchen, curled up together, the latter of the two nodding off.

Pearl nudged at Gretchen. "Babe, it's Bee."

Gretchen's eyes fluttered into focus. "Oh, hey, Bee. Good first day?"

I gave them both two thumbs-up. "A dream come true, actually, now that I think about it." My first day on set moved so fast that I could barely process any of it in the moment, which was probably for the best, because now it was all coming back to me in overwhelming snapshots. Blocking the kiss. Declarations of undying love. The evening scene where the duke divulged his tragic backstory. Actually kissing. My breath hitching as my tongue flicked against Nolan's. By the end of our final take, my body was aching for more as I began to wonder what else he could do with that tongue.

I still couldn't believe it. I shared a kiss with the object of my teenage obsession, Nolan Shaw. Teenage Bee was dying. Adult Bee was dying. It was no mistake that the ceiling above my teenage bedroom was covered in INK posters. Of course, I had a crush on Kallum and Isaac, but Nolan was the boy whose thousand-yard stare felt like it was meant just for me. Every post. Every photo shoot. Nolan's piercing blue gaze was teenage Bee's number one withdrawal from the spank bank.

"Sit down for a sec, if you don't mind," Gretchen said, motioning to the leather ottoman.

I obeyed, because who could say no to Gretchen? *The* Gretchen Young. I'd been so in my head about starring opposite Nolan that I hadn't even taken a moment to consider the fact that I'd be working so closely with Gretchen, the ultimate *it* girl of my teen years. She was in Disney movies, young adult book adaptations, and also a few indie films that made her even more impossibly cool. If you didn't want to kiss her, you wanted to be her, and if you did want to kiss her, you probably still wanted to be her.

"You were great today," she said genuinely.

"So natural," Pearl confirmed.

"And I don't want to interfere with your process," Gretchen continued. "But I just wanted to let you know that there's no pressure to be so . . . full bodied in your kissing scenes."

"Full . . . bodied?"

Gretchen pursed her lips as she thought for a moment.

Pearl leaned forward, like the three of us were just a few girls talking at a slumber party. "Tongue," she said with a wink. "Hopeflix doesn't even let us show that kind of stuff, so a good old chaste stage kiss is all we need."

My whole body froze, the blood draining from my face. "Oh." I couldn't hide how horrified I was. Of course the kiss this morning was meant to be a stage kiss, and of course I stuck my tongue down Nolan Shaw's throat like we were filming some kind of soft-core foreplay. "I—I guess I just got caught up in the moment."

"And that's what we love about you," Pearl said, her voice bordering on otherworldly.

Gretchen nodded, her gaze of endearment lingering on Pearl as if even she knew that her girlfriend and screenwriter was some sort of fairylike being made of cotton candy and moon rocks. "We just don't want you to think that's required of you."

I stood then and nodded. I had to go upstairs before my entire body burst into flames of embarrassment. "Totally," I said. "And thank you. I appreciate that."

"Good night," they both cooed as I waved goodbye before disappearing into the stairwell.

Great. *D*elightful. First day on the job of an actual movie that wasn't a porno and I snaked my filthy tongue into my costar's mouth like I was clearing his dang pipes. Just lovely. Maybe tomorrow I would unhinge my jaw and swallow him whole while the crew watched.

In my room, I traded my opaque tights, corduroy skirt, and slouchy sweater for my ex-boyfriend's old undershirt that I couldn't seem to get rid of. (It was soft, okay?) After threading my septum piercing back in place and putting on a freshly opened sheet mask, I settled into bed with my laptop and did something I'd been meaning to do since I arrived.

"Proof! Of! Life!" Mama Pam shrieked the moment her face lit up my screen, and I saw so many of my features reflected back to me. Our button noses and rounded jawlines with full cheeks and the same ivory complexion with warm undertones.

"Hiiiiiii," I said sheepishly, trying not to move my face too much so that my face mask didn't slide right off.

"Del!" she called over her shoulder for my other mother, Delia. "Bee's on the phone! Get in here."

Even through the speakers of my computer, I could hear the pounding of Mom's steps as she came back downstairs, already midway through her bedtime routine, surely. I didn't know when or why, but Mom had always been Mom and Mama Pam had always been Mama Pam and my relationship with each of them was equally distinct. Mom was more of a hard-ass, with near impossible expectations at times, while Mama Pam was always there to remind Mom that I wasn't perfect and didn't have to be.

Mom saddled up next to Mama Pam at the kitchen table, taking the phone from her and turning it sideways so they were both in the frame. Mom's long dark hair was twisted into a thick braid pulled over her shoulder and over her heart. She wore the baby-pink terry cloth headband that she used every night to hold her hair back during her multistep skin-care routine.

"It's not proof of life if we can't see your face, baby," Mom said. "But I'm glad to see you taking care of your skin."

I rolled my eyes, and Mama Pam, who used bar soap and two-in-one shampoo and conditioner, shrugged.

"Your text message said you were going to Vermont?" Mom asked.

"Must be quite the job if you're filming on location," Mama Pam said.

The both of them had always been deeply supportive, even if it did take Mom a few months to catch up with Mama Pam's enthusiasm. And even though they never shied away from calling me an adult-film performer or a ClosedDoors model, they mostly referred to my actual job in general terms. *Filming. Gigs.* Those were easier words for us to communicate in.

"Is it snowing there?" asked Mama Pam, who, unlike Mom, was born and bred in small-town Texas and whose winter coat was a windbreaker.

"Actually, the flurries just started again when I was on my way back to the hotel."

Mom sighed. "How lovely to experience a little bit of snow around Christmastime."

"Speaking of Christmas . . ." I said.

"Yes," Mama Pam interjected. "We need to talk about Christmas Eve. The Turners invited us over for their annual party. Apparently, they've got the gay men's choir from St. Paul's Episcopal as entertainment, but we wanted to leave it up to you."

Mom leaned her head against Mama Pam's shoulder. "Oh come now, tell her the truth. We just don't want to share you with anyone else while you're home."

I needed to tell them. Mama Pam might cry and Mom might crawl through this screen to kill me herself, but I had to tell them.

Mama Pam nodded. "But the choir is very tempting. They're nearly impossible to book these days and—"

"I won't be home for Christmas," I blurted.

The two of them were so silent that I had to check and make sure they hadn't frozen. "Are y'all still there?" I asked, my voice creeping into its Texas roots. "Moms?"

Mom cleared her throat after a long moment. "Yes, dear, we're still here, but I don't think we heard you correctly."

"Did you just say you would not be celebrating Christmas with us?" Mama Pam asked.

"Well . . . when you put it like that . . . It's just that I'm on location and barely even have a full day off. I'd have to fly home and get right back on my return flight," I tried to explain. Mom responded well to logic. Surely she would see my dilemma here.

Mom leaned forward so that I could barely see Mama Pam, making it very clear that this conversation was between her and me. "What exactly are you doing in Vermont? I can't imagine an adult film would need to film through the holidays, Bianca." And nothing about the way she said my birth name and subsequently my porn name was at all sexy. "Dear, is there something you're not telling us? Are you seeing someone?"

"Are you back with Spencer?" asked Mama Pam in the background. "It's okay. We won't be mad."

Even though that was definitely a lie. They'd be very mad if I got back with Spencer. I'd be mad with me if I got back with Spencer, the struggling screenwriter I was in an on-again, off-again relationship with for a year and a half until eight months ago, when I thought for sure he was cheating. Turns out he wasn't cheating. He was just attending a string of family weddings over the summer that he was too embarrassed to take me to. If I hadn't immediately dumped him, Sunny would have done it for me.

A loud knock rapped against my door. Loud enough that they could hear.

"Who's that?" they asked in unison.

"Does it look like I'm expecting someone?" I asked, motioning to my face mask and ratty T-shirt.

"It would be fine if you were," Mom said. "You're an adult woman who is perfectly capable of making safe and informed sexual decisions."

I stood up and left the laptop on the bed.

"But perhaps you could put on pants first," Mom said through the screen.

"Del," Mama Pam scolded.

I looked through the peephole in my door to see Nolan tracing his jawline with his thumb . . . the same jaw I'd touched just this morning. I could practically feel the stubble against the pads of my fingers even now. Heat coiled in my abdomen. "Shit," I muttered.

"Who is it?" Mom asked again, more loudly now.

I ran back to the computer and tore the mask off my face. "I gotta run, y'all, but I'll call back soon, I promise."

"Don't forget to squeeze the excess product out of the face mask and massage it into your skin," Mom urged breathlessly. "Especially your neck! That's where you age first. That and your hands."

"We love you, baby," Mama Pam said.

"Love y'all too." I slammed the laptop shut before they could get another word out about Christmas or excess skin-care product, and I ran into the bathroom in search of a bathrobe.

"Shit, shit, shit," I quietly shrieked.

He knocked again, and this time called, "Bee?"

I took one look at Spencer's undershirt, which was ripped around the collar and one of the few mementos I still had of our relationship. Quickly, I tore it off over my head before pulling the inn robe off the back of my bathroom door. One size fits most? More like one size fits most people who don't have any tits, ass, or internal organs in general.

I knotted the sash tightly under my bust and made the absolutely ludicrous decision to wrap my hair in a towel. *It's a whole look*, I tried convincing myself.

And holy shit. Bad boy Nolan Shaw was knocking at my hotel room door. This was like my favorite INK fan fiction come to life. In fact, I think the opening scene of *18 Hours in Tokyo* started just like this. After the band broke up, I circled fanfic sites like a vulture, hoping that the stories I found there might give me the kind of closure INK themselves never had.

I don't know if they gave me closure, but they certainly

helped deliver some of my first orgasms. Written in first person, *18 Hours in Tokyo* opened with Nolan making strong, meaningful eye contact with a stranger (the reader) on an elevator during a tour stop. The stranger slipped him a key card before getting off on their floor, and well . . . let's just say that the imaginary things that imaginary Nolan did to the imaginary mystery person had lived in my imagination for years to come.

The way my nipples instantly hardened in the balmy hotel bathroom at the sheer memory of that fic told me one thing for certain: I might have grown out of my INK phase, but I definitely hadn't grown out of my Nolan Shaw crush.

One last quick knock pounded against the door.

"Coming!" I said as I pulled the gaping robe closed around my hips, unable to help the sliver of thigh peeking out. I held my hands to my cheeks. They were so warm and flushed. I wished I could dunk myself in an ice bath.

I ran across the room and swung the door open before stepping out into the hall. "Hi. Good evening," I said, sounding like a hostess at an Outback Steakhouse. Party of one?

His brows shot up for a brief moment before settling into an expression of indifference. He yanked his beanie off his head and shoved it into his back pocket before tugging a hand through his hair, like he was actually trying to yank it out of his scalp.

It took everything in me not to reach up and pull his hand away, begging him to just go easier on himself.

"Uh, sorry to interrupt anything. I know it's late." He looked both ways down the hallway. "Embarrassingly enough, I couldn't get the phone in my room to work and I couldn't find that directory thing they gave us so I couldn't text you and—"

"It's okay," I said, taking a step toward him. There was a nervous energy about him tonight, like I could feel his body thrumming with electricity, and all I wanted to do was place a hand against his chest to remind him to breathe.

"Right. I just . . . you were great today."

"Thanks." The poorly lit hallway hid the blush gathering on my cheeks.

"I was thinking we could run lines tomorrow? Our call time is pretty late."

"We could do that."

"The dance studio around noon?" he asked. "I think we have to meet up there later this week to rehearse for the ball scene."

"Oh God," I said. "I almost forgot we had to dance."

"Can't be any harder than kissing," he said softly.

"Can't be," I replied.

"Well, good night, Bee Hobbes," he said.

"Good night, Nolan Shaw."

I watched as he walked down to the very end of the hallway. The last room on the left.

And as he reached into his pocket for his key, waving at me once more before ducking inside his room, I remembered that I definitely slipped Nolan Shaw some tongue earlier that day during our kiss.

And Nolan Shaw had returned the favor. Tongue and all. I guess I wasn't the only one who forgot to keep it PG.

He really was the bad boy of INK, wasn't he?

I SLEPT WITH the curtains wide open, because if I didn't, I would definitely sleep through all my alarms. Sleep didn't come easy. I was too frustrated and horny. Every time I closed my eyes and let my fingers trail down my breastbone, I saw Nolan wringing his beanie in his hands. Biting his lip. Standing in an elevator. Holding my gaze. Sliding a key card into the door of a hotel room with me waiting on the other side. And finally I gave in—if anything, just so I could get some sleep.

Something about masturbating to my costar felt like a slippery slope that led straight to breaking all of Teddy's rules, but it certainly wasn't enough to stop me and soon I was biting into my pillow, thankful that I'd remembered to pack the charger for my vibrator.

When I finally fell asleep, I couldn't stop myself from dreaming of our kiss over and over again. I hadn't been so turned on by a kiss since Robert Pattinson and Kristen Stewart kissed at the end of *Twilight* with Iron and Wine playing in the background. (Turned out I wanted to be *and* kiss both Edward *and* Bella. I still mourn the fact that the porn parody of *Twilight* was shot before my time.)

As I sat up early the next morning, still slumped against my headboard, the sound of someone jiggling my doorknob woke me up completely. *Please don't be a Christmas-themed serial killer.* I tiptoed carefully to my door and peered out the peephole.

"Angel?" I asked as I unlocked my dead bolt to find a surprised, partially drunk, and partially already hungover Angel standing in the hallway, limply holding his room key in his hand.

"Oops," he said through a hiccup. "Wrong room. I can't find my room, so all the rooms are the wrong room."

I snorted out a laugh and pulled him inside before closing the door behind us. "Let me get you some water. Please tell me you haven't just been wandering the halls of this place all night."

"No, no, no," he said with a yawn. "We stayed at the bar until two-ish. And then Prancer gave us a ride home." He nodded with eyes closed. "Salt of the earth. Strippers are. Salt. Of. The. Earth."

I reached into my minifridge that didn't actually work and handed him a room-temperature bottle of water, which he chugged in three gulps. "And then Luca and I went back to his room—"

"Oh?"

He held a finger up and shook it in my face. "And we fell asleep watching an old Celine Dion concert."

"Oh," I said, somehow both unsurprised and disappointed. "That actually sounds really romantic."

He stumbled over to my minifridge, taking my second and last complimentary bottle of water. "Do not. Do not even go there. My brain hurts too much to even consider what it might mean that I was perfectly content to fall asleep to an old Celine Dion concert and innocent cuddles, because that could only mean two things. Either I'm old or I'm in love, and I am neither of those things."

"Or you're both," I offered.

He chugged the second bottle and crushed the plastic before tossing it into the small recycling bin. "Unspeak your curse, witch."

After a moment, he stretched with his whole body and opened his eyes widely. "Okay. Okay. Okay. I'm awake. I'm sober. And dear God, I need a shower."

"Oh, oh, oh wait!" I jumped up from where I was perched on the edge of my whirlpool tub. "Before you go, could you do me a favor? I forgot my tripod, and I really need a shot for my ClosedDoors page."

He held his hand out for my phone.

"Thank you, thank you, thank you!" I squealed. "Give me just, like, ten minutes. I need to get ready. I'm going for that oh-I-had-so-much-sex-all-night-I-can-barely-open-my-eyes-but-here's-my-cute-little-tush-ready-and-waiting look." Surely there's some sort of compromise to be found in keeping my supporters happy and not pissing off Teddy. And I was reasonably certain a few more paywalled posts on an already porny ClosedDoors account wasn't going to fundamentally change the risk calculus with my Hope Channel morality clause.

"So, natural?" Angel asked.

"Exactly," I said as I dug through my suitcase for the perfect pair of barely there panties.

CHAPTER SEVEN

Nolan

Don't look at her ClosedDoors account. Don't look at her Closed-Doors account.

I sat on the edge of my bed, freshly showered and with my phone in my hand. I'd just gotten the notification that she had a new post, and I wasn't going to look, I absolutely was not going to look. Because if I looked, I was going to break, and I didn't want to break, not on the very first morning implementing my new and improved Bee Strategy.

The new strategy went like this: *no orgasms in Christmas Notch*. Like at all. My junk was now verboten to me.

As yesterday's shower session had shown me, I was incapable of keeping my mind off Bee when I jerked off, and after the kiss yesterday . . .

I groaned remembering it. The silky whisper of her tongue against mine. The wicked coax of her lips. It had been a kiss that said *I'd like to sit on your face, please*, and there was simply no way in heaven, hell, or Vermont that I'd be able to stroke myself without thinking of it. Or without thinking of the two kisses that had come after—each as filthy as the first, and yet hauntingly innocent too, because whenever we'd break off the kiss, I'd pull back to see her looking up at me with wide, pretty eyes, and her expression showing nothing but total commitment to Felicity. It was like she had no idea stage kisses were a thing. And she definitely had no idea what they did to me. Even though they were the most carnal kisses I'd ever felt in my life, she clearly wasn't trying to be carnal at all, which made me a total perv for kissing her back.

Sure, sure, I could always say that I hadn't wanted to ruin the take, but the truth was cutting through my conscience like scissors through wrapping paper: I had wanted to kiss her back. I had wanted to feel her tongue on mine. Professionalism be damned, Steph's warnings be damned, I'd *wanted* it.

But for reasons both moral and practical (but okay, more practical than moral, let's be honest), I now had to stifle all Bee-related thoughts. We had only one other kiss scene to shoot, and if I wasn't going to end up panting after her like a dog, I needed to cut all my fantasies off at the source.

Which was why it was a terrible idea to look at her Closed-Doors post. Terrible idea. Simply terrible.

But maybe just a quick peek . . .

My thumb moved on its own, muscle memory taking over as I woke up my screen and tapped the app notification to take me to her latest post. And *fuck*, it was a good post. I bit my knuckle as I looked at it, a low groan working its way out of my chest.

Bianca von Honey in lacy little panties, hair tousled, bottom up in the air as she stared into the camera with hooded, come-hither eyes.

Unf.

God, to be in the same room as her, to be walking toward that bed knowing that curvaceous ass was mine to smack. To be *with* her, near her, able to kiss her for real with no one watching . . .

My cock filled and lengthened, pushing against the towel I had wrapped around my waist, and you know what, screw the strategy, screw the plan, I would need superhuman strength to resist a picture like this, and maybe it was smarter to stop when the gingerbread lotion was all gone anyway, like how smokers quit when they're done with a pack—

Before I could get off the bed to find the bottle, something in the picture caught my eye.

Something that looked an awful lot like a reflection of someone in the window behind Bee.

It was blurry and half-obscured by the candy-cane-print curtains, but after I zoomed in, there was no doubt it was someone holding up a phone, like they were taking the picture for her.

And then I remembered last night when I'd knocked on her door, having spent a full thirty minutes psyching myself up to ask her to read lines, and she'd answered wearing a bathrobe and an expression that made it seem like I'd pulled her away from something. And the way she'd stepped out into the hall instead of staying in her doorway, like she hadn't wanted me to see inside . . .

It hit me like a baton to the knee. She hadn't been alone last night.

She'd been with someone else.

IT WAS A mistake suggesting the dance studio for reading lines. I should have suggested Frosty's Diner (now serving Blitzen blini!) or maybe the lobby of our kitschy inn. Or better yet, the town square, where there'd be no chance of me thinking non-Benedictine nun thoughts because I'd be freezing my beanie off.

But no, I had suggested the dance studio. Which apart from being completely empty aside from me and soon my costar, also came with mirrors. And a barre.

Which looked tailor-made for resting a lover's leg on while I fucked them from behind.

But maybe Bee Hobbes already had someone else to do that with?

I paced around the dance studio as I waited for her, rolling my script into the tightest cylinder possible and feeling stupid. Normally, I found a dance studio to be a comforting place. No matter what ridiculous thing was happening in our lives, no matter what was going on between Kallum, Isaac, and me, once we got into a studio, everything became easy. Simple. Learn the routine. Practice till you got it right. There had never been a problem that music and sweat couldn't fix.

Of course, it wasn't that easy anymore, in these post-INK

times. Which was why I was waiting for Bee when she was probably still saying goodbye to whoever had stayed the night in her room.

As soon as I'd thought it, I wanted to hit myself in the head with my rolled-up script, like I was a bad dog. What did it matter if she wasn't alone last night? She had every right to be with whomever she wanted!

But God—how I wanted it to be me. I wanted those sultry eyes on *me*, I wanted that hair all tangled and messy from *me*. I wanted to kiss her and have her melt the same way I melted when she'd kissed me for the scene yesterday.

You couldn't anyway, I reminded myself. Even if she wanted me to be the person in her room, I couldn't be. There was too much at stake for me to risk getting caught behaving badly, even for a woman I'd built a thousand behaving-badly fantasies around. In fact, maybe *especially* for that woman, because getting caught fucking around would be bad. But getting caught fucking around with a porn star? *Extra bad.*

So why had I picked a room full of mirrors and lined with a very inviting barre again?

The unexpectedly sexy environment of the dance studio wasn't helped by Bee showing up in skintight leggings and a clingy sweater, which was cropped above her waist so that I could see a strip of warm, suntanned skin between the bottom of it and the top of her leggings.

I actually had to turn away while she shucked off her coat and started stomping her boots on the rug in front of the door. She was doing it to get the snow off, but it had the fantastic effect of making her thighs and ass move as she did, and her breasts too—and if I watched her any longer, I was going to have problems keeping things at Steph-approved levels of flaccidity.

I suddenly needed to be anywhere but here. Anywhere but with a woman who couldn't be mine for so many reasons, and who was nuking the slouchy-cool control I'd taken years to master.

Just get this over with and escape, I told myself. *Then you can get yourself together before you're actually on set with her again.*

"Thanks for meeting me," Bee said.

"Yeah," I said, my voice coming out shorter than I'd meant it to. "No problem."

Since I didn't hear any more stomping, I assumed it was safe to turn around. As I did, I carefully kept my gaze above her shoulders. I couldn't avoid seeing her soft mouth or those striking green eyes, but at least she wouldn't think I was leering at her. But then I felt my gaze drawn back to her mouth in a way that was both leering *and* not helping with the new Bee Strategy of total denial, and I forced my eyes past her to the windowed door and the snowy main street outside.

"We should get started," I said, avoiding looking at her as I glanced at my watch. "We won't have long before hair and makeup."

"Sure," she said, her voice cooler than before, and when I finally braved a look at her, I saw something almost defiant in her expression. It was gone before I could decipher what it was.

"Okay," I replied pointlessly, a little bothered and not sure why. I gestured toward the far end of the studio, where there was a small table and two chairs set against the wall. "Shall we?"

"Yes," she said, and started making her way to the table. I followed after making sure my phone was on vibrate. I couldn't miss any calls from home, especially if they came after Mom's appointment today.

Bee sat down and set the week's pages on the table in front of her. Her hair slid over her shoulder in glossy waves, and all I wanted on this earth was to wrap some of those waves around my fist and tug.

I blew out a long breath. How was I going to survive being in a room alone with her for as long as it took to read through these lines?

I sat down too and carefully unfurled my script from the tight scroll I'd rolled it into, trying to signal that we should get started, when Bee pressed her hands to the table and looked at me. It seemed like she'd lost a bet with herself or something, like she didn't want to say what she was going to say next, but she had no choice.

"So I have to ask," she said, her voice still cool, but her words a bit rushed too. Maybe she was curious or nervous . . . or both. "What is Naughty Nolan Shaw doing making a Christmas movie? For the Hope Channel of all places?"

Well, Bee, I need the money. I need the veneer of safe celebrity. And aside from having been famous once, I have no skills other than getting into trouble and painting theater sets, and so smiling pretty for the Hopeflix camera was my only option.

But I couldn't say all that, not to my dream girl. So I fed her the spiel Steph had cooked up. "I've always loved acting, and this project grabbed my attention." That was PR-speak for *This was the first project I could get hired for.* "And knowing

that it was directed by Gretchen Young made it irresistible,"
I added.

That part *was* true. I'd been around manufactured fame and
engineered talent long enough to recognize a genuine gift when
I saw it, and Gretchen was phenomenal. Which was why it was
so fascinating that a made-for-TV Christmas movie was where
she wanted to make her directorial debut. I would have thought
something indie and sad-quirky, or maybe some big-budget
woman-led superhero film. But nope. The Hope Channel.

I suspected her bendy-looking screenwriter girlfriend had
something to do with it, but who knew? Maybe Gretchen just
really liked Christmas movies.

Bee was looking at me as I fiddled with the pages of my
script, and I had the uncomfortable feeling she could see right
through my PR-speak and that she wasn't very impressed by
it. I tried not to care; I never used to care about anything! But
this was Bianca von Honey we were talking about. My pride
prickled hard at her disapproval.

"What about you?" I asked, trying to deflect the conversation away from myself. "What brings you to *Duke the Halls*?"

Bee pulled her lower lip between her teeth for a moment—
long enough for me to greedily trace how the white points of
her incisors dug into her plump flesh—and then did a quick,
preparatory inhale. "I guess I've always loved acting too," she
said quickly. "I've been doing, um, freelance modeling stuff
in L.A., but my real love has always been for theater and film.
I've been trying to break into acting for a while, but—"

A shrug, which sent more glossy hair sliding every which way.

"It's hard for a fat actress. Either no one wants to cast you at all, or the roles they do cast you for aren't exactly awesome. It's like being in high school theater all over again."

I tried not to cringe when she called herself fat. Bee was the sexiest goddamn woman in the world to me, so it was hard to wrap my head around a word that felt like a schoolyard insult. The way she said the word *fat*, though, was so matter-of-fact, like it was just a neutral truth.

It made me see that Bee wasn't the problem. Fat wasn't the problem. But the way the world, and especially the entertainment industry, treated people like Bee . . . *that* was the problem.

"I'm sorry," I said, and I meant it. I'd seen some of the headlines directed Kallum's way for his dad bod, and they were pretty crappy. I imagined it was a thousand times worse for a woman in the industry.

She lifted an eyebrow at my response. "Well, fatphobia is everywhere." There was a pointedness to her voice that I couldn't quite identify, and before I could even try, she flipped open her script. "Should we get started?"

"Um. Sure."

I paged through the script until I found tomorrow's scenes. Because the fake Frostmere Manor also hosted weddings and assorted other events, along with the occasional filming of a movie, we had it booked for weird chunks of time. Tomorrow at the manor we were shooting both Felicity's first Victorian dinner with the duke and the mutual declaration of love that came before the final kiss.

The memory of the kiss flooded through me, sending heat straight to my groin.

I cleared my throat. "Which scene would you like to do first?"

"Can we do the last one in our pages?" Bee asked. "The scene right before the kiss?"

"Yep," I said, trying not to think too much about the kiss. But it was difficult when she was running her finger along the edge of the page, because her nails were painted a shade of pink that made me think of the pink places of her body. Like her lips. Among other things.

Pure as the driven snow, Nolan. Celibate as a nun.

I shifted in my seat, and imagined nuns and snow. And nuns making angels in the snow while wearing wimples and big wooden rosaries and stuff.

"Your Grace," Bee started reading, keeping Felicity's contemporary American accent, "I finally understand what the witch wanted me to learn. I finally understand why she sent me here. To you."

"Don't say 'Your Grace' as if we were strangers, dear Felicity," I replied, my eyes on her, since I already had most of my lines memorized. "Or as if you were beneath me. You aren't. You are my everything. You make up my entire world."

Bee glanced up. The sunlight winked off her septum ring. "I forgot to tell you yesterday. You have an *amazing* British accent."

Despite everything, I couldn't help the smug grin that was spreading across my face. "I know."

"*How?*" she asked. "That's not something they taught you on that *Bootcamp* show, is it?"

I shook my head. *Boy Band Bootcamp* was the reality show

where I got my start; boys from all over the country came to learn to dance, sing, and wallow in pettiness. Zero accent lessons. Although, weirdly, lots of etiquette lessons.

"It's a pre-INK skill," I said. "You're not the only high school theater geek here, you know. You're looking at the youngest ever Wadsworth to grace the stage of Olathe North High School."

"You were the butler in *Clue*?"

"Sophomore year," I said proudly. "And I was Prince Eric in *The Little Mermaid*."

There was a subtle dimple in her cheek, like she was fighting off a smile. "I'm imagining you as a Disney prince now. It's very hard."

I pressed a hand to my chest in mock hurt. "I'm wounded. You don't see how all this hair makes me the perfect prince?" I tugged off my beanie and ran my hands through my hair so that it swept off my face all prince-like.

The dimple was getting deeper now. "Maybe I can see the prince thing . . . if you were Beast from *Beauty and the Beast*."

I sighed dramatically. "The one that got away. Kallum got that role. I had to be Gaston instead."

"Kallum?" Bee asked, her face lighting up. "Like Kallum Lieberman? He was Beast?"

I fought off a little sulk. I didn't expect people to fawn over me because I'd once been a teen pop sensation or whatever, but I'd assumed that Bee had a blanket apathy for all former boy band members. *Not* that she'd be interested in Kallum with a K instead of me.

"He was," I said. Sulkily. "But he did trip over Cogsworth

and knock over the set on opening night, so he wasn't great at it."

"So you two really did go to high school together?" she asked. "That wasn't, like, a cute, manufactured backstory thing?"

Hmm. So she knew that little tidbit of INK lore, did she? Maybe she cared more about my history with INK than she'd let on.

"We grew up basically in each other's backyards. I was the troublemaker, and Kallum was the kid who always went along with whatever wild idea I had." (The wildest idea I'd ever had? That we should drive to L.A. and try out for a show called *Boy Band Bootcamp*. Sigh.)

"We were sort of like Pinky and the Brain," I said. "Any trouble we ever got in was always my fault. Luckily in high school it was mostly contained to pranking the theater teacher and the occasional heavy petting sesh on the cast sofa."

"With each other?" Bee's eyes were as round as saucers.

I laughed. "I wish." I'd gone through a big Kallum crush phase, but it'd never gone anywhere. Kallum was pretty flexible as far as heteroflexibles went, but he was never truly *available*. Starting with Kayla Schechter, he always seemed to be either falling in love, actively in love—or nursing some kind of post-in-love heartbreak.

"It's hard to imagine Kallum being a theater kid," Bee said after a minute. "I'd always assumed he'd played high school football or something."

Kallum definitely looked like a former jock, but what could I say? The man loved to sing and dance. "He was the one who got me started in theater in the first place," I told her. "In middle school. I agreed to try out for *Once Upon a Mattress* on the condition that he let me borrow his Game Boy Advance, and then somehow I made it into the cast. And I ended up loving it."

Offstage, I'd been just another crappy student with a bad attitude. But onstage, I could be anyone. And when I sang— even silly musical songs that had nothing to do with my actual life—it sometimes felt like the words and the melodies were coming together to express a part of me I would have never been able to explain otherwise.

"Do you still talk to him?" Bee asked, and I didn't bother hiding my sulk this time.

"Why are you so interested in Kallum?" I asked. My pout was more real than pretend, but the coy little smile I got in return was worth it.

"No reason," she said, looking back down at her script.

But now her dimple was here to stay. And suddenly I wasn't so interested in rushing through the reading so I could escape. I wanted to do everything I could to see that smile again.

"Hey," I said, putting my fingers over the top of her script. "I meant to tell you that you were fantastic yesterday."

She looked up at me, her eyebrows lifted in surprise. "Really? You think so?" she said, and then shoved her face in her hands and groaned. "That sounded so needy. I'm *sorry*."

"We're all needy here. Isn't that why we're performers and not test engineers for software companies?"

She laughed and peeked at me through her fingers. It was so flipping cute.

"And for real," I said softly, "you were so good. You've got a knack for this, you know? For showing all a character's corners and edges. No shade on Pearl, but that's not the easiest task with the source material. And transitioning from theater to screen isn't something everyone can do."

God knows I'd had a hell of a time with it myself. It had taken countless music videos and eleventy million photo shoots to learn how to emote with the small, subtle precision that was so contrary to the big acting I'd been used to in theater. My early bad boy persona had been more John Travolta in *Grease* than perfectly curated teenage apathy.

"I just . . ." She shook her head. "I feel so out of place here. This was Winnie's role. You should be sitting here with the sweet and wholesome Winnie Baker right now."

"Winnie isn't my costar. You are. And you're a fucking scene-stealer in the best possible way. Christmas-obsessed audiences everywhere are going to gobble you up. Five out of five Yule logs. Would costar again."

She lowered her hands to reveal bright pink cheeks, which she seemed a little embarrassed of. She coughed a small cough, adjusted her script on the table, and then mumbled something that sounded like *thank you shut up.*

I grinned and nudged her foot under the table. "It's true. I'll remind you of it every day if I have to."

And somehow, I managed to behave for the rest of our mini table-read. Even after she shifted and her knee brushed against mine, and the warmth of her skin seeped through my jeans. Even after she gave me a parting smile that was so big and bright, it felt like summer itself had come to Christmas Notch.

I wondered if she'd smiled at the person she'd spent the night with like that.

I wondered if they'd felt like they could move mountains afterward.

So anyway, I behaved, which was a very good thing, because it wasn't until I got back to my room that I fully digested the fact that Bee hadn't mentioned anything about porn or Bianca von Honey when she was explaining why she was here. In fact, no one had mentioned it at all that I could remember—not Pearl or Steph or Teddy.

Which must mean that *they* didn't know.

Which meant it was a secret.

Which meant that like me, she was trying to keep her past from getting in the way of her future.

CHAPTER EIGHT

Bee

Nolan Shaw had a soft side. Like, a mushy-to-the-touch soft side. And his encouraging words were all I could think of as I walked with a little skip in my step into the costume department, where Luca held a clipboard to his chest as he quickly flipped through a rack of extremely normal street clothes while Angel sat behind the fake toy shop register with his feet propped up on the fake toy shop counter.

"Yeah, their breakup is turning out to be the porn divorce of the century," Angel said as he eagerly scrolled his phone. "This is like ten times worse than when my actual parents got divorced. At least my mom left Uncle Ray-Ray's mostly intact."

"Your mom produces daytime talk shows," Luca said. "She probably paid Teddy to keep his porn biz to himself."

"Whose breakup?" I asked as I fiddled with the dress labeled FELICITY NIGHTTIME PRESENT-DAY MONTAGE. A green knee-length velvet dress with a Peter Pan collar and an ivory wool coat topped off with black tights and a red scarf. It was cute. Nothing I'd ever wear, but cute.

"Do you like it?" asked Luca. "Does it say time-traveling virgin?"

"Precisely," I said as I began to take off my coat.

"Jack Hart and Levi Banks," Angel said with a sigh. "Things are getting messy."

I frowned. Jack and Levi had been together since I started in porn, and last year they got married in a huge wedding where they both wore denim tuxedos à la Britney and Justin. In fact, they planned it the same weekend as the AVN Awards after Levi was snubbed for a second year in a row, and their reception was better attended than the AVN after-party at the Virgin Hotel in Vegas. The porn industry had taken the news of their breakup badly to say the least. "I thought their split was amicable."

"Not according to Jack's latest Instagram post," Luca said. "Think of it this way. If this were a custody battle, it looks like Levi is getting everything, even the dog."

"Miss Crumpets?" Poor Jack—oh crap, *Jack*! I let out a loud gasp and pulled my phone out. "Shit."

"What'd you forget?" Luca asked as he held open the door of the makeshift dressing room.

"I just need to text someone." I stepped inside with my costume and began to type out a message to Jack. I knew I was forgetting something when I left town. I'd taken the whole month of December off. It was something I'd worked for all year. It would be the month I learned to bake or went to a restaurant on the other side of town just because. But then a few weeks ago, Jack called me, saying he was desperate for a scene partner for a gig he'd booked. He was light on details, but Jack had once fished me out of a bad situation when I was starting out, so I owed him. Plus I'd felt bad about the divorce.

> **Me:** Hey, I hope you're okay. I know things aren't easy at the moment. I'm really sorry to do this, but I'm in Vermont (long story), and I'm going to have to reschedule our shoot. I'll text you when I'm back.

"Everything okay in there?" Luca asked.

I dropped my phone into the pile of clothes I'd slowly shed. "Yup! All good."

I HELD BOTH hands over my face, trying to contain my laughter at the sight of Nolan.

"Oh, come on," he said, touching his hair while Denise, the hair stylist, swatted at his hands. "It's not that bad."

I'd encountered Denise on a few shoots for Uncle Ray-Ray's, and no matter how many times we met, I had to reintroduce myself, so this time I didn't even bother. Denise had some major Midwestern-mom energy. Her thick auburn hair was very permed, and her matching tracksuit gave off *I have a van and I'm not afraid to use it* vibes.

"When you get paid to touch your hair," she said, "you can touch it. Until then, it's mine."

Nolan slumped down in his chair. His normally reckless locks had been slicked and parted so that—

"You look like a Young Republican," I blurted.

He slapped a hand to his wounded heart. "It's for the *art*, Bee. The art that will send me a nice, non-arty paycheck. This might come as a surprise, but even ex–boy band members need affordable healthcare."

"Porn stars too," I muttered.

"What was that?"

"Out of work actors too," I said with a smile.

"Well, you look like a librarian." He patted the director's chair next to him, and for the first time I realized the back of the chair had my name on it.

I fumbled for my cell phone in the deep pockets of the coat I'd bought from the town's tiny department store, a coat much better suited for Vermont in December than the one I brought from L.A. "Is it nerdy to take a picture of that?" I gushed.

He grinned. "Are you kidding me? Your name on a chair? That's boss shit."

I held my phone up. "Say 'boss shit.'"

"Boss shit," he said through his warm, broad smile.

Before I forgot, I sent the picture right to Sunny. She was going to lose it.

I hoisted myself up and managed to wedge my hips into the unforgiving chair with a grunt. "My ass was not made for this chair."

He shook his head, unbothered. "No, it's the chair that wasn't made for your ass."

I tried to swallow, but my throat was suddenly dry and my

tongue felt like it was too thick and I couldn't form words. So instead I just let his comment sink in between us, slowly sucking the air out of my lungs as waves of want rolled through me. Was Nolan Shaw an ass man? Was he an ass man for my ass?

A few moments later, Gretchen strode toward us. "You two look great," she said. "Tonight, we're just looking for some really playful moments for the montage. We'll be in the diner and then reset for some street scenes. I don't want to keep you both too late since we have an early call time tomorrow. We've finally got almost all the crew replaced, so we're ready to get moving at a quicker pace starting first thing in the morning."

Nolan and I both nodded along. Gretchen always presented herself as in control, even when she wasn't, and there was something very calming about that. She was like that one friend who always volunteered to be the designated driver.

"Nolan, tonight should be cake for you. A montage is just a music video," she said.

He nodded confidently, and the two of us were led inside the diner, which was decked out for Christmas in red and silver. All the extras inside were bundled up in scarves and hats, and the waitresses wore roller skates with peppermint wheels and diner uniform dresses to match.

As we sat down in our booth, I was thankful that our scriptwork for the night was light. After Nolan's ass comment, my brain could barely string together sentences.

We were only a few days in. I had no idea how I'd survive the next few weeks without actually imploding, and I honestly couldn't tell if my little jerk off sesh last night had made things better or worse.

"Bee?" he asked. "They need to know if you're a vegetarian."

"Huh?" I shook my head, trying to dislodge the horny, angsty memories of teenage Bee.

"For the chili cheese fries," he clarified.

I smiled up at the props master, who was not so patiently waiting for my answer.

"Um, no. I'm a failed vegetarian. Maybe it'll stick one day."

"You don't have to swallow," he said with a shrug. "You can spit if you need to. Just take a bite for the money shot." He walked off down the narrow aisle.

Nolan tilted his chin up. "Did he just . . . ? Was that . . . ?"

I leaned out of the booth and squinted at the guy from across the restaurant. He looked vaguely familiar now that I thought about it. Must be one of Teddy's. "Yeah, that felt a little dirty," I said with a snort.

"A failed vegetarian, huh?" Nolan asked.

"I'm mostly fine in L.A., but that Texas barbeque gets me every time."

"Inferior," he coughed into his fist.

"Excuse me?" I said, crossing my arms defensively over my chest.

"Listen," he said, reaching across the table to touch my arm gently. I felt the heat of his fingertips through the velvet of my sleeve and held back a trembling breath. "It's not your fault you've been led astray your whole life and have never felt the gospel of Kansas City barbeque deep in your bones, but it's not too late to accept our Lord and Savior, Z-man Christ, into your heart and belly."

"The Z-who?" I asked.

His jaw dropped. "The Z-man. Only the greatest sandwich known to mankind. Brisket, smoked provolone, kaiser bun, onion rings, and Joe's Kansas City Bar-B-Que sauce. Perfection."

I waved him off and rolled my eyes. "Texas barbeque doesn't require bread. That's how good our shit is."

He recoiled from me and opened his mouth to counter just as a tower of chili cheese fries was placed down between us.

As we began to film take after take, Nolan and I took turns feeding each other cheese fries. Every few minutes, they'd replace our plate with a fresh tower.

"I'm never going to look at chili cheese fries the same way again," Nolan said in between takes.

"Okay," Gretchen said as she suddenly slid into the booth next to me. "I've got a thought. How do you two feel about giving us a little *Lady and the Tramp* moment with the fries?"

I looked to Nolan, who shrugged. "I think we can handle that."

I pointed to his side. "Should I go over there or should . . ."

Gretchen stood. "Nolan, you come over to sit with Bee. God, I love her in this light." She turned to him. "Isn't she perfect in this light?"

He cleared his throat as he sat down next to me. "She is," he said evenly.

We sat there for a moment, our hips brushing up against each other, waiting for direction.

"Maybe some canoodling?" Gretchen called from the other side of the camera.

Nolan nodded and stretched his arm over my shoulders. No, no, no. It was the duke. The duke and Felicity. The duke wrapped his arm around Felicity's shoulders.

"This okay?" he asked.

I nodded because the words . . . they were hard to put together.

"I don't know which fry to choose," he said, a hint of panic in his voice.

"Better make it a good one," I whispered as Gretchen called, "Quiet on set!"

With a devious smile, Nolan diligently pulled one fry out of the middle of the pile like he was playing Jenga.

He held it up for me to take into my mouth as he gripped my shoulder, pulling me closer.

As I did, he bit into the opposite end with a laugh. The both of us kept biting along the fry until his teeth were so close to my lips that I could feel the snap of his jaw.

His bottom lip brushed mine, and despite the chili cheese fry breath and the cameras and the prop guy whose only experience was probably with dildos and lube, I panted into his mouth.

I felt unhinged.

"Cut!" Gretchen called.

Thank fuck.

AFTER THE DINER scene, Nolan and I were led around the town square by the crew. We walked the length of a sidewalk, reset, walked it again, reset, walked it again, and so on. I quickly began to see how parts of this job could be tedious. In porn, we definitely had to work with the camera and sometimes you had to redo a specific moan or position transition so the right camera could capture it. But for the most part, filming sex was pretty straightforward. The shot didn't have to be perfect as long as it was hot.

A little after eleven, Gretchen called it a night and sent us to get out of hair, costume, and makeup. "You're doing great, Bee," she whispered with a wink before I set off.

Maybe she was just being nice or maybe she really meant it, but either way her words worked a little bit of magic on me. I found myself standing a little taller as I walked to hair and makeup. My mind wandered and I let myself imagine what it might be like for *this* to be my job. I hated myself for it a little bit. It felt like a betrayal in a way—to myself and all the sex workers I loved and respected—but there was something wonderfully simple about having the kind of job that your grandparents could easily explain to their friends. And that was a thought I couldn't shake.

After I was back in my street clothes, the van took a few of us, including Nolan, back to the inn. When we arrived, Luca and Angel nearly fell out of the sliding door as soon as the van came to a stop.

"Anyone want to take a trip to the North Pole?" asked Angel.

"Me!" Luca sang. "Bee, you in?"

I shook my head as I checked the time on my phone. "Uh, it's almost midnight and my call time is six in the morning, which means yours is at least five."

Angel rolled his eyes and tugged Luca onto the trolley. "Exactly, which means it's not even really enough time to actually sleep, so why bother?"

"Good evening, Ronald," Luca said to the driver with a deep bow as the doors shut behind them.

"Should someone tell them that's not how sleep works?" asked Nolan.

I sighed. "I don't think it would matter."

"Do I want to know what the North Pole is?" he asked.

"Would you believe me if I told you it's a Christmas-themed strip club?"

His brow furrowed as his lips fell into a soft, delighted O.

My phone began to vibrate in my hand, tearing me away from Nolan's amused expression, as a picture of Jack Hart at his bachelor party in very tiny underwear with whipped cream on his nipples lit up my screen. "Uh, I've gotta take this," I said quickly.

"Good night. See you in a few hours," Nolan called after me as I pulled my coat tight around me and stepped out from the protection of the carport.

I swiped to accept the call and immediately Jack's stunned face greeted me with volume on high as he asked, "Is there a reason you're in Buttfuck, Vermont, and not sitting on my dick later this week as previously discussed?"

I held my finger to my lips, shushing him, and looked over my shoulder, hoping that Nolan had already gone inside. "Can you not?"

I turned down the volume as low as it would go without muting it entirely. Not only was Jack loud, but the snow made everything else painfully quiet.

"How about *you* not?" he asked.

I loved Jack and that was something not everyone could say, but even I could admit that Jack was a real bitch at times. I couldn't blame him entirely. He was one of the few male performers out there who truly did queer and hetero porn. You would expect that an industry built on people filming themselves having sex would be pretty open and accepting, but when it came to men in porn, there was very little stream crossing. Jack's now ex-husband, Levi Banks, was the king of male/male porn. His website, The Cockery, was so popular, there were once rumors of several mainstream streaming services attempting to purchase it.

To say they were a complicated pair was an understatement.

"I know it's bad timing," I told him, "and I swear I'll make it up to you when I'm back in town, but I'm here working on a thing for Teddy."

That silenced him for a moment as he digested this new piece of information. "Teddy Ray Fletcher? Teddy sent you to Vermont to film a porn? Teddy doesn't even take his own kids on vacation."

"Not true," I said, coming to Teddy's defense. "He took Angel and Astrid on that cruise last summer. Teddy got food poisoning, Angel broke the lifeguard's heart, and Astrid won first place in the karaoke competition."

"Cruises don't count as vacation. It's like camp, but on a boat with people you don't know or like, and the food is just as bad," Jack said emphatically. "Anyway, why would Teddy take you to Vermont? Do people in Vermont even watch porn? Don't answer that."

"I mean, everyone watches porn," I said with a shrug. "And it's not a porn . . . it's a thing. It's a thing I can't talk about, and I wouldn't have bailed on you if it wasn't important."

He thought for a moment, before shaking his head. "You have to come back. You have to come back this week. Don't you get a day off from your secret Vermont not-porn thing?"

"Next month," I told him again. "I promise."

"No one will let me fuck them," he blurted. "And by next month I'll be fifty in porn years and completely irrelevant."

"Well, you're not everyone's cup of tea," I said weakly. There were the gay guys who didn't want to work with a guy who also fucked women and then there were the women who didn't want to fuck a queer guy and then there were the people who just didn't fuck Jack Hart, because like I said, Jack Hart could be a bitch. So even though he had a loyal fan base, the list of Jack's potential scene partners was dwindling.

"It's not that," he said. "It's Levi. He's blackballing me. He's putting in calls to everyone, Bee. Performers. Studios. Producers. Directors. Anyone who will listen, which is actually a whole ton of people. If I don't get some new work under my belt post-divorce, I'm going to be persona non grata faster than you can say Berlin gloryhole."

"I'll try to see if I can find anyone to take my place," I offered. "How about—"

"Don't you dare say Sunny," he said. "Do not even speak her name."

"I guess you're still upset about the incident with your mom."

"Don't. Even. Bring. It. Up," he said through gritted teeth.

It wasn't Sunny's fault she took home a stunning silver vixen at Jack's wedding and that it just so happened to be the mother of one of the grooms.

"Bee, I don't know what the hell you're doing out there for Teddy, but if you screw me over, I will take you down with me. You know I will."

And then he disappeared, ending the call before I could say another word.

I slid the phone into the pocket of my coat and let out a wild-sounding groan. I hated this feeling. All the lies and not quite truths and secret identities felt like they were pressing against my chest, holding me under.

"Let it all out," a voice said from behind me.

I spun around to see Pearl lying with her eyes shut in a silver sleeping bag that closely resembled a space suit and was positioned in the middle of the snow-covered grass outside the front of the inn. "Pearl, I didn't see you there! Are you okay? What are you doing out there? It's freezing."

She crossed her arms over her chest, like she was lying in her own casket. "It's a full moon," she said. "I left the set a little early to tweak the last page of the script and recharge in the moonlight."

As I stepped closer, I noticed the crystals encircling her. "That sounds kind of nice," I admitted. "But aren't you freezing?"

"Mother Moon warms me," she said solemnly.

"Right, well, I hope I didn't bother you with my phone call." Like, really, really hope.

She shook her head. "I was attempting an astral projection, so my senses were occupied."

My shoulders sagged with relief. "Are you sure you're okay out here?"

"Are you sure you're okay out here?" she mimicked.

Ouch. That actually stung a little bit. I looked at her for a long moment before deciding to believe that she didn't hear my conversation with Jack. Wherever she was mentally, it wasn't here. "Okay, well, good night, Pearl."

"Be well!" she called as I walked back toward the inn.

As I stepped into the lobby, I found Gretchen sitting by the fireplace with a notebook.

I hiked a thumb over my shoulder. "Um, Pearl is . . ."

"Lying in the freezing snow. Yes, I know." She checked her watch. "I'll give her five more minutes to cook or whatever."

I laughed. "You two make a good pair."

Gretchen's gaze drifted out the window to Pearl. "She's a poet, you know," she said, her voice softer than I'd heard it yet. "That's how we met. I stumbled across a chapbook of hers in a local bookstore, and I was totally captivated by how ethereal—and weird—her words were. They were like being inside someone else's dream." A smile, as soft as her voice. "I had to meet her, and the rest is history, I suppose. She pulls my head into the clouds and I pull her feet to the ground. It works."

"It must be incredible to translate her words into film, then."

She lifted a shoulder, still looking at her girlfriend out in the snow. "I unapologetically love Christmas movies, but this is all a little more practical for Pearl. No health insurance in poetry, see. But screenwriting is a different story."

"I know that pain well," I said. It wasn't like affordable PPOs for porn stars were growing on trees or anything.

Gretchen finally turned back to me. "Was everything okay out there a moment ago? Looked like a pretty intense phone call."

My hand flew instinctively to the pocket holding my cell phone. "Oh. It was nothing. Just—just a friend in crisis."

"The world is never quiet, is it? Somehow even in a place like Christmas Notch, the chaos seems to find us."

I nodded my head, a tightness settling in my chest.

"Good night, Bee. You were rock solid today."

She was so good. So kind. It wasn't fair to her that something as simple as my identity could bring this whole thing to a screeching halt.

"Good night," I said as I stepped into the stairwell, finally letting my guard down.

My heart pounded in my chest as I began to fully understand what a liability I was to the whole production. Not just to Teddy, but to Pearl and to Gretchen, who'd worked so hard to be taken seriously after years of being written off as nothing more than a child star.

And Nolan. I couldn't understand why he would ever take a job like this—a silly Christmas movie for Hopeflix. But he was here for a reason, and my presence alone could ruin all of this. For him. For everyone.

CHAPTER NINE

Nolan

The wreath on the door looks great, Mom," I said as I propped my phone against the windowsill so she could still see me. Through the window, I saw Gretchen coaxing Pearl to come inside from the snow. "Like magazine great."

"It's not my best," Mom said with a sigh. "I ran out of floral wire halfway through."

"I like that it's asymmetrical," I told her as I unspooled a length of thread. In front of me was the brocade dressing gown the duke would be wearing tomorrow when he and Felicity got sucked back into the present day. I'd been wanting to wear a dressing gown since I saw Shakespeare in the Park legend Bruce Roach rocking one for *The Winter's Tale*, but that was before I'd met Luca. Before I'd known that in order to wear a dressing gown, I'd have to rehem the whole thing and restitch the belt loops by hand so it would fit me.

At least Luca had relented and let me use his sewing machine for the hem.

"And I've seen asymmetrical wreaths all over Instagram and stuff," I assured her. "You're very hip with the wreath times for an old lady."

She huffed a small laugh. It was a little flat, but she still sounded miles and miles better than she had on Sunday night. "I try. Now show me this dressing gown again. Is your needle thick enough for that shit?"

My mom was like a foulmouthed Martha Stewart. She'd been the one to teach me how to sew when I was in middle school, since all our costumes came straight from the high school's theater program trash can. She'd also been the one to teach me how to paint, how to transform random thrift store finds into incredibly specific props, how to garden, how to cook, how to do hundreds and thousands of tiny, amazing things that made the world a sweeter and more interesting place.

She was also the mom who brought everyone pizza and pop during long nights in the theater, who carpooled for all the kids whose parents couldn't pick them up from rehearsals, who saved all my show programs as keepsakes and helped me wash stick glue out of my eyebrows after a long night in special-effects makeup. And when I went to her one day with a printed-out casting call for a boy band reality show in L.A. and told her that Kallum and I were going to do it, she was the one who convinced Kallum's overprotective mom to let him go, who drove us to California, and who made sure we had plenty of Gatorade and PowerBars during the sixteen-hour-long audition days.

I held up the dressing gown to the phone camera, and she leaned in, squinting at the brocade.

"And there's no way you can coax the costume designer to do this for you?" she asked, giving the fabric a critical look.

"He's at a strip club right now," I groused as I threaded the needle.

"And you're not with him at this strip club?"

"Mom!" I said. "I've cleaned up my act! I don't do that anymore!"

She gave me a skeptical look.

"I'm serious," I promised her. "I've been a total saint, and there's even someone I like here and everything."

It was maybe a mistake to tell this to April Kowalczk, because her face immediately turned into a Nosy Mom face. "Ooh, someone you *like*, hmm?"

"Mom."

"What? I can't want my son to stop sneaking boys and girls up to his room like he's still a teenager? I can't want you to settle down with someone nice?"

I ducked my head over the dressing gown so she couldn't see me chew on my lip. Even though Bee was sexy beyond belief and also witty and silly and sharp in real life, I also knew that most people wouldn't consider a porn star *someone nice*. Mom probably would . . . but Steph wouldn't.

Neither would the producers of a singing competition show.

"You know," Mom said, and I heard something careful in

her voice. "If you *do* meet someone, I want you to know that it would be okay if you moved out."

I looked up at the screen, trying to read her face. "Mom . . ."

She looked away from me, and I could see the shine of tears in her eyes, sudden as a spring rain.

"Mom," I said again, softly. "I'm happy at home, I promise. And who knows? If I get more stuff after this movie, I'll be traveling a lot anyway, and it wouldn't make any sense to move out."

I didn't say the real reason I lived with them, which was that Mom and Maddie needed all the money I made at my crappy theater job. Mom barely got by on her Social Security and the flimsy pension Dad left behind.

I also didn't say the *other* real reason I lived at home, which was that Mom needed me there. Not always, and not even very often. But when she did need me, I wanted to be close by.

A tear slipped free and she quickly wiped it away. "Okay," she said, in a voice that indicated she wanted to change the subject. "Well. If you want to. Just know that you can. I'll be okay. Even after Maddie goes to college, I'll have Barb." She gave me a thin smile. "And Snapple."

"Snapple is better than any son," I agreed, turning back to the brocade draped over my lap before I asked my next question. "How are the new dosages treating you?"

"Fine," she said quietly. "I'm feeling better than I was on Sunday."

It was the cruelest thing about bipolar disorder, I thought; there was never one thing that worked forever. No one med, no one dose, no one routine. My mom said it was like walking on a rope bridge, where every step was slightly different from the last and sometimes you had to stop and just hold on until you could find your balance again. But she also liked to remind me that sometimes the views from her bridge were incredible too.

"If you need me to come home . . ." I started, but she was already shaking her head.

"I didn't get low because you left," she said firmly. "And I'm feeling better now. Remember? I made a wreath today?"

"You and I both know you made that wreath to get Barb off your back." Barb was a lovely woman with a heart full of kindness, but she was the kind of person who used to work sixty-hour weeks, and in her retirement sewed an entire quilt every month. She seemed to think that the cure for depression was keeping busy, and so she was always encouraging Mom to make things or bake things or volunteer at the community garden by our house. She meant well, but it was also exhausting to have to explain over and over again that *depression didn't work like that.*

Mom smiled a little, a real smile this time. "Okay, yes. Maybe I did."

"Will you let me know how your follow-up with Dr. Sam goes tomorrow?" I asked. "And if you need to call or talk at any time, and you can't get ahold of me, Kallum can come over right away."

"I know, I know." She gave me another real smile. It was weary and I could see the strain of the last week in her eyes, but it was still a genuine April Kowalczk smile. "Stop feeling guilty," she said. "I'm excited you're there, doing this. I'll be okay, I promise."

"Okay," I said, regret squeezing me everywhere. If only I'd known what a shitty contract INK was signing with our old manager; if only I'd kept a better hold on the money I had managed to get; if only I had more skills or more degrees or more *something*.

If only I'd been like Isaac and stuck the landing on a successful solo pop career instead of accidentally throwing it in the dumpster at the Duluth Olympics.

But I couldn't go back and change the past. I could only fix the future.

ONLY A FEW hours after falling asleep—damn you to brocade hell, whoever invented the dressing gown—my phone jolted me awake with a sound like I was on a submarine that had just been struck with a missile.

"Shit, fuck, shit," I sputtered, my heart racing as I slapped at the phone, trying to get it to shut up. I finally succeeded, glanced at the window, where it still looked like midnight outside, and briefly hated my life. If there was any good thing about professional theater, it was that it skewed nocturnal. These early movie mornings *sucked*. Especially when I also woke up with a hard-on that felt like it was ready to go to war.

And of course, when I finally did sit up, the first thing I saw was the bottle of gingerbread lotion on my end table, taunting me with its silky, Christmas-scented goodness.

It would only take a little dollop, and then I could feel so much *better*—

No! *No.*

I swung myself out of bed and raced into a lukewarm shower—I tried a cold shower, but I was shivering too hard to wash my hair—and tried to psych myself up for another day of implementing the No Orgasm Component of my Bee Strategy. But all I could remember was the way her bottom lip felt against mine last night as we Lady and the Tramped that cheese fry and the way the hem of her costume dress had fluttered around her plush thighs as we'd walked around the town square.

The way it had felt to hold her close and stroke her tongue with mine at fake Frostmere Manor . . .

I can help youuuuu, the gingerbread lotion called from the table. *Let me fix it with the moisturizing glide of gingery, cinnamony wonder. Let me be the holiday salve to your poor, aching, throbbing—*

I stalked over to the end table, grabbed the bottle, and then locked it in the room safe under the bed, where its siren song would be silenced. For now.

I managed to dress, gathered my things, including my newly re-belt-looped dressing gown, and headed to the fake toy shop. All with an angry boner that only abated to a semi once I found the Danish tray and helped myself to a flaky breakfast treat.

Luca wasn't there, which wasn't surprising, and after I was haired and makeuped into a Victorian duke, I changed into my costume on my own. Tight, dark breeches and a puffy shirt, followed by the dressing gown, belted tight against the cold.

Fifteen minutes before call time, I was in the town square, where Felicity and the duke would be spat out into the present day. I stood by one of the portable heaters and watched Pearl write furiously in a notebook, then scratch out what she'd written, and then scribble something new. I really, really hoped it was the last page to the script, since none of us still had any idea what the real meaning of Christmas was going to be.

Cammy the PA was darting around making the movie happen, except that at some point it became clear that the movie *couldn't* happen because we were missing Bee.

"Did anyone see her at the inn this morning?" Gretchen asked as Cammy tried calling Bee's phone.

"I did," one of the camera guys volunteered. "She was on her way to the toy shop."

"She made it to the toy shop," Denise said, "because she got her hair and makeup done before Nolan. She said she was going to find Luca to help her with her costume."

"I'll grab her," I offered. "I left my water bottle in there anyway."

Just then a gust of icy wind threatened to blow papers and cups everywhere. I was waved off while everyone else wrestled their things back into submission, and so I strode down Main Street to the toy shop and went inside.

"Hello?" I called, expecting to hear Bee's laugh or the drone of another *True Crime in Ice Skating* podcast. But I heard nothing. The hair and makeup room was empty. The *entire place* seemed empty.

"Bee?" I tried again, and this time I heard something muffled from the back of the space. I passed the makeup tables and the stacks of totes and racks of costumes to find a door, which I knocked on. "Bee? Are you in there?"

"Yes," came the faint, dismayed answer. "Nolan, is that you?"

"C'est moi. Is Luca in there with you?"

"No," she said grumpily. "He never showed up this morning. And I need—I need a second person for this costume."

My pulse kicked up, threading through my veins at a double clip. "You need help getting dressed?"

"Ugh. Yes."

I tried to summon every ounce of pseudo professionalism I sort of had. "You know, my day job back at home is working at a theater, and I help with costumes a lot, especially historical ones. I'm happy to lend a hand if you need it." *Or two hands.*

"You have a day job?" she asked after a minute. "Why do you need a day job? Didn't I see you posed on a bed made of solid gold on a private jet once? In the liner notes of *INKredible*?"

"It was a rented jet." I was glad she couldn't see my giant grin. "You've looked at our liner notes?"

She went silent, like she was pleading the fifth, so I relented. Although I did tuck that little nugget away to warm me up later tonight, that little Ms. Bee was almost certainly a former INK fan.

"Actually—this is a boring story—but we signed a pretty shitty contract when we formed the band," I said through the door. "It gave our manager nearly total control over our money, and then one day he up and left with almost all of it. And by then INK was dead, and my attempted solo career after that quickly went south—"

"Because of Duluth."

"Because of Duluth," I affirmed, leaning my shoulder against the door. "And so the only thing I knew how to do other than sing, dance, and sign posters was theater. But I knew if I tried to act locally, it would get weird fast—and I didn't want people crashing the show because of me, or critics panning it just because a washed-up pop star was in the cast, so I decided to work behind the scenes. As Nolan Kowalczk, not Nolan Shaw, so I could be sort of discreet."

And it had mostly worked. There had only been a few awkward moments—usually people waiting after shows to try to catch me coming out the back door so they could get a selfie or an autograph. I was the Kansas City theater scene's worst-kept secret.

Bee took a moment to answer after my explanation, but then she finally said, "Okay. You can help. But you have to promise not to laugh."

I turned the knob and opened the door.

"Why would I laugh—oh my God." I couldn't help it. I did start laughing. Bee clearly had been attempting to tighten her own corset, and she'd looped the lacings around the inside doorknob and also around a curtain hook to try to pull it tight. I had to duck under a tangled web of lacings just to get inside the dressing room.

She gave me an adorable pout as I straightened up in front of her. "You said you wouldn't laugh."

"That's before I knew how funny it would be. Hold still," I said, and slowly followed the twisted lacings to the doorknob, where I unhooked one of the rabbit-ear laces. "This is like some weird Spider-Man cosplay. This is like shibari gone wrong."

There was a note of interest in her voice when she said, "And you know about shibari gone *right*?"

I could hardly say that I'd learned about it from watching

some of her scenes, so I settled for a mysterious *mmm* noise instead.

I got the other rabbit ear unhooked from the curtain holder, and then, with the crisis solved, I had a moment to really take in what Bee was wearing.

Or rather, what Bee *wasn't* wearing. Because while she was wearing a corset on top, she wasn't wearing any of her historical underthings on the bottom yet. Meaning that she was wearing tiny little boy shorts trimmed in black lace.

Somewhere deep inside the folds of my newly hemmed dressing gown, my cock jerked fully back to life.

"Uh," I attempted, my throat dry. "Um. Would you like me to tighten it for you now?"

"Yes, please," she said. Did her voice sound strange too? *Too* casual, maybe? Or maybe she actually was this casual about a near stranger lacing her into a corset, since her day job meant people saw her in various stages of undress all the time?

I cleared my throat, trying to sound casual too. "Straighten your shoulders a little," I said. "And make sure your, um, chest is where you want it." I knew from several years of helping performers at Shakespeare in the Park that no one liked having their boobs cinched with their nipples pointing down at the floor.

She laughed a little, but did as I asked, adjusting herself ever so slightly, and I reminded myself that I could do this. I could be alone in a room with Bee, lacing her into a corset. This was fine.

I carefully swept a long curl off her shoulder with my fingertips so that it wouldn't get caught, moving it so that it draped over her collarbone and down to her chest. She shivered as my fingers brushed her skin.

I felt that shiver in the pit of my stomach.

Working methodically, trying to keep myself focused and trying to keep my fingers from lingering on the soft skin underneath the lacework, I tightened from the top and from the bottom, working my way to the middle, where I'd give her a final cinch and tie the laces off.

"Almost there," I told her, and she nodded.

Finally, she was fully corseted, and I stepped back, grateful that I was wearing a giant, heavy robe and she couldn't see my body's response to lacing her up.

"What are these?" she asked me, turning around to show me two ties dangling from the front of the corset. "Should we tie these too?"

"Ah, yes," I said. "It's the bust drawstring. It fits the corset better to your chest." There was no way to tie the drawstring without my fingers being in dangerously close proximity to her breasts, so I didn't move to help her until she pouted at me again.

"I'm afraid of doing it wrong," she admitted, and then jerked her chin down at her chest in invitation.

"Are you sure?" I asked, my heart thudding against my chest. I felt fifteen years old. What grown-ass adult has palpitations at the prospect of tying a bow?

Bee smiled up at me, her deep green eyes sparkling. "I promise it's okay—I ask people to do shit like this all the time. For the modeling," she added quickly.

"Right," I said. "Modeling. Okay, one sec." I stepped closer to her, reaching up to the drawstring, which hung from the top center of her corset. We'd cinched the thing tight enough that her breasts were plumped above the top, and when I moved my hands to tie the knot of the bow, my knuckles brushed against the warm curves of her breasts.

She sucked in a breath at the same time I did, and our eyes met. I could have drowned in her eyes just then, because they were open, so very open, and soft and curious. There was no wariness in them right now, no walls.

Only her.

Without breaking our stare, I finished tying the drawstring in a little bow, my fingers caressing over her skin twice more before I was finished.

"There," I said quietly. "All corseted up."

She looked up at me for a moment more, and then her face registered a blip of panic. "*Shit!*" she exclaimed, turning toward the table where the rest of her costume was draped. "I'm supposed to wear stockings too. There's no way I'm going to be able to bend in this thing enough to put the stockings on."

"I can help," I heard myself offering. "I can help you put them on."

She looked back at me over her shoulder, her pink lower lip caught between her teeth. I could see the indecision on her face—the necessity of it all warring with something else I couldn't decipher—and then she nodded. "Yeah, that would be great. Sorry."

"Totally fine," I said, trying to stay cool and not have a heart attack. "Luca will just owe us all a drink tonight."

"Definitely," she said. "Should I stand here or—"

"Actually," I said, "if you could sit on the table, that would probably be easiest."

"Table," she said. "Right."

While I tried to focus on anything other than the fact that I was about to put stockings on my wet-dream girl, Bee perched herself on the edge of the table and then grabbed the stockings, which she held out for me to take.

Our fingers touched as I took them, and I was proud of their steadiness. Proud, that is, until she spread her legs so that I could help her more easily, and then I felt a slow shaking all over my body, like every muscle was trembling from the sheer proximity to her.

"I think Luca got them from his stash," Bee said after a minute, and I realized that I'd been staring down at the stockings as I gathered my breath. "I know they're not historically accurate, but they'll fit me, and there shouldn't be much more than a glimpse of them on camera anyway."

She was nervous, maybe. She was rambling in a way she didn't normally, running her words together instead of delivering them with her usual cheeky, confident edge.

"These will be fine," I said, and I did mean it, but also I could be about to roll fuchsia fishnets up her legs and I would still be reassuring her because I didn't want her to change her mind. I didn't want this surreal, wonderful moment to end.

I slid the stockings through my hands—they were thigh highs with stretchy lace at the tops—and then looked at her, where she sat on the table, her legs spread and her corset exaggerating every breath she took.

It looked like she was breathless, but that couldn't be it, she couldn't actually be trying to catch her breath around me. It had to be the corset. Right?

I slowly got to one knee, which dropped me down to where I could more easily tuck her foot into the stocking. Her toenails were painted a delicate lavender, and I wanted to kiss them. Kiss her toes and the arch of her foot and the knob of her ankle, and then trail my mouth with slow kisses all the way up her leg . . .

Why hadn't I used that gingerbread lotion, again? Why had I thought that starving myself of orgasms would make this any easier? Because there was *nothing* easy about this. About kneeling between Bianca von Honey's legs while she was in her panties and pretending it didn't affect me in the least.

I tucked my lip between my teeth and worked open a stocking so that I could slide it over her foot. Her breathing stuttered as I did, as I worked the silky fabric over the top of her foot and the curve of her heel, as I carefully smoothed it up her calf and then over her knee. She reached for the top of the stocking as I rolled it into place, her hands tangling over mine, which were now trapped between the soft skin of her thigh and the weave of the lace. I looked up at her, and she looked down at me, neither of us seeming to breathe.

She didn't tell me that she could fix the top of the stocking herself. She didn't push my hands away.

Instead, with our eyes still glued on each other, she kept her hands tangled with mine as I gently smoothed the top in place. And then as I slid my hands free to do the other stocking, she let go and curled her fingers over the edge of the table. Her knuckles were white.

I slid the second stocking over her foot and then up her leg and knee, and this time, she didn't reach for the top. She let me tug it into place and then smooth it. She let me take longer than I needed to do it too, and when I looked up at her, she was breathing hard, a flush blooming on her chest.

I was touching her. I was touching her and kneeling in front of her and if I leaned forward, I'd be able to press my face to her silk-covered pussy and kiss her there.

I felt wild inside, unsteady and roiling like a storm at sea, and then something inside me just broke. Snapped right in half, because I couldn't do it anymore, I couldn't pretend I didn't want her with every fucking fiber of my being.

I turned my head and kissed the inside of her stocking-covered knee.

Her breath hitched. "Nolan," she whispered.

I looked up at her, begging for forgiveness. Or begging for more, I wasn't sure.

And then suddenly she was grabbing at my dressing gown, urging me up to my feet, and I caught a glimpse of dark green eyes and a soft pink mouth before her hands sank deep into my hair and we were kissing.

Hard.

Her lips opened under mine, coaxing my mouth open in return, her tongue flicking wickedly against my own, and I groaned into her, my hands finding her hips and yanking her into me. Which is when I discovered that with her on the table and me standing between her legs, I was in the perfect position to rock my throbbing erection against her pussy.

"Oh God," she moaned, her hands moving from my hair to

my shoulders to my chest, where she found the lapels of the dressing gown and tried to shove it off me.

I helped, stripping it off my shoulders and then off entirely, letting it crumple to the floor as I dropped my hands to her ass and held her tight against me. I gave her a long, searching grind, relishing the moment I lined us up perfectly and gave her clit the friction it needed.

She broke off our kiss to drop her head against my shoulder. "Nolan, holy shit," she said.

"Yeah?" I whispered, rocking against her again, dying at the feel of her cunt so soft and so hot and only a couple layers of fabric away. I slid my hands to her thighs, my erection surging against the inside of my breeches, aching to be let out.

"God, yes," she panted as I kept fucking her through our clothes, holding her tight while I worked against her clit, and then she panted again as I dipped my face to her neck and kissed her there. Kissed her like I'd dreamed of kissing her for the last six years, with lingering lips and little sucks and nips that left behind tiny red marks that immediately faded after I moved on.

"Pretty girl," I breathed, kissing her neck one last time before kissing my way back up to her mouth. "I want to play with those sweet little panties of yours. I want to push them to the side and see exactly what they're hiding from me."

"You—you do?" she said under my mouth, her words breathless and dazed.

"I do," I said. "I want to see where you go all pink and wet. You are wet, aren't you? If I touched you, you'd be so slick that my fingers would slide right inside?"

"God," she said. "*Yes.*"

I wanted to wedge a hand between us and do all the things I'd just talked about, but then her head dropped back and her lashes were fluttering as if she were struggling to keep her eyes open. "I think I'm—" She huffed out something that was half a moan and half a laugh, as if she couldn't believe it. "I think I'm going to come. Jesus Christ. I'm going to come from this. Don't stop, please don't stop."

As if I could keep myself from rocking against that hot pussy. As if I could keep myself from being the one to make Bianca von Honey orgasm with nothing more than a dirty little dry hump before seven A.M.

And orgasm she did, her hands finding my ass and gripping hard as her mouth dropped into a big O and the flush crawled all the way up her neck. I could feel her body tense against me, I could feel the faint flutters of her sex, and the way her thighs wrapped tight around my hips, as if to make sure I wasn't going to go anywhere until she was done using me.

Like I would. If I had my way, I'd stay here in this room with her forever, letting her use me as many times as she needed to get off. It was the hottest thing I'd ever felt, the sexiest thing I'd ever done, and then I was lost to the feeling of it, to the need to move and rut and come.

"Yes," she purred in my ear, her hands sliding between us, and then suddenly my breeches were undone and my cock was free, burning against the cool air of the room like it was a brand.

She leaned back a little and then finally made all my dreams come true. She tugged the crotch of her panties to the side, showing me her cunt, and before I could finish having an out-of-body experience at the sight, she took hold of my erection and pressed it against her. We were able to grind together like we were doing before—but now we were skin to skin. Sex to sex.

We met eyes as she tucked the top of her panties around me. My shaft was inside her boy shorts, the fabric keeping us pressed together, and now when I moved—

"Oh shit," I said, shuddering so hard I was sure I was about to shudder all the way apart. "Your pussy, holy *shit*—"

She giggled, her eyes flashing all sweet and teasing and green up at me, and it was so different from how she was on her ClosedDoors account. She wasn't being sultry or pouty, but *happy*. Like she was having *fun*.

And her pussy was so very slippery; it was so very warm and so soft, and even just grinding against it was too much, I'd never survive being inside, never ever.

My balls drew up tight to my body, full and ready, and then I pushed against her again, feeling that inevitable fire at the base of my spine, that tension in my thighs and stomach as my body prepared to give her everything I had. I was about to come all over my perfect obsession, erupt all over my dirty fantasy come to life.

One final wet grind, and I saw stars.

"*Fuck*, Bianca," I groaned. "You feel so fucking good. I knew you would, I knew it would feel like fucking heaven."

With a heavy jolt, my cock swelled and then pulsed its release all over her, making everything very, very messy between us. My entire body was wracked with it, shuddering and trembling and contracting, until I'd drained myself of everything I could give, until I was completely dry.

I could barely breathe when it finished. I hadn't come that

hard in years, maybe ever. And we hadn't even gotten all the way naked.

Holy shit.

But when I could finally breathe again, when I could finally *see*, I found Bee staring back at me with a shocked expression on her face.

A shocked, *unhappy* expression.

For a floundering half second, I wondered if she was mad that I came—or mad that I came on her without checking that it was okay first—but then it crashed into me like a tidal wave, the memory of the last thirty seconds. The name I'd said as I'd rubbed myself against her until I erupted.

It hadn't been *Bee* that I'd groaned. But *Bianca*.

And now she knew that I knew. That she wasn't just a struggling actress who'd also done some modeling. That I didn't just *know* about her porn but had probably watched it. Was familiar with it. And she could probably guess that I'd jerked off to it too.

We were staring at each other, and she still looked so shell-shocked, and I needed to say something, anything, to explain—

"Bee," I started, not sure where to begin. "I—"

A series of quick knocks on the door made us shoot apart, startled, and then we were both scrambling for clothes, straightening and smoothing hair, fixing lipstick.

"Shit," Bee muttered, and I was right there with her. "Shit, shit, shit."

"Bee?" Cammy's voice came from the other side. "Are you in there?"

"Yes," Bee said, and I was in awe of her acting skills, because even as she was cleaning herself with her T-shirt with one hand and rubbing at stray lipstick smears with the other, her voice sounded totally normal. "Sorry, I had a costume mishap, and Nolan was helping me."

The doorknob turned, and Cammy came in, stopping once she saw me standing in what I hoped was a super casual pose by the window.

"Okay," she said, her eyes sliding between Bee and me in a way that was far too astute.

I could feel the panic simmering in my blood, could already see the tweets from Dominic Diamond, could already hear Steph telling me she was dropping me as a client.

Could already feel the future in which I took care of Mom and Maddie slipping away before it had even started.

Was Bee panicked too? Surely she wanted to keep a low profile while she was here, because there was no way the Hope Channel would go for a porn star heroine in one of their films—and I really didn't think the crew was in on this particular secret.

"They're waiting for you both on set," Cammy finally said. "Do you need any more help with your costume, Bee?"

Bee shook her head, and even though she was technically smiling, there was a sharpness to her voice when she said, "I think I can finish dressing on my own, thank you very much."

CHAPTER TEN

Bee

The moment he left, I almost regretted sending him away. Partly because I was still ready for round two, and partly because actually getting dressed by myself was simpler said than done.

Thankfully, though, the mock buttons of my dress, a maroon gown with filigree embroidery around the neckline, hid a very sturdy and well-made zipper. After wrestling the dress on and using a wire hanger to pull the zipper up, I was hopelessly out of breath and had sweat gathering at my hairline.

Great, hair and makeup would just love that. *Hello? Yes, I just humped the shit out of my costar's erection, was nearly caught, and then wrestled my way into this dress like I was Dwayne "The*

Rock" Johnson. *Could you please powder my nose and smooth out my frizzy hair? TYSM. I am one hundred percent a professional actress.*

I slumped against the table—the same table Nolan and I had just defiled. The sun wasn't even up yet and I'd already broken one of Teddy's most important rules. Not only that, but Nolan *knew*. He knew about Bianca, and if he knew about Bianca, it was for one reason and one reason only. Heat flushed in my chest, and I somehow felt both deeply desired and deeply embarrassed at the exact same time.

But how could I have resisted him in that moment? His lips lingering there on the inside of my thigh . . . My whole lower body had been scorched with evidence of him. Like he'd left a trail of heat with every touch. And then the moment his hardness had pressed into me . . .

Fuck, I needed a cup of coffee. And a cold shower. But I was likely to get only one of those things anytime soon.

"You okay in there, Bee?" Cammy called through the closed door.

"Coming," I called as I rolled my shoulders back, trying my best to emit got-my-shit-together energy as I strolled out the door. "Do we have time to swing by craft services?"

She brushed past me in a hurry to get the door for me and my dress, which felt more like an entourage than any piece of clothing should. "Officially, no, but unofficially, no one can make this movie without you, so if you need coffee, we need coffee."

The rush of cold morning air immediately turned my sweat into a cold chill as Nolan's eyes caught mine from where he stood down the street, talking to Pearl. Or rather, where Pearl talked *at* him while Nolan's hungry gaze followed my every move. "Yeah, I'm gonna need that coffee."

"Pearl, Nolan! Do either of you want anything from craft services?" Cammy bellowed down the street.

Pearl shook her head as she pulled up the hood of her floor-length lilac puffer coat. "I usually don't eat before I've had my morning kombucha."

"Nolan?" Cammy asked.

"I can always eat," he said, catching his lower lip between his teeth.

THIS MORNING WE were filming the scene where Felicity said a tearful goodbye to the duke in the gazebo at the center of town, after accompanying him to his Christmas ball the night before only to decide she had to return back to modern times to apologize to her sister for stealing their deceased mother's gingerbread recipe.

In between takes, Luca slithered into the crowd of crew members and tilted his sunglasses down in my direction with a grimace. I was pretty sure that was his attempt at apologizing. By the looks of it, though, his hangover was punishment enough.

"I guess it's a good thing we didn't tag along with them last night," Nolan said under his breath as Maya patted my under eye with a tissue before retouching my makeup.

I'd surprised myself (and, I think, everyone else) when I was able to muster honest-to-goodness tears on camera. Gretchen assured me we had several products on hand to stimulate the tears, but all it took was imagining what would happen if

Nolan weren't the only person who recognized me on set. Or maybe that wasn't it. I don't know, but over the last few days, I could feel something inside of me that I'd been pushing away for years begin to rise to the surface.

When Teddy called me about this job, I thought I'd come here, deliver a few cheesy lines, and wear some pretty dresses. But I didn't expect for this unsettling yet thrilling vulnerability to take hold of me every time the cameras started rolling. I could feel myself really and truly starting to want this, and that terrified me.

We did two more takes of me blubbering and Nolan staring into the distance as the duke morphed back into his chilly self in the face of heartbreak before Gretchen called, "Cut! This is looking great on my end. The connection between you both is so on point."

Nolan glanced over to me, but I kept my eyes trained on Gretchen.

"I think you two are on your own for a few hours but check in with Cammy before you disappear. We had a few last-minute changes to the call sheet. One of the horses had a dental exam yesterday and is still feeling a little woozy."

"So no horses tonight?" I asked with relief. I didn't have a problem with horses. It's not like I wanted to see the hooved demons get shipped off to the glue factory. I just planned on doing everything in my power to avoid them. A shiver rolled through me as I imagined their creepy humanlike teeth . . . just chomping.

My question went unanswered, but Cammy was already shoving new call sheets into our hands with updated scene numbers. "You're both free until three. Go wild," she dead-panned.

I clutched the sheet to my chest and marched over to Luca, who stood waiting with the puffy, insulated shawl-blanket I wore between takes.

"Good morning," I said, trying and failing to sound brisk.

"Is it morning?" he asked as he searched his head for his sunglasses.

"They're on your face," I told him as I stepped past him with the shawl pulled tight around my shoulders. "Is there something you want to tell me?"

He nodded. "Tuesday night is half off apps and Jell-O shots at the North Pole."

"I was thinking more along the lines of *sorry*, but that certainly does explain your no-show this morning."

"I *am* sorry," he admitted. "Things got . . . sloppy last night."

"Sloppy bad or sloppy good?"

His lips split into a slaphappy grin. "Sloppy good. Real good. Like best-I've-ever-had good."

My jaw dropped. "You and Angel?" Finally. The two of them had been making fuck-me eyes at each other for the last year. I guess all either of them needed was to get the hell out of Los Angeles.

He nodded. "And then that after-sex sleep hit, and before I knew it I'd slept through three alarms. It didn't help that my phone was technically on silent and inside the pocket of my leather Balenciaga fanny pack."

"You need a smartwatch or something. Don't those things tell you to move every thirty minutes?"

"And look like I'm in *Spy Kids*? No thanks." He opened the door to the toy shop and lingered there for a moment as Angel walked past the storefront and gave him the kind of smirk that made even *my* heart flutter. Luca didn't stand a chance.

As I walked to the inn, my phone chirped with a voicemail notification and a missed call from Teddy.

"Bee. Call me back. I'm trying to wake Angel up. I got a call from a very serious-sounding PA saying he no-showed this morning. Him and Luca both. Did I mention it might as well be the middle of the night here? The yoga moms aren't even awake yet. If you see my son, could you remind him this isn't summer camp? Actual livelihoods are on the line here, particularly mine." The voicemail crackled on for a few seconds longer before Teddy said, "This goddamn phone."

And then the line cut.

I'D SPENT PLENTY of time fantasizing about Nolan Shaw knocking at my door, but this time it was me waiting in the hallway for him to answer.

He opened the door after two quick knocks, rubbing the heel of his palm into his eye. "Bee?"

I was not prepared for how cute Sleepy Nolan would be. How had he made it back here so quickly and already started a nap? Was he a cuddly napper? It didn't matter. Napping with Nolan Shaw was definitely not in my star chart anytime soon.

Inhaling through my nose, I took a step closer but was careful not to cross the threshold between his room and the hallway.

"We need to talk," I said.

He stepped aside, his normally cool indifference replaced with a brief, unexpected warmth. "Come in, come in."

I shook my head.

His brow furrowed in that familiar brooding way. "And let the whole hallway in on our conversation?"

He was right. "Okay, but we have to leave the door open," I said.

"Is your mom going to check in on us to make sure we're six inches apart and to see if we need more Chex Mix?"

"The snacks, yes," I said as I slid through the narrow gap between him and the door. "The inches, no. Pam and Delia Hobbes are deeply progressive and sex positive."

"Well, I guess that's lucky for you," he said as he sat on the edge of his bed. "And me."

He patted the space beside him, but I perched on the red-and-green-plaid armchair instead. I couldn't be too careful. Being this close to him in private made me feel like a sex robot.

"You and I can't sit on beds next to each other, because we'll do a whole lot more than sitting."

"Right. Yes. And that—"

"Can never happen again."

He nodded. "Never again. Bee, I'm so sorry."

"We can't let it happen . . . and no one can know about Bianca, Nolan." The desperation in my voice was uncomfortably raw.

His eyes met mine, and for a brief moment, all the pretenses dropped, and I could see beyond *the* Nolan Shaw. He needed this movie to pan out just as badly as I did, if not more so.

"Pure as the driven snow," he muttered.

"Pure as the what?"

"Nothing—just—never mind, but I'm with you . . . I mean, don't get me wrong. Bee, that was—you were . . ." He bit down on a knuckle and let a slow, controlled sigh-whistle through his lips.

I nodded and stood. "Good. Okay. We'll be good. Saints. Pure as whatever you said."

He rose to meet me, and oh God, these rooms were smaller than I thought. I had to get out of here. I had to get out of here and go call my moms. That would crank down the rising temperature in my abdomen faster than Sunny could pack an emergency bag of sex toys.

But I just had one question first. "Nolan?"

"Hmm?"

"When did you realize who I was?"

"The moment I met you." He tucked his lower lip between his teeth in an attempt to stop a grin from forming, but he was too late. "That first day on the street with Pearl."

"How did you—had you seen one of my—"

"Loyal subscriber," he said, his eyes darting from the floor to me . . . and then on me and only me. "Three years and counting. At the Honey Pot level."

ClosedDoors allowed users to subscribe at different levels, which gave the subscriber access to more and more content depending on the level. Honey Pot level meant that Nolan had seen and consumed every inch of me long before our encounter just hours ago. It was impossible not to smile at the thought.

"It's not often I get to thank my subscribers in person."

"Yeah, I didn't see Morning Grind listed as a perk on my account."

"For Nolan Shaw, I can make a one-time-only-never-to-be-spoken-of-again exception. I better go get some rest. Call my moms."

"Tell them I said hi," he said as we walked to the door.

"I don't know, Nolan. Mama Pam still holds a grudge from the time you left your loyal fans in the rain on your *Fresh Ink* tour in Dallas."

"I did what now?"

"You and the guys disappeared after the show, but left the tour bus at the stadium, so all your fans—myself included—stood in the rain for hours waiting for nothing."

He clutched his chest. "You went to see INK? In concert?"

"For my birthday, you jerk," I said with a laugh.

"I guess an 'I'm sorry' doesn't cut it." He went to reach for my hand but then pulled back. "Maybe this morning made up for it?"

"Only if no one finds out," I said as I strolled down the hallway and back to my room. But I was still smiling.

I TRIED THE house line and each of their cell phones, but neither of my moms answered. As I hung up on Mom's voicemail a second too late past the beep—a personal pet peeve of mine—an automated email from ClosedDoors lit up my screen.

BIANCA VON HONEY,
Your fans haven't heard from you since yesterday. Click here to share an update and let them know what's new.

The ClosedDoors Account Support Team
Where social media has no limits.

It was the longest I'd gone without at least logging on since my moms took me and Sunny on an Alaskan cruise for their anniversary last summer. (Despite Sunny's insistence that I was missing great content opportunities. She wasn't wrong. My boobs and glaciers at the same time would've been a real hit.)

Even though I didn't *explicitly* promise Teddy I wouldn't be updating my ClosedDoors account while I was on set, posting so soon after this morning's incident felt like playing with fire.

And yet, I knew of only one truly effective way to stop the hammering in my chest and the heat in my belly that I'd felt for hours now.

I set my phone up against the television and opened my app. After framing the camera on the bed so that it wouldn't give away any clues to where I might be, I hit the Go Live button.

Nolan was a coincidence. A really big fucking coincidence. Surely I didn't have any other fans tucked away in Christmas Notch, Vermont. And I couldn't just ignore them. They paid my bills. They would be there for me with or without *Duke the Halls*.

I pulled off my jacket and sauntered over to the edge of the bed, where I looked up to the camera and in my poutiest voice said, "Good morning to my little B-hive out there."

People really responded to live posts, and I could see why. There was something dangerous about knowing anything could happen and that whatever unfolded wasn't rehearsed or planned.

And I had to admit, it got me going too. But that wasn't the only thing that had me going today.

I crossed my arms over my abdomen and pulled my sweater over my head before letting my thighs spread as I ran my fingers up the front of my thigh highs. The same thigh highs Nolan had rolled up my legs and over my knees until his hands were so close to the damp heat pooling between my legs. I'd forgotten to take them off at the toy shop, and after this morning, I didn't think I'd ever be able to give them back. No, I'd sleep with these babies under my pillow until I was on my deathbed and pass them on to one of my grandchildren in the hopes they'd have the same joy of fucking—or almost fucking—their former celebrity crush one day.

Instead of taking the time to strip down completely, I pulled my skirt up around my waist and let my heavy breasts spill out of the light pink lace bralette I'd changed into after getting out of the corset.

Propped up on one elbow, I slid my other hand down the front of my soaked lace boy shorts.

I didn't last long. All it took was the thought of Nolan, a few doors down with his phone in one hand and his hard cock in the other.

Bee was nice. She could survive the next few weeks without a whiff of naughty behavior.

Bianca? Not so much.

CHAPTER ELEVEN

Nolan

Sticky with fluids both gingerbread-scented and not, I set my phone down on my bed and scrubbed at my face with my not-sticky hand.

Would this be any easier if we hadn't shared a petite mort together in the costume department this morning? Surely, it would be; surely not having felt her, the soft wet heat of her, would mean I'd be that much stronger when it came to resisting her siren Bianca song. It was always easier to quit when you didn't know what you were actually quitting, when you could pretend it was probably an overblown fantasy anyway.

But unfortunately for me, nothing about that fantasy was overblown *at all*. Which meant that my dick was still stirring valiantly for more, even after treating myself to her live video. A live video that felt like a slightly cruel touch, by the way. She knew I was a Honey Pot subscriber, so surely she'd known I would see it. Did that mean something?

Did it matter if it did?

I decided to take care of my renewed hard-on in the shower—might as well put all that soaping and rubbing to good use—and then afterward, I dressed and gave myself a sermon about making sure Bee and I had plenty of room for the Holy Spirit between us whenever we were together. Maybe I'd cave and satisfy myself with her ClosedDoors posts from time to time, but Bee needed her identity to stay a secret, and I needed my new identity to remain so clean that it merited an Outkast song.

It made me wonder, though. Whoever had taken the picture from the other night, certainly they knew about Bianca von Honey? And if they knew, did that also mean they got to—

I tried to cut that line of thinking off at the root. It wasn't my business. Bee got to touch whomever she wanted, and if she felt safe enough to be with someone else while filming, then that was her right. The main thing was that we stayed away from each other and didn't do anything to mess up our respective opportunities with this movie.

No Bee, I told myself, like a prayer. *Pure as the driven snow. No Bee, pure as the driven snow.*

Silently repeating my new mission and vision statement, I went downstairs and out to Frosty's, where I caught up on the-ater TikToks and had the best BLT of my life. Kallum texted right as I was contemplating ordering five more.

> **Kallum with a K:** Have you talked to Isaac today? This week is the week.

He'd capped off his text with a crying emoji—the one with the single teardrop, not the super dramatic one—and then he added:

> **Kallum with a K:** I tried calling, but he didn't answer.

I sat back in the vinyl booth, a new heaviness in my chest. Isaac hadn't answered a call from Kallum or me since his wife's funeral, which was almost exactly a year ago. While Isaac and Brooklyn's relationship had initially been manufactured—him the boy band heartthrob, her the mega pop starlet—they really had been in love. Not the way Kallum had always thought himself in love, calling me at all hours of the night to dissect three-word DMs or to do a blow-by-blow of a six-week anniversary date. But like *real* love. The kind of love boy bands sing about.

So when Brooklyn died so unexpectedly, it was like a part of Isaac had died along with her. And while there had always been a quiet gap between Isaac and both me and Kallum before Brooklyn's death, that gap had turned into some sort of uncrossable chasm after she'd gone. Isaac's normal songwriter brooding had turned into outright seclusion—including from his former bandmates.

> **Me:** I'll try calling him too. And texting. Sometimes he answers texts?

> **Kallum with a K:** He needs to get out of that house. It's got to be like living in a tomb.

Isaac was still in the Malibu home he and Brooklyn had shared, the Malibu home Brooklyn had died in, cradled in Isaac's arms as she breathed her last breath. It was very sad, very Victorian.

And so Kallum and I worried about Isaac still living there sometimes.

> **Kallum with a K:** Also I dropped some garlic knots by the house tonight. Everyone is doing fine. Maddie had a boy over.

> **Me:** WHAT???!?!

> **Kallum with a K:** Hey there, big guy. Sun's getting real low.

> **Me:** What BOY???

> **Kallum with a K:** They were preparing for some mid-term economics presentation. Like little baby corporate lawyers. It was very cute. Also, in case you forgot, Mrs. K is still Maddie's actual parent, and she said it was okay.

> **Kallum with a K:** Also, remember what you were like when you were seventeen?

I scowled at my phone. I did remember what I was like when I was seventeen. That's why I was worried!

Kallum with a K: So if you're done being a schmuck about your sister having an active social life . . .

I ground my teeth. God, I wished I were home. Home, where I could keep an eye on everyone and have everything running the way it should, with no random teenage boys ping-ponging around my sister.

Me: It's fine. I'm fine. How's Mom?

When I'd talked to her earlier today, she'd mentioned that a pharmacy delay had meant she hadn't been able to get one of her new medications yet. Transitioning between meds and dosages already required some real choreography, and this was the kind of thing that could send the entire chemical dance off-kilter.

Kallum with a K: She's fine, Nolan. You know I'd be the first to tell you if Mrs. K needed you home.

I had to concede that was true. While he loved his own mom with a fierce devotion, there would always be a special place in his heart for the stage mom who'd fed little Kallum all the fruit snacks he'd wanted.

Me: Thank you again.

Kallum with a K: Stop stressing out. You're gone only a couple more weeks. It's going to be fine.

Right. Only two more weeks.

It was going to be fine.

"I GUESS ALL those music videos paid off," Gretchen said the next day as I trotted up to her and Pearl on my horse, which was named One Hundred Percent That Horse.

"Oh come on," I said, making One Hundred Percent That Horse do a perfectly executed circle. "This is just natural talent! I rode a horse in only two music videos!" And two summers of riding camp, but I didn't mention that part.

Gretchen scoffed right as my phone buzzed in my ducal jacket pocket. She glanced down at a page that Cammy the PA was handing her, and I took advantage of her inattention to slip my phone out of my jacket and glance quickly at the screen. I wasn't *technically* supposed to have my phone on set, but it was silenced, and it's not like I was using it to write skeevy DMs or anything. I just needed to be available for Maddie and Mom.

> **Mads:** hey can you call me

Okay, maybe not that available.

> **Me:** shooting a scene real fast, call you once I'm done, promise

I put my phone back in my pocket in time to see Bee walking from the manor house, a thick winter jacket and snow boots paired with her present-day Felicity costume, her hair pinned up and set beneath a snug-fitting cap, presumably to keep her waves camera-ready for later in the day. Her green eyes were like summer amid all this snow.

In case she hadn't seen it the first time, I had One Hundred Percent That Horse do another circle.

"Stop showing off," Gretchen said, and That Horse and I chuffed at the same time.

"I'm not showing off."

"You are a little," Bee said in her signature husky voice, stopping next to Gretchen. "Um, that's close enough," she said as I stopped the horse in front of them.

"You don't like horses?" I asked.

"I don't like being kicked in the head," Bee clarified, wariness narrowing her eyes as she regarded That Horse as it tossed its head. "Or flung to the ground like a rag doll."

"A horse would never do that," Pearl soothed. "They can sense a resonant soul."

"And," Gretchen cut in firmly, "a horse on this set would never do that because we don't use dangerous horses. You'll see when you meet yours."

"Mine?" Bee asked, the wary look not leaving her face.

"I could go with you to meet yours, if you'd like," I volunteered, and I realized too late that I was flirting, I was definitely flirting. Inviting Bee on a horse date where we'd be alone together was not a good way to keep our mouths apart, or our genitals, and Bee seemed to be thinking the same thing because she said, "I don't know—"

Pearl said, at the same time, "Inspired idea, Nolan! I'll go with you!"

I lifted my eyebrows at Bee, as if to say, *How much trouble can we get into with Pearl as a chaperone?*

Bee screwed her mouth to the side in a cute little knot, and then she let out a sigh. "Okay. After you're done here."

"We won't be long," Gretchen said. "We just need one take of him riding in his ducal glory, and then another take of him riding more . . . sadly."

She wasn't being reductive; that was actually what the script said.

EXT. FROSTMERE MANOR
Duke rides horse sadly.

"And let's be on the ball, everyone," Gretchen said so the nearby crew could hear too. "We don't have much good light left, so let's try to get this as quickly as we can! Nolan, to your mark, please."

I couldn't resist showing off a little and cantered down the snowy field, turning the horse with a flourish. I knew that Bee and I had said sex was off-limits, and maybe while I was on Steph's roster, Bianca von Honey would always be a PR no-no, but goddammit, I wanted to impress her.

Once the camera started rolling, I nudged One Hundred Percent That Horse into a gallop and acted the hell out of a smoldering duke, riding his way smolderingly to his manor house. I felt the coat flapping around my thighs, the ease of my seat in the saddle, the wind rushing through my hair, and I hoped Bee was watching and thinking about how great my thighs looked in these breeches—

Bzzz. Bzzz.

A familiar vibration rumbled from inside my jacket. This wasn't a text, but a call. And a call could be anything, it could be so many insignificant things that weren't worth pissing off Gretchen Young for, but if it wasn't insignificant, if it was Maddie and there was something scary happening and she couldn't get ahold of Barb or Kallum—

Muttering a German swear word I picked up from a tour bus driver back in the day, I slowed the horse to a halt in the middle of the field. We were only halfway through the shot, and I was ruining the take, and I knew I looked like a gigantic dickhead as I pulled out my phone and answered it.

"Hey, now isn't a good time," I said breathlessly, turning the horse toward Gretchen and the crew. Pearl looked baffled, the cameraman looked downright ticked, and Gretchen's face hadn't changed at all, in a way that felt like it didn't mean great things for her opinion of me.

And Bee? The disappointment on her face was enough to shrivel my heart, lungs, *and* balls.

But all of that was forgotten as soon as I heard Maddie's teary gasps.

"Hey," I said quickly, panic rising, "hey, hey. It's okay, Maddie. It's okay. Can you tell me what's going on?"

"Nothing's okay," she said in a watery voice that made my own throat ache. "I'm at the pharmacy, and they said Mom's medicine was going to cost over a thousand dollars for a month's supply, and I don't have a thousand dollars, and then they said I had to call the state Medicaid people, and so I did, and they're being so mean to me right now, and I don't know what to do, because I still don't have a thousand dollars, and if I don't have that, I can't get the medicine for Mom."

Her words came so fast, right on top of one another, that it took me a moment to understand.

"Oh Maddie," I said.

"And I know you said that if I ever have to call for something for Mom that I should just pretend to be her, but the pharmacist was right there, and I didn't feel like I could lie right in front of her, and—"

"I'll figure it out," I promised. "It's okay. Sometimes places like Medicaid deny things for reasons that are really easy to fix."

And sometimes the fixes weren't so easy—or possible—but I elected not to say that to Maddie right now.

"Is Medicaid still on the other line?" I asked.

A sniffle. "Yes."

"Give them my number. I'll deal with them and that should bring the price down. Can you come back to the pharmacy later this evening?"

Another sniffle. "Yeah, after band practice."

I couldn't sigh right now, not without her hearing, but I let out a long, slow breath instead. If I were there, Maddie wouldn't be crying. If I were there, I could fix everything and Maddie could be at band practice like a normal high school student and not dealing with the pointless dickery of subsidized health insurance.

"Okay, then that's what we'll do. You'll give them my number, I'll handle everything with them, and then all you'll have to do is come back and get the medicine—hopefully for less than a thousand dollars."

Very much hopefully. While I'd gotten my first sprinkle of *Duke the Halls* money, it had all gone to—ironically enough—my own health insurance premium. So if Maddie and Mom were going to have enough for food and gas for the next week, I needed the new medication to be much, much less than a grand.

"Okay," Maddie said quietly.

"Love you, Mads," I told her. "I have to go now, but I'll—"

"—fix it. I know, I know. Bye, Nolan."

The sound of her hanging up felt like a mallet to the skull. A hammer bludgeoning one very simple fact into my brain: I should be home.

I should be home right now.

"If you're done," Gretchen said, her voice loud enough to be heard across the field, but still unreadable in a way that was *very* readable to me, "we can try the shot again."

"I'm sorry," I called over. There was only so much I could shout from horseback, and then I glanced over at Bee, who was risking everything to do this movie, and then back to Gretchen, who'd escaped every single trap and foible of early celebrity, and I abruptly felt very stupid.

Who cared if I had shit going on at home? Everyone had shit going on at home. That was just how it was, and I could hardly ask for special treatment because they used to print T-shirts with my face on them.

I gave an apologetic wave to the crew—which no one returned—and then trotted back to my mark to begin again.

CHAPTER TWELVE

Bee

The fact that I would eventually have to ride a horse during the filming of *Duke the Halls* was something my brain had selectively chosen to forget. Maybe it was because the thought of making it this far into the filming schedule without being found out and fired by the Hope Channel with a blazing red P for *porn star* stitched to my chest felt unlikely at best.

But here we were. In exactly two days' time, I would be galloping across a snowy valley alongside the duke, and I would have to find it in me to not only get over my fear of horses, but also appear to be a carefree time-traveling kindergarten teacher who was falling hard for a man who was confused by zippers and had a sudden passion for chili cheese fries.

Some people had absolutely no real reason to be scared of

things like snakes or spiders, but I had an actual, valid reason to be scared of horses.

My scarring horse incident *started* with one of my moms' out-of-touch but well-meaning fancy art-curator friends renting a pony so her old gang of lesbian gal pals turned lesbian soccer moms would make the trek to her chic modern home in north Dallas for a brunch of mimosas and a vegan breakfast taco bar. The incident *ended* with a six-year-old Bee, a broken nose, and a white sundress drenched in blood. I barely remember the incident itself, but I'll never forget the sound of Mom speaking soothing words to me about how I would be okay after a quick trip to the hospital as I took in the horror of my blood-covered hands and Mama Pam sat with her head between her legs, on the verge of passing out.

I had learned the hard way that horses didn't actually like to be tickled. And while I would never try that again as an adult, the fear of my head being crushed by a horse and how close I had been to that actually happening had only crystallized with time.

"You're like some kind of horse whisperer," I told Nolan as we walked a few feet behind Luca and Angel back to the inn after a long day of shooting town square scenes.

"Whitneigh Houston warmed right up to you." He shrugged, the crisp Vermont air rushing through his open jacket, like it didn't even faze him. At the stables, he'd been so in his element, and that made coming face to muzzle with Whitneigh Houston, my white horse with a brown belly, a little less terrifying.

"You call trying to eat my fingers warming right up to me?"

I asked. After I'd changed out of costume for the day, Pearl and I were supposed to meet up with Nolan and the animal trainer at the stables to see my horse, but Pearl bailed at the last minute, claiming she was having a creative crisis. So it was only Nolan escorting me, and while I knew being alone with him wasn't a good idea, going solo to the stables wasn't going to work either.

"He wasn't going to eat your fingers!" Nolan insisted. "You had a handful of carrots that we both agreed you would feed to him when we approached his stall. But then you just stood there! It was like standing next to a wax figure version of you."

"I froze, okay? I saw his blood-hungry death stare and chomping human teeth, and I froze. And speaking of wax figures, I definitely have a picture of myself with INK at the Madame Tussauds in Orlando."

A slow smile curled along his lips. "Do you really?"

I buried my face into my hands. It had been four whole, very long days since our . . . encounter in the toy shop. And while his hands on me were the first thing I thought of every morning and the last thing I thought of every night, the fact that he'd seen me in such a moment of vulnerable want made it somehow easier to reveal all the embarrassing truths about my INK obsession. "It was the lock screen on my phone for two years," I admitted.

"Sadly . . . my favorite picture of you isn't lock-screen appropriate," he said, so quietly his words were almost swallowed up by the wind.

Warmth crept up my neck despite the constant, teeth-chattering chill.

Like a godsend, Luca whirled around as we stepped under the awning. "Bee, you're coming with us tonight."

A groan rumbled in my chest. I was tired and wanted to try out the panda face mask I had bought from a beauty vending machine at LAX. Not to mention I was actually getting back early enough to call my moms and Sunny.

"You can't come all the way here to this winter wonderland and not experience the magic of the North Pole," Angel said in a much less demanding tone.

And then, as if by actual Christmas Notch magic, the door to the trolley wheezed open. "Where can I take you fine folk on this fine night?" asked the sweet old man with rosy cheeks from where he sat behind the wheel. His name tag indicated his name was Ronald.

I turned to Nolan and then Luca. "Only if Nolan comes with."

Nolan cleared his throat into his fist, hesitant to make eye contact with Luca, like he was either scared of Luca or making it clear that this was Luca's domain.

"Whatever," Luca said as he stepped onto the bus. "It's not like a private event or something."

"Thank you so much for the warm invitation!" Nolan called after him, and I couldn't help but snort.

ANGEL WAS RIGHT. It would have been a crime to deprive myself of a visit to the North Pole. I was sure this outing definitely broke at least one rule on Teddy's list, but if I went down with this ship so be it.

Every inch of the place was decked out in multicolored

Christmas lights and vintage blow molds of everything from Santa and his reindeer to giant flickering candles.

"Does anyone else hear a tooting noise?" Nolan asked as a hostess named Peppermint, who was dressed as a sexy elf, escorted us to our seats.

I tilted my head to listen and sure enough I heard it just in time to see a toy train chug over the top of the stage.

"Is this your first time with us?" Peppermint asked Nolan and me as she sat the four of us at the end of the stage where the runway jutted out into the club. "Those two have turned into regulars quicker than you can say Santa's little stripper. I tried to tell them we've got only ladies dancing up on that stage, but that hasn't stopped them."

"We're patrons of the arts," Luca clarified.

I smiled at Peppermint. "Yes, this is our first time."

"Well, tonight's drink special is Grinch Punch: peach schnapps, Sprite, rum, blue curaçao, and orange juice. Appetizers are half off until midnight. Don't try the egg rolls, and don't ask me why."

"Don't have to tell me twice," Nolan muttered.

Angel ordered Grinch Punch and mozzarella sticks for the table, and just as Peppermint slipped away, blue light washed over the stage as "Santa Baby" began to play and a sexy Mrs. Claus slinked out onto the stage.

Luca let out a wolf whistle. "That's Prancer," he told us. "Well, actually, her name is Whitney, but all the dancers go by reindeer names."

I glanced around at the kitschy decor and the limber dancer

as she slid effortlessly down the pole. I'd done a little bit of pole dancing for scenes before and was forever impressed by anyone who could make it look easy. "This place would kill in L.A."

I let the corner of my vision drift to creep on Nolan as discreetly as possible. I couldn't blame him for drooling over Prancer, but instead his gaze met mine as though he'd been watching me become fully consumed by the seasonally appropriate pole dance in front of us.

Luca interrupted the moment as he reached past me and tossed some dollar bills in our laps. "I expect repayment with interest and inflation."

Nolan held up a dollar and said, "I don't typically borrow money from anyone, but who am I to deny local entrepreneurs of their hard-earned cash?"

Just then, Prancer reached off the stage and plucked the dollar from his fingers with a wink.

"And for that," I told her over the music, "you get more dollars!"

With a giggle, she laid down in front of us, arched her back, and slid out of her bra to reveal two Santa hat pasties as we showered her with dollar bills. Merry Christmas to me!

The four of us ordered more appetizers and drinks as the club began to fill up a bit more without ever feeling crowded. Something about this slightly musty place with its glowing lights dripped in tinsel made me feel like the outside world didn't exist and there was no danger of what would happen if all this came crumbling down. Inside here, it was only holiday joy, too-sweet drinks, and half-off appetizers.

After a few more numbers, the dancers began to circulate the floor, and I made a beeline for the ATM because Sunny would kill me if I left without a lap dance. Sunny collected lap dances in new destinations like people collected key chains, so if she couldn't be here to be on the receiving end, I at least had to get the full experience to properly relay the magic of this place to her.

As my fingers hovered above the keypad and I decided how much to withdraw, I glanced back to where Nolan sat in front of the stage. He seemed to be doing his best to only make eye contact with the dancers, which was far from the bad boy persona he'd so purposefully embodied for years.

Nolan deserved to have fun. He deserved to be a little irresponsible in a safe space, and I could be that for him. At the very least, maybe that tension threaded across his shoulders might ease a little with a pretty girl in his lap, even if that girl couldn't be me.

I turned back to the ATM. Half the fun of buying a lap dance was also buying one for a friend, right?

"I JUST ORDERED a fresh plate of nachos," Nolan said as he followed me through the club to one of the private rooms. "So what exactly are we—?"

He stopped midsentence as I paused in front of the curtain. There were only two things worth exploring at the back of a strip club: the bathrooms, which should not be visited unless it was an emergency, and the private rooms where private dances happened, which was likely familiar territory for Nolan.

"Bee," he said firmly. "This feels like a bad idea."

"We wouldn't be touching each other," I said innocently. "In fact we wouldn't even be touching her."

"Her who?"

I peeled the curtain back to reveal Prancer sitting like a gift on a red velvet sofa, in a sexy reindeer costume complete with a harness made of bells.

Nolan looked to me, then to Prancer, and then back to me before shaking his head. "No."

"What if I pouted and pleaded?" I asked, fully pouting and pleading.

His jaw twitched, and the vein in his neck jumped before he finally sighed with resignation. "And the Hope Channel can't find out either."

"Obviously. And this is *private*. Who's going to know except us?"

He nodded, a rueful smile tugging on his lips. "Good point."

Prancer squealed as we walked in and settled in on either side of her. "I love couples! How romantic!"

"Oh no, we're not a couple," Nolan said so quickly that it hurt my feelings even if it was true.

"Just friends," I told her with a wounded smile.

"Cool. Who's up first?" she asked.

Nolan and I pointed to each other.

Prancer stood gracefully, which was truly impressive in her red patent leather six-inch platform heels. "Stripper's choice, then. Since she paid, she goes first."

"You hear that?" Nolan asked. "You paid. You go first." Just then my phone vibrated.

> **Sunny Dee:** Where are you? You promised me a catch-up call tonight! I demand details on what Nolan Shaw's ass looks like in period-appropriate trousers or pantaloons or whatever the fuck.

I flipped to the camera on my phone and held it up above me and playfully bit my lower lip as my eyes widened innocently and took a quick series of pictures. I had to ham it up for Sunny, obviously.

Just as I held down the capture button, Nolan mumbled, "*Fuck.* Bee."

I looked over at him. Those two words sounded unfairly good coming out of his mouth.

I sent one of the pictures off to Sunny and quickly typed: At the Christmas strip club of your dreams. More details later!

Prancer hit a button on a small remote, and a sleepy jazz version of "Jingle Bells" began to play. "Now," she said, "no touching, but look all you like."

"Yes, ma'am," I said as she slithered down into my lap with her back to my chest and her perfect ass grinding into me.

Who knew Christmas could be this hot? Even without Nolan here, this little town had plenty of temptations tucked away.

"You're, like, really good at your job," I told her as my body began to respond to her and my hips rose to meet hers.

"Thanks," she said as she turned so that she was straddling my thighs and her pouty C-cup breasts were within inches of my face. "I really love it. I love making people happy and nothing brings more joy than Christmas and titties."

I turned to Nolan, whose sharp gaze watched me intently. "You're not wrong."

"Are you two in town working on that duke movie?" Prancer asked.

I nodded.

"You're actually dancing in the lap of the star," Nolan told her.

With that, Prancer plopped down like I was Santa Claus and gasped. "Are you serious?"

"And that's the one and only duke right there," I told her, selling Nolan out.

She clapped a hand over her mouth, but that didn't stop the words from tumbling out in quick succession. "I knew it! I heard Nolan Shaw was starring in a Hope Channel movie, and I thought it was you when I was up there onstage, but I've never seen a famous person in real life before and my sister looks like a discount-bin Jennifer Lawrence and clueless people are always asking her for pictures and I didn't want to be one of those people, because if Nolan Shaw was actually here in Christmas Notch, why would he even come to the North Pole to begin with?"

"Why indeed?" he asked with a laugh.

"But you're here! In my club! You've seen my boobs—I'm so honored! Could I get a picture?" she gushed. "Please!"

Nolan nodded almost automatically, and I could tell he was used to saying yes to pictures even when he didn't feel up to it.

Prancer pulled a cell phone out of her bustier and held it up for a selfie. "You too," she said to me. "I'm sorry I didn't get your name."

"Bee," I told her as I leaned into Nolan. "And would it be okay if you just kept these photos to yourself? The Hope Channel is super intense about their brand and stuff."

"Oh, yeah, yeah," she said. "This is totally going in the vault, I promise."

After she took several pictures and quickly scrolled through them, the DJ's voice crackled through the speakers. "Last trolley back into town leaves in two minutes. After that you're on your own or at the mercy of whoever's got a vehicle left in the parking lot at closing time. Last call, folks."

Prancer, still in my lap, looked to both of us, her lower lip protruding. "I didn't finish your dance! And I didn't even get to yours," she said to Nolan. "Here. I can refund you."

"No, no, no," I said as I began to scoot forward and she stood up. "We're good. Your company alone was worth the price of admission."

Nolan stood. "She's right. Thanks, Prancer."

"It was so nice to meet you both. Good luck with the movie! And if you want to make the tabloids think one of you is dating Jennifer Lawrence, I could get my sister to pose for a photo with you from far away. And maybe at night would be best."

"We'll certainly let you know," Nolan said as he held the curtain open for me.

My phone lit up with a text.

Luca: We're getting a ride home with Peppermint.

I held the phone up for Nolan to see.

"At least tomorrow is our off day, so we don't have to worry about another early morning no-show," he said.

On the trolley, we sat in silence across the aisle from each other as the driver watched us suspiciously with a giant smirk on his face from his huge rearview mirror.

In the soft, dark silence of our drive back into town, all I could think of were Nolan's eyes on me all night and the gravelly tone in his voice as he said, "*Fuck.* Bee."

For a moment, none of it mattered. The movie. My secret. His reputation. All I wanted was his body pressed into mine, satisfying nearly a decade of lust.

The trolley lurched to a stop, and Nolan waited for me to exit. He helped me off the trolley's narrow steps and then escorted me inside the warm, well-lit inn. My heart did a little twirl of joy when I saw that the Out of Order sign was off the elevator.

Nolan followed close behind as I stepped inside and pushed the button for our floor, standing near enough to touch me as the doors closed and the elevator heaved itself upward. Either the elevator was older than porn itself or time was moving like molasses, because the ride up felt torturously slow. The moment the doors opened to our floor, he stepped into the hallway and as far from me as he possibly could, like he was finally coming up for air.

I tried to be flattered instead of offended. We didn't have very much luck with keeping our hands off each other, but still it made me feel like a pariah.

"Good night, Nolan Shaw."

"Kowalczk. It's Polish. The, uh, label thought Shaw was more accessible," he said dryly.

"Kowalczk," I repeated carefully. "I like it. I like multiple syllables."

He half smiled and let himself into his room. "Good night, Bee."

After unlocking my door, I sank down to the edge of the bed and pulled out my phone, flipping to my camera reel full of photos I'd taken for Sunny. A few of them showed me looking at the phone and the others captured me as my eyes darted away from the camera and to Nolan.

I scrolled over to my ClosedDoors app, uploaded the photo of me with my gaze drifting to Nolan, and quickly typed, When you want them, but you can't have them.

It wasn't my typical sort of post. It felt more exposed and raw than any topless photo or video of me having sex that I'd ever shared.

I tossed my phone onto my bed and went to the bathroom in search of my panda face mask.

I hadn't even flicked on the light when two firm knocks shook my door.

Quickly, and with sparks of electricity strumming through my veins, I rushed over and opened the door.

Nolan, his lips pursed and his whole body vibrating with determination, stepped inside without waiting for an invitation. "Are you trying to kill me?" His words came out like a painful accusation.

"No," I squeaked. "Yes. No."

"Well, then what is it?" he asked with a desperate urgency.

"I don't know," I said, helplessly. "But maybe . . . maybe we just need to get *it* out of our system."

"*It?* As in?"

"This. Us." The next word was out of my lips before I could stop it. "Sex."

CHAPTER THIRTEEN

Nolan

I was moving before I even realized it, kicking the door shut behind me. I had my hands in her dark, silky hair and my mouth hovering over hers as I pushed us back, back, back until she was against the wall and panting against my lips. Each pant tore a new hole through my already flimsy control when it came to her.

God, I needed this; I needed this like I needed nothing else.

The few days since the Dressing Gown Incident had been hard enough—watching her getting a lap dance nearly impossible. But that picture she posted, all big green eyes and soft, soft pout . . .

When you want them, but you can't have them.

She *wanted* me. And suddenly nothing else mattered. Not

the movie, not relaunching my career. Not staying good and manageable for everyone else.

I fisted my hand tighter in my costar's hair and held her still as I brushed my mouth over hers, tasting lip gloss and Grinch Punch, my feet crowding against hers and effectively trapping her between me and the wall that looked like a Christmas-themed blazer from 1989. Heat crawled up my thighs and seared all the way up to my lungs.

"I take it that's a *yes*," she breathed.

I growled in assent, sealing my mouth over hers and wasting no time licking inside. Her lips were so warm, so soft, and her tongue was a slick welcome that had me straining against her. Her body, pressed against mine, was nothing but dips and swells and curves, all for me.

Tonight, it was all for me.

"Just to get it out of our systems," she repeated between kisses, gasping as I dragged my mouth from her lips to her jaw, and then sought out her neck. My cock—which throbbed more than it should considering the amount of gingerbread lotion I'd been going through—pushed against the zipper of my jeans, ready for more.

"Just to get it out of our systems," I agreed, burying my nose behind her ear and smelling the sugary smell of her. She smelled like utter sweetness and innocence, but she *felt* like sin incarnate. Like she'd been formed for filthy fun and nothing else.

My hands shook as they dropped from her hair to her waist. Underneath the hem of her cropped sweater, I could feel the bare skin of her stomach before getting to the tight waistband of her leggings. When I slid a finger under the wide elastic and ran it over the skin there, she shivered. "We can't get caught, though," I cautioned.

"I know," she said on an exhale as I dropped both hands to her thighs and skated my palms up to her hips and squeezed. "Teddy will kill me if we get caught."

"*Steph* will kill me," I said, "and then desecrate my corpse with bunting or something."

"*Bunting?*" she asked breathlessly. "Like . . . for bandstands in old-timey town squares?"

"Bandstands," I confirmed, palming her ass and hitching her hips even closer to mine. "But it doesn't matter because I can't fight this thing anymore. I have to give in before it kills me."

She let out a long breath at that, meeting my eyes as I pushed my hand down the front of her leggings and into her panties. And when my fingers parted her folds to find her clit all swollen for attention, her head dropped back against the wall.

"Nolan," she whispered.

"Shh."

Her wet arousal coated my fingertips as I searched for the tight well between her legs and then skimmed back up to the needy button at the top. She was almost too slick to properly finger, my fingers sliding on her skin, everything too slippery and too wet. But the moment I made it work and gave her a good, firm stroke, her knees buckled—and fuck, mine did too. I didn't know how I was supposed to keep standing when she was like this; I didn't know how I could keep thinking, keep *breathing*.

I was fingering Bianca von Honey, and she was loving it.

I rubbed her again, and she became frantic, pulling at my

hair, and then at my Henley, stripping it off and then sucking in a sharp breath at the sight of my bare skin. "Nolan," she said weakly. "You still have the tattoos you had when you were in INK."

I grinned at her, still touching her with dirty, steady strokes that had a flush crawling up her throat. "Can't be a bad boy without the tattoos," I purred, sliding my free hand up to her neck. "And I was the bad boy, remember?"

"Oh, I remember," she breathed. A hand reached up and ghosted over the one on my chest, a pile of tangled Christmas lights that I'd gotten after my first Christmas away from home, and then the one on my hip of my very first tour bus, complete with wings on the side, like it was the bus of dreams. I had a glimpse of bright green between her dark lashes as her eyes fluttered closed, and then I bent in to kiss her again, using my hand around her neck to tilt her face up to mine. "It's a shame you had to change your ways."

"Who said the change was permanent?" I murmured right before I bit her lower lip and tugged. Hard. She whimpered, her hips bucking under my touch, but then she sucked in a breath and held her body almost completely still.

She was weirdly tense, when before she'd been all heat and give.

I pulled back to check in with her.

"Don't stop," she said, her brow furrowing as she looked at me. "Why would you stop?"

She was still pressed back against the wall, and still breathing short, shallow breaths high up in her chest. At first I thought maybe she didn't actually want to go any further, that her pleading words and those pleading eyes were somehow not the entire story, but when I started to slide my hand free, she hissed like a cat and then shoved my hand back where it belonged.

I laughed a little as I began playing with her again. "Okay, I won't stop."

"*Good*," she huffed indignantly.

But as I rubbed her, it happened again. The strange breathing, the tense posture. Like she was trying to keep only her pussy near me and nothing else. Like she was trying to keep her stomach from pressing into my forearm as I fingered her.

"Bee," I said softly. "Don't do that."

She looked at me, all confusion. "Don't do what?"

I let go of her neck and skated my fingers down her ribs to her waist. And then to her stomach. A new kind of tension stole over her.

"Let me feel you," I murmured to her. "Please, baby. Let me feel you."

She swallowed. "Okay," she said, but there was hesitation written all over her face, as if I wasn't hard enough to pound nails just from touching her. As if I hadn't spent years rubbing myself raw thinking of her body.

She shook her head, as if internally chastising herself. "Sorry," she said, shaking her head again. "I'm so used to having to think about the camera—about the angles."

"You don't *need* angles, Bee," I told her, gliding my fingers down to her entrance and slowly penetrating her, watching her melt bit by bit. Feeling her body arch and press into me the way it should. "You make me lose my mind. You make me fucking feral."

I grabbed her hand and molded it over the stiff bulge of my erection. "Feel. Feel what you do to me."

She shivered, scraping her hand up and down my denim-covered cock as I fucked her deep with my fingers. Her eyes flashed green, and then she said, "Christ, I can't wait any longer. We have to fuck. Right now, we have to fuck."

She was still in her sweater and leggings; I still had my boots on and I hadn't even made her come yet.

"But—"

"I've been wanting this for ten years," she said, yanking at the button of my jeans. "I can't wait a second longer. I *need* this."

"Shit, me too, oh shit—" She'd pulled me out of my jeans and was working my rigid flesh with rough, expert pumps that had fluid beading at my tip. "But let me make you come first."

"Oh, I'm going to come," she said, tossing her hair over her shoulder. "Do you have a condom?"

"Ah hell," I said, clearly and painfully visualizing my wallet back in my room, keeping the gingerbread lotion and a half-drunk water bottle company on my nightstand. "I don't."

"It's okay, I came prepared," she said, and she pushed away from the wall toward her suitcase. It took a superhuman effort to slide my hand out of her panties to let her go, but I did, following her across the room with my dick jutting from the open zipper of my jeans.

I sucked on my fingers as she dug through the suitcase, and when she turned and looked at me licking my hand clean, she gave a low laugh that went straight to my balls.

"God, you're so sexy," she said, laughing again, and I remembered how she'd giggled and smiled in the dressing room with me, how different it had seemed from her pouty Closed-Doors persona. She laughed because she was having fun and having fun with *me*.

I wanted *this*, I realized. Well, okay, I wanted the sex too, but hearing her giggles and seeing her smile and have fun with me, I finally understood my uncertain feelings over her ClosedDoors post the other day. It didn't bother me that she was sharing her body; even if I hadn't known about her sex work, my own sexual history was hardly a study in monogamy. But knowing that she might be *falling* for someone else, that someone else might be making her light up with laughter and might be occupying her thoughts . . . *that* imaginary person I was jealous of.

Determined to see more of her smile, I licked my fingers all the more dramatically.

"I like a man who cleans his plate," she teased, and I stepped forward, ready to stop this condom nonsense so I could bury my face in her pussy and show her *exactly* how I would clean a plate if given the opportunity, but then she began tossing brightly colored objects from one side of the suitcase to the other and my horny brain short-circuited.

"Are those toys?" I asked.

A naughty smile. "Obviously."

"And lube?"

"Sugar cookie flavored."

I stared at her Mary Poppins sex suitcase with my entire central nervous system on fire, unable to process the sheer amount of debauchery I could accomplish given enough time and enough suitcase access. Dizzy, delirious lust buzzed all over me, along my skin and in my chest and inside the throbbing stiffness currently shoving its way out of my jeans.

I hadn't been bad in *so long*; I'd been such a good, good Nolan. I'd been so good that I'd forgotten how very exciting being bad could be.

Bee stood up with a condom in hand, her full lips curved in a knowing smirk as she saw how I was eyeing her suitcase. "A fellow connoisseur, I see."

Without my being entirely aware of it, I'd dropped my hand to pump myself. "You could say that," I said hoarsely, my eyes going back to the buzzy things and the pluggy things currently piled in her suitcase. My dick leapt in my hand just thinking about using them on her . . . or her using them on me.

"Come here," she said, her voice huskier than normal, and then she swatted my hand away from my own flesh like it no longer belonged to me. She tore open the condom packet with her teeth—something I'd always found terminally sexy—and then pulled out the latex, sheathing me with a practiced smoothness that had my toes curling.

When she stole a hand down below to cup me, I lost it. I dug my hands into her hair and kissed her hard as I walked her back to the bed.

"Have to fuck," I grunted, biting her lip and then spinning her around.

"Yeah, dude," she panted as she and I both yanked at the waistband of her leggings. "That's what I've been saying—" Her words cut off with a moan-giggle as I gave her now-bare ass a hearty smack and pushed her forward onto the bed.

I wish I could say that I slowed down to savor this moment, that I took my time as I knelt behind her on the bed and spanked her again, but I was a mess. I was a mess and she was a mess. We were both still mostly dressed—her leggings were pulled down just enough to expose the slick seam I was dying to get inside of—and we were already half-tangled in the hotel bed's duvet and there were candy cane–shaped throw pillows everywhere.

She was telling me to hurry, hurry, hurry, and when I grabbed her hip and pressed the plump tip of my cock against her, she rocked back against me, trying to spear herself on my sex. "Come on," she panted, looking back at me like I was denying her on purpose. "I can't wait, don't make me wait—oh *shit.*"

That was the first thrust, which brought me halfway into her wet, tight grip. She was slippery, wet enough to glisten from the light of the Christmas tree in the corner, but I still had to work for it, grabbing her hips with both hands and screwing myself into her with short, rough thrusts until I was completely buried. Sheer, shivery sensation rushed up my dick; it practically punched me in the stomach with a building orgasm that felt as brutal as it did urgent.

I dragged in several breaths to claw back some control, although I didn't stop fucking. I *couldn't* stop. Short of Bee telling me to knock it off, nothing could have stopped me from sinking inside her over and over again. The literal bed could have been on literal fire, and I still would have been there, pumping into my girl like a man possessed.

"Oh shit," I finally managed to echo, still hardly able to breathe because Bee Hobbes was sucking my soul out through my dick. I was maybe dying the world's best death here on this plaid-and-candy-cane bed.

She seemed to be feeling something similar, because her head had dropped down between her shoulders and I could see her sides heaving as she breathed. "That's good," she said, sounding a bit uneven. "Nolan, that's . . . really good."

"Yeah?" I asked.

"Go deeper," she begged, reaching between her legs. Her fingertips grazed me as she rubbed herself, and I groaned. "I need it deep. I never get it as deep as I want because we have to show certain angles for the camera—oh my God, yes, yes, exactly like that. *God.*"

I spread my knees to get more leverage and then pushed in as deep as I could go, giving her hard, filthy strokes as she moaned in front of me. Behind her like this, I could see the arch of her back and the spill of her hair, and I could see the way her supporting hand fisted in the cover as she started rocking back into me, meeting me thrust for thrust. Her leggings around her thighs kept her legs cinched together, making everything tighter, hotter, as if I'd tied her up like this.

The thought had a gorgeous tension clenching hard at the base of my spine, and I went even harder, driving into her as she fell onto her stomach, laughing and moaning, and then bearing into her hard enough to scoot us closer to the edge.

"Don't stop," she gasped, still half laughing, her face lit up with a smile as she turned her head to the side. Her hand was underneath her, still stroking, and even though I was fully on top of her now, her hips were restless and squirmy underneath mine, as if she needed more friction. I gave it to her, piercing her rough and deep, and I was going to come any minute—*but not before she did, goddammit.*

We were almost at the edge of the bed now, the blanket moving underneath us and sliding to the floor, and I could feel her tensing around my dick, could feel her fingers moving faster and faster. She choked out, "I'm going to—Nolan—holy fuck . . ."

She moaned as I let myself go, rutting with mindless, feral need, stroking hard enough that I fucked us both right off the edge of the bed, blanket and all. I managed to half catch us as we tumbled to the floor, but I didn't stop seeking, I couldn't stop the churn of my hips as my orgasm tore out of my body, and I finished just like that: on the floor, on top of her, tangled in the blanket, a candy cane pillow somehow resting on top of my ass.

I dropped my head, panting into her neck as I filled the condom.

"That was nice," Bee breathed faintly.

"Oh, we're not done," I growled, and rolled her onto her back as I slid free. I found her wet sex and started fingering her again. "You interrupted this earlier, remember?"

"But I already—" She shook her head, her hair spread around her on the floor like a dark halo as she grinned up at me. "We're doing this out of order."

I pushed my free hand under her sweater and palmed her breast, kneading her as my other hand stayed very busy. "Tell me about this order of events. Is this another porn thing?"

"Like you don't already know," she teased, and then her breath hitched. "Yes, faster, *ohhhh*." I'd moved closer to her and started sucking on her neck, kissing her throat and collarbone and jaw as I massaged her stiff little clit.

"Normally," she managed to squeak, "in het porn, the guy's orgasm is the end of the scene. There's not another orgasm for the girl."

"There is for this girl," I murmured, nipping at her earlobe as she arched her hips into my touch. All I could smell was her—sugar and sweat—and she was also all I could see, all I could feel. And when she came again, she looked at me and whispered my name as if she'd whispered it a thousand times before.

As if she'd been waiting to whisper it to me all her life.

I held her close as she came down from her climax, burrowing my nose into her hair and stroking her hip with long, soothing caresses.

"Okay?" I asked after a minute.

"I feel like the human version of the one hundred emoji," she said, and I laughed.

"Me too," I said. "And also maybe like the human version of the water droplets emoji."

"Yes, you are sticky." She sat up, making me sit too. "Go unstickify, and I'll see if the bed situation can be salvaged."

With more reluctance than anyone not about to visit the DMV should have, I rolled to my feet and went to the bathroom to take care of the condom (and the stickiness). I kicked off my jeans and boots while I was in there too, because there was no way I was going back to my own room yet.

Bee laughed when I walked out of the bathroom completely naked with a fresh erection all ready to go.

"We might have to revise the 'getting this out of our system' timeline," I admitted as I went to help her pull the duvet over the bed.

"No problem here," she said, sitting on the newly made bed to peel off her leggings. "We've got the whole night, and I'm not tired in the least."

"Hmm," I replied, and dropped to my knees in front of her. I pushed her thighs apart and gave her my most Nolan Shaw, Bad Boy of INK grin. "We'll have to see what we can do about that."

CHAPTER FOURTEEN

Bee

When I woke up, Nolan's arm was hooked tight around my waist, anchoring me to him as the morning sunlight seeped in through the crack in the plaid blackout curtains.

I gasped softly as I fully realized he was still here. Nolan Shaw—no, Kowalczk. Nolan Kowalczk was here in my bed. Not only that, but we'd had a literal sex marathon last night. It was all out of order and full of laughter and panting and honesty. It was a fantasy come to life, as though I'd stepped into every fic I'd ever written about bad boy Nolan Shaw in my head and I got to make it all come true. Like we were two poseable dolls.

And maybe it wasn't just *my* fantasy. Maybe it was Nolan's too. Even though, with every touch and moan, I felt more like

Bee than Bianca. There were no cameras or fans or angles. Just me and Nolan.

I let out a long yawn, and as I arched back, a hard bulge pressed into my bare ass that made my nipples immediately tighten through the crop top I'd fallen asleep in. Last night was supposed to be our one go at it. Our chance to get it out of our systems, but maybe this morning still counted as last night since he hadn't left my room yet.

I pressed my ass into his growing erection and guided his hand up my breasts and over my stiff nipples.

"Good morning," he growled in my ear.

"I didn't know if you'd still be here," I said.

"And miss the chance to sleep in with you on our day off?"

I'd forgotten! Today the entire cast and crew had a day off, and tonight Gretchen and Pearl had invited anyone who wanted to go out to dinner and karaoke for a cast and crew night out. I didn't know how likely it was, but the thought of Nolan singing to me was enough to make me come on the spot. Before that happened, though, I had other plans.

His fingertips dragged along my hips as I rolled over and sat up onto my knees, straddling him. We both let out searing moans as our naked lower halves came into contact.

His eyes darkened as he dug his fingers into my hips and prepared to spear my wet cunt with his dick. I nearly whimpered at the thought, but managed to pull myself free, as I slid along the length of him, the head of his cock briefly gliding across my throbbing clit.

"Fuck," he whispered.

I panted in response. It was so tempting to just give in to a furiously fast fuck, but if this was really our first and last hurrah, I was going to milk it—literally. "In a minute, I promise. But I never skip breakfast," I said as I slithered farther down the bed and lowered my head to his shaft, already dripping with precome. I gripped the base and ran my tongue along the underside.

His legs stiffened as he groaned. "Bee. You're going to kill—"

I devoured his arousal, letting it sink to the back of my throat before he could finish that thought. His fists burrowed into my hair and pulled as he thrust into my mouth. I moaned around him, because *fuck*, this was so hot, this was so hot, and I'd had enough hot sex in my life to base a six-season HBO drama on. And when he swelled and came down my throat, I had to slide my own hand between my legs to soothe the need there. In a few slippery seconds, I was right there with him, brought to the edge by nothing more than sharing space with him, touching him, tasting him. I never knew my body could feel like it was made for someone else.

But of course, it would be made for someone I could never fully have.

"Oh my God, oh my God," Nolan said breathlessly, his chest heaving. "You killed me. You literally sucked the life out of me. Holy fuck, Bee. I'm done. I'm dead. I'm—tell my family I love them. If this is how I go, so be it."

A wild giggle rippled through me as I bounced to his side, completely invigorated by the toe-curling orgasm I just gave him and myself. I tore off my shirt and said, "Male, age thirty-one. Deadly blow job. Doc, we're losing him!" I pulled his limp arms to me and held his warm hands on my tits as I rubbed them together like two defibrillator paddles. "Charging!" I said, and made a buzzing noise before shaking both our hands, my heavy breasts bouncing. "Clear!"

He pulled me down to him so that my chest was pressed against his. "That's better," he whispered with new life in his eyes. "I think I needed close contact for it to work."

After a few more positions—including one Nolan said Kallum called Tossing the Dough—we both lay in a sweaty, spent pile on the floor, sheets tangled around us.

"Fucking on a bed has never felt so inadequate," Nolan said.

"We didn't even make use of the heart-shaped tub," I said, hoping that maybe this one-time thing didn't have to actually be a one-time thing, even though I knew better.

"It would have been my first heart-shaped tub," said Nolan, sounding a little sad that he'd missed out on that. "I don't have very many firsts left, you know."

"Me neither," I said in a deadpan voice, and he laughed, turning his head on the floor to look at me after he did. The smile slowly slid off his lips as his bright blue gaze searched my face.

Despite the sex hanging in the air—despite the silvery winter sunshine pouring in through the window—it almost felt like we were teenagers staying the night at each other's houses. Like we were about to whisper secrets to each other while sad indie music played in the background.

"Do you like doing it?" he asked. "The porn?"

There was no judgment in his tone, no disbelief. Only curiosity.

I wasn't bothered by the question. It was one I was used to

fielding, and given that I was currently doing something that was very much *not* porn, it was a fair one for someone to ask. But I still took a moment to answer, trying to fuse all of my disparate feelings and dreams into a single, coherent response. "I *do* like doing porn," I finally said. "And I've carved out this career for myself where I have almost as much control as a performer and creator can have. I've taken something I loved to do and made it work even better for me. But porn isn't forever, and I guess I feel like if I need to be aware of my future, then why not use something I've always wanted to do anyway?"

"And being here?" Nolan asked, still looking at me. "Has it made you feel like you want to keep doing mainstream work?"

"I think so," I said, turning my head to smile back up at the ceiling. I thought of the dizzy pace of filming, the flurry of preparations, the dopamine-laced high of shooting a really strong take. "I mean, yes. It has. When I'm Bianca, I *am* the fantasy, but as Bee Hobbes, actress, I get to live inside the fantasy too. I love doing both, but they're not the same, and I think I hadn't realized how much I needed the latter until I came here."

"So after *Duke the Halls*, will you keep doing . . . you know?"

"Porn, you mean?" I picked idly at the carpet. Even though it was only a couple weeks away, the post–*Duke the Halls* future felt like another world—another dimension, even. One I couldn't see into yet. "I wish I had some strategic five-year plan for that, but I don't know yet. I want to do more mainstream acting, but I don't think I'm ready to give up performing either. And doing both at the same time feels like it will take becoming a wizard or lots of lying, and I'm not a wizard. And I don't want to be a liar either."

"That makes sense," Nolan said, and there was more than sincerity in his voice now. There was empathy too.

But when I looked at him and opened my mouth to ask what he thought, an insistent buzzing noise filled the room.

Nolan sat up. "Shit. What time is it?" he asked as he stumbled to his feet and reached for the jeans I'd thrown over the TV last night. He took his phone from the nightstand and stepped over me and into the bathroom.

I didn't want to be a creep. I was totally *not* going to be a creep and scoot closer to the closed bathroom door so I could hear his muffled, suddenly serious voice. So instead I held my breath and tried to listen from the exact spot on the floor where he'd left me. It was still early, and we were on the East Coast. Maybe . . . maybe it was someone back home. Maybe family. Or maybe not. Maybe a girlfriend or boyfriend . . .

The door swung open, and Nolan stepped out, his lower half clothed for the first time since last night. His jeans sat on his hips, begging to be tugged off again.

"I better, uh, go," he said as he gathered up his shirt and shoes.

"Is everything okay?" I asked.

"Yeah. Everything's fine, I think."

I stood with absolutely zero grace and wrapped the sheet around my chest. "This was good," I said, like I was giving him a quarterly review.

He nodded, abruptly awkward and very businesslike. "I really think that . . . this was the way to go. Now we can just concentrate."

I fought with my sheet to make it look like anything other than sex-drenched hotel bedding. "Concentrate. Yes."

"On the movie."

I nodded. "Our jobs. The movie. The one without an ending. Concentrate." Without thinking, I held two thumbs up, and the sheet fell, like a curtain on a stage, into a puddle at my feet.

He bit down on his lower lip and covered his eyes, but then uncovered them the moment he remembered he'd literally fucked me off this very bed just hours ago.

"We can't let this make things weird," I said as I gathered up the sheet.

"Why would it be weird?" he asked. "This is the opposite of weird."

"The antithesis!" I called after him.

"The antonym!" he said as he closed the door. "See you tonight!"

It wouldn't be weird.

Unless it was weird.

I SPENT THE afternoon talking my moms off the your-daughter-isn't-coming-home-for-Christmas ledge and trying to reach Sunny so I could spill my Nolan Shaw/Kowalczk–penis-shaped secret, but no answer.

So instead, I ate ramen and tried to memorize my lines for the rest of the week.

But the whole room smelled of him. The sheets. The bedspread. Hell, even the floor. Especially the floor.

I left for dinner too early, but I couldn't stay in my room any longer. I turned the door hanger so the HOUSEKEEPING

PLEASE side faced out. The rhyme and reason of when and how rooms were cleaned at the inn was random at best, but if I returned to my room tonight and it still smelled like Nolan, I might have to change rooms.

When I walked into Kringle's, the classy-ish Italian restaurant on the corner of Silver Bells Boulevard and Tinsel Lane, I spotted Angel and Luca sitting so close together at the bar they looked like they might melt into each other.

"Bee!" a voice called.

I turned to see Gretchen and Pearl at the head of a long banquet table covered in a white tablecloth and piled high with baskets of garlic bread.

"Over here!" Pearl called.

Luca glanced at me from over Angel's shoulder and made a subtle shooing motion. I couldn't tell if he was nudging me toward one-on-one time with my director and screenwriter or if he was trying to preserve alone time with Angel. Probably a little bit of both.

"We're so glad you could join us tonight," Gretchen said as I sat down under a web of twinkling lights.

"Why wouldn't I?" I asked.

Pearl leaned forward. "Well, the Hope Channel schedule doesn't really allow for many days off."

"Which is why this is totally optional," Gretchen added. "So please feel free to eat and run or drink and run or whatever."

I shrugged. "I've been cooped up in my room all day, so I'll take any good excuse to get out."

"Told you so," Pearl said in a singsong voice.

Gretchen rolled her eyes playfully. "I've been toying with the idea of hosting a Christmas dinner for the cast and crew, but I don't want anyone to feel obligated to spend the day—"

"Oh, I think that would be so nice," I told her. "My moms usually go all out . . . it would be great to have something like that to look forward to."

"A Yule feast!" Pearl said with dreamy delight. "It'll be after the solstice, but we can improvise. Are you familiar with the festival of Saturnalia, Bee?"

"Let's save the ancient Roman festival talk for later," Gretchen said. "But I'll see what we can whip up."

"Saturnalia doesn't have whipping," Pearl said. "You're thinking of Lupercalia."

Gretchen turned to her with a smile and Pearl nuzzled against her cheek. I loved the contrast between the two of them so much.

Cast and crew began to trickle in, some of whom were already pretty well tipsy. Angel and Luca drifted over and sat by me, saving me from Maya the makeup artist, who was very intensely involved in the world of cat breeding and finding her cat an eligible bachelor. Catchelor?

With every swing open of the door, my breath hitched as I waited for him to come in. But maybe Nolan was staying in tonight. Maybe he realized that lobster ravioli and karaoke were very un–bad boy of him.

Or maybe it *was* weird. Maybe our sex marathon had made things so weird that now there was nothing we could do to unweird it.

I placed an order for eggplant Parmesan, because I had a

masochistic sense of humor, and then I leaned into the various conversations around me as my wineglass was filled to the brim with a cheap and delicious white.

Angel and Luca argued passionately over an anime with giant monsters that had eyelash tentacles as Cammy casually asked Pearl about the still MIA last page of the script (while Gretchen tried to jump in and save Pearl before she turned into a skittish deer on a highway). The infamous last page, as it were, was still cooking, apparently.

Across the table, the props master—who was definitely one of Teddy's porn people—tried to have a serious discussion with the sound mixer about ball-gag sizes.

And then the bell above the door chimed, announcing Nolan. I sighed softly as he pushed his floppy hair off his forehead and hung his leather moto jacket on the coatrack before searching the table for an open seat. He wore fitted houndstooth slacks and a black turtleneck that hugged his biceps.

It took every ounce of self-control I possessed to not call his name.

"Nolan!" Pearl called. "Over here!" She looked expectantly to the PA, who took a moment to realize she needed to find a chair and a space for the duke himself.

I attempted to exhale, but it came out shaky as my chest tightened with expectations and nerves.

A chair was quickly procured and shoved in beside Gretchen, just across from me.

"Good of you to join us," Gretchen said in a low voice.

"Here." Pearl shoved a menu in front of his startled face. "There's still time to order."

Behind him, an older woman with white hair and a red velvet vest appeared, ready to take his order.

Nolan's eyes scanned the offerings. "I'll take the lobster ravioli."

My lips split into a wide grin as Nolan's gaze caught mine.

He raised one brow in question, and I smiled, my cheeks flushing, as I shook my head.

As the food trickled out to the table, Gretchen and Nolan traded war stories about teenage fame and figured out the few occasions they'd been in the same place at the same time.

"But surely you were at the Teen Choice Awards the year Kallum dropped his surfboard on Winnie Baker's foot?" Nolan asked.

Gretchen's jaw went slack. "He what?"

"Oh yeah. And then he took that picture of her passed out in the car during the after-after-party, and there was that whole thing about how 'virginal, girl-next-door role model Winnie Baker' was actually a secret party girl who drank too much."

"That I do remember," Gretchen said, shaking her head. "So that must have been the same year the paparazzi climbed up to Isaac and Brooklyn's room at the Sunset Tower."

The light reflected off the dark sapphire flecks in Nolan's eyes as they widened, and I found myself polishing off my second glass of wine. "Oh my God . . . I remember reading about that," I said.

Gretchen nodded solemnly. "I think we all blocked out more during that time in our lives than we even realize."

I had never really thought about it. My memories of Nolan from then were elaborate fantasies in my head based on someone I didn't even know, but puberty and high school were hard enough. Experiencing that under a microscope? That was a recipe for trauma if I'd ever heard one.

After a round of champagne and tequila shots for courage, the bravest among us filed down the sidewalk to the Dirty Snowball.

"What an awful name for a bar," Angel said.

"I think it's sort of charming," Pearl mused.

The props master, who I'd learned went by Tall Ron, held the door for the whole group. "Well, it depends on what kind of dirty snowball you're referring to."

"There are different kinds of dirty snowballs?" Gretchen asked.

"Oh yeah," Nolan and I said in unison.

"Multiple kinds," Nolan added.

He looked to me with a knowing, half-cringing smile. Well, aren't we just a couple of pervs.

"I'm pretty sure this place has no relation to the dirty snowball I'm thinking of," Tall Ron said as the door shut behind him.

Gretchen's smile turned into a disgusted frown like she might gag. "Trying my best not to yuck someone's yum here, if you know what I mean, but, uh, I'm really not looking forward to searching for this online when I sit down. Have human beings always been such deviants?"

"You have no idea," I said.

As we settled into the booths lining the back wall, easily doubling the population of the bar, I elbowed Nolan. "So are we going to get a one-man INK concert tonight?" I asked, the drinks from Kringle's making me feel warm, fuzzy, and a little too fearless.

He smiled, catching his bottom lip between his teeth. "Karaoke is a spectator sport for me these days."

A round of Jell-O shots, ordered by I didn't even know who, landed on our table. Angel held one out for me to take, and then Pearl passed me another. I didn't want to be rude, and liquid courage was the only thing that could get me on that stage in front of Nolan, so two Jell-O shots it was!

"Oh, come on!" Luca said as he looked up from the water-stained menu. "The satisfaction of an INK original Christmas song is the least you could do."

"What does that even mean?" Nolan asked. "The least I could do?"

Luca sat up straight and pointed right at Nolan. "When you robbed Emily Albright of her gold medal at the Duluth Olympics, not only were her dreams shattered but so were mine and those of a whole generation of figure skating fans. Team Emily Albright forever and ever, amen. So yes, the least you could do is sing one of your ridiculous Christmas songs for me."

Nolan thought for a moment before rising to the challenge. "I'm not going to argue with you over the Duluth Olympics, because trust me, I could. But I am going to make you an offer. If I get up there and sing a song from the *Merry INKmas* holiday album, you'll help me with my costumes."

Luca narrowed his gaze. "I'll do any future costume alterations for you."

"Or . . . you could have just been doing that the whole time since it's your job," Nolan said firmly, while somehow managing not to sound like an asshole.

"Fine. I'll do your alterations and I'll be nice . . . *ish* to you."

Nolan shook his head but held out a hand to shake. "You've got a deal."

Luca hesitated. "And I get to choose the song."

"Done." Nolan stood and walked dutifully to the bar, where he signed up. Luca followed, making his song selection, and they both returned with another round of shots.

"More Jell-O shots?" I asked as Luca set the tray down.

"Not for me," Nolan said. "I am too-old-for-Jell-O-shots years old."

Luca handed me two shots. "Bee will take yours."

"Y'all have to stop feeding me boozy Jell-O," I whined.

"Was that a 'y'all' I just heard?" Nolan asked.

"That's how you know she's drunk," Luca explained.

"I'm not drunk," I said in a way that definitely proved that I was drunk.

"All right, Santa's little helpers," one of the waitresses said, stepping in front of the microphone as the man I recognized as the pharmacist at the drugstore took a bow after his heartfelt rendition of "Christmas Without You" by Dolly Parton and Kenny Rogers, in which he sang both parts. "Next up, we've got Nolan with 'All BeClaus of You.'"

I shrieked gleefully and clapped like a madwoman as Nolan made his way to the stage. "This is my Christmas gift for eternity," I said to Luca. "You literally never have to buy me another present for the rest of time."

The opening notes of the song—bells mixed with the kind of dance music you heard only during basketball game halftimes—crackled through the shitty karaoke speakers, and

Nolan sang the opening line, "Sometimes it snows, sometimes it blows, but I'll always be home for Christmas, baby, and it's all beClaus of *youuuuuu*."

That was it. This moment was too good. I shot to my feet, ignoring the slight wobble in my knees, and let out a *wooooooo* so enthusiastic it would have made Mama Pam proud.

I knew this song (and its choreography) by heart. In fact, it was still in my Christmas playlist rotation, so I did what any diehard INKling would do and sang along at the top of my lungs as I fumbled through the choreography. "It's all beClaus of *youuuuuuu*," I crooned.

Nolan pointed to me and the rest of our table dramatically as he let himself get back to his INK roots with his fingers snapping on the beat and his hips swaying in a way that made teenage Bee feel like she might drown.

When Nolan finished, the whole group cheered for him, pounding our fists on our rickety tables. Even Luca conceded with healthy applause.

Nolan sat back down, and soon Luca and Angel treated us all to Mariah Carey's "All I Want for Christmas Is You." Pearl sang some Polish Christmas carol none of us had ever heard of, including the karaoke catalog, which is why she had to sing it a cappella. And soon I was yawning as my body slumped against the booth.

"I need bed," I said with a pout as my head rolled onto Nolan's shoulder.

"We can take her," Angel offered.

I let out another yawn and tried to stand but slithered right back into my seat because Nolan had me trapped in the booth.

"I'll get her back," he said in a husky voice as he held two hands out for me and pulled me to my feet.

"The duke!" I said. "The duke will escort me back to my chambers!" I gave the table a grand curtsy. "Good eve to all until I see you on the morrow . . . which means tomorrow in fancy talk. You would know if you were fancy."

Nolan stuffed my arms into my coat as I groaned and fussed like I was being subjected to an awful injustice. "Why do I even have to wear thisssss? I'm cold either way."

"Well, while I can agree that this garment barely constitutes a coat, you're better off with it than without." He looped my arm through his, which offered a surprising amount of stability as we stepped out into the crisp chill.

"Oh, does the sophisticated Kansas City man have big feelings about weather-appropriate clothing like he does about barbeque?"

"In fact, I do, and we could start with those delicious leggings and short skirts you always seem to wear that do absolutely nothing to keep you warm. Are you okay to walk?" he asked.

"I think I can, I think I can, I think I can," I said, quoting the cultural icon, Timothy the Train.

Or maybe it was Thomas? Tillie? Whatever.

"We don't have far to go," he promised.

I let my head droop to his shoulder. "When you said that thing about my clothes being delicious, did you mean just my clothes or me too?"

"You," he said without hesitation. "In your clothes and out of them."

"Mmm . . . good answer. You should go on *Jeopardy*."

"I was a question on *Jeopardy* once," he said with a chuckle.

"No shit?"

"The rebellious member of the pop sensation INK made infamous at the Duluth Olympics," he said from memory.

"Who is Nolan Shaw?" I offered as we stepped into the toasty lobby of the inn.

"Maybe you're the one who should go on *Jeopardy*."

"You're more than that, you know," I said softly as we stepped into the elevator and I slumped against the wall with my eyes closed. "You're more than a stupid *Jeopardy* question."

He was completely silent as the elevator took us to our floor and he guided me into the hallway.

"Bee, where's your key?" he asked.

"I don't know," I said with a shrug. "I guess you'll have to come and find it." And then because I'm a good person, I decided to make his job easier, and I slipped out of my coat, letting it fall to the ground. I crossed my arms over my stomach and began to peel my sweater up and—

"Oh, no, no," he said as he rushed toward me, his eyes dark and hooded but his hands cautious as he threw my jacket over my bare stomach. "Come on. Come with me."

He led me down the hallway, my eyes barely open as I listened to the sound of a key entering a lock.

The door opened and I tumbled inside, kicking off my white cowboy boots and sinking immediately onto the bed as my brain tried to tell my hands to take off my bra, but all my mental wires were too crossed to get the message to my fingertips.

"Ugh. It smells so much like you in here." It was the best and the worst. I burrowed my nose into the pillow and inhaled deeply. "Get over here," I demanded as he locked the dead bolt and pulled the curtains closed.

"I think it'd be best if I took the floor tonight, Bee."

I shook my head. "No. You can't. I never get cuddles. No one cuddles in porn. Bianca wants dirty shit *and* cuddles. Pleaseeeee." My eyelids grew heavier no matter how hard I tried to resist. "Please," I mumbled.

And then finally . . . *finally* I felt him settle in behind me as his head bowed into the crook of my neck and he slipped an arm around my waist. My body eased under the weight of him as I let every muscle uncoil.

He pulled my hair to the side as his lips brushed the skin at the back of my neck, the heat of his breath clinging to me, as he said, "This isn't a porn, Bee. This is real life."

CHAPTER FIFTEEN

Nolan

*T*hud.
Thud.
THUD.

The porn star in my arms sat bolt upright, elbowing my face in the process.

"Ow," I complained sleepily, shoving my wounded face into the pillow. Shit, it was bright in here. The last thing I remembered was finally finding Bee's key and then helping her back to her room—where she immediately lured me into another snuggle trap. I'd meant to stay for only a few minutes—just until she fell asleep again—but I hadn't set an alarm. And now it was so bright outside and I'd been elbowed in the head and someone was pounding on Bee's door.

Thud.

"Bee!" I heard a man call. "Open this door right now!"

"Do you have a stalker I don't know about?" I mumbled into the pillow. "Do you need me to valiantly subdue him?"

"Shh," Bee hissed. "It's Teddy."

"Teddy? The producer?" I hadn't officially met Teddy yet, but it was hard to imagine a good reason why a Hope Channel producer would pound on his young starlet's hotel door first thing in the morning.

"*Shh!*" Bee hissed again. "Don't let him hear you!"

I blinked against the horrible sunlight, my entire body feeling as rumpled as the duvet underneath us.

"Bee," Teddy called through the door. "If you don't open this door, I'm calling your moms. And then they will call you. And we both know you don't want that."

Next to me, Bee swore. And then she looked down at me.

"You have to hide," she whispered in an urgent voice. "If he calls my moms, it's all over."

"How does he know your moms? And what's all over?"

"Peace! Equanimity! Separation of church and state! *Nolan!*"

"Okay, okay," I mumbled, and squinted around the room. There was a bathroom, a heart-shaped Jacuzzi that for some reason *wasn't* in the bathroom, and a closet with an ironing board and dusty children's skis. "I'm not sure where to—"

Bee was shoving at me, rolling me onto my side. "Hurry," she pleaded.

"Wait, Bee, wait—" I was tangled in the blanket and couldn't sit up all the way, and my legs were trussed together with the fluffy duvet. Then she pushed me again, and I fell right off the bed.

"Ow," I said into the carpet.

"*Stay there*," she whispered, all bossy and hot, and so I stayed on the floor, hidden between the bed and the wall, as she got to her feet and went to the door.

"Finally," Teddy said as she opened the door. "You're alone, right?"

"Obviously, I'm alone," Bee huffed.

"Well, then you won't mind if I come in," Teddy said, walking into the room.

I knew I was hidden from view unless he walked to the far wall and peered at the slice of floor between the edge of the bed and the window, but I still did my best *Law & Order* dead body impression, staying extra still and trying not to breathe. Because now that I was awake, the stakes of getting caught in Bee's room by Teddy the producer were very clear.

He might tell Steph. Steph might kill me.

Then she will fire my corpse and Maddie and Mom will have to fight the Medicaid people with only Barb and Snapple to help them.

Shit.

And to think this was after an evening of innocence too! We hadn't even done anything X-rated last night! Ahhhh, the injustice of it all.

"You look like you slept in your clothes," Teddy said to Bee suspiciously.

Why does he care? This seemed well outside a producer's

business, and I was ready to jump to my feet and defend Bee's boundaries and stuff when she answered, sounding bored and not at all like a producer was being creepy with her.

"I did," Bee replied. "So what? The rules on the Chili's menu didn't say anything about no hangovers."

Chili's menu?

"You're young," Teddy said. "Just wait until you're forty-six and your adult children make you do a bicycle bar for their birthdays, and then you wake up puking, with your hamstrings cinched like strips of rawhide left out in the sun. *Then* you'll know what a real hangover is."

"Teddy, why are you here?"

"It's ten in the morning, Bee. I get to this schlocky hellhole, learn you're supposed to be meeting with some horse trainer in thirty minutes and that you're nowhere to be found."

"So you came here to yell at me?"

"Yes!" Teddy said. He sounded like he was waving his arms, and I couldn't help it, I needed to get a better look, mostly to make sure Bee was doing okay. I slithered a little closer to the foot of the bed and peered around the edge to see a tall, stocky man wearing a Hawaiian shirt, snow pants, and sandals, all while carrying a white plastic bag in one hand. He had a big, scruffy beard, and the hair above his upper lip was longer than the rest, like he'd been sporting a mustache initially and then had forgotten to shave the rest of his face for a month.

Or a year.

And he was indeed waving his arms at Bee, but in a hapless Muppet sort of way.

"We have to be above reproach for this!" he told Bee, the

plastic bag bouncing up and down. "If you're late, then people will wonder why. If they wonder why, they might start poking around your past. And if they start poking around your past—"

"Yeah, yeah," Bee said. It was hilarious, because even though she was a grown-up woman who'd done very grown-up things in the last forty-eight hours, she resembled nothing more than a sullen teenager right now. She even scowled at the floor as she kicked at the carpet with her bare feet. "I *know*. Above reproach and all that."

"I mean it," Teddy said. "I have to make this work for Angel and Astrid, and you have to make this work for you. Isn't this what you've been wanting? A chance to make a brand outside of Bianca?"

Bianca. So he knew about her other career.

Bee's shoulders fell. "Yeah," she said, suddenly sounding very small. "It is."

Teddy lowered his arms. His mustache moved. Then he said, "I brought you breakfast."

"You did?"

He dug around in the plastic bag and pulled out a smaller paper bag. "Pain au chocolat," he said, a little gruffly. "And a banana."

Bee abruptly flung her arms around Teddy, and after a minute, he patted her awkwardly on the back.

"Thanks," Bee said, sounding brighter. "You know I like bananas when I'm on set."

"Yeah, but usually it's to prevent leg cramps because someone's folding you into a kinky pretzel. *No kinky pretzels in Christmas Notch.*"

"I *know*," Bee said. "Now let me get changed in peace. I promise I won't miss my horse date."

Teddy narrowed his eyes at her, his mustache still moving with some deep Teddy emotion, and then with a chuff, he turned on his heel and made to leave the room.

"Bye, Uncle Ray," she called as he walked through the door. He gave her a middle finger without looking back, and then the door slammed shut behind him.

Uncle Ray. Uncle Ray. Where have I heard that before—

Ohhhh.

Oh shit.

No wonder Bee and Teddy knew each other.

Uncle Ray-Ray's was the traditional studio Bee worked with most, and it was presumably owned by the titular Uncle Ray. And if Uncle Ray was *Teddy Fletcher*, that meant *Duke the Halls* was being produced by the same person who'd made *Trapped on Co-Ed Island 17* and *Spider-Peen: Homecoming*.

I didn't even want to think about what would happen if Steph found out, but even worse was the possibility of the media finding out. Of Dominic Diamond finding out. If he learned that Nolan Shaw was filming a movie produced by a porn mogul . . . and if he learned that Nolan Shaw was starring in that porn mogul's movie with a bona fide porn star . . .

That couldn't happen. No matter what, that couldn't happen.

Bee sank down onto the bed after the door shut, clutching

her pain au chocolat with both hands. "Holy shit," she whispered. "We almost got caught. We almost got caught."

"But we didn't," I said, trying to reassure her and myself at the same time, wiggling like a worm until I was free of the duvet and then getting to my feet. "We're all good, Bee. It's okay. We'll just be more careful is all."

She looked up at me.

Too late I realized what my words implied. That there would be more sneaking around. That there would be *more*, period.

I should have taken it back right away; I should have explained. Because we couldn't do more, we absolutely couldn't. Not with the stakes this high. Not with her and Teddy's pasts at play, and not with my future at risk.

But I didn't take it back.

And she didn't ask me to.

LATER THAT DAY, I felt my phone buzz in my pocket.

> **Steph:** Coming to Christmas Notch tonight.

> **Steph:** Want to make sure things are going well.

That was surprisingly thoughtful from Steph, and I was about to text her back and say so, when she added:

> **Steph:** If they're *not* going well, I will personally remove your eyeballs and string them onto a cranberry-and-popcorn garland for my tree.

> **Steph:** ♥

With a sigh, I texted back a thumbs-up and was sliding my phone into the inner pocket of the Duke of Frostmere's riding jacket when I got another text.

> **Mads:** Whatever you did with the insurance people worked! They filled Mom's prescription and she was able to pick it up this morning! We're going to the craft store after my half-day at school is over. There's a sale on Christmas tree stands. Or something.

Relief flooded through me.

> **Me:** That's great, Mads. I'm shooting all afternoon, but I'll call tonight to check in.

I put my phone inside my jacket, suddenly feeling so light I might float away. I didn't feel burdened by Mads and Mom needing my help while I was gone, but I also couldn't fuck up this opportunity by looking like a dickhole who cared more about answering his phone than filming his scenes. How ironic would it be if I ruined my only shot at taking care of my family . . . by taking care of my family?

Ugh.

But that *wasn't* going to happen today, because Mom's insurance issue was all taken care of, Mads was consigned to an afternoon of Christmas bargain hunting, and I was going to act the hell out of my scenes today. And then I'd call Maddie and finally call Isaac, and so I'd be a good brother and a good former bandmate to boot.

If I wasn't missing Christmas—and also missing the taste of Bianca von Honey's mouth—then life would be perfect right now.

There was a bounce to my step as I walked over to Bianca herself, who was currently walking in small circles, her fists clenching and unclenching as Luca hovered around her, trying to fuss with the bonnet tied under her chin. She was wearing a light blue gown and a crimson cape, and her face was framed by locks of hair hanging in big, pretty curls. More Pinterest researched than period accurate, but she looked absolutely stunning.

"Where did Denise *go wrong* with these front curls?" Luca asked, like a history professor about to deliver a lecture on a failed invasion of Rome.

"She was distracted," Bee said, sounding plenty distracted herself at the moment. "Maya was talking her ear off about cat breeding because she was waiting on a call about a boyfriend for her cat. A catchelor, you know."

Luca gave up trying to fix her hair under the bonnet and sighed. "If you don't stop moving, I can't un–Jane Austen you."

"Hey," I said, approaching and taking her hands. I dropped them when I saw Luca looking at us. "Everything okay?"

Bee glanced up at me. Her cheeks were rosy from the cold and her face was shadowed by the bonnet's brim. "It's not okay," she said fiercely. "I hate horses, I hate them, I hate them—"

"Aw, but horses have always spoken so fondly of you," I said.

She gave me the dirtiest look I'd ever seen, and I'd once sat between Martha Stewart and Gwyneth Paltrow at Rihanna's

Diamond Ball. "This isn't funny, Nolan," she said. "I'm going to get on that horse, and it's going to throw me into the snow and then it's going to prance on my body until I pop like a grape and then I won't even be able to say I told you so because I'll be dead. Dead as a popped grape."

"It's going to be safe, I promise," I soothed. "No deaths, no grapes. I'm going to be right here with you, okay? The whole time."

She blinked those bright, vulnerable eyes at me, and everything inside my chest turned to warm, squishy putty.

"You mean it?" she asked.

I pressed my palm to her jaw. Luca be damned, any nearby crew be damned, I couldn't be near her while she was unhappy and not need to make it better. "I mean it," I swore. I brushed a cool cheek with my thumb. "I won't let anything happen to you."

She sucked in a breath, her eyes searching mine, and in that moment, it felt like it was just the two of us, alone in the entire world. "I think I believe you," she whispered.

"AH. HEM," a put-upon voice interjected. "I'm not sure what is happening here, but this seems less than strictly equine-related."

Bee and I jumped apart, clearing throats and shuffling our feet. Luca stared distrustfully at us both.

"Let's go ride some horses," I said with fake enthusiasm, and with a weak smile, Bee took my arm and allowed me to escort her away from Luca and to where the rest of the crew was getting ready.

CHAPTER SIXTEEN

Bee

Anxiety coiled in my chest as we approached Whitneigh Houston and her trainer, Tabitha, a fine and nice woman, except she barked out a dry laugh when I admitted my fear of horses during our training session earlier this morning. I thought she assumed I was being sarcastic, and I couldn't blame her, because what normal adult was scared of horses? They're like the animal kingdom's big derpy version of Fabio.

I inhaled deeply and then let my breath out slowly and shakily. Big derpy Fabio. Big derpy Fabio.

And then there was Nolan at my side. He felt like the sun—his touch was enough to spread warmth and calm. But he wouldn't be there next to me while I sat on big derpy Fabio. He'd be on his own big derpy monster.

"You ready?" Nolan asked in a whisper that made me feel like it was only me and him snuggled up under the covers all over again.

I nodded wordlessly. I felt like I could barf, and if I was going to barf at least it should be in an attempt to say my lines.

I glanced all around the snowy valley. Pearl and Teddy sat lined up in the video village, where they could easily watch the playback. Gretchen watched with her arms over her chest and her incisor tugging on her lower lip. Teddy smiled under his walrus-like mustache—or maybe it was a grimace. I couldn't be sure. Even though him being on set meant Nolan and I would definitely have to turn the heat down to zero, he was a familiar source of peace in all his mismatched clothes, seasonally inappropriate shoes, and grumpy demeanor.

Nolan took a step back and held out a hand for me as I walked up the wooden steps that would allow me to mount Whitneigh Houston without trying to hoist myself up and risk ruining my exquisite blue dress and Austen curls.

Guiding my hand safely to Whitneigh Houston's reins, Nolan looked up to me, his intense blue eyes demanding my attention. "I'll be right beside you. For every step and every take. I promise."

I nodded and breathed out softly: "Okay." And it was okay. I wasn't excited for this moment, but I also felt like maybe I would at least survive it.

Nolan mounted his horse without the help of a ladder and with complete ease. Some of the more seasoned Hope Channel crew members let out impressed noises, but nothing too loud. These horses might be trained for a life on camera, but you could definitely sense the crew's efforts to keep the set a little more quiet and calm than usual.

"Quiet on set!" someone called.

"When you're ready, Bee," Gretchen told me.

Thankfully my lines were minimal as this scene opened up into one of the film's many montages.

The trainer stepped back and out of frame. Just like I'd been instructed, I squeezed gently on Whitneigh Houston's rib cage with my legs as I took a deep breath and forced my body to push through the anxiety and become a woman in love who couldn't be more thrilled to be riding a murder beast through a snowy valley as her love interest playfully chased after her on his own murder beast.

"Oh, duke!" I sang. "Catch me if you can!"

And then I squeezed a little tighter as Whitneigh Houston went from trot to full-on gallop.

I looked over my shoulder, and my heart nearly broke out of my rib cage at the sight of Nolan and One Hundred Percent That Horse cantering after me, the breeze rushing through his hair and his debonair Duke of Frostmere laugh rippling through the valley.

And it was almost like this could be . . . fun. Like this might not be so bad.

Without even intending to, I threw my head back as real, genuine laughter rolled through me.

I let the tension in my thighs ease and gently maneuvered Whitneigh Houston's reins as she circled us back, and Gretchen called, "Cut!" She added, "Good, good! Bee, you're a natural! Let's do another now that you're a little more relaxed. Nolan, you were just as dashing as I expected."

Nolan chuckled as he trotted up alongside me. "See? That wasn't so bad."

"I didn't die," I conceded as I patted Whitneigh Houston gently. "Thank you for not unaliving me," I told the horse.

And then several things happened at once.

Nolan's phone rang at full volume. "Just a minute," he said as he glanced at his phone. "Oh shit, I have to take this." He jumped off his horse with his phone pressed to his ear. "Maddie? Calm down!"

At the exact same time, a violent gust of wind rolled down from the mountaintops and picked up three canopies, flinging them into the air and right toward us.

Whitneigh Houston immediately reared up onto her hind legs. I held on as tight as I could, which turned out to be too tight, because she tore off quicker than Teddy does anytime he sees his ex-wife at one of Astrid's or Angel's functions.

It all happened in the slowest four seconds of my life, and then I was airborne and the last thing I saw was the crystal-blue Vermont sky.

Turns out your life doesn't flash before your eyes just before you die.

Instead your brain turns to static and nothing else.

"YOU KNOW SHE hates horses!" someone said.

"No, actually, I didn't know she hates horses. Horses on my sets aren't exactly a normal thing."

"I can't believe that very cute dickwad had his phone on."

"Yeah, not exactly professional. But don't act like you haven't ever answered your phone midscene."

"It was a close-up of me receiving oral, okay? And do you know how hard it is to get a call back from my doctor's office? I'd been waiting on that bloodwork for, like, three weeks."

"Besides, it wasn't the phone that startled the horse. The gale force winds that literally turned craft services into a salad spinner did that."

My throat was so dry. Is that what happened when you died? Your throat mummified first? I tried to cough and then clear my throat, but I needed water.

"She's alive!"

"She was never dead," the heavier, gruff voice said.

"Bee? Bee? Can you hear me?"

Minty-berry bubblegum-scented breath tingled over my nose. I knew that scent anywhere. My whole house smelled of it.

"S-Sunny?" my voice croaked as my eyes fluttered open.

Sunny hovered an inch above my face, her deep brown eyes wide and bright, her signature gum hanging like it was about to—

"Oh shit!" she said as the gum bounced off my chin. "I'd been building up that ball of gum since LAX."

A few feet behind her, Teddy stepped forward and pushed her to the side. "Let's get you some water and maybe a brush. I promised your moms I'd have you on FaceTime the moment you woke up. We should get you camera-ready for them."

"So that ferocious monster definitely did not kill me?" I asked, my voice scratchy.

I glanced past him to Sunny, and that's when I realized that not only was I not dead, but my best fucking friend in the whole wide world was here. And that's when I began to sob— like, snotty, ugly, meltdown cry. "You're here," I managed to say.

"Oh for fuck's sake, please don't cry," Teddy begged.

"Too late," I said as Sunny flung herself on top of me and joined me in my tears, because my best friend was a bubblegum-chewing empath.

But most importantly . . . she was here.

And Nolan was not.

CHAPTER SEVENTEEN

Nolan

"Mr. Kowalczk, there is nothing more I can tell you right now," an impatient doctor explained on the other end of the line. A hard, cold wind whipped around the corner of the farmhouse I was standing behind and gusted right into the phone's speaker, which I knew was probably irritating for the doctor, but it couldn't be helped. The farm, and more importantly its field, had been rented for today's horse-riding scenes, but the farmhouse was closed to us, and the only thing that counted as inside right now were the canopies the crew were huddled under while they froze their tits off and grumbled about the still-missing last page of the script.

Not exactly where I wanted to handle a family emergency.

"We won't know anything more until we get the CT scan," the doctor kept saying. "And until the rest of her labs come back."

"She just started a new medication," I said, trying to sound calm and not at all like I was *flipping out*, which I had been since Maddie called to tell me that Mom had fainted in the middle of a Michaels parking lot and hit her head on the concrete. "Could she have passed out because of an allergic reaction? When I Googled it, there were all these warnings about severe allergic reactions—"

"We don't think that's what's going on," the doctor said.

"And her head—"

"—has been stitched and she's due for her scan at any moment, so we'll be able to conclusively rule out stroke or concussion." His voice softened a little. "She's in good hands. I promise."

I knew that on an intellectual level. I knew this doctor was probably very good at his job, and that Barb would harass anyone she came across who wasn't good at their job, and that Kallum would make sure everything outside the hospital was handled. I knew that Maddie was way more mature than she should have to be at this age and had done everything right after Mom collapsed—called 911, given the hospital a list of Mom's meds, called Barb and me and Kallum.

But knowing something intellectually wasn't enough, because I should be there. I should be there right now, making sure everyone was okay, and . . . and I should also be on the other side of the farmhouse doing my job.

Doing my job with Bee, who was terrified of horses and had been relying on me to help her get through the day.

"Nolan?" I heard my sister say. The doctor must have handed the phone back to her.

"Hey, Mads," I said, trying to exude calm-older-brother energy. "I think I should probably come home tonight—I haven't had a chance to look at flights yet, but I'm sure I could find one out of Burlington in time for me to drive to the airport—"

"Shut up. You're not doing that," Maddie said.

"Maddie—"

"Mom is doing okay for now," Maddie went on, "and if she stops doing okay, then she's in the best possible place. And I'm officially on winter break, so I can be here the whole time."

"But—"

"And before you say that I shouldn't have to be because blah blah you're the grown-up, I'd be here anyway even if you were here too, because I'd want to be with Mom."

"But I should still be there," I said stubbornly. How the hell was I going to concentrate on being a fake duke when my mom was unconscious in a hospital? With a head wound that we didn't yet know the seriousness of?

"Barb and Kallum said you'd say this," Maddie pointed out. "So you need to consider whether or not you want to be this boring and predictable."

I was pacing now, tugging at the cravat around my neck. "I'm not predictable!"

"You *are*, and you're micromanaging this family even though you're in Vermont for only two dang weeks," Maddie said. "Stop it. I got this. Barb has got this. And once Mom wakes up, she'll have this too. So just chill *out* until I call you again."

My fingers twisted in the fabric of the cravat as I sucked in a deep breath. I wanted to grab my horse and gallop straight to Burlington, but I had responsibilities here too—responsibilities that also mattered to the family in a big way.

"You'll call me the minute she wakes up?" I asked. "Or when you hear something from the doctor?"

"Yes," Maddie said. "Now go away and do acting things. Bye, Nolan."

Feeling helpless, I hung up and stared at the farmhouse wall. I still wanted to go home, but Maddie was right. Everything was stable now, and I'd already dicked over my cast and crew by ducking out before a scene. Leaving the entire movie would screw things up for countless people, including Bee.

Bee. Shit. I needed to apologize for running out on her while she was on the horse. I knew how nervous she'd been, and I'd meant what I'd said about staying with her the entire time. But as I rounded the corner of the farmhouse to go back to set, my mind went blank.

The well-organized outdoor set that I'd left to answer my phone was gone, and in its place was a cluster of crumpled canopies, a mess of blown-over equipment, and crew members scattered everywhere trying to clean up. In the distance, I could see the trainer walking an agitated Whitneigh Houston around the field.

A riderless Whitneigh Houston.

"Where's Bee?" I asked Cammy as I got closer, my heart starting to pound all over again.

"The horse threw her," Cammy said briskly, bending to pick up a canvas chair. "After you left to take your call, there was a big wind and it got spooked."

"It threw her?" I breathed. A crackling hiss of panic filled my mind.

Cammy took pity on me. "She's fine, but they took her to get checked out by the town doctor. The rest of the day's work has been postponed."

"Where?" I asked, not caring that it was probably unprofessional to ask. I had to see her. I had to know she was okay. "Where is she now?"

THE BEAUTIFUL WOMAN in front of me crossed her arms. "Nein. Nyet. Non."

"Please," I begged. *"Please.* I just want to make sure she's okay."

Sunny glared at me. "She *is* okay, no thanks to you and your obnoxious ringtone. And the doctor says she needs to rest." At the hopeful lift of my face, she added, *"All night."*

My shoulders fell. "Are you sure I can't see her for only a minute?"

"Uh-uh," Sunny said, snapping her gum. "You're not her doctor, best friend, or mom. You are a fuckboy and fuckboy visiting hours don't resume until tomorrow. And that's only if I decide I'm less pissed off at you."

Sunny had shut the door behind her when she'd answered my knock, and so I couldn't even try to peer around her to see Bee in the room. And short of unsexy wrestling, I didn't see a way to get past Bee's new bodyguard. Who—according to Cammy—also happened to be our new makeup artist.

I was starting to feel vaguely cursed.

I left Bee's door with a final apology/plea, which was met

with no mercy whatsoever, and then I went to my own room, where I stood in front of my suitcase for a long minute, trying to organize my thoughts. I decided to halfway pack my things, just in case Maddie called with bad news, and then I sat down and texted Bee. And called her.

And DMed her on ClosedDoors: I'm sorry I wasn't there during the accident. And that I sort of caused the accident to begin with. Can we talk when you're feeling better?

There was no answer. And no texts or calls from Maddie—or Kallum or Barb. I even tried calling Isaac and got no answer. It was like everything had gone wrong today and I had no way to fix any of it. All I could do was hold this metal and glass rectangle and hope it eventually lit up in my hand.

THE INN'S DINING room doubled as a sort of bar, but it was barely used and its bottles were dusty enough to warrant concern. It had also never been staffed that I'd seen, and Stella the innkeeper was nowhere in sight as I came downstairs. So I stuck a twenty under a coaster and helped myself to some bourbon, which I drank alone in the dark, listening to the cheerful Christmas music playing in the lobby as it filtered into the empty room.

I'd just finished talking to Maddie and Mom. Mom had been awake and feeling much better, although a little tired from the events of the day. The good news was that her scan came back free of any signs of stroke or concussion, and the doctors didn't think her fainting was an allergic reaction to anything. They diagnosed the event as a vagal response to some pelvic pain she'd been having and had been trying to grit her way through without bothering any of us about it. She would be released from the hospital tomorrow and see her gynecologist later in the week to investigate the source of her pain, although she insisted it was normal for her and that this was a big fuss over nothing.

"Mom, passing out in the Michaels parking lot is not nothing!" I'd protested.

"Well, it's not a good look, I'll admit that," Mom had said. "But they're just going to tell me to take some ibuprofen and to eat more fiber or something. Joke's on them—I have a Metamucil smoothie every morning. I excrete like a champ."

"Ew, Mom," I'd heard Maddie say in the background.

I'd told everyone to call me tomorrow and also reminded them that I would be on the first flight home if anything changed, and then hung up, trying to pep talk myself into staying here. Trying to convince myself to stay and do my job when it felt like I was still needed back home, even though everything was sort of fine now.

But what if it didn't stay fine?

Or what if Maddie's right and you're micromanaging your own family?

And that was when I'd decided I needed some dusty bourbon.

My newly arrived manager found me in the dark sort-of bar with my head in my hands and the uncapped bourbon next to my elbow.

"That bottle might be older than you are," Steph said by way of greeting.

I didn't bother looking up as she mounted the stool next to me, but I did gesture to the bottle, since I was nothing if not a gracious host, and she grabbed it by the neck and took a long swig.

"You just got here," I said. "It can't be that bad."

"Oh yes, it can," Steph said, setting the bottle down with a *thunk*. "I just came from the production office, where I had a long meeting with Teddy and Gretchen. Teddy, by the way? A total fucking disaster. That's my professional diagnosis; he doesn't even have to pay me a consulting fee for that."

"Is that why you came to Christmas Notch? To meet with Gretchen about me?"

Steph tapped maroon-painted nails on the bar. "No, I came because I wanted to make sure things weren't a shit show here. This is Teddy's first movie for the Hope Channel and your co-star is brand new. It's more variables than I'd like."

And that wasn't even including me, the biggest variable of them all.

"What did Gretchen say?" I asked. "Was it about this afternoon?"

"Yes, and about every other day that you're running some kind of PTO phone tree instead of being a duke. You're on thin fucking ice with her, Nolan, and I think we've established that I will make my grandmother's traditional Christmas gravy from your neckbone if you screw this up. Being vetted by the Hope Channel and its viewers is the first step to the new Nolan Shaw. Without this we have nothing. Zero. So I hope these phone calls have been worth the risk."

It sounded so shallow when Steph put it like that. Like nothing could be worth the risk of messing up a fresh start.

"It was my mom," I said after a minute. My voice was soft against the strains of Nat King Cole drifting in through the open double doors. "She had to go to the emergency room today."

When I looked up at Steph, she was leaning forward to put her hand on my face. Her trademark pearls glinted from underneath the lapels of her tailored pantsuit.

"I'm sorry, Nolan," she said, not unkindly. "I'm sorry your mother had a thing. And I know why you're doing all of this, I really do. But directors don't have time to care about your personal shit. Producers especially don't."

Producers. That reminded me that she still didn't know about Teddy being Uncle Ray-Ray, or Bee being Bianca. And for Bee's sake, I was a little relieved that it was only my own messes that needed to be cleaned up at the moment.

And I could do that; I could fix my mess. I could apologize to Gretchen and—and well, I didn't know what else yet. Maybe find someone I trusted to hang on to my phone while I was on camera and hope that my run of bad phone luck was over.

Maybe even tell her the truth.

Steph was right that directors and producers didn't have the bandwidth to care about what each individual cast member was going through, but my family stuff was such a big part of my life right now . . .

Steph correctly interpreted my pause. "I don't like lying, even though it's part of my job," she said. "Normally, I might even advocate for telling Gretchen the truth. But if the word gets out that your home life is complicated—the kind of complicated that causes problems on set and ultimately costs time and money—you'll develop a reputation in this business that even I can't fix."

"Gretchen's not like that, though," I protested. "She wouldn't see it like that."

"I agree," said Steph. "But can you promise that Pearl wouldn't? Or Teddy Fletcher? Can you promise that Gretchen wouldn't need to tell someone else because she thinks they should also be aware? A PA? A Hope Channel exec worried about delays? There are no secrets on a movie set, Nolan. None. And there are even less in Hollywood. If people know you have divided attention for a semipermanent reason here in Christmas Notch, they will know it everywhere. And if that happens I can't promise that you'll be able to get another job with the Hope Channel. And I definitely can't promise you any kind of prime-time gig where they'll need you to be dependable above all else."

The truth in her words felt like bottom-shelf whiskey. A deep-chest burn I needed, but not one I particularly liked.

She was right, though. I couldn't risk anything tarnishing my new reputation. I'd known that it meant keeping my nose clean of any visible debauchery, but I guessed it also meant pretending all my priorities began and ended with whatever gig I was working.

"You're right," I said finally. Heavily.

"Of course I'm right," Steph said. "Now knock off this un-professional shit before I use your teeth as earrings."

She patted my cheek and then grabbed the bourbon again. In the dim light filtering in from the lobby, I could see that her first swig was already putting a smirk on her impeccably lipsticked mouth and pinkening her normally fair cheeks. "What does a woman have to do to get a cherry around here?" she muttered to herself, getting up to poke around the back of the bar.

I checked my phone while she did, seeing that Bee still hadn't responded to any of my messages. Maybe she was really resting like Sunny and the doctor wanted her to. Or maybe she was furious with me for being a faithless horse companion and she planned on never talking to me again. Maybe I'd lost any chance to laugh with her again, smile with her again, *kiss* her again . . .

I texted one more time and then finally gave up. With a glum wave at Steph, who'd found a dusty jar of cherries in some mysterious bar cranny, I trudged up the stairs to my room.

UNSURPRISINGLY, I SLEPT like shit, but when I finally pushed myself out of bed, I had a message from Maddie telling me that the night had been uneventful and the plan was still to discharge Mom today.

There was nothing from Bee.

I was due at ten for hair and makeup—and makeup with *Sunny*, so that would be fun—but I showered and dressed early so I could catch Gretchen at the production office before things got moving for the day. I found her in the ground-floor office with a laptop open in front of her and Pearl curled into a human apostrophe on a nearby sofa, fast asleep.

"Hey," I said, coming in with a light knock on the open door. "Can we talk?"

"You can count on me," I finally told Gretchen. "There will be no more trouble for *Duke the Halls* of the ex–boy band variety."

And I meant it. After all, I had less than a week left here.

What could possibly go wrong in a week?

CHAPTER EIGHTEEN

Bee

My body felt like it had aged fifty years in one night as I rolled over with a bone-cracking yawn to find Sunny with a Twizzler dangling from her lips and her magnifying glasses and headlamp on as she embroidered what appeared to be a red-and-green vulva framed with holly.

"Why does it feel like the TV has been getting progressively louder?" I asked with a moan.

"Because it has been," she said simply. "I was inspired by one of those expensive alarm clocks that wakes you up slowly."

I squinted at the glowing screen on the other wall. "What are you even watching?"

A cheery version of "Rudolph, the Red-Nosed Reindeer"

piped through the speakers as the words *A Barista for Christmas* in a red curling text unfurled across the screen.

She turned down the blaring volume as the music swelled. "Old Hope Channel movies. It's pretty much the only channel that works here. Well, that and the Weather Channel, and I already know I can recite the hourly update, including the Santa tracker status. Plus the weather people just say the same jokes over and over again. You can only hear someone named Todd say 'Baby, it really *is* going to be cold outside' so many times before you start to wonder if the matrix is resetting itself or something."

"Didn't the internet cancel that song?" I asked as I sat up on my elbows.

She turned to me, her brown eyes magnified so much that she looked like she had walked right out of an anime. "I don't know if cancel culture has hit the Weather Channel yet. Trust me. It definitely hasn't hit Todd."

She pushed up her magnifying glasses and switched off her headlamp before handing me a not-so-fresh cheese and cherry pastry. "Eat up, buttercup. We'll get you real food later, but for now it's continental breakfast leftovers."

I grumbled as I scooted all the way up and took the flaky Danish from her. It was less offensive up close and personal, and even less so when I bit into it and my stomach grumbled for more. "What are you even doing here?" I asked with a full mouth.

"Well, darling, they needed another makeup person after one of the makeup artists had some sort of cat emergency?"

"Maya? Is her cat okay?"

She shrugged. "Something about a cat in unexpected heat and a future cat dad waiting for his big moment. I don't know. Kind of sounded like a bad porn premise. A cat sex emergency. So anyway, here I am! Working makeup for my first penetration-free film. My dad is so proud."

"Aw, Papa Sammy! You could have texted me a heads-up, by the way."

"Teddy wanted to surprise you," she said.

"What a sweet little Krampus he is." And then I gasped, nearly choking on the last of my pastry. "Oh shit, what time is it?" I scrambled out of bed, glancing down to see I'd been haphazardly dressed in whatever dirty laundry had been crumpled in the corner next to the minifridge.

"It's four o'clock in the afternoon," she said as she leaned back against my headboard. "You've been pretty much out of it since we brought you back to the inn last night."

"But I'm supposed to be on set . . . oh my God, does this mean I have to reshoot the horse scene?" My chest tightened and my eyes began to burn at the thought.

"Okay, deep breaths. Good news: you don't have to reshoot. Bad news—"

"I have to pee." I rushed to the bathroom and left the door cracked as I groaned with sweet relief the minute my tush hit the porcelain. "What's the bad news?"

"The bad news is your dear Nolan Shaw is a piece of shit fuckboy."

I finished in the bathroom and kicked the door open as I washed my hands. "He's not, though. He really isn't." But I didn't buy it. I didn't believe it. Not even from myself. Nolan had promised me he'd be with me every step of the way yesterday. It was such a small, simple promise to keep, and one that was actually his job. And sure, maybe his phone ringing was an accident. But when I really thought about it, Nolan had been tied up and distracted by phone calls since day one.

I walked back out and plopped on the bed—the same bed where I'd done very filthy things with said fuckboy.

Sunny's jaw fell as she threw her Christmas vulva embroidery to the side and gave me her full attention. "Bee 'Bianca von Honey' Hobbes. You fucked the fuckboy."

"It's more like"—I grasped for the most artful phrase I could find, but it all came down to—"friends with bennies."

She gawked at me. "Bee, that makes it even worse! Not only is he a fuckboy, but he's fucking *you* and abandoning you in your hour of need. He's basically the reason Whitneigh Houston—great horse name, by the way—startled to begin with."

"Well, there was a really violent gust of wind and—"

She pulled my hands into her lap, like she was trying to transfer all her concern and sincerity with just the touch of her fingertips, and to be honest, it was working. "You know I'm Team Friends with Bennies. But this could go toxic super quick, and not only would that mess *you* up, it could very easily mess up this whole opportunity. For you and Teddy. You've been doing so good post-Spencer. I don't want you to end up in that kind of cycle again."

She was right. Sunny always had a way of being right. I'd almost always been the secret of everyone I'd ever been in a relationship with. Sometimes it was because I was fat. Sometimes it was because I was a sex worker. And sometimes it was because of both. But being the secret of someone like Nolan Shaw . . . that was on a whole new level.

I threw myself back on the bed, and she maneuvered around so that I could lay my head in her lap.

And then I told her every detail. How Nolan and I had just wanted to get it out of our systems, and then it turned out to not be out of our systems. I told her all about the absolute terror I felt going into my scene yesterday and how Nolan swore up and down that he'd be there for me. But then he was gone, and I was suddenly flying through the air.

Even though we'd known each other for only a week and in just over a week's time he'd go his way and I'd go mine, I couldn't ignore how deeply hurt I felt by the fact that when I woke up from being thrown, he hadn't been there. And that he couldn't ignore his phone or the outside world for a short amount of time to be with me.

That's what it always came down to. It was all I ever wanted in any relationship—for the person I was seeing to not only be with me at night when things were fun and sweaty and full of delight, but to be there in the harsh light of day when there was no hiding from reality. I wish I could go back in time and tell little Bee that the dark was nothing to be scared of and that the hardest things in life usually happened in broad daylight.

And maybe that was all Nolan could or wanted to give me. Those nighttime hours wrapped in bedsheets. But I owed it to myself to find out. And at the very least to yell at him about his stupid phone.

I stood up abruptly. "I need to talk to Nolan."

"Yes, mama!" Sunny hooted.

I marched over to the door full of determination.

"Oh, Bee?"

I glanced back over my shoulder. "Yeah?"

"Maybe brush your teeth?" She grimaced. "Deodorant might not hurt either."

I nodded and doubled back to the bathroom.

"And maybe take some lube too," Sunny offered. "Just in case! Anger is always a motivator for great sex!"

AFTER A QUICK shower, a change of clothes, and yes, brushing my teeth and applying deodorant, I plugged in my very dead cell phone and, leaving Sunny to her seasonally appropriate embroidery, walked down the hall to Nolan's room. According to this morning's call sheet, he should've been done shooting his solo scenes by now.

My fist made it through only half a knock before Nolan swung the door open. His drawn expression began to dissolve into relief as he pulled me inside, his arms coiling around me as he held me to his chest and inhaled deeply against the top of my head and my still-wet hair. "I was so worried about you."

My resolve began to crumble. *You're here to talk*, I reminded myself. *You are here to talk. And maybe even get a little shouty.*

God, his room smelled even more like him than mine did. This was not fair. I was in enemy territory here.

I stumbled back from him and shut the door behind me, locking us both in this Nolan Kowalczk hot-boxed room.

The only chance I had at getting through this was to leave middle school dance levels of distance between us.

"We need to talk," I said, just as he said, "Bee, I think I need to tell you something."

"You first," we said in unison.

He took a breath, and so did I as he motioned for me to talk first.

"Look," I said as I perched on the armrest of his red velvet love seat. "I know that . . . whatever we are is casual and . . . likely to wrap the moment this whole film does and I know that we are a secret. For both of our sakes. But, Nolan, I need you to know that I don't take promises lightly, and when I was thrown off Whitneigh Houston after your phone rang and that wind rolled through the valley . . . and then you weren't even there when I woke up . . ." I shook my head. I could feel my train of thought wandering, like I was suddenly unsure of what I needed to say or why I was here. I tried my best to shed the onslaught of intense invalidation and soldier on. "What I'm trying to say is that no matter how serious this is or how long this lasts, I need you to not make promises you can't keep."

He sat down on the small coffee table in front of me. "Bee, I—I'm so sorry. I don't want to unload all these excuses on you, because it doesn't matter. I wasn't there for you when I said I would be, but I also . . . I think it's important you know why I'm here and what's waiting for me back home. Steph doesn't want me to tell anyone at all, and I wasn't going to, but then I thought more about it today, and you have a lot at stake too, and I just feel like I can trust you, and—"

"Wait," I interrupted him. "What's waiting for you back home?"

Oh, fuck no. I was already the other woman for plenty of people across the world, but that was different. This was . . .

"My mom," he said slowly. "And my little sister, Maddie, who's had to grow up way too fast. They're all I have, Bee. See, my mom . . ." He took another breath, then met my eyes with his clear blue gaze. "She has bipolar disorder, and after Dad died, her mental health took a real hit. As a family, we all had to find our new normal without him, and it meant being there for each other, as much as possible. It still means that. Even when I'm here, I need to keep a piece of myself there."

Waves of sympathy and guilt washed over me in equal measure. I never even took a moment to stop and think what kind of calls he might be fielding. I was so wrapped up in the idea that I didn't deserve to have him—even in a physical and fleeting way—and so it was all too easy to believe that he was being reckless with his promises and my feelings.

"Oh, Nolan." My voice came out like a soft breath, and the stiffness in my posture and in my heart began to melt. There had been so many small moments when it felt like his head and heart were in a different place . . . and that's because they were.

"It's fine," he said a little gruffly, like he was all too used to saying those two words. "But that's why I need this to work. That's why I need to rebound enough to get out of the theater tech job that I actually love but pays shit. I fucked up once and lost everything, but I won't do it again. I can't. But anyway, that's what all these calls have been for, and then yesterday, Mom fainted and hit her head in a parking lot. She had to go to the emergency room."

"Holy shit. Is she okay?"

"Yes," he said on a tired exhale. "She's okay and was discharged earlier today. Maddie—well, she's too young to be as capable as she is, but she did everything she was supposed to. She did all the right things."

"I'm so sorry, Nolan. This . . . this is a lot to carry around while on set."

He shook his head. "I don't mean to make it sound like a burden, because it's not. Mom is fucking awesome, and she's hilarious and crafty and has so much love for everyone she meets, even this demon dog named Snapple. Our family just needs a little flexibility is all. And you'd think that would be an easy thing to get, right? Just a little bit of give around the edges. But it's almost impossible, and *that's* what's hard. Not the being there for her—but the having to fight off the world so she can be there for herself."

I leaned forward and let my fingers graze his shoulder, which was rigid with tension. "She sounds amazing," I said softly. "Maddie too."

His body relaxed a little under my touch. "Maddie is the best teenager ever. No little sister has any business being as cool as she is. The best part is that she's just young enough for her and her friends to give zero shits about me or INK."

"And that's the best part?" I asked.

"If your cousin had ever sold your underwear on eBay, you'd be pretty grateful for any family members who were also unimpressed by you."

"Well, the real question is: Were they clean? Because the ones that are good and sweaty go for some serious coin."

He looked up from under those dark brows and with a helpless grin said, "You have one delightfully perverted mind, Bee Hobbes."

I stood from my perch and let my body drift toward his. "You can take the girl out of the sex work, but you can't take the sex work out of the girl."

"I'm not complaining," he said as he gazed up at me, his head resting against my stomach now.

"What can I do to help?" I asked. "I want to do whatever we can to set your mind at ease during this last week of filming. Maybe we could find someone trustworthy to monitor your phone while we're on set?"

"That's not a bad idea, but who? Steph is adamant that no one knows about this, so I don't get the *needy actor* label slapped on me."

I shrugged. "Half the crew are porn people brought in by Teddy. They're better at keeping secrets than Tom Hanks."

"Is he . . . known for that?"

"No, but he should be. He looks so trustworthy."

He craned his neck back as realization settled over him. "Huh. That . . . makes so much sense about the porn crew members. Luca and his tote of assless chaps."

I nodded. "Yup. And Angel. You remember when I told you he was Teddy's son? Tall Ron too. Well, he's not also Teddy's son, but he is a porn person."

"Uncle Ray-Ray," he said. "Teddy Fletcher *is* Uncle Ray-Ray, right?"

I nodded. "The one and only."

"That guy is a porn king. What's he even doing producing a movie for the Hope Channel?"

"Diversifying his income streams," I said simply. *Planning for the future*, I thought. *Like I should be. Like I'm trying to do.* "People don't pay for porn like they used to, and Teddy might be a lot of things, but he's a good dad. Angel's fancy-ass art school tuition is a boner crusher, and Teddy's also trying to help Astrid, his daughter, finance the prototypes for her eco-friendly sex toys."

"And that led to joining forces with the Hope Channel how?"

"These Christmas movie shoots might run longer than a usual adult film schedule, but other than that, they're pretty similar. Replicable story lines, tight budgets. When Teddy lost so many crew members to the UnFestival accident, he started filling in the holes—pun intended—with porn people."

"If this weren't my attempt at launching a brand-new, clean-as-a-whistle Nolan Shaw, I would say this was genius."

"I know there's a lot at stake here for you, Nolan. I do. But Teddy's a good guy, and I think he might just get away with this. Have a little faith."

His lips twitched into a reluctant smile.

"Oh! And Sunny too," I added. "She's here taking over for Maya. Oh, oh! Sunny would be the perfect person to be on Mrs. Kowalczk cell phone watch!"

Nolan blew out a low hiss. "Does she do favors for fuck-boys?"

"Ooooh, that would be a good nonprofit name. Favors for Fuckboys."

"Do you forgive this fuckboy?" he asked, nuzzling back into my belly.

"Yes," I whispered, warmth coiling just under the skin. "And thank you for being honest with me."

"Where do we go from here?"

My sigh came out as shaky and unsure as I felt about our future. "I think . . . we . . ." The good and right answer would be for us to go cold turkey and remove the benefits from our friends with benefits situation, but after this thing wrapped, I didn't know if I'd ever see Nolan Shaw again. If I could have only one more week with him, I didn't want to waste it hoping and wishing for more. "I think we should be careful."

His hands slid up my hips and over the waistband of my bike shorts. "How careful?" he whispered.

As his fingers traced up my sides, a small bottle fell out of the pocket of my hoodie. He reached down to inspect it. "Is—is this lube?" he asked with a laugh.

"Travel size," I admitted, my words coming out a little breathier than I'd intended, because now that he'd touched me and pulled away so suddenly, the soft skin of my stomach felt like it was burning. "Sunny always insists that I'm prepared."

He inspected the bottle. "Sugar cookie flavor again? Mmm." He set it down on the table and pulled me closer to him, his breath hot on my abdomen.

With a gentle care I hadn't yet seen from him, he pulled down the waistband of my shorts, letting them slowly slide down my thighs like he was unwrapping a present with every intention of saving the paper.

My knees weakened, and I forced myself not to suck in or hold myself still as he kissed along the seam of my lacy light pink boy shorts.

A soft sigh lingered on my lips as his teeth dragged along the supple flesh, and with his dark, hungry eyes Nolan peered up at me like I was something to be worshipped. Treasured.

He stood then, pulling my sweatshirt over my head, and pressed the full length of his body into mine.

I slid my hand down to his waist, to his erection bulging against the zipper of his jeans, and used a gentle grip to guide him to the bed.

His voice was raspy and grating when he said, "This is . . . you are *everything* I want."

I wanted to respond, but I didn't know the words to say. I didn't know how to explain that I felt the same way too, and the possibility of this ending hurt too much for me to admit that *he* was everything I wanted.

We stood there framed by his open window, as the sun hovered above the slopes crowding this town that was picture perfect from a distance until you looked close enough to see all its little rough and endearing edges and imperfections. Sort of like me. And Nolan. And whatever we were.

He pressed his mouth against mine, pushing his tongue past my lips, and I hadn't realized how thirsty I'd been for his kiss until his tongue danced with mine. Scraping my nails over his back, I pulled his shirt over his head, and we both fell onto the bed, him heavy between my thighs as the seam of his jeans rubbed against the wet lace covering my aching slit.

"I need you," I whimpered into his mouth, like a confession.

With a growl, he left a trail of licks and kisses down my

neck and over my heaving breasts. Wonder and lust in his eyes, he pulled the cups of my bra down, letting my nipples spill out. With his warm tongue painting circles around my puckering tips and his teeth poised to bite, he said, "Tonight, I'll take my time with you."

CHAPTER NINETEEN

Nolan

S hh," I told Bee, putting my hand over her mouth as my other hand continued kneading her hip. No shrill phone alarm for me this morning—instead, I'd woken up to a porn star kissing my neck. Which had quickly turned into Bee riding me like her life depended on it. "Noisy girl."

Her next moan was muffled by my palm, but she was nodding like my telling her to be quiet was some sort of sexy revelation. Like it turned her on to be scolded for feeling so good, and watching her get turned on turned *me* on. When she made another noise against my hand, I gave her a hard swat on the ass.

"Make any more noise, and I'll take you over my knee," I purred, savoring the way she shuddered on top of me. Loving the way her half-lidded eyes strayed all over, from my eyes to my mouth to my chest, like she couldn't get enough of look-ing at me, at us, like she couldn't get enough of *this*.

Her job meant that she was everyone's dirty girl all the time, and never her own dirty girl, never doing dirty things *only* for fun and *only* for her own pleasure. There was always the image to consider, the brand, the performance. It was all give and no take, and I understood that all too well. It was a lot like being a pop star, actually. There was a real high that came after performing—an incredible high, even—but some-times you just wanted to sing for yourself.

I found her clit with my thumb, pressing and rolling as she fucked herself on my cock. "It's morning now," I murmured, still keeping my hand over her mouth. "We've been fucking all night, and you're still not satisfied, are you? And every per-son walking down our hallway this morning is going to know it. They're going to know you can't come enough to keep that pretty pussy happy, aren't they?"

I felt the moment my words sent her over the edge. Her eyes flew wide and she fell forward, her hands splayed on my chest and her hair tumbling over her shoulders to tickle my face and collarbone as she panted against my palm. Her thighs were tense, her chest heaved, and her core was hot and flut-tering around me. I could feel her smile against my hand as she came, and all I wanted was for time to stand still so that I could finally drink my fill of her, of her body and her smile and her wicked sense of humor. Because last night hadn't been enough—this morning wouldn't be enough.

I can't get enough.

The moment her climax receded and she began to get lax

and slumpy, I flipped us over so she was on her back, and I was on top. I was back inside her in an instant, moving between her thighs with hard, rutting strokes as she ran greedy hands up my biceps and over my shoulders. She grinned up at me, her eyes still glittering with the dozy sparkle of the recently orgasmed and her cheeks still stained pink.

"What about you?" she teased, scratching her fingernails up my back, drawing a grunt from deep in my chest. "Will you be able to stay quiet when you come? Or is everyone going to know how much you love fucking me?"

I grunted again. There was no hiding it, no staying quiet. Whether I was inside her hot, slick sex or her hot, slick mouth, whether I was in her hand or just pressed against her, Bee Hobbes drove me out of my goddamn mind.

Needing her mouth, I bent down to kiss her, sliding my arms underneath her shoulders and laying my entire body over hers so that we were pressed together as I fucked the churning orgasm out of my body and into hers. I kissed her the whole time, licking into her mouth as I screwed her, and only stopping once I'd drained myself into the condom.

And I'd been plenty noisy while I did it.

Bee bit my lip, tugging at it with a smile, as I reluctantly eased myself from her body and got up to take care of the condom. After cleaning up, I found my pajama pants and pulled them up around my hips while I walked over to the small coffeepot near the bathroom.

"Coffee?" I asked the temptress currently tangled in my sheets.

"Only if it's some obnoxious seasonal flavor," she said. "Nothing plain."

I looked down at the coffee pods organized in a dish shaped like a snowflake. "There's chocolate peppermint, white chocolate peppermint, and . . . figgy pudding. That feels like a bold choice for a coffee flavor."

"Figgy pudding, please," she said cheerfully.

I grimaced but complied, making us each a mug of coffee—white chocolate peppermint for me, thank you very much—and then I walked carefully back to the bed with them in hand.

It was then, with the steam curling from the top of the mugs, with Bee sitting up and reaching for her disgusting coffee with adorable grabby hands, that the truth punched me in the chest.

I didn't want this to end.

Not this morning, not tomorrow. Not when I left the set. Not at any point in the foreseeable future.

I wanted her. This.

And I wanted this for more than just a handful of days.

I handed her the mug and then sat down on the edge of the bed, wanting to etch this moment into my memory forever. The morning sun glowed in, the kind of pale light that promised cold noses and snow-blanketed hills, and it loved Bee, caressing her lush mouth and high cheeks, fanning shadows underneath her long eyelashes. Her hair was tousled and tangled over her breasts and shoulders, and on the end table was an empty condom wrapper, a scrunchie, and her phone, scattered in a mess that felt so girlfriendy it made my throat ache. Everything smelled like sex and coffee and Christmas, and it was heaven.

It was actual heaven.

"What if—" I started, my heart flipping over as I realized what I was about to ask. What I was about to risk. Because what if she said no? Or worse, what if she thought I was like those creepers in her ClosedDoors comments, the men who craved her not as a person, but as a disposable fantasy?

But I had to ask, didn't I? Because the thought of *not* having this when *Duke the Halls* wrapped felt like getting hit by an INK tour bus *and* its caravan of cargo trucks. So I cleared my throat and started again.

"What if this didn't end?" I asked quietly. "What if it was like this all the time?"

She blinked at me. "Like this? Drinking figgy pudding coffee in Vermont?"

I set my mug on the table and turned so I could face her completely. "Like *this*," I said, curling my hands around hers cradling her mug. I looked deep into her gaze, which was as green as a Kansas prairie in spring. "Us."

Her lips parted, but she didn't speak at first, her eyes searching mine. Then she said, slowly, "Us?"

"I like you," I whispered, taking her coffee from her and setting it on the table next to mine. "I like you so much that it scares me. And when I think about leaving and never seeing you again, it makes me feel like something's being yanked out of me. Something important, something that I need to breathe and eat and live. I want more than memories with you, Bee. I want moments upon moments."

She swallowed, her eyes dropping to our hands, which were now laced together.

"I like you too," she murmured. "More than is good for me. But I don't know, Nolan." She looked back up to me again.

"You feel like a mirage to me, like the closer I get, the less real you'll become. And sometimes I wonder if it's better to keep you at a distance."

Her voice was soft, but the words made me ache, both for her and for myself. "I'm not a mirage," I said, leaning in to brush her lips with mine. "I'm real. I'm here. And I'm not going to disappear."

She pressed her forehead to mine. "You promise?"

"I promise. Not a mirage."

A small sigh. "I want to see you after this too."

My heart surged against my chest, and I couldn't help it, I kissed her again. I dug my hands into her hair and moved my lips over hers until she impatiently deepened the kiss like she always did, as if she were hungry for my taste.

"But," she said, breaking off, "you'll be in Kansas City. I'll be in L.A."

"We'll make it work," I pledged.

"Hmph."

My stomach pulled on my heart, and it was my turn to sigh a little. "What you said last night, though, about being careful. We'll have to be careful after Christmas Notch too."

"Oh," Bee said. "Right."

I didn't want her to misunderstand. "Not because I want to be," I said quickly. "I'd love for us to be together for all the world to see. But—"

"Your career. Your manager. Bunting." She didn't sound angry or hurt, but there was a carefulness to her words where there hadn't been before.

I tried to read her expression, tucking my finger under her chin so she couldn't duck her face away. "Bee, if I didn't have to make this rebranding thing work, I swear I would . . ."

"I know," she said. "I understand." Then she moved her head so she could kiss my knuckles. "I'll take it, Nolan. Just so you know. I'll take you however I can get you. But maybe we should think about cooling things down here."

"What? No!"

She laughed a little, although it sounded forced to me. "I know. I don't want to stop either, but I have me and Teddy to think about too. And you're here for less than a week, just until a couple days after Christmas, and I'll wrap a few days after that, and then we'll have as much time as we want in the privacy of our homes or in the privacy of a hotel. A real hotel, not a hotel with a heart-shaped bathtub next to the bed." She pressed a hand to my chest, her green eyes locked on mine. "It doesn't make sense to risk everything when we don't have very long to wait."

She was right. I hated that she was right because I wanted to spend every spare moment in bed with her, but her logic was undeniable. "So we'll be dry until after the movie wraps?" I asked to clarify.

"Think you can handle it, Mr. Bad Boy?" she asked, looping her arms around my neck.

"Maybe," I answered. "As long as I don't look at you. Or think about you. Or smell anything with sugar cookies or figs."

She leaned in, her exhales ghosting over my lips. I could feel the stiff tips of her breasts moving over my chest as she pressed closer. "Maybe the whole going dry thing could start after today—"

My phone erupted into the opening bars of "Fresh INK," a ringtone chosen especially for Kallum, since that was his least favorite song from our debut album.

If Kallum was calling . . .

Panic fizzed through me as I thought of all the things that could be going wrong right now. As I imagined Mom back in the hospital and me all the way out here in Vermont.

"One second," I muttered, dropping a kiss onto Bee's forehead and then retrieving my phone from the counter with the coffeepot.

I answered as quickly as I could. "Oh my God, is it Mom? Is she okay?"

"No, man, it's way worse," Kallum said glumly. "My sex tape leaked."

CHAPTER TWENTY

Bee

"Eyes closed," Luca reminded me as I steadied myself on his shoulders and stepped into the wedding gown. "You know what I see every time I close my eyes? Kallum Lieberman's sex tape. Holy hell. That man is rocking the dad bod. I didn't think straight porn could be hot until I saw that video."

"Uh, excuse me? Are you saying my straight scenes aren't hot?"

"Aw, Bee. You know I think you're smoking, but P in V is just not my flavor." I felt a chill roll through him as he fluffed the skirt of my dress. "But Kallum, he was always my fave. You would think Isaac was tailor-made for me, but something about that doofus Kallum always got me so hot. And Nolan . . . well, Nolan had big dick energy, but Kallum *is* big dick energy if you get what I mean."

I laughed to myself. I hadn't told Luca about me and Nolan yet, but I could confirm that when it came to Nolan, his big dick energy was more than just energy. I hadn't seen Kallum's tape yet, but it was everywhere. And not only that, but apparently the media was now sniffing around INK's past, looking for any juicy details they could possibly dig up on any past or current scandals. The moment Nolan got off the phone with Kallum, he'd dressed in a hurry and gone in search of Steph. We'd barely spoken since.

"I sort of feel bad for Kallum," I said. "He's moved on with his life. He's a small-business owner. I can hardly imagine he wanted this out there."

Luca scoffed. "There is no world in which a man who can fuck that good doesn't want his sex tape publicly broadcasted." He tugged on the underskirt, and I nearly fell over.

"Are you sure this isn't some kind of Hopeflix trust-fall exercise?" I asked.

"No, but this dress is absolutely chef's-kiss perfect on you and even better than my sketches. I attempted a wedding dress before I dropped out of fashion school, but I didn't have a movie costume department budget at my disposal. Even a dinky Christmas movie budget is better than a fashion student budget."

"I never took you for a wedding dress designer," I told him as I forced myself not to cheat and squint.

"Wedding dresses are just the first layer of lingerie." A metallic sound sliced through the air as the teeth of the zipper connected.

"Huh. That is a deeply sexy way to think of it."

"As are you, my dear." He let out a squeal that was somehow both delighted and exasperated. "It's perfect. God, I am so good at my job. You are a goddamn work of art. Open your eyes. Drink it up!"

I opened my eyes and my hands slowly drifted up to cover my O-shaped lips. "You made this, Luca?"

He studied his work in the reflection of the three-way mirror. "Well, sort of. I designed it. The seamstress constructed it, and I put on the finishing touches."

I glanced over my shoulder at him, a touch of admonishment in my tone. "We have a seamstress and you made Nolan fix his own dressing gown?"

He shrugged noncommittally. "What doesn't kill him, et cetera, et cetera."

I turned back to the mirror to fully appreciate Luca's work. The neckline was a low swoop with delicate straps that cut over my shoulders and down my back into a ballet-style back that curved dangerously low. Floral lace crept up the bodice, gathering tightly at my waistline and then spreading down into the skirt, which flowed out into soft, full layers of delicate tulle.

When Luca told me I wouldn't need a bra or a corset and that he'd built all the correct undergarments into the dress, I was hesitant. I loved and trusted Luca, of course, but fat girls were specific about our clothing, especially our undergarments. We knew what worked. We knew what was available to us. And I didn't mind showing a little bit of skin or letting a pretty bra strap stick out, but I also didn't know if I'd ever worn something as fine and delicate as a dress like this without any hint of bands or lines. And while wardrobe actually was always a bit of a trust fall for me, something about the idea of stepping into a wedding gown for the opening scene of *Duke the Halls*, when Felicity left her modern-day fiancé at the altar, made me feel even more vulnerable in a way I had no interest in parsing apart.

"Well, holy fucking shit," Sunny said as she froze in the doorway. Teddy stumbled to a halt behind her, holding a turkey leg in his fist. "I'm not going to say you look like a virgin, because I don't believe in virginity, but you look like a virgin. Hi, how are you? May I sex your body, please?"

I glanced down at myself once more, my chest and cheeks flushed pink. "Are you sure this is okay on me?"

"How dare you?" Luca demanded, sounding out each syllable. "How dare you question my creative intuition and also my ability to make you look so incredibly hot in a wholesome Christmas movie?"

Teddy cleared his throat and took a bite of his turkey leg. "You look great, Bee."

Sunny held her phone up and snapped a photo. "For your moms . . . and my spank bank."

"Forward that to me," Luca requested.

I rolled my eyes, even though it felt a little—okay, a lot— nice to be drooled and fawned over.

Teddy turned to me. "Bee, your moms are hounding me about scheduling a Christmas call with you and finding out what your wrap time on Christmas Eve is. Can you please, for the love of cheesy tots and Natty Light, call them back? Every morning, the first thing I feel is the sting of regret that I ever gave them my phone number that time they visited the set of *Camp Stepbrother*."

"Every time I try to call, they're already asleep," I whined.

Teddy held his hands up, turkey leg included. "Not my problem. Sunny, Luca, we've got some logistics to work through."

"Hey," I said, "have you heard anything about the last page of the script yet? I was supposed to get the updated version with my call sheet yesterday."

Teddy shook his head. "Gretchen's the Pearl Wrangler."

Luca held a hand out for me as I stepped down from the platform, and then he picked up the train of my dress before leading me behind the partition so I could change in private—even though everyone in this room had seen my boobs so often that they were about as exciting as an Applebee's menu.

Luca unzipped me and helped me step out of the dress, but before he could leave, I turned with my arms crossed over my tits, and said, "I never really dreamed of having a wedding dress, but now if I ever do have those dreams, this is the one I'll be wearing. It's perfect." It was true. We'd already filmed the scene in which I wore a tattered tulle skirt and overcoat—the scene where the duke found me stumbling through a snowstorm in what was left of the wedding dress—but the actual dress was better than anything I could have imagined.

He sighed with satisfaction. "It really is." Which was basically *thank you* in Luca's language. "You okay in here? I think we're going to drink our way through this last week of filming at the Dirty Snowball."

I nodded and he left to hang up the dress as I began to dig through my pile of clothing to find my chiming phone.

Mom: Call your mothers, dear.

Missed Call from Jack Hart

Jack: You might want to call me back if you don't want this whole vanilla movie thing to blow up in your face.

Jack was still pissed at me for canceling on him. I'd planned on making it up to him as soon as I got back to L.A., but this text sounded more like a threat than anything else. I'd call him back later, but shooting with him was out of the question even if I did feel bad about how things were shaking out for him post-divorce.

Nolan: Asking for a friend. Are you free around . . . now?

I couldn't hold back my grin as I pulled the straps of my bra up.

Me: What does your friend have in mind?

Three little dots appeared in his text bubble, then disappeared, and then appeared again.

Nolan: My friend says that you have to come and find out for yourself.

And then a moment later, a picture of the small ice-skating rink beside the church loaded, and I put on my sweaterdress, tights, boots, and jacket as quickly as I could. I took one last look at the wedding gown, hanging from a hook high up on the wall so that the train did not touch the ground, and then left the toy shop. I walked against the wind to the rink, going past the Mistletoe Theater, the one-dollar, twenty-four-hour, Christmas-themed movie theater where I had planned on spending my downtime before my downtime turned into Nolan time.

I saw him before he saw me. His cheeks were red as he puffed out white air, like a little boy pretending to smoke a pipe in the cold. I stopped walking, letting myself blend into the early Thursday evening crowd. Over the last couple weeks, the town had become more bustling as visitors arrived to overdose on Christmas endorphins. But I wanted to watch him for a moment longer. Just to observe him as him. A fleeting moment where Nolan wasn't trying to be anyone or anything for someone else. From where I stood, he didn't have any worries or concerns beyond enjoying the burn of the crisp Vermont air in his lungs.

And then he turned, and his face lit up with a slow grin as he saw me, like I'd stepped right into his trap.

We'd decided to cool it until after filming wrapped, but that didn't stop me from hoping he had a dirty little surprise in store for me. I circled around the skating rink to where he sat on a small viewing platform with two steaming cups of what I assumed was hot chocolate beside him.

"I guess they didn't have any figgy pudding syrup?" I asked as I sat down and nearly kissed him hello like we were an honest-to-goodness couple before I suddenly remembered that we were neither in the privacy of our own rooms nor were we pretending to be the duke and Felicity. Here we were just two people in a very public place. Two people who definitely did not fuck each other.

He growled. "An abomination to hot beverages everywhere."

"So where's your friend?" I asked.

"He had to go. Trouble back home. Something about putting his sleigh in the shop and rerouting some deliveries."

"Well, when the home front calls," I said very seriously. "So. Nolan Kowalczk . . ."

"Yes, Bee Hobbes?"

"Would this be considered . . . a date?"

"I guess we have done it all kind of backward, haven't we?"

I let myself scoot an inch closer to him so that I could feel a little warmth from his body. "I like it that way, I think."

"Do you?" he asked as he slid a hand under my ass.

A thrill rippled through my chest. "We are in public. Just as a reminder."

"My hand was cold," he said innocently.

I shimmied my hips a little. "That should help."

"So what do people talk about on dates?" he asked. "I never really did the dating thing. It was more like, hey, let's hire a petting zoo to come to my suite on the thirtieth floor, do a little ecstasy, and have a minirave."

"Tale as old as time," I said.

He shook his head at the memory of his party boy days as he picked up his hot cocoa. "I'm curious, though. How did Bee Hobbes become Bianca von Honey?"

"Ah, yes, my villain origin story," I said with a laugh.

"I can tell you from experience that Bianca von Honey truly brings joy to the world. You are no villain."

I want to kiss him. I want to kiss him. I want to kiss him. "Well, it started with me sending a nude to the first boy in high school who gave me the time of day. When I asked if we could go to prom together, he said no, because people would think we didn't make sense together. He wasn't even, like, a jock or something. Just some show choir loser."

He groaned with disgust.

"And then after graduation, when I told him it was over and that I was done trading nudes and making out in secret, he threatened to post a topless photo of me on some revenge-porn website, so I posted the photo before he could."

"Wow." His whole body tensed as he slammed his cup of cocoa on the bench beside him. "That little fucking twatface."

I appreciated his outrage on my behalf. "The story went viral, and my photo was taken down because of Instagram's community guidelines, but I liked the attention. It made me feel powerful. I went to college for a semester but started my ClosedDoors account while I was there, and then I dropped out without telling my moms and moved to California. It was pretty much zero to sixty in terms of people looking at me as a sex symbol. I went from cutesy fat girl to a fantasy in a matter of months. I met Teddy and that was pretty much it. He was the only porn producer out there who didn't require an exclusive contract or expect me to split some of my ClosedDoors profits."

"Teddy's a little . . . odd, but I'm glad you found him. A lot of people in the entertainment industry are vultures. I should be shocked that anyone would expect a cut of your Closed-Doors paychecks, but I'm not. I think I told you that our contract with our manager was laughably bad? He basically let us sign our identities away to the label."

"You did tell me. God, that's so awful," I said quietly, feeling a little bad for feeding the label and manager monsters with my INK obsession.

"Yeah, when things started falling apart, our manager left town and took whatever money he still owed us with him. Isaac was fine, he was always going to be fine. And Kallum had saved enough money to start Slice, Slice, Baby. But I'd been hemorrhaging cash faster than a gushing artery on *Grey's Anatomy*."

"Which is why you need this movie to pan out."

He nodded.

"I have to know," I said. "McSteamy or McDreamy?"

He grinned and bit down on his lower lip. "Both."

And that thought, of him with two impossibly hot, salt-and-peppery ER doctors in a sexy Nolan sandwich, gave me a thrilling rush straight to the groin. "I have to ask you a very serious question."

He turned to me with a nod, his rigid shoulders bracing for the worst.

"As a hard-core INK fan, I could die happy at this very moment if you would finally answer the question that has burned in my brain since ninth grade. Did you or did you not hook up with either Kallum or Isaac?"

He threw his head back in a laugh. "I'm afraid the answer might disappoint you."

My shoulders drooped, and my lower lip pouted.

He leaned over, his shoulder knocking against mine. "We did fool around once or twice."

A shrieking giggle so loud that some of the skaters turned to look at us tore from my chest. "I think my brain is exploding. I feel like I'm in heaven and asking God or whoever what happened to the dinosaurs."

He gave our onlookers a dashing but firm smile that said *Nothing to see here.* "Well, at the risk of you combusting, I'll admit that Isaac and I had a very enjoyable heavy petting sesh on the road one time, but the rumors about wild threesomes on the tour bus are sadly untrue. That's mostly Kallum's fault. He's basically a one on the Kinsey scale. God bless his mostly straight soul."

I threw my body back against the bench, my chest heaving like I'd just completed the most astounding orgasm. "I don't know what to do with this information, and my legs feel like Jell-O."

He laughed as his gaze dragged up my neck and to my lips, his Adam's apple bobbing as he swallowed.

"You were one of my bi icons," I admitted. "I loved that it was never a question for you. Though, I gotta be honest, it didn't really prepare me for how much porn would be interested in only the straight-male fantasy version of my sexuality. So much of it has felt like a man using two women as his blow-up dolls."

He sighed heavily. "It doesn't make any sense to me. Porn is a business where women should hold all the power."

I booped him on the nose. "Correct. Teddy is good, though. He knows that for everyone who wants the fantasy of porn, there's someone out there who wants the reality of intimacy.

The stuff he produces really runs the gamut, but even with him being better than most, you sometimes still get a director who treats you like a poseable Barbie or someone who won't work with a plus-size performer."

His nostrils flared. "That's fucking nonsense. Is it bad that I want to go all macho asshole right now and tell you that I'll beat the shit out of all them?"

"It's kinda hot," I confessed. "But only in theory. Anyway, it was just so amazing to see someone like you—in the spotlight—owning your bisexuality."

"I've had it easier than a lot of people in the business. Unlike, say, Isaac—who was the heartthrob and was supposed to be every girl's potential fairy tale—being bi fit my INK narrative. I was the party boy. The epitome of the slutty bisexual. And sure, I was bi and I was slutty, but I was more than that too, even if I didn't always believe it myself at the time. But so goes the tale of the bisexual disaster."

Even though we sat there on display for the whole ice-skating rink to see, I touched my hand to his thigh and said, "If two bisexual disasters find each other, does that negate the whole disaster part? Like how two negatives equal a positive?"

"It's so sexy when you talk math to me," he rasped.

"I think I might have to start making a list of all the things I want to do to you after this movie is done," I told him.

"Well, to tide you over, you might as well watch Kallum's sex tape. The man is an artist."

"Oh, I've heard about it," I said, and then remembering the anxious mess Nolan was this morning, I added, "Are you doing okay?"

He sighed. "Yeah, Steph is trying to put out little media fires everywhere. Suddenly every magazine, website, and celebrity gossip show wants to relive the downfall of INK. Kallum is flipping out. His mom, whose biggest dream is for her son to meet a nice Jewish girl, is convinced the only path forward is to move and abandon the family name."

"Poor Kallum," I said.

He nodded. "He'll charm his way out of this. I just wish it didn't coincide with me trying to rebrand myself as this squeaky-clean reformed bad boy."

"Yeah," I said softly. "There is that." I did feel bad for Kallum. And Nolan too. But my whole life was one giant sex tape. If Nolan's reputation was in danger over his best friend's sex tape then what did that mean for us? Nolan said he wanted to be together after all of this was done, but what did that actually mean? What did that reality even look like for us? If his career couldn't withstand an ex–band member with a sex tape, there was no way it could handle a porn star girlfriend.

"Welp," he said as he stood, "my hot chocolate is no longer hot, so I think that means it's time."

"Time for what?"

"Ice skating, baby."

"I don't know how," I said as he pulled me to my feet. "How do you even know how to ride horses and ice skate? Are you secretly rich? That's too many advanced-skill hobbies for one person to have."

"The music video for 'All BeClaus of You,'" he said simply as we walked over to the skate-rental hut. "Plus, you know, I did pick up a few tips at the Duluth Olympics."

As we requested skates in our sizes, I tried to breathe through my nose, thinking of every possible outcome, including me falling and accidentally slicing off one of our limbs.

We settled onto a bench by the shoe cubbies. Nolan knelt in front of me, loosened the laces on my boots, and removed them before helping me pull a skate on. It all felt intensely intimate.

"What if someone sees us?" I asked.

"You mean what if someone sees Nolan Shaw helping his costar with her ice skates because she's never skated before?"

"Well, I guess when you put it like that, it doesn't look as salacious as it feels. And I *have* ice skated before, by the way. I just don't actually know how to."

He ran a hand up the back of my calf, making my breath hitch, as my foot slid into my other skate. "Salacious, you say?"

The exhibitionism kink switch in my head officially flipped on. But my horny ice-skating moment was interrupted as a man in a puffy pink snow jacket and matching pants sauntered behind Nolan with his arms crossed. With his icy-blond hair and reflective ski goggles artfully placed like a headband, he definitely stood out in the cozy Christmas village. "Well, well, well."

And it took only those three words—those three signature words that opened every video and article he'd ever published—for me to recognize him. Dominic Diamond.

"Oh my God," I stuttered.

Nolan looked up at me, and I could see the dread furrowed into his brow as he stood and turned. "Dominic," he said through gritted teeth.

Dominic's smile dazzled, like he'd been waiting for this

moment his whole life. "Nolan Shaw, I never expected to see you ice skating on a Thursday night. Well, fully clothed and sober at least. How . . . innocent."

Nolan's jaw twitched, and I could see his brain cycling through every possible version of what he could say in response—most of which would get him in enough trouble to turn him into Steph's old-timey bandstand bunting. He took a deep breath, and his lips curved into the same charming, rehearsed smile I'd come to associate with the duke. "'Tis the season for new beginnings."

CHAPTER TWENTY-ONE

Nolan

I stepped forward, still smiling, but also inserting myself ever so slightly between him and Bee. It was probably a mistake, because there was a snakelike gleam in his eyes now, as if he'd just smelled a juicy young vole nearby.

"And who might this lovely lady be?" Dominic asked, his gaze running over Bee in a way that pissed me off. Smiling through the anger currently tightening every muscle in my body, I stepped even further between Dominic and Bee, blocking his view.

"This is Bee Hobbes, my costar," I said.

"Hi," said Bee, peeking her head around my hip. "We were just about to go skating, as you can see, so . . ."

It was clearly an invitation for Dominic to screw off, but

he only leaned against the rink wall with a smirk. He had his phone in his hand, and I could see the lit screen between his fingers. It was on, and probably recording. That fucker.

"Lucky girl," Dominic said lightly. "I never would have guessed that Nolan would do the skating before he did the skater. Or *skaters*."

"That's enough, Dominic," I said, as pleasantly as I could while my entire body vibrated with the need to . . . to . . . punch. Punch something. Many punches. "Bee is new to the business, so let's have some respect, shall we?"

"Interesting. Would you say that respecting young women is something that's important to you? Given what happened in Duluth?"

Dominic was trying to get a rise out of me, I knew he was.

The problem was that it was working.

I could viscerally recall the moment I'd opened the door of Emily Albright's Olympic Village room with her cradled in my arms. I could remember the fresh laundry smell of the blanket I'd wrapped her in, and underneath it, the sharp scents of mint toothpaste and food-poisoning-induced sick. The two speed skaters had been naked behind me, panicked and speaking in rapid-fire Dutch, which had sounded enough like English to be incredibly distracting—as if all the naked-ness wasn't distracting on its own while I was also trying to rescue a puking figure skater.

And then the flash of a phone camera.

The flash that had been the beginning of the end of Nolan Shaw and Emily Albright both.

How Dominic Diamond had gotten into the village, I never

found out, given that I had to leverage quite a few Nolan Shaw smiles and selfies myself to be let in, and it was still a near thing. I also never learned how he knew to linger outside Emily's door. But linger he did, and as I opened the door to carry her out and down to the clinic, he captured her glassy-eyed and half-naked in my arms, with the two fully naked speed skaters behind us.

He'd posted that picture the moment he could, then recorded the speed skaters wrestling for his phone. He'd managed to capture the inside of Emily's village room—a room that had transparently been the site of an athletic fuckfest, with strewn sheets and condom wrappers everywhere, including on top of the minitrampoline.

With a few taps of his fingers, Dominic ruined the career of a talented athlete whose only crime was horniness (and eating an iffy fish dinner before taking two speed skaters up to her room to work off a little steam).

He hadn't been so worried about respect then.

I took a deep breath and then calmly offered my hand to Bee to help her stand. She wobbled for a moment on her skates, clutching my arm, and Dominic gave us a reptilian smile as he lifted his phone. "What a charming pair you make. Any comment on that? Is Bee your next Emily?"

A chill sluiced down my spine. I had the sudden vision of Dominic digging into Bee's past and finding Bianca von Honey; I had the sudden vision of Bee's past work being smeared all over the press and the internet, of her career being spun as something immoral or tawdry, when it was neither of those things.

Her non-Bianca career would be over. Teddy's Christmas movie attempt would be over.

And *my* career . . . well. The optics would not be Steph's favorite. If Steph would even keep me after the truth came out and my name was irrevocably tied to porn.

"What do you want, Dominic?" I asked, too sharply.

His smile spread wider across his face. "What I've always wanted, Nolan. For the world to know the real you."

"They have Wikipedia for that," I said, and then with a hand on Bee's back—her upper back, pure coworker territory—I nudged her toward the rink entrance so we could escape from Dominic and his phone.

"ARE YOU SURE you're okay?" asked Bee as we walked back to the inn in the chilly dark. From the town square, we could hear the faint strains of music and laughter coming from the Christmas fair that had popped up overnight and would stay for another two days until Christmas Eve.

"I'm fine," I said, a little glumly. I wished I could hold her hand. Or kiss her. Or press her against a wall and shove my hand up her cute little sweaterdress. But I couldn't do any of those things, and I especially couldn't do them *now*, not when the press and Dominic were this eager to juice up the sex tape news with some fresh Nolan Shaw misbehavior. Already the first wave of articles had hit the internet, gleefully dredging up all my past sins and musing about what future scandals I might start.

And I was straining every fiber, cell, and mitochondrion in my body toward the hope that my *Duke the Halls* costar would remain a gossip afterthought. All it would take was one person who loved celebrity gossip *and* progressive porn to recognize Bee.

"I hope Dominic doesn't do something that makes things crappier for Kallum," said Bee as we reached the inn.

"Me too, although Kallum has a way of landing on his feet." We tromped up the salted path to the inn's front door. "And while his mom isn't happy about any of this, the internet is. Apparently Kallum is our Dad Bod Messiah and has come to save us from our thirst. Or something."

"Mm-hmm," Bee said, maybe a little too appreciatively, and I gave her a look as I opened the door.

"No Dad Bod Kallum for you, missy."

Her pout was cute enough to lift my mood as we stepped inside the inn—at least until I saw Steph sitting in the dark bar, her face underlit by her phone like she was about to tell a ghost story. The dusty jar of cherries was open on the table in front of her.

"Nolan," Steph called. "I need you for a minute."

No sense in delaying the inevitable. I turned to Bee as she turned to me, and then we both seemed to realize in the same instant that we couldn't kiss good night, or hug, or do anything else that wasn't strictly coworkerly.

And it hurt. It hurt not kissing her good night.

Fuck.

"Good night," I managed to murmur.

"Night," she murmured back. And then added, "It's just until we wrap, Nolan. Only until then."

I nodded, but as she walked away and I started toward the

bar, my stomach felt hollow. Because even after *Duke the Halls* wrapped, I'd still have to be in Clean, Unobjectionable Nolan mode. No way would Steph let me openly date a porn star, even if that porn star was successfully siloing off her new career.

Bee and I would still have to hide.

Steph reached her fingers into the jar as I sat, pulling out a cherry and holding it like a jeweler inspecting a diamond. Judging by the whiskey and vermouth bottles next to her, she'd been here for a while, although she was still wearing the jacket of her pantsuit, as if she was going to take an important bar meeting at any moment.

"More cherries?" I asked.

"It's a deconstructed Manhattan. Shut up."

I slumped back. "I hope you have good news," I said. "Dominic Diamond is here, and I think he's out for blood. Is there, like, some kind of amazing Steph D'Arezzo plan for this circumstance?"

"Plan? *Plan?!* For the goddamn pizza boy releasing a goddamn sex tape?" She waved the hand holding the cherry around. "There's no plan for that! And now all anyone wants is to remember every scandal INK has ever been associated with. They're dredging up stuff about Brooklyn and Isaac. They're even running clips of the time Kallum dropped a Teen Choice Award surfboard on Winnie Baker's foot. And—okay." She sat forward, suddenly looking very sober and very kind. Which was unusual enough for Steph to send a bolt of alarm through me. "Speaking of dredging up, have you checked your tags tonight?"

"No," I said warily. "I've been ice skating and fending off Dominic Diamond. Why?"

Steph unlocked her phone and then pushed it toward me. Her face was apologetic. "I'm sorry, Nolan. I really am."

The headline on the screen was the sort of pseudosympathetic verbiage made to garner clicks and yet deflect criticism at the same time: "Nolan Shaw's Tragic Secret." And then the subhead: "Troubled former pop star struggling to support ailing mother and young sister."

My face numbing, I scrolled quickly through the article. There was a picture of my house, small but neat as a pin, festooned in the Christmas decorations I'd put up before I left for Vermont. A tire swing hung from the big tree in the front yard, the top humped with snow. Maddie's battered Honda Civic was parked on the street in front of the house.

My mom's asymmetrical hipster wreath hung on the front door.

Invasive was not the right word for this—or maybe not the only right word—because I didn't feel this like it was an army at my gates or a navy sailing into my harbor. I felt this like it was weeds growing inside my chest, like many mouths gnawing on my bones. Eating at my life.

Deeper in the article was a picture of my mom and dad, and then all sorts of details about our family that weren't public. *Recent* details. Like my mom's diagnosis. Like that my mother had just been in the hospital.

Luckily, the actual reason for her hospital stay remained private, but unluckily, it opened the door to all kinds of speculations. And when I opened up a new browser on Steph's phone and typed in *nolan shaw mother*, I saw that the internet had spent the entire night spitballing about why my mom had been in the hospital. Spitballing that was three percent totally absurd, and then ninety-seven percent really shitty about bipolar disorder and mental health in general.

I felt sharp stabs and dizzy tingles, like I was being pricked all over with needles, and my voice was shaking when I asked Steph, "How?"

Because *how* was the only question I needed to ask. Certainly not *why*—I knew why. Because I wasn't a person to the internet, and my mom wasn't either. We were bags of blood for the gossip vampires, and we were content fodder for everyone else. Disposable, moldable. Easily flattened into a joke or hammered into a soapbox. Or worse.

"And I didn't tell anyone on set, like you said not to," I added, not mentioning that I had told Bee. I trusted Bee completely, so I knew this had to be something else.

And it was.

After fortifying herself with a cherry, Steph reached over and tapped something open on her phone, pulling up a social media account I hadn't seen before. It belonged to Maddie, but it had a cutesy username.

"Your sister has been posting on this account," Steph said. "Normal teenage stuff. Very diary-like, very detailed. About everything."

"Shit," I mumbled. "I didn't even think . . ." When I'd first been cast as the duke, I'd asked Maddie to scrub her socials of anything with any identifying details, where she lived, what school she went to, things like that. But it looked like she'd made this account, thinking that a different username would make it private enough, and then went on posting about whatever she wanted. Including posts about our mom that ranged from loving to teenage-angst-infused.

"We'll have her make it private," Steph said. "But in the meantime, there's a lot on there that you hadn't planned on making public."

My hands curled into fists on the table. I was so fucking *angry* that people had found this and thought it was okay to use for articles and posts and tweets, and I still felt like I was being stabbed all over with hot, burning needles. It was one thing to bring up all the shit I'd done. I deserved it. But my mom and sister were off-fucking-limits.

"Look," Steph said, leaning forward. "I know I said we had to keep this locked down, but the situation has changed since then. Which means we need to reframe the narrative, and quickly. *We* need to be the ones to sell the version of the story that's going to stick—not Dominic, not random Twitter citizens. Us. And if you could step out and talk about your mom and your sister and why—"

"I don't want to use my family as a prop," I said tightly. "I'm not interested in that."

"Not a prop, Nolan," Steph said. "A reason."

"But a prop is what they'll get reduced to." I jerked my head toward the phone. "Mom is already being turned into a stereotype as we speak."

"Then make sure that your version of the story can't be reduced. Make sure you give it all the nuance, all the context you need."

I snorted. "Yeah, like Dominic will write a nuanced, contextual post about this."

"Maybe not. But if you did a filmed interview, then you'd have more control. It would be your words, directly, exactly as you want them to be."

I thought for a moment, trying to shake off the haze of anger that clouded my thoughts. I wanted to protect Mom's and Maddie's privacy more than I wanted to protect my own pride, but it still stung to think of giving that asshole anything to work with. "He won't do it, Steph. He doesn't want a sob story or a comeback narrative. He doesn't want my reasons or my repentance."

"Then give him what he wants," she said matter-of-factly.

"And what is that?"

Another apologetic smile. Another cherry. "Duluth."

I WAS SO tired the next morning that I had those weird tired shakes, like my body couldn't decide if it was jittery or ready to collapse onto a snowbank. I'd spent the night on the phone with Mom and Maddie, making sure they were okay, and seeing what they were comfortable with me sharing in an interview, and then I'd gotten up at dawn this morning to talk with Emily Albright, who was now a coach in Colorado Springs and still kept the godforsaken hours of a competitive athlete.

We hadn't spoken since that night in Duluth, when I'd left her in the care of the Olympic Village doctors, which was funny because I felt like our fates had been so strangely intertwined. But the truth was that we'd barely known each other before that night and then the fallout from the Olympics had been so catastrophic that I hadn't really had the bandwidth to talk to my fellow scandal survivor. I guessed that she'd felt much the same, because she'd never reached out either.

But despite all that, our conversation was warm and friendly, and Emily was more than willing to talk through what she was ready to make public.

"I don't think I ever thanked you," she said toward the end of the call. "For being there that night. For coming when I called. Bram and Sem were so scared of getting in trouble, and too panicked to be of any help, and you were the only person I could think of that wasn't my coach. And then you didn't even flinch when you found me naked and puking."

"It was nothing," I assured her as I pulled on my duke boots. Steph wanted the optics of me looking like a Committed Actor during the interview, so I'd be in full ducal garb while I attempted to wrestle the human eel that was Dominic Diamond.

"It wasn't nothing," Emily said. There was a hollow sort of echo, like she'd just walked into an empty rink. "It was the end of your career. And I never said anything to contradict all the stories they made up about us."

I gave a rueful laugh. "My career was already ending. Any good buzz I'd had around my solo album was swallowed up by all the trouble I was getting into. This was just the nail in the coffin I'd built for myself. Seriously, Emily, there's a reason everyone believed that I'd corrupted you into a night of minitrampoline depravity. It was an ironic sort of justice that the one time I'd actually been innocent of any debauchery was the time when it all exploded in my face."

"Do you ever regret it?" she asked after a minute. "The trouble? The debauchery?"

I thought for a minute. I regretted not playing the game well enough to secure my family's future, and I regretted squandering opportunities that I'd kill for (or wear fake side-burns for) now. I definitely regretted all the times I'd been burdensome or disrespectful or selfish—or all three.

But the actual misbehavior? The sex, the adventures, the batshit hijinks? Honestly, I would've probably found all those as Nolan Kowalczk anyway. Nolan *Shaw* just had more oppor-tunities and a tour bus with lots of sex-friendly flat surfaces.

"No," I finally said. "I don't."

"You know what?" Emily said. "Me neither."

I stood and pulled on the duke's jacket and then found my peacoat to tug over it all. "Are you sure you're okay with all of this?"

"I am," she said. "We should have made a real statement a long time ago, but I was too embarrassed at first, and then when I was done being embarrassed, I was so scared of feeling that kind of humiliation again that I never even let myself talk about it. And that's stupid, because I did nothing wrong. Well, except for ordering tuna tartare in Michigan."

I couldn't argue with her there.

After the phone call was finished and I was dressed, Sunny did my makeup and Denise did my hair while Steph sat next to me and coached me on all my answers. We had long, compli-cated flowcharts about all things Duluth, Emily, and my fam-ily, and I had all my sound bites memorized. Steph would be standing just out of view to coach me through any curveballs.

"Hey, duke," Sunny called as I was walking out the door with Steph. "Tell your former bandmate that his sex tape was really, really good. And that's an informed opinion, because I basically have a postdoctoral fellowship in sex tapes."

"Sure thing," I said with a salute, and then Steph and I walked out to the town square.

Steph had framed the entire scene perfectly for the Committed Actor tableau. Dominic and I would sit under a production tent near the town square, with the Christmas fair in full swing behind us, and enough production equipment staged nearby to make it very clear that I was taking precious time away from the shoot to talk. With me in my costume and the sparkly flurries drifting down from the sky, it was equal doses of Christmas and earnest, humble celebrity. It was good.

Now all I had to do was manage Dominic.

When I sat—grateful for the warmth of the small outdoor heater just out of frame—Dominic gave me a delighted look. "I am so glad you agreed to this," he said, his voice overly friendly. "I think this will give so many of your disappointed fans some closure at long last."

Ugh, what a gaping dickhole.

Steph gave me a quelling look, though, and so I said, "Thanks so much for the chance to talk," and crossed my legs, like there was nothing I wanted in the world more than to talk with the guy who'd ruined my career.

His delight didn't fade. He was planning to provoke me into giving up *something* scandalous, and he had an entire interview to do it in, but little did he know that Steph had drilled me harder than a championship spelling bee coach to get my answers right. I was ready.

We kicked off with his signature *Well, well, well*, and then he went right in. "Nolan Shaw, you're probably most famous for the events of the Duluth Olympics. When you dragged

Emily Albright into one of your signature bacchanals, you started a chain of events that led to her missing her free skate and her shot at the gold. She never skated competitively again. Did you know the cost she would have to pay for spending time with you that night?"

It was a shitty question, but Steph and I had prepared for it.

"It's interesting you ask that," I said pleasantly, "because I've often wondered if you knew the cost she'd pay when you posted your pictures from that night."

The response didn't ruffle him, because he didn't care that people thought he was pond scum, but I didn't give him a chance to find a new angle on his leading question. "But truthfully, I had a lot of other things on my mind that night," I continued. "Because contrary to the rumors that sprung up after, Emily and I hadn't known each other very well. I won't deny that I'd wanted to know her better when we met the night of the opening ceremony; it's why I gave her my phone number and hoped she would use it. And she did—but not for the reason I'd planned."

I leaned forward a little, like I was preparing to divulge something secret and heavy. It wasn't really going to be either, but I did need to be careful here, because there were a few parts of the truth that Emily and I had agreed not to speak aloud. And I supposed it did feel a little heavy to tell the truth after so many years of staying silent and hoping it would all go away.

"What most people don't know is that the night the pictures were taken, Emily was sick. Really sick. She was later diagnosed with food poisoning, but at the time, all we knew was that she was too sick to move. She called me because she needed help, but she didn't want to call her coach and none of her teammates picked up the phone." I didn't mention that she hadn't wanted to call her coach because her room hadn't exactly been a coach-friendly scene, what with the naked Europeans and all. Before the food poisoning had hit, she'd been in the middle of getting her epic Olympic Village sex on. (Sex that I hadn't been a part of, sadly enough.) "She was so sick that I had to carry her down to the clinic. Which was, of course, seen in the famous picture you posted that night."

From behind Dominic, I could see Steph nodding her head—I'd gotten through that part without fucking up, at least. Teddy Fletcher had come to stand next to her while I'd been talking and was eating sugared almonds from a paper cone. Steph looked over at him with genuine confusion on her face, like she had no idea how to categorize him in her brain.

"But it's not just you two in that picture," Dominic goaded. "You're forgetting about the naked men too. You really want us to believe that you and Emily had nothing to do with the extra people in her room? That you and Emily hadn't been together before that moment?"

"The truth is that it's no one's business what happened that night," I said, giving my biggest, dukeliest smile to balance the frankness of my words. "Emily and I—and the two skaters—were adults at the time. If we had spent the night together, if we had spent the night with anyone else there, it would have been our own business and no one else's. But for the sake of clarity, no, Emily and I were not together that night or any other night. She called me for help when she got sick, and I went."

Dominic opened his mouth to interrupt, but I kept going, not giving him a chance to derail me.

"And even though I firmly believe what happened in her room that night isn't anyone else's business, I want the world to know what did happen, because they have entirely the wrong idea about Emily. She didn't get sick because of drinking or drugs, and she wasn't blowing off the biggest moment of her career. She happened to get very, very sick because of something she ate, she happened to be with two people who weren't able to help, and I happened to be the one who could. And you know what? If it all went down the same way again, I'd pick up the phone and go help, even knowing what the consequences would be. Some things are more important than a reputation."

I could see Dominic run his tongue under his teeth, as if deciding what to say next. Which meant I'd given him a good enough answer that he needed to change tactics.

That was a positive thing, but I still braced. I knew this next one was going to be about Mom, and I needed to get it right. I needed the world to understand what my family meant to me while also making it clear that they were not available for gossip consumption.

But Dominic didn't ask about Mom. He didn't even ask about Maddie. Instead, he mimicked my posture and leaned forward too, a pen in hand. He looked like a congressperson about to scold me for spilling oil on some baby seals somewhere.

"But what about your fresh-faced costar Bee Hobbes?" he

asked. "Even though you've only been on set together for a couple of weeks, it seems like you've got her thoroughly under your spell. I suppose old habits die hard."

There was a distant ringing in my ears, and blood prickled my face as alarm slid through my veins, icy and slippery and awful. I hadn't expected a question about Bee when Duluth was on the table, and since Steph didn't know anything about Bee's other job—or the many, um, *jobs* Bee and I had shared over the last week—she hadn't thought to prep me.

From behind Dominic, I could see that Teddy was frozen right in the middle of eating a sugared almond.

But somehow, despite the panic humming through me, I found that I was answering the question. I was answering with an easy tone and an even easier smile, and hell, maybe I wasn't such a bad actor after all.

"Bee is an incredible actress for a newcomer, and she's a wonderful colleague to have," I said. "But she's nothing more than a colleague. I'm not in a place right now where I can focus on romance or a relationship. Or even a place where I want to. I'm all about Nolan Shaw for the foreseeable future."

Teddy's shoulders slumped in what looked like relief, and he finished putting his sugared almond into his mouth. Steph gave me a thumbs-up.

Relief trickled through my body, blunting the panic somewhat. It was more than my career at stake if Dominic got too interested in Bee. But it did feel weird to deny our . . . our . . . whatever we had so directly.

And then between the shoulders of the crew members who

were standing around watching, right behind Tall Ron, I saw a glimpse of dark, glossy hair as the person it belonged to walked away from the tent. I knew that hair; I'd buried my nose in it, tangled my hands in it.

Bee was walking away after my answer, and I couldn't see her face, or even watch her as she went, because this interview still needed all of my attention.

Was she upset? Or relieved that I hadn't given us away?

I bet she was relieved. We both needed our thing to stay hidden, right? I'd find her later to make sure, but I knew she'd get it. She'd get why we couldn't own each other openly, now or anytime immediately in the future.

Eyes a little narrowed, Dominic changed tack once more and veered back to the subject of Duluth, which I deflected and reframed according to Steph's plan, and then he turned to the subject of my mother. He knew he couldn't say anything directly insulting and still have *me* look like the shithead, so he did the next worst thing, and made it sound like my mom was some damsel in distress I was rescuing.

"And we were all so concerned when we heard about your mother's suffering. She was in the hospital for her mental illness recently, wasn't she? Do you want to talk a little about how you've managed to take care of her while trying to re-launch your career?"

I folded my hands in my lap, remembering Steph's coaching about how to look thoughtful and assured. Even though I still wanted to do punch-related violence to this man.

"My mother isn't a victim," I said, grateful to hear that my voice came out gracious and not irritated. Steph and I agreed that I should be passionate about my family—because I was—but that passion couldn't in any way be interpreted as confrontational or defensive. "So I'm not a fan of the word *suffer* or the idea that I take care of her because she can't take care of herself. I'm not going to speak very much about this, because this is her life and her story to tell, but I want everyone to know that my mother is brilliant, fierce, compassionate, and creative, and the thing I'm proudest of in this world is being her son. And if people want to know more about mental illnesses and bipolar disorders in particular, then there's plenty of information written by people who've experienced these disorders firsthand. In the meantime, I'd like to ask for some empathy and respect—and most of all, privacy. I signed up to be a celebrity and to be in the public eye. My family didn't."

And by the time the interview ended, Dominic seemed a little grumpy that he hadn't found any gaps in my interview armor. He didn't shake my hand or even make any small talk before he left the tent. Instead, he got up and looked at me.

"You and I should talk again soon," he said, in a voice that could have been friendly coming from anyone else. "I can't wait to see what other secrets are buried deep behind those blue eyes."

"Mmm," I said noncommittally, wanting to break a camera dolly over his stupid head. But I behaved.

After he left, I turned to go find some coffee before I actually had to work and encountered Gretchen standing right behind me.

"Hey," she said, giving me a small smile. "Can I have a minute?"

"Of course." We stepped out of the tent and into the middle

of Main Street, which had been closed down for the Christmas fair. The smells of sausages and apples and gingerbread filled the air. Flurries danced down, small and glinting, like we were living inside a static-ridden television set, and I could hear Eartha Kitt crooning to Santa about all the things she wanted.

I loved it. I loved the smells and the sounds and the snow, and I suddenly wished I was at home with Mom and Maddie right now, stringing popcorn and cranberries into garlands and complaining about all the dishes left over from cooking the latest batch of cookies. I wished that I could bring Bee home with me too, wished that I could have her cuddled in my lap while the Christmas tree lights winked from the corner of the room. Wished that I could see her snuggled in fuzzy Christmas jammies, not bothering with mistletoe to steal whatever kisses we wanted.

"I want to apologize," Gretchen said.

Huh? "Apologize?"

She touched my arm. "I didn't know until I saw it on the internet. That your mom's had something going on and you've been helping. The phone calls—that's what those were for, right?"

"Yes, but—"

"No *but*s," she said with a small smile. "You are a better version of Nolan Shaw than I gave you credit for, and I'm sorry for that. What's more, I was looking over the schedule, and if we cram an extra scene in today and two extra scenes in tomorrow, we can have you wrapped before Christmas. You could go home, Nolan."

It was like someone had just poured liquid sunshine down

my throat. I could be home for Christmas. I could see Mom and Maddie as soon as tomorrow night. "Really?" I asked excitedly. "You think so?"

"I do. And I think you've earned it."

I lunged at her and picked her up to swing her in a circle. She batted at my shoulders, laughing. "Put me down! I'm not a music video girl!"

"You're the music video girl of my heart, Gretchen Young! Thank you so much." I set her down, beaming at her as she batted my shoulder once more for good measure and went off to find Cammy to change the schedule.

I might float right off the ground. I'd stopped Dominic from doing something Dominic-like, I was heading home for Christmas, and after this movie was over, I'd have Bee back in my arms and bed, where she belonged. It was like Christmas Notch had summoned up a little Christmas magic just for me.

CHAPTER TWENTY-TWO

Bee

"Close your eyes for me," Sunny said patiently.

Sighing, I obeyed and cradled the phone in my lap as it played the video of Nolan's interview.

"It's okay to turn it off," she said. "You already watched most of it live anyway."

With a pout, I looked up at her from where I sat in her makeup chair. Today was my runaway-bride wedding scene. It was the moment when Felicity would leave her present-day fiancé at the altar, and it was also one of the rare scenes I didn't film with Nolan.

If I was being honest, I was a little more nervous without him. We'd just stumbled into a routine. He always brought me coffee from craft services and moved our chairs so that

I was sitting closest to the portable heaters. I brought gum for us to share in between scenes, and he always gave me one of his AirPods so I could listen to whatever playlist or podcast he was tuning in to. And the moments we did share on-screen . . . well, they were beginning to seem more and more real. Leaning against his chest or holding his hand felt like applying aloe to sunburnt skin. It was exhilarating, too, to do the things with him on camera that I dreamed of us doing during daylight hours as if we were a normal couple.

In so many ways, this whole experience was reminiscent of summer camp, and I leaned into the idea that while we were here in Christmas Notch, we could be anyone and do anything. And that meant being Nolan's person and getting to live out all of the acting dreams my younger self was too scared to hope for.

"Close," Sunny commanded.

I hit the button on the side of my phone to turn off Dominic Diamond's grand inquisition and turned it facedown on the makeup counter before leaning back in my chair and closing my eyes.

An incredible actress for a newcomer . . .

All about Nolan Shaw . . .

Nolan's words felt like they'd been branded into my chest. There was no pause or moment to collect himself. He simply answered Dominic's question about me in such a genuine way that I began to believe his answer myself.

In the logical corner of my brain, I knew that Nolan was doing exactly what he needed to do—for both our sakes.

But . . .

"It just sounded too easy," I blurted.

"Huh?" Sunny grunted.

"What was too easy?" Luca's voice asked as he stepped into the trailer we were using as a home base while shooting the church scenes.

I opened the eye Sunny wasn't currently applying shimmery, smoky eyeshadow to. "Nothing," I said just as Sunny said, "Probably Nolan's full-on dismissal of her and their—"

"Sunny!" I said her name like a shush.

"You haven't told him?" she asked, like we didn't both fully know that Luca—despite how much we loved him—treated secrets like trading cards.

"Secrets? You have *secrets*?" Luca said with outrage. "From *me*? Secrets are only sexy when I'm the one who's keeping them."

I looked up to Sunny with my one open eye for a moment, before my shoulders dropped and I nodded for her to just go ahead and spill. Maybe it wasn't smart on my part, but I couldn't imagine Luca outing our . . . our whatever it was.

In her best church-mouse voice, Sunny said, "Bee and Nolan are—" And then in true Sunny fashion, she made a creaking noise to mimic a mid-coitus bed frame.

"Don't be mad at me," I interjected, and closed my open eye before he could say anything.

"Whoa," Luca said as I heard him sitting in the chair beside me. "Whoa. First the truth about Duluth—which I'm still processing, by the way, and have already left a voicemail for my therapist. And now this. I just . . . everything I thought I knew is wrong. Talk about a turn of events."

He paused for a moment. "However, let the record show that I do maintain my healthy suspicion of Nolan Shaw, FYI—as should you, Bee—but I really didn't see the food-poisoning plot twist coming . . ."

Luca was having a real existential crisis about this, and I was just relieved to know he didn't hate me for insert-bed-squeak-noise-ing with Nolan.

"I'm just having, like, a real am-I-the-villain moment here," Luca said.

"Should you tell him or should I?" Sunny asked with a snort.

I smiled, but Sunny must have seen right through my forced expression.

She sighed. "You can't have it both ways, right? Nolan can't talk about how much he loves being around you and also boning you in a live interview without absolutely ruining everything for a lot of people, but I also totally get why you would be in your feelings about this."

"So basically," Luca deadpanned, "don't overthink it, but follow your gut."

"Open your eyes," Sunny said.

I did.

She shrugged. "I mean, yeah, essentially. Luca's not wrong."

I laughed. "That's awful advice."

She frowned. "Well, it's not the ideal situation, Bee. But, I mean, you should still get that nookie."

"Excuse me," Luca said with one finger held up, like he was just going to ask the waiter for *one* more thing. "But did you just say *nookie*?"

"My dad was a Limp Bizkit fan," Sunny said simply. "Don't make fun of my culture."

Luca shook his head. "Wow. Wow, wow, wow."

Cammy opened the door of the makeup trailer and popped her head in. "We need you in wardrobe, Bee." Then she eyed Luca with disdain. "Uh, Wardrobe, we need you in wardrobe."

"I have a name," he called, but the trailer door had already slammed shut.

Sunny applied some natural-looking but false eyelashes and dusted my cheeks with a soft pink blush before the three of us shuffled across the street to the church, where my dress was waiting for me in the tiny robe room behind the altar. Luca had moved my costume over here so that I wouldn't have to walk very far in the gown or get it dirty. I never realized how much pressure was involved in wearing white.

The church was full of extras who would be strategically moved around for different camera angles. I briefly met Brian, the local theater actor in the role of Felicity's present-day fiancé and who played Fred Gailey every year in the Christmas Notch production of *Miracle on 34th Street*. When he began to tell me about his ill-fated attempts at Broadway, Sunny stepped in to powder his nose and let me escape to the robe room with Luca.

As Luca zipped me up, I watched out the window as Nolan was loaded into a van in full costume. "Is he filming today?" I asked out loud before I even realized I was speaking.

"B-roll," Luca said. "I delivered his costume to the inn this morning for the interview and then Gretchen has him squeezing in a few things with the second unit so he can go home in time for Christmas."

"Christmas?" I asked, my voice nearly cracking. "Nolan is going home for Christmas?" I was one part sad I'd been excluded from knowing this information and another part even sadder that I wouldn't be able to go home myself and see my moms, which sounded so comforting right now that I could cry.

And for maybe the first time ever, Luca said nothing. He simply patted my shoulder and said, "Come on. You look amazing—thanks to me. Now, take a deep breath and channel our lord and savior, Julia Roberts, as we film the second greatest runaway-bride scene in cinematic history."

"Third," I said. "*My Best Friend's Wedding*. You can't forget *My Best Friend's Wedding*." The movie my moms got into heated arguments over anytime it came on TV. Mom loved it. Mama Pam thought it was manipulative trash. *Looks like a rom-com. Feels like a rom-com—until oof! It's about as funny as* Titanic. Mama Pam loved Mom, me, racquetball, and her romcoms. In that order.

Gretchen buzzed with energy as we filmed, like she'd been struck with inspiration. Brian, whom my brain had affectionately begun to call Not Nolan, was very dedicated to his job and even sank to his knees for one take as I fled the chapel.

We wrapped just as the sun began to slip past the snowy mountaintops behind the church. All the extras were herded out, and the crew made quick work of clearing out all their equipment.

I slumped into the front pew, wedding gown and all.

"Bee," Luca, a little frazzled, said as he approached. "I've got to go deal with all the extras and their costumes, so I can get you out of costume now or . . . much, much later."

The idea of standing up in this at that exact moment was too much. "Can you just start the zipper for me?" I asked. "I'll hang everything up, and you can come by for it in the morning."

Luca shrugged. "If you're sure."

I slumped back against the pew. "I'm very sure."

He reached over me and pulled the zipper partway down my back before chasing after the crowd of extras surely lined up at the toy shop, waiting for him.

What I didn't say to Luca and could barely admit to myself was that I wasn't ready to take the gown off. I wasn't ready to say goodbye to this moment, especially when all I wanted was to share it with Nolan.

"Hey," Gretchen said as she passed her headset over to Cammy. "You need help with that dress?"

"Nah, the zipper is already halfway down. That's the hard part."

She wavered for a moment, and I realized it was only me and her now. "You okay? Did that feel all right to you today? I know we're moving at a pretty quick clip."

"It was good. It was great, actually. You really seemed to be in it today."

Bouncing a little on her toes, she began to smile. "Some days are like that. It's pretty exhilarating, though. Seeing all these people come together for one common thing, to make something out of nothing."

"The magic of movies," I said, and it really was magic. I'd been so wrapped up in me and Nolan that I'd almost forgotten about what I was actually here doing and how in so many ways I was living my wildest dreams. And not only that, but what would come next? Who would I be after the knowledge that I could work in a mainstream movie, and as the leading lady too? Would I go back to porn and ClosedDoors and maybe even become Nolan's little secret? That didn't sound so bad. I loved my career. I loved the people I worked with. I wasn't ashamed of any of it, but if I could be both Bianca the porn star and Bee the actress, I would in a heartbeat.

But what if that wasn't possible? What if I had to choose? Or worse yet, what if this was my only shot, and the choice to stay in porn or go mainstream wasn't even a choice at all? This could very well be my first and last acting gig. And . . . Nolan . . . well, sure we could make it work for a little while, but the wall between our two worlds would only grow taller and taller.

"You sure you're okay in here?"

I nodded as the last of the daylight shined through the stained-glass windows, creating a kaleidoscope on the hem of my gown. "Just first movie feelings and, weirdly, wedding dress feelings."

She laughed. "Costumes have a way of fucking you up." Her phone began to ring and she quickly silenced it with a swipe.

"Go on," I said. "I'll see you bright and early tomorrow."

"Do you want me to leave the lights on?"

"Nah," I said. The clouds had cleared, letting in plenty of moonlight, and the idea of sitting alone under the dim yellow lights of the church somehow seemed more depressing than sitting alone in the dark. "I won't be that long."

She gave me a good look and a final discerning nod before jogging down the aisle and out the door, hitting the lights as she went.

And then it was me alone, sitting a few feet from the altar in this wedding gown that somehow felt like it was a part of me even though I'd never once hoped or wished for a moment when

I might someday walk down an aisle myself and in such a traditional dress. And not in a church. Especially in a church. A porn star with two moms wasn't often the kind of girl who found herself getting married in a church or even outside of one at all.

Behind me the heavy door to the church swung open, and for a moment there was only a silhouette.

"Bee?" the silhouette asked.

I stood and stepped out into the aisle. "Nolan?"

He stepped into the church in the same Duke of Frostmere costume he'd done his interview in.

His whole body froze, his lips parting and his gaze dripping over me.

I smoothed my hands over the bodice of the dress, feeling both uncertain and also radiating excitement, because I hadn't realized how much I'd wanted this. For him to see me in this dress. In this church.

The door swung shut behind him, leaving us in the silvery almost darkness of the sanctuary. Moonlight filtered in through the windows, leaving slanted rectangles on the floor, glimmering islands in the dark.

I heard him take a breath, and not the kind of breath that came before speaking, and not the kind of breath that came in a moment of reverence. It was a rough breath, a deep breath.

The breath of someone fighting for control.

I had heard that sound a thousand times in my job. It was part of my profession to make people lose control, after all. But any other time someone had made that noise in my presence, I'd been stripped down and—I don't know—*available*, with my mouth or hands or body. Never wearing a dress that symbolized promises and forever and cuddling and making dinner together and shopping for fitted sheets and towels and things.

This feeling was something new, something that sank deeper into my body than physical lust, deeper than knowing I was craved. This was the type of want I'd never known anyone could have for me.

Nolan did also crave me, that much was clear. He stalked toward me now, his strides purposeful and hungry, the knee-high boots of his costume gleaming and his eyes glittering in the dark. But desire wasn't the only thing scrawled across that gorgeous face, and his stare wasn't burning along my breasts or my mouth. No, our eyes were locked instead, and the only time his gaze left mine was to drop to the train of my gown where it rested in a filmy swirl around my feet.

When he reached me, I started to speak, even though I didn't know what I wanted to say.

Do you like my dress, maybe. Or maybe *Were you going to leave Christmas Notch without telling me?* Or maybe my deepest fear, the loose end that could unravel me if tugged just right.

Will I only ever be a fantasy to you?

But Nolan didn't let me speak, he didn't let me do anything. He dug his hands in my hair and slashed his mouth over mine in a scorching kiss.

"Nolan," I murmured, finding the lapels of his costume jacket and pulling him close. He was already inside my mouth, licking and tasting me, and then his hand dropped to my hip and fisted in the silky fabric there, yanking our pelvises flush together.

Every bit of me burned at the feel of him. At the artfully

tousled hair and his hot, firm mouth. At the possessive grasp of his hands and the evidence of his need pressed against my stomach.

"You can tell me anything right now," he said roughly. "But don't tell me to stop."

Stop? When all I wanted was for him to keep going? For this moment to fractal out like a snowflake and never, ever end?

"Don't stop," I breathed against his lips, and then again. "Please don't stop."

He leaned down, his lips burning over my throat and collarbone as he did, and scooped my train over his arm before he straightened and slowly walked me backward. Backward until I hit the thigh-high rail separating the altar area from the rest of the church, and I was trapped.

Nolan draped the train over the rail, and before I could anticipate what he might do next, he dropped to his knees like a sinner and shoved my skirts up to my waist.

No. Not like a sinner.

Like a *groom*. Like a groom who couldn't wait another goddamn second to have his bride, who couldn't stand one more moment without her taste on his tongue. That's what we looked like right now, with him in his formal duke clothes and me in a wedding dress, situated in front of the altar, right where a couple would stand.

A bride and a groom.

With a ragged noise, Nolan used his thumb to hook my seamless thong to the side and kissed the curls he found underneath. My hands searched for the rail behind me and gripped hard as he kissed me again, seeking out the wet heat of my body and licking a hot stripe up my center.

I let out a begging moan as he impatiently pushed my thighs apart and began eating me properly, his hands fisting in my skirt once more and keeping the fabric rucked to my hips. His hands were trembling in the silk. Shaking, like he was overcome.

Like he was dying and this moment was his heaven.

Pleasure curled up from my core, whorls and eddies of it, spun into being by his hot mouth and his clever tongue. Nolan Shaw was an artist at his canvas, painting sensation with his mouth, sketching lust with his teeth and lips. But even Nolan's wonderful mouth wasn't enough to explain what I felt right now—which was a dangerous cocktail of lust and misery and . . . and *nostalgia*, maybe? Nostalgia for something that hadn't happened yet?

Nostalgia for something that would never happen?

I looked down at the man kneeling in front of me, his hands still clenched in my skirt, his dark head bent toward his work, and everything was silk and tulle and boots and moonlight, and suddenly my chest hurt so much I couldn't breathe. I couldn't breathe even as an orgasm began to build somewhere behind my clit.

"Nolan," I choked, knowing that I didn't want him to stop—that I didn't even think I *could* stop—but also knowing that this was too close to something that was going to hurt me. Too close to goodbye, even as we stood where generations of lovers had pledged till death did they part.

What if this was the closest I ever got to a wedding? Or worse, what if I *did* get married one day but all I would be able to think of then was Nolan Shaw, staring at me in a fake wedding dress like I was the only thing on earth that could save him?

Nolan tilted his face up to mine, his eyes dark and his mouth wet. His hair had fallen over his forehead, just like a careless duke's would, and the moonlight glowed along his cheeks and perfectly cut jaw. He lifted his hand from the bunched skirt at my waist to my chest, where he laid his palm flat over my heart, like he needed to feel the wild beating of it for himself.

For the first time, I saw nothing of the pop star in front of me, and nothing of the fantasy I'd concocted of him in my teenage head. I only saw *him*. Nolan Kowalczk, my fellow bisexual disaster. Nolan, who was trying to be a good son and a good brother, who was trying to clean up after his years-old messes. Nolan, who somehow knew parts of me I had yet to uncover myself.

Nolan, who shouldn't be here, who needed to lay low during the post-Kallum news storm, but who still couldn't stay away.

The truth was that I couldn't stay away either, and maybe that was part of the problem. The porn star and the newly wholesome celebrity were never meant to have a happy ending; they were never meant to stand in a church wearing gorgeous clothes and pledging eternity to each other.

So if this—this moment of make believe—was all we would ever get, then I'd take it. I'd take it with both hands and no remorse, because I couldn't imagine a world where I'd regret the time I'd had with Nolan. It had been every fantasy come to life, even the ones I never knew I had. Even the ones where

I was a bride and he was a groom and he was choosing me in front of the world. Forever.

He knew what I needed, of course. I needed the promises and vows we could never speak aloud, so he wrote them into my body instead. I needed the memories, the moments to hold on to, because after he left, after *Duke the Halls* was over, there would be no guarantee that we'd find our way back to each other, or if we could, that we *should*.

And if this was the last time we were together, then I wanted nothing held back.

He didn't hold back, because of course he didn't. Nolan Shaw unleashed was a beautiful thing, and he treated my body like it was his to plunder and a shrine to worship all at once. And when he slid his fingers inside me, stoking a fire with his touch as well as his mouth, I was done for.

He sucked and licked the climax free of my body as I clung to the altar rail and fought to keep standing. With his free hand, he held my hip firmly, refusing to let me move or escape. He continued to kiss me as my cunt pulsed again and again and again.

I'd barely finished when he stood, his hands dropping to the waistband of his pants and making short, easy work of the buttons. From his pocket came a condom, which he rolled on with his booted feet braced and his hair tumbling over his forehead. His sheathed cock gleamed in the moonlight, but otherwise he was still fully clothed as he said, hoarsely, "On your knees. Now."

His words moved my body to action like I'd been hypnotized. I'd been asked to kneel scores of times—I'd dropped to my knees three or four times a week for the last six years. But never, ever, had it felt like this. Like I'd die if I didn't give him what he needed. Like making him come was as necessary as drawing my next breath.

I went to my knees in front of the altar rail, the dress rippling and rustling all around me, and then he easily flipped me onto all fours, already shoving the gown up around my hips and plunging inside of me before I'd even caught my breath.

"Fuck, you're so wet," he groaned, giving me a deep, urgent thrust that had my toes curling. I rocked back into him, and he hissed. "Yes, that's it. Just like that, beautiful girl. Just like that until I'm done."

He was so raw when he fucked. Like once his lust took over, he was nothing but unvarnished, primal animal until he got what he needed. God, it made me hot.

"Touch yourself," he breathed. "I want you even wetter."

I pushed my hands down between my legs, my cheek pressing into the floor, and obeyed, the first touch of my fingers to my clit telling me that it would take no time at all to get off again, and then he started screwing in short, filthy strokes, chasing his release as his fingers dug into my hips.

I came first, clenching around him, and then he gave a sharp, low grunt and began surging, filling the condom as he held me still against him. My lips were tingling, and static danced at the edges of my vision. I could barely drag in breath after breath as my body was flooded with every hormone known to humankind, and Nolan was right there with me, each breath labored, his thighs tense and straining against mine.

I crumpled forward and panted into the floor like a freshly fucked heathen while Nolan pulled out and rearranged himself. He gathered me into his arms after, holding me against his chest as he sat with his back braced against the rail, and we caught our breath together in a pile of crushed silk and tulle, the faint strains of the music from the Christmas fair somehow making it inside the old building.

I didn't know how to feel about what we'd just shared, and thinking about being cuddled here—simultaneously satisfied and all twisted up inside—while I was dressed as Felicity and Nolan was in full duke regalia made the situation that much stranger. Because even though I was ninety percent sure Pearl had written this script in a crystal-gridded, sage-scented fever dream, there was a clear prism of truth at the heart of Felicity and the duke's story. And it was that even if fate could triumph over separate timelines and separate lives, no destiny, no love, ever came for free. Love—even love decreed by fate— always demanded sacrifice and risk.

But whose risk? Whose sacrifice? And was that fair to ask of anyone? Even people who didn't have their future dreams and livelihoods on the line, like Nolan and I did?

I didn't know if the shiver that followed that thought was from being uncertain or cold.

I decided to pretend it was the cold, even though Nolan's arms were so very warm around me. "We should go to our rooms separately," I murmured. "To avoid suspicion."

He didn't answer for a long moment. "Yeah," he said, his voice reluctant. "That would be the smart thing to do."

"We'll see each other tomorrow. We'll have a real goodbye."

"I want more than tomorrow, Bee," he said softly. "More than a goodbye. You know that."

Yes, yes, I did know that. He'd told me as much before. But then why didn't it *feel* real? Why did a future still seem as fleeting as the moonlight moving across the church floor on a cold December night?

Maybe . . . maybe it was because that sometimes wanting wasn't enough.

CHAPTER TWENTY-THREE

Nolan

I woke to thick flurries falling from the sky, and after a long
stretch and a moment spent looking at the other side of my
bed, wondering what it would be like waking up next to Bee
every morning, I padded over to my window and looked outside. It was early enough that the streetlamps were still lit, and
I watched as snowflakes fluttered down to the already snowy
lane. Just at the edge of my vision, Caroler's Creek glinted as it
wound through ice-crusted banks, and in the other direction,
I could see the glow of the giant Christmas tree in the town
square.

It was Christmas Eve, and tonight I was going home.

Bouncing a little as I got ready, I brushed my teeth and
dressed quickly, knowing there was no time for an onanistic

reliving of last night's memories if I wanted time to pack and still get down to hair and makeup on time.

God, I wanted to relive them, though. Remembering how that wedding dress felt bunched in my hands, the taste of her in that dark church . . .

I'd never considered myself the kind of person who thought much about marriage, who thought about weddings or vows or sticking with one person for the rest of my life. It wasn't that I *didn't* want those things, necessarily, only that they felt like opening a Roth IRA or downloading a meditation app: all good ideas, but good ideas for a future Nolan who had his shit together.

But seeing Bee in that dress . . . suddenly that future Nolan felt like he could be *right now Nolan*. My heart had leapt into my chest and heat had seared my body everywhere—my blood, my groin, the backs of my eyelids—and if there were such a thing as a Christmas wish, then I knew in that moment exactly what my wish would be.

Except *right now Nolan* still had a career to launch and a sanitized public image to maintain, and all of that precluded a porn star girlfriend. Or a porn star wife.

It'll work out, I told myself firmly. I was fuzzy on the details, and I didn't love the idea of asking Bee to sneak around, but I also couldn't lose this chance to claw back what I'd lost, and I would never ask her to quit her work as Bianca von Honey at the same time. If she loved doing it, then that was good enough for me. We'd figure out the rest.

It wasn't until I was ready to leave that I saw the page that had been slipped underneath my door at some point during the night. An updated call sheet. With a scene I'd already shot before.

Puzzled, I tugged on my beanie, did one last visual sweep to make sure all my shit was packed, and then headed down to the toy shop.

"NOLAN, BEE, THERE you are," Gretchen said as she walked into the wardrobe department.

Bee was already made up and dressed, once again wearing that dark red silk she'd worn for the very first scene we shot together. I'd had to be careful about how much I looked at her as Sunny did my makeup, because that corset did things to my body that were very visible in my precostume sweat-pants.

"I have the final page of the script here, and I know I said we'd shoot it on its own and stitch it onto what we already had, but I think it will be stronger if we reshoot and do it all at once. And," she said, looking at me, "because you were such a B-roll hero yesterday, we have the time." Gretchen handed Bee and me each the final page of the script as she talked, her other hand curled around a reusable coffee mug. I placed the page on my lap and started reading while Sunny messed with the fake sideburns Denise had put on me, trying to make them more symmetrical. "We'll be heading to the mansion in thirty minutes, but we have the location only for the morning, so we'll need to be snappy. And let's use the same blocking, if you're both still comfortable with it, and—"

"Gretchen," I said, lifting my eyes from the page. "Is this really the script?"

"Well, I didn't hand you the script for the next *Fast and Furious* movie."

"No, but—" I met Bee's eyes, which were wide. She was currently trying not to laugh. I changed tack. "Have you read it?"

Gretchen gave me a look. "Of course I read it."

I glanced back down to the page, which read:

DUKE

Felicity. With you, I understand the real meaning of Christmas. With you, it all makes sense.

They kiss.

DUKE (CONT'D)

Come, my love. Let's find the others and let them know what we learned about the real meaning of Christmas.

FELICITY

And what's that?

DUKE

(fondly)

That the real meaning of Christmas is just to love, and to be loved in return.

"Gretchen, the last line is from *Moulin Rouge*," I finally said. She shook her head. "No, I don't think so."

Bee finally broke into giggles as Sunny grabbed the script page from Bee's hand. "This is definitely from *Moulin Rouge*," Sunny said.

"'There was a boy,'" I started singing, to prove our point. "'A very strange, enchanted boy.'"

"If we're getting technical," Bee said over my rendition of "Nature Boy," "I think it was from David Bowie's brain first."

"Not to be the *well, actually* guy, but actually it was Nat King Cole's song first," said Luca, wandering in from parts unknown. "And I cannot *believe* you are just glossing over the iconic Gaga version with Tony Bennett."

"*Iconic* is not the word that comes to mind," Sunny said.

I kept singing, but Luca talked over it. "Nolan Shaw, no one wants to hear your Bowie impression if you're not going to back it up with a Yamamoto jumpsuit," he huffed. He waved his hands at Sunny before he swiped the script out of my lap. "And what would you call a Gaga-Bennett duet if *not* iconic?"

"I don't know. Noisy? Stop slapping me, that's how I feel!" Sunny said while Luca accosted her with the script page as Gretchen stared down at her phone.

"Shit," Gretchen mumbled. "It really is from *Moulin Rouge*."

"By way of Nat King Cole," added Luca. "And enhanced by Lady Gaga."

"Don't worry," Bee said, trying to swallow her laughter. "We could use a less well-known line. Maybe the meaning of Christmas is that God bless us, everyone?"

"The meaning of Christmas is that love, actually, is all around?" I suggested.

"That nobody puts Baby in a corner?" said Sunny.

"There's no crying in baseball?" contributed Luca.

"I am Spartacus," Sunny said for good measure as Gretchen glared at all of us in turn.

"This isn't funny," she said, pressing her coffee mug to her face and rolling it on her forehead like she was trying to roll away a headache. "Okay, okay. Pearl's been having a rough time finishing this script, and I don't want to make her feel worse. How about the real meaning of Christmas is that love is a gift that we can give year-round?"

We stared at her.

"I weirdly like it," Luca said after a minute. "It's like the perfect amount of cheesy and true."

"That's the formula," Gretchen said with a sigh. "Okay, write the new shit on your scripts, please. Before I forget what I said."

"Why are you doing this movie again?" Sunny asked curiously as Bee and I groped for something to write with. Bee grabbed a brow pencil. I grabbed lip liner. "This whole Hope Channel thing doesn't seem cohesive with a Gretchen Young brand."

"I like Hope Channel movies," Gretchen said, pressing her mug to her head again. "They make me happy. And *happy* and *formulaic* are not incompatible with *smart* or *important*. Also I want my girlfriend to have health insurance. Okay, Bee, Nolan, see you up at the mansion. Goodbye, all."

After she left, Luca was grinning at Sunny. "She told *you*."

"Shut up."

After I was dressed, Bee and I got in the van to take us up to the mansion. I had a scene to shoot after the kissing scene, and she had scenes scheduled for later this afternoon that required a costume change, so this was our last moment together semi-alone, save for the driver. I turned to her.

"Hey, I'm sorry I didn't get a chance to tell you I was leaving early. I meant to last night, and then . . ."

She gave me a little smile. "Then you screwed my brains out instead?"

"Apparently, I have a fetish."

"For wedding dresses?"

"For you in a wedding dress," I said, and then realized how that sounded. "I mean . . . not like . . . I'm not trying to—"

"It's okay." She laughed. "I know you're not proposing right now."

Was it weird that I kind of wanted to?

"I just didn't want you to think that I was running off because I was done with this. With you." I found her hand and fitted my fingers between hers, keeping our hands hidden in her skirt so the driver wouldn't see us touching if he happened to look back.

"Oh Nolan, I know," she said, meeting my gaze. She wore a lipstick that highlighted every tilt and curve of her full mouth, and her lips turned up now into a very soft smile. "I know you want to see your family. Hell, I want to see mine too. I'd kill for my moms right now."

"Just tell me that you'll pick up the phone when I call after this," I said.

"Tell *me* that you'll pick up the phone when I call, and you have a deal."

I squeezed her hand. "Deal."

THE SCENE WENT perfectly, and if Pearl noticed the change to her script, she didn't show it. More importantly, even though it happened in front of an audience, the scripted kiss in the scene was the only chance I had to kiss Bee goodbye.

I was almost sad that we got it in one take, because the warm brush of her lips was drugging, inviting, incredible. I wanted to kiss her for the rest of my life, until the mansion fell down around our ears, until there was nothing left but her sugary scent and soft little sighs and the snow outside.

When we finished, I looked over at Bee, struggling for a way to say goodbye that would seem totally normal for coworkers, but that conveyed at least some of how much I wanted her and hated leaving her. Some of that twisty, needy feeling that was so much more than lust or respect or affection—the feeling that scared me when I thought about naming it.

"It's okay," Bee said, seeing my hesitation. Cammy was waiting to get me upstairs, where I'd shoot my last scene, and Bee needed to get back to the toy shop for her costume change—there was no time left, no privacy to be had. This was it for us until after the movie.

If there was an after.

"Remember our deal," I said so only she could hear.

"*You* remember our deal," she said back, and then gave me the world's biggest smile. "Goodbye, Nolan Kowalczk."

My entire body itched to touch hers, to haul her into my arms and never let her go. But Cammy was walking toward me now and Gretchen and Pearl were nowhere in sight—probably already upstairs waiting for me.

"Goodbye, Bee Hobbes," I said softly, and then I left.

I thought about her for the rest of the day. I thought about her as I shot my last scene, and someone—Tall Ron, maybe—passed around a flask of Baileys to toast me after Cammy announced, "That's a wrap on Nolan Shaw!" I thought about her as I rode back to the inn, hoping I'd catch a glimpse of her but seeing only the bustling Christmas fair and the crowded main street, and on the way to Burlington, and while boarding a plane for home. And all I thought of was Bee Hobbes in a wedding dress and of a future that stretched far beyond the borders of Christmas Notch, Vermont.

CHAPTER TWENTY-FOUR

Bee

I wished every day on set could have been as good as today was. Well, except for the part where Nolan and I had to say our final goodbyes. But this morning in the toy shop with Luca, Sunny, Nolan, and Gretchen, it felt like something had finally gelled between us all and it didn't seem fair that we were hitting our stride just as it was nearly time to wrap *Duke the Halls*.

As I walked back to the inn, I watched the sky, wondering if Nolan was somewhere up above me looking down on Christmas Notch for one last time.

I turned the corner past the thinning crowds heading home for Christmas Eve and pulled out my phone to find a text.

Nolan: Going on airplane mode. Talk soon. ♥

And then a notification for *eight* missed calls and one voicemail from Jack Hart. I pulled up my voicemail and tapped on his message, hearing nothing at first. For a moment, I thought he'd meant to hang up without leaving a message, but after a few seconds and some muffled noises, Jack's irritated voice said, "You're gonna want to call me back."

My first reaction was to bristle, but then every possible reason why Jack Hart might call me eight times on Christmas Eve spun through my brain. I called him back as fast as my fingers would move, but I went straight to voicemail. Again. One ring and then to voicemail.

I tried once more as Sunny came sprinting out of the inn toward me. "Bee!"

I looked at my phone in my hand and shot off a quick text to Jack.

Me: I can't call you if you won't answer.

"Hey," I said to Sunny as she collided with me, white air puffing from her lips. "What's going on?"

She swallowed and then caught her breath for a moment. "You hate surprises, right?"

I nodded. "Yeah. Almost always."

She nodded quickly. "Okay, just checking. It's, like, one of those things you always say about yourself, but I wasn't actually sure if it was like when people say they don't celebrate their birthday, but then when no one remembers, they're sad."

"Yeah, it's not like that. Surprises stress me out."

She gave me two thumbs-up. "Cool, cool, cool. So . . . your moms are here."

My eyes began to tingle as tears pooled, and I let out a partially excited, partially overwhelmed shriek. "My moms! They're here? Like, here-here? In Christmas Notch?"

Sunny pulled my arm and dragged me toward the inn. "Yes! Here-here! And there wasn't a room ready for them yet, so they left their bags in your room and gave Teddy a bouquet of beef jerky for Christmas, like he's your fourth-grade teacher or something."

"My room?" I asked.

"I dumped your bag of toys in the minifridge. Don't worry. As if they don't already know what an avid collector their daughter is."

"Oh my God, I can't believe they're here!" I bounced as we walked under the carport and into the lobby. "Sunny, were you in on this?"

"I wouldn't say *in* on it, but yes, they did take my temperature. P.S., Mama Pam is looking fiiiiiiine after ditching the highlights and letting the grays come in."

"Drop it," I said, like she was a very naughty German Shepherd.

"I can admire without touching and exorcize my mommy issues from a distance, thank you very much."

"There she is!" Mom said from across the lobby bar as she stood to meet me. Next to her, Mama Pam immediately welled up with tears.

I pushed past the crew members all congregating at the bar

in search of Christmas cheer, and within seconds my moms' arms were wrapped around me in a familiar embrace. "You're here," I whispered.

"Couldn't miss out on sharing Christmas with our Bee," Mom said. "And a white Christmas no less!" She stood back, and I noticed she and Mama Pam wore matching monochromatic outfits except in different colors. Mom, tall and slender, wore red pants with a red cable knit sweater and matching puffer vest while Mama Pam, more round and petite, wore the exact same thing except in hunter green. After I moved out, they began to coordinate their outfits a lot more than I remembered them doing before.

"You both look great," I said.

Mama Pam wiped tears from her cheeks. "Well, thanks, dear. According to Sunny, the gays love to match." And then she wound her arms around me again for another hug.

I waved to Teddy at the bar as he saluted me with a stem of beef jerky. On the televisions hanging above him, a weatherman in a navy-blue sweater embroidered with snowflakes pointed at some charts as the scrolling headline read "An Even Whiter Christmas for Vermont!"

"Fuck that fucking fuck!" someone behind us snapped, and half the lobby bar froze like they were in trouble.

I almost used my hands as earmuffs on Mama Pam even though she'd said worse while bowling with her Rainbow League bowling team, the Twink Ladies.

The source of the voice was none other than Nolan's sexy and absolutely terrifying manager, Steph. She shook her fist at the weatherman on-screen as she barreled through the crowd with her suitcase rattling behind her. "Every plane in this maple-soaked hellscape is grounded for weather."

Teddy silently laughed into his fist as Steph plopped down beside him and whistled at Stella behind the bar. "What's bigger than a double?" she barked.

"Looks like we got here just in time," Mom said as she eyed Steph.

"Seriously," I muttered. "Gretchen and Pearl are planning a really nice dinner for everyone who's not going home for the holidays, so I'm sure you can both—"

"Actually," Sunny said as she stepped into our tight circle. "They both had to go back to L.A. at the last minute because someone's sister was going into labor or . . . something. I'm not sure. But I guess they were on the last flight out, so Teddy is hosting the dinner."

"Oh. Lovely," Mom said. "I can't say I ever wondered what Christmas Eve with Teddy might be like, but we're just so thankful to be with you here." She pulled Sunny to her. "You too, Sunny."

The four of us melted into another reunion hug and for a moment, I felt like I could have it all. I could star in the silly Christmas movie and have the ex–boy band member boyfriend. I could have my ClosedDoors fan base and one foot in the porn industry. I could be every version of myself without any sacrifice at all.

WHEN TEDDY LEARNED he was now in charge of the crew dinner, he moved it from Kringle's to the Dirty Snowball and announced that everyone was entitled to cheese fries, wings, and a pitcher of beer, which according to him was a Christmas feast.

I walked with my moms and Sunny through the snow as the thick flurries began to come down in heavier bursts. I showed my moms around the town, though all the shops were now closed and just a few lights glowed within.

As we passed the church, my chest swelled at my last memories there with Nolan. Because he booked his flight last minute, he had two layovers but should be landing in Kansas City within the next hour. This morning felt like weeks ago, and I didn't know how I'd survive not existing in the same zip code as him. Even when we were apart here in Christmas Notch, I could feel him. I could sense his presence, and it was the kind of knowledge that soothed me.

With a curtsy, Sunny held the door of the Dirty Snowball open, and we all filed inside and tucked ourselves away into a quiet booth at the back.

Sunny pointed to me. "Beer?" And then to my moms. "Beer?"

Mama Pam and I nodded as Mom said, "A cab sav would be ideal."

"Roger that," Sunny said, and wandered off toward the bar.

Mom, whose heart was always buried a little deeper than Mama Pam's, made the frowning-smiling face that she always made when she was so happy she could cry—thus the frowning.

"Bee," she said. "Our sweet Bee. We're just so proud of you."

"We always have been," Mama Pam added, reaching across the table just as I noticed Teddy taking a call at the bar before walking back outside into the heavy snowfall with his phone pressed to his ear.

"Your grandmother is so excited she can watch this one," Mama Pam said.

And then, because I hadn't said so out loud or realized this was even a decision I had to make for myself, I said, "I think I'm still doing ClosedDoors and probably adult films, too, just so y'all know. I . . . don't want to disappoint you, but it's possible this Hope Channel stuff might be a one-and-done type of thing, ya know? And—and I love my job. I really, really do."

All softness shed from Mom's expression. "You could never disappoint us, and don't for a minute think we are more proud of you for this than we are of your adult work. We raised a self-assured, confident young woman who is compassionate and clever. Whatever makes you happy makes us happy."

My heart swelled. Knowing I had them both at my side made my very uncertain future feel a little less terrifying.

"We couldn't have asked for more," Mama Pam added as Sunny returned with a pitcher of beer and a glass of wine.

"I managed to find one menu for us all to share," she said as she pulled the water-damaged paper from where it was wedged under her arm.

My mothers took it from her and began to deliberate over the very limited list of bar food.

Just as Sunny began to pour the pitcher of beer, Teddy appeared and leaned over the booth as he did the throat-clearing thing that he did when he was uncomfortable, which was sometimes the case around my moms. Mainly because other performers' parents weren't usually as involved as mine. "Uh, Bee, could I borrow you for a moment?"

I nodded.

Sunny briefly stood so I could squeeze past her, and I followed Teddy as he led me through the bar.

We stopped at the exit, and from the coatrack he threw at me some random stranger's coat, which was huge and black and puffy and much more like a real winter coat than anything I'd ever owned. I held it over me like a blanket.

We stepped outside into the bar's narrow alcove, the wind gusting past us, and I said, "What's the deal, Teddy?" I couldn't imagine what he would need to talk about that couldn't wait.

He looked out into the street and pressed his lips together for a moment, like maybe if he just tried, the words would stay inside of him and never truly exist. Something about the way his shoulders slumped and how he couldn't quite find the right words reminded me of many times in my life when my parents had to tell me about problems there were no solutions to.

"It's not good," he finally said. "They found us out, kid."

It took a minute for my mind to process what he'd just said and for my smile to melt away. "But . . . how? What does this mean for the movie?"

"Hell if I know," he said, gritting his teeth against the cold. "It's just now hitting Twitter."

My hands flew up to cover my mouth, but I couldn't stop my voice from shaking as I said, "Oh my God. Nolan."

At that moment the door swung open, and Steph held the glowing screen of her phone up for Teddy to see, her whole body vibrating with fierce anger. "Tell me this isn't true. Tell me you didn't just sink this whole motherfucking ship. Tell me you didn't just turn my client's career into the *Titanic*."

Teddy opened his mouth to speak, but nothing came out.

"It's not his fault," I blurted as some sort of need to shield Teddy after he'd spent years protecting me bubbled to the surface. "He didn't know!"

On the screen of her phone was a very topless picture of me on Dominic Diamond's website; he'd covered my nipples with Santa Claus hat clip art. The headline read "Nolan Shaw's Christmas Costar Is on the Naughty List." Teddy scrolled down to the next photo, of me and Nolan with Prancer, our favorite stripper.

The one who'd promised not to share her picture.

Dammit.

Steph's gaze flew to me. "You. I had a feeling about you. Do you have any idea the kind of damage you've done to Nolan's career? He'll be lucky if this movie even makes it on air and—"

"Enough," Teddy said firmly. "I cast Bee in this film. I knew all about her . . . because she works for me at Uncle Ray-Ray's. Which is *my* porn studio."

She turned back to Teddy, her jaw slack. "You . . . you produce porn? What kind of farce is this?"

He shrugged. "It's not so different from producing one of these Christmas movies, you know. And we have core values and everything."

"We're all fucked," she declared, and then looked to me. "We'll be lucky if the Hope Channel doesn't level this whole fucking town once they find out their brand is connected with a porn star—*a porn star*, for fuck's sake! I'm not even supposed to be here. I'm supposed to be at David Duchovny's Christmas party!"

"Isn't he Jewish?" Teddy had the nerve to ask.

"Half," Steph said as she opened her purse and tore the lining aside to pull out a cigarette and a matchbook. "My emergency cigarette. Don't tell my daughter. And some Jewish people like Christmas, you dumb shit."

As she began to smoke, and as Teddy scrubbed his hands over his face, everything inside of me began to fall apart.

Steph was right. We were fucked. And it was all because of me.

I needed to call Nolan.

"He should have landed an hour and a half ago," I said as I hung upside down off my bed, hoping my tits would just suffocate me already.

After we quickly ate, my moms, Sunny, and I walked back to the hotel. I said good night to my exhausted moms and pulled Sunny into my room, where I told her the gig was up. Thankfully, by the time we left the bar, none of the cast and crew seemed to know what was going on, which either meant that the story hadn't gained a ton of traction just yet because of the holiday or they were all too drunk to care about what was happening on the internet.

I sat up, the blood rushing to my head. Whatever shot Nolan and I had at a future after all this was now done for. I was right to doubt it could ever work, but I still felt ridiculous for holding on to the hope that our friends with bennies relationship could ever turn into anything more.

I checked my phone once more. I'd called him nineteen times. No answer.

As I putzed around some more on my phone, I gasped as I

realized I had his flight number in our text thread. My thumb scrolled and scrolled until I found it. Switching over to a browser, I typed the info into a flight tracker.

FLIGHT #335: ARRIVED AT KANSAS CITY INTL 34 MINUTES AGO

"He landed," I said, my voice wrought with confusion and hurt.

"Call him, call him!" Sunny urged.

"Half an hour ago," I said, trying to hold back a sob. God, I hated for anyone to see me like this, but if it was going to be anyone, I was glad for it to be Sunny. "He landed half an hour ago, and he definitely knows what is going on and is choosing not to return my calls."

"Listen," Sunny said gently. "It might be time to think about Bee priorities. You know the moment he got off that plane, he had like thirty-seven messages from Steph. There's no telling what kind of defense she has in mind. It might be every bisexual for themselves right now, babe."

I shook my head frantically. "Nolan wouldn't . . . he wouldn't do that."

She threw a supportive arm over my shoulders. "Maybe. But what I do know is that nothing is getting fixed tonight and you need to chill out and get some sleep." She pulled a large bottle of gummy vitamins from her purse. "Try these."

I held the purple bottle in my hand. "Your women's multivitamin?"

She snorted and took it back from me, and then popped the lid open. "They're edibles, Bee."

I stared at her blankly.

"Pot gummies?"

"Ohhhh!" I might have been a total sexual deviant, but my interactions with substances started and stopped with beer and fruity drinks.

"I'm going to take a shower in my room, but I'll come back and stay the night here with you," she promised.

The thought of her being there for me to cuddle or at the very least stare at while I couldn't fall asleep helped me breathe just a little easier. "Are you sure you don't mind?"

"And miss your anxiety spiral? Never."

She left me to her bottle of gummies, but not before turning on the TV and finding some Christmas Eve true crime special, like she was turning on the Discovery Channel for her dog.

I whimpered my thanks, because I truly appreciated the thought.

After she left, I put my phone on the charger, pulled the blankets up to my chin, and popped a gummy in my mouth before I could overthink and change my mind.

They didn't smell or taste so different from regular gummies. In fact . . . they reminded me of the wine gummies Mom would bring back from her yearly business trips to Munich when I was younger.

I dug around for another—this time a green star-shaped gummy.

For a brief moment, I wondered what the recommended serving size was as I cherry-picked a third.

Maybe it was wishful thinking, but I could already feel the

edges of my mind and body blurring and my nerves slowly beginning to ease.

Maybe being fucked wasn't so bad. Maybe we were always meant to be fucked.

Suddenly everything felt so much smaller and more manageable, and was the green flavor supposed to be apple or pear? The only way to know for sure was to try another . . .

CHAPTER TWENTY-FIVE

Nolan

y plane landed, but then took forever to get from the icy landing strip to the even icier gate area. After about an hour of trying to nap through the plane creeping over the tarmac, I stepped off feeling tired and scruffy and unsettled. I was excited to be back home and to surprise Mom and Maddie, but I kept having that feeling like I'd left something really important back in Vermont, like my phone or my right lung.

It was Bee.

I missed Bee.

I scrubbed at my hair and then yanked on my beanie as I slouched through the terminal toward baggage claim. It was delusional to miss someone this much after only two weeks, right? To feel like this woman was back in Vermont, holding my gasping right lung while I struggled to breathe apart from her? That was moon man talk. Like lyrics from a song that Isaac would have taken lead vocals on, and *not* like real life at all.

I slumped against a cold window in the mostly empty baggage claim section and waited for the carousel to spit out my bag. As the other passengers straggled over, I found my phone and bent my face over it. There weren't very many people here, and I never minded giving out autographs or pictures when people recognized me, but I was too off-kilter for unexpected selfies right now.

I should call Bee. That was what I should do. I would call her and let her know I landed, and just hearing her voice would make this awful *missing* go away.

I turned off airplane mode and waited for my phone to scratch its belly and yawn before it decided to connect to the network. I glanced up as the carousel juddered into motion, and that's when it happened.

That's when my phone became radioactive.

Seventy-two missed calls. Fifty-eight texts.

And social media notifications numbering in the thousands.

Whaattttt? I mouthed silently at the screen as I tapped open the messages from Steph first. There were seventeen voice messages from her, and I pressed play on the most recent one.

"You knew nothing," she said, sounding like she'd already deconstructed several Manhattans by the time she'd left the message. "If they ask, *you knew nothing*. You were supposed to do a movie with Winnie Baker, you were a good sport with the last-minute replacement, but of course you had no idea that you were a little baby boy-band bird in a nest of pornographers. You don't watch porn and you never would. And you were pressured into taking that selfie with the stripper—you were just being polite to the nice lady with the nipple pasties and stuff. No, I'm still eating this, why would you assume that the woman clutching a fistful of nachos is done eating them? In fact, I want another order, and I'll give you two hundred dollars to bring me the cherries from the bar."

That was where the message ended. I didn't listen to or look at any others. I went straight to my phone icon and saw that nineteen of the seventy-two missed calls were from Bee. *Shit shit shit.* What had *happened* while I was in the air?

I called Bee, looking up in time to see my bag glide by on the carousel, and walked over to grab it.

"Hey, this is Bee," came her husky, recorded voice. Just hearing it made me close my eyes and breathe deeply for the first time since I left Christmas Notch. "If you're calling about a job, make sure to leave your name, number, and what date you'd need my test results by. If this is Mom or Mama Pam, I'm sorry about the thing I just said about test results. If this is Sunny or Luca and you need to be rescued from a boring date, pretend this is me telling you that my goldfish just died and I'm inconsolable. I need a friend. I need a fish wake. I need my friend in the depths of my fish grief, et cetera, et cetera."

Beeeeep.

Popping up the handle of the suitcase, I began rolling it toward the door as I spoke quickly into the phone. "Bee, it's Nolan. I just got off the plane and turned on my phone. I'm catching an Uber home, but then I'll try calling again. I just want you to know that I—"

I stopped, the word I'd been about to speak sitting on my tongue like a note waiting to be crooned. But I couldn't say that word to her. It was too early and probably not reciprocated and I couldn't even be sure *what* it was that I felt for Bee, because I'd never felt this way before. And if I was thirty-one and hadn't felt this way before, how could I trust it?

Instead, I finished with "I just want you to know that I care about you. And we'll figure this out." The first sentence wasn't the entire truth. And the second?

It was a version of the truth I desperately wanted to believe.

WHEN THE UBER rolled in front of my house forty-five minutes later, I was carsick from looking down at my phone while riding in the back seat and worse than carsick from what I'd been reading.

Dominic Diamond's article was gossipy and salacious, but at least predictably so. The more reputable outlets were thankfully somewhat restrained, but the social media storm was . . . It was bad.

Stills, clips, and GIFs from Bee's scenes were everywhere, splashed all over with commentary about her body, about her career, about *her*, even though no one knew her at all. She was called a slut, a performative bi catering to the male gaze, a pervert, a profiteer complicit in the fetishization of her own body. They had a lot to say about her trying a different kind of movie—most of it awful. And they had a lot to say about her being plus-size—*all* of it awful.

Between her and Teddy, the *Duke the Halls* shoot was being framed as some kind of Christmas orgy, all on the Hope Channel's dime, and sure enough, my reputation as a former orgy enthusiast was being brought into it.

Not that the stripper selfie helped with that *at all*.

DiamondDom @domincdiamond · Dec 24
Breaking: Former bad boy Nolan Shaw's plus-size costar hiding secret identity as hard-core porn star Bianca von Honey!

josiegrosie @comejosephine · Dec 24
there's no way NOLAN SHAW wasn't all over a porn star while he was filming (albeit a fat one). am i the only one who hasn't forgotten the sex train in germany???

Olive is on hiatus ✦ @travelwitholive · Dec 24
so much for the bad boy phase being a "phase." i bet the whole emily albright story was a lie too. i mean, it wasn't like *she* was coming forward to talk, so why wouldn't he tell a version of events that made him out to be a hero?

Thanos is my daddy @darlingspence · Dec 24
FINALLY A HOPE CHANNEL MOVIE I WANT TO WATCH

Moms for Clean Media @momswhocare9 · Dec 24
We will not stand for this from the Hope Channel!!! We are boycotting anything with the Hope Channel or anything with so-called Nolan Shaw from INK. What happened to sanity and DECENCY???

silver bells ❄ ▶♫ @bellabellabella · Dec 24

I think it's funny that *anyone* thought Nolan Shaw had changed. Bianca von Honey is the proof that you can't take the dirty out of the dirty, dirty boy.

Josiegrosie @comejosephine · Dec 24

no joke. bet hope channel is rethinking a lot of things right now, esp. with the clean image they have to maintain. this nolan shaw comeback is dead on arrival.

Moms for Clean Media @momswhocare9 · Dec 24

@thehopechannel, I hope you are ready for this BOYCOTT. We have relied on your network for family-safe, wholesome content for years, but now we know better!!! @NBCnews @ABCnews @frontline @twitter @facebook

I turned off my phone and tried to choke down a few deep breaths. This was bad. *This was really fucking bad.* It wasn't just that Bee and Teddy were exposed as Bianca and Uncle Ray-Ray. Now everything about the movie, about me and my attempted rebranding, was in jeopardy. And I'd known that could be a possibility, that this was something that could happen, but shit.

It felt so much worse than I ever could've imagined.

But even with all the oh-shit chemicals dosing my blood, I knew with absolute clarity that Bee had the worst of it right now. I was a gleeful sex-train reference. She was performative or fetishizing herself or just plain perverted. I was getting called a dirty, dirty boy. She was getting called a slut.

The stuff you got away with when we were younger . . . do you think I would have gotten away with it? Gretchen had asked me that day in the office. The answer for my younger self had been *no*—and now, six years later, it was the same. Maybe my career was over, but Bee's *life* was actually going to be worse for this.

I tried calling her again as I exited the Uber, thanked the driver, and rolled my suitcase up the salted path to the door. Despite everything, the sight of our house with fake candles perched in every window and strung with lights and garland sent a ripple of warmth right through me. Not the hot, twisty sear of Twitter-induced panic, but the slow, sweet glow of coming home.

Bee's phone went to voicemail again, and just as I was about to leave another message, the wreath-hung front door swung open, and there was my mom. Short and soft and wearing cozy jammies. The cold hit her fair skin immediately, making her nose and cheeks rosy, but she rushed out onto the porch any-way and flung herself into my arms.

"Hey," I said, hugging her tightly back.

She pulled away enough to smile up at me. Tears glimmered in her blue eyes. "You're home early," she whispered.

"Home for Christmas, Mom," I said, and then went *oof* as a teenage-size ball of pajamas and hair crashed into me. "Hi, Mads," I wheezed, and then for a long moment, none of us moved, even though our breath made clouds and clouds around us, and the warmth of the house was pouring out the open front door.

We just stayed there on the porch hugging, freezing cold and all.

ON CHRISTMAS MORNING, I woke to the smell of pizza.

I stretched in bed and sat up, my mind blissfully blank. It could have been any Christmas morning in recent memory, with Kallum coming over to make us breakfast while holiday music filled the house.

And then my phone gave an indignant chime and the events of last night came rushing back in.

I went to brush my teeth as I checked to see if Bee had called me back—or texted. She hadn't done either, so I called her after I was done in the bathroom and got no response. I left another voicemail, and then finally called Steph.

The phone rang twice, and then a groggy man's voice greeted me. It was a familiar voice. A voice I associated with Hawaiian shirts and food. "Hello?" it asked.

"Um," I said, not sure what the hell was going on. "Teddy?"

"Yeah?"

Holy shit. Could they have . . . ?

No. No way. Steph wore pearls. She did not spend the night with men who ate turkey legs. "Is Steph there?" I asked doubt-fully.

"I don't know. Are you here, Steph?"

"Give me that—give it!" snapped Steph, and then there was the unmistakable rustle of blankets. "Nolan?"

"Um. Hi," I said, stunned. "Is this a bad time?"

"Thanks to *Uncle Ray-Ray*, it's all a bad time now," said Steph. There was protesting from her end of the phone. I was guessing from Uncle Ray-Ray himself. Jesus.

"Sorry, did you and Teddy actually spend the ni—"

"So here's what we're going to do," Steph went on, ignoring my question. "Deny, deny, deny. You had no idea what was going on, you're heartbroken that the Hope Channel was deceived, yadda yadda, and then I unlapse my Catholicism so I can light a candle for you in every church from Vermont to Eugene."

"So you're not dropping me as a client?" I asked hopefully.

There was a pause. A pause that did not feel good. And when Steph answered, she sounded more careful than I'd ever heard her.

"Depending on how we come through this week . . . maybe there's a chance I can still get you somewhere. But I won't lie to you, Nolan—my job is to turn ships around. Not bail out sinking ones."

"Got it," I said weakly.

"Buck up, kiddo," she said. "It might all work out. In the meantime, you know what you need to do. Deny, deny, deny. Just like St. Peter. Oh, look at that! Maybe I'm unlapsing already!"

"If I do deny knowing anything about it—"

"No *if*, Nolan. I'll put together a statement now, short and sweet. Once you approve it, I'll blast it everywhere."

A statement. Essentially disavowing Bee.

"I don't know," I said hesitantly, and she made a scoffing noise into the phone.

"Of course you don't. That's what you pay me for."

After I hung up and pulled on a hoodie to wear with my pajama pants, I called Bee again but still got her voicemail. I wanted to make sure she was okay and talk about what the last twelve hours had been like, and also to let her know that Steph wanted to put out a statement on my behalf—but none of that felt like it could fit into a voicemail.

How could it, when it didn't even fit inside my own thoughts?

I went downstairs to see if Kallum needed any help in the kitchen. He was standing at the kitchen counter, weighing marshmallows on a kitchen scale with the seriousness of a drug dealer weighing out product. He was so tall that he practically had to reach down to the counter to pour the marshmallows in the measuring bowl, and he was wearing fuzzy footie pajamas with pizza slices on them. Christmas music played from the living room, and the curtains were pulled open on the big picture window to show a fresh layer of snow sparkling over the world outside.

"Merry Christmas," I said, shuffling over to the coffeepot. "Where's Mom?"

"She went with her book club group to serve a pancake breakfast to the needy or something. She dragged my mom too."

"Are your parents not going to the casino this year?"

Kallum's family was Jewish, but they also took advantage of the unlimited crab-leg Christmas buffet at their favorite riverboat casino every year. Since nothing about our Christmas celebration was religious and since Kallum was allergic to shellfish and preferred to be in his pajamas anyway, he was a Kowalczk come Christmastime.

"They're going to the casino after the charity thing." Kallum stepped back and reached for a container of cocoa powder.

"And Mads? Is she up yet?" I asked, pouring a cup of coffee and then looking down at the stack of bills next to the coffeepot. They were all printed on pink or blue paper. The big deal bills. I'd taken an unpaid leave of absence from the theater to go to Vermont, and I had received only my first payment from filming *Duke the Halls*, which had gone toward my own health insurance premium. Which meant there definitely wouldn't be enough between my and Mom's money to take care of the entire stack of bills, or maybe even only one of them, depending on how bad they were.

I resisted the urge to whiskey up my coffee.

"Maddie is still asleep, I assume," Kallum said as he attached a dough hook to the stand mixer.

"What are you making for us today?"

"Eggy breakfast pizza is in the oven, and I'm currently getting the stuff ready for a hot cocoa pizza for when your mom gets back and your sister finally awakes from her coma."

The idea of the hot cocoa pizza almost soothed the sting of carrying the stack of bills over to the table to sort through. Kallum pulled out the breakfast pizza and set it on a rack to cool, and then he started working on the cocoa dough.

"Hey, man, I'm sorry about all the gossip around this Christmas movie thing. Even though I'm not sorry it took the heat off me for the sex tape," he said, measuring the dry ingredients into the mixing bowl.

"Don't think we're not going to talk more about that later, by the way."

Flour was now being sifted as he slid past my pointed remark. "Did you have any idea that Bee was Bianca von Honey?"

"Yeah," I said. "I definitely had an idea." I picked up the first brightly colored bill, this one from Mom's psychiatrist and stamped with a big Final Notice on the outside, and abruptly felt the weight of the world drop onto my shoulders. "Steph thinks I should deny it, though. Claim I didn't know anything."

Kallum was measuring the wet ingredients now. "Not a bad idea."

"I fell in love with Bee," I said without meaning to, still looking at the bill.

And then I froze. I hadn't even used that word with *myself* yet. Did I really mean it? Could that really be something Nolan Shaw could do? That Nolan Kowalczk could do?

Meanwhile, Kallum was slowly turning in the most dramatic circle ever turned, his mouth hanging open and his eyebrows raised up to meet his dark blond hair. He had flour in his beard. "You fell in love with a porn star? In the last *two weeks*? This is why you can't go places alone, Nolan, I'm serious."

I set down the bill, swallowing. "I was kind of a fan of Bianca's before the movie, actually. I've been super into her for years, and then she was just there, like a wish come true. Except suddenly my wish wasn't only sexy and gorgeous, she was also witty and silly and brave, and we understood each other . . . and then one thing led to another. For the last week or so, we've been together. Hiding, but together."

Kallum studied my face. "Methinks that would make it harder to throw her under the PR bus."

I squished my eyes closed, because they suddenly burned in that about-to-cry way, and I didn't want to cry on Christmas morning. "But if I don't throw her under the bus . . . if the attempt to restart my career doesn't survive this scandal, then

I'm fucked. I'm back to having no money for me and Mom and Mads; I'm stuck in this pit of final-notice bills and praying that we can keep the lights on and get Mom what she needs. I'm stuck knowing that it will never, ever get easier."

I opened my eyes to see Kallum shaking his head. "No matter how hot the hottie, family comes first. Kin before sin."

"But I don't want to lose Bee either," I said softly, looking down at the bills. "With her, everything felt so doable, so *light*. Like everything would work out. I felt like the old me and the new me, but also like the best parts of both."

"Okay, look," Kallum said, starting to pace. "This is a solvable problem. Because maybe Nolan Shaw can't have a porn star girlfriend, but he can have a *secret* porn star girlfriend."

I'd basically suggested the same thing to Bee, but hearing it from someone else's mouth made it seem kind of crappy.

"You know how people have a desert-island book?" Kallum went on. "The one book they'd bring to a desert island? She'll be your desert-island hottie. Love, longevity, the whole works, just in secret. Maybe you could get together at a resort every few months, like at a Sandals."

"Sandals," I echoed.

"They're really nice," said Kallum. "I went to a wedding at a Sandals once."

"I don't think that's what I want," I said. "Or at least not all of what I want. The sex is amazing, and I'm not saying no to that, but I want all the other stuff that comes around it too. I want to be with her. Like really *be*. Just in our normal, everyday lives. Doing chores and sleeping in and shopping for new blinds together."

"No, you don't," Kallum said, shaking his head again. "That living together part is bullshit."

"What would you know about it?" While Kallum was perpetually in love, none of his soul mates ever stayed mated to his soul for longer than three months. He'd only ever lived with his parents or INK, and currently had a cat named Bread. "You've never even attempted to move in with any of those bridesmaids you keep finding."

"Shh!" he hissed, dampening the air between us. "Do not speak that evil word here!"

"Bridesmaid?"

He glared. "This is about you," he said sternly. "And about what you're going to choose if the choice is between family or hottie."

With that, he slung a tea towel over his footie-pajamaed shoulder and turned back to the important business of mixing his cocoa dough.

I finished my coffee in silence as I reviewed the bills one by one and organized them into those I could pay now and those for which I'd have to call to beg for an extension. We were going to be in the hole no matter what, and if I didn't get another Nolan Shaw job within a month, I didn't know that we'd ever be able to climb out. Hell, even *with* another Nolan Shaw job, it was still going to take months to tackle all the medical bills. And that wasn't even counting my mom's last visit to the hospital, which hadn't been processed yet.

My phone chimed and I looked down to see a message from Steph.

> **Steph:** got the statement ready. check your email.

I opened my email, ignored the scores of interview requests, and found Steph's statement. It was short and blunt. Reading it made me feel slightly sick to my stomach. But looking at the pile of bills also made me sick to my stomach.

When had everything gotten so goddamn hard?

I was about to call Bee again when Maddie scampered down the stairs and then slowed to a slouching sort of stroll once she was in view of the kitchen, all forced casualness and calm. She claimed she was over her girlhood crush on Kallum, but she performed Not Having a Crush so emphatically that it was almost *more* annoying than when she did have the crush. And then Mom came in the back door, snow caught on the shoulders of her coat and her smile as big as I ever remembered it being. The kitchen immediately became noisy and crowded and perfect.

With a twist deep in my chest, I texted Steph a thumbs-up in response and then set my phone facedown on the table.

"Who wants to open presents?" I asked, and received a resounding cheer in response.

CHAPTER TWENTY-SIX

Bee

For the first time in my human life, I slept straight through Christmas morning. And afternoon. Turned out pot gummies were not meant to be eaten like movie theater snacks.

"What flavor of coffee do you want?" Sunny asked through my post-sleep-marathon haze.

My eyes hurt to open, so I just sat in bed with them closed. "Anything but figgy pudding."

I squinted at her with one eye as she zoomed her finger around before landing on a random coffee pod and popping it into the machine. Pawing at the end table, I searched for my phone and found it looking dead.

"Oh, I just went ahead and turned that off last night," Sunny told me. "Your notifications were off the charts and you were sleeping so hard. I checked in with your moms this morning to let them know you were still down for the count."

I groaned. "My moms. Oh God. I ruined Christmas. Do they know? Have they seen?"

She sat on the bed next to me and handed me a peppermint mocha–scented cup of coffee. "Do they know that you're a porn star? Uh, yeah, Bee. They know."

I took a sip, letting the liquid scald my throat. "You know what I mean."

Sunny set her mug down on my nightstand and turned to me. "They saw before I could tell them. I guess it was on their Yahoo home page. Should I tell them no one uses Yahoo anymore?"

I took another sip as my phone powered on. Everyone in my parents' inner circle knew what I did. But this would be news for some. Neighbors . . . coworkers . . . people they had to interact with on a regular basis but didn't actually know.

Once my phone came back to life, headlines began to appear.

Hope Channel INKS Deal with Porn Star

Nolan Shaw's Raucous Night at Strip Club with Porn Star

Hope Channel Lands a Bag of Coal This Holiday Season with Porn Starlet

"Oof."

"How did this even get out?" Sunny asked.

My brain took a moment to recalibrate before I fully re-membered everything that happened yesterday. "I think I have an idea," I said through gritted teeth as I scrolled through my contacts and then held the phone to my ear.

"Are you calling Nolan?" Sunny whispered. "I can leave, or just be, like, super quiet. Oh my God, please let me stay."

I nodded my head at her and then rolled my eyes after it rang twice before going straight to voicemail.

"This is Jack Hart. I never check my voicemails, so don't bother. Text me or try my manager."

After a long beep, I let loose, unleashing all the rage I felt for him and his weird threatening calls and texts and for Dom-inic Diamond and his awful catchphrase and his disgusting entitlement to private information. "Jack Hart, you piece of shit. How could you? I was nice to you! I was one of the only people still in your corner and you go and sell me out to that human leech! I hope you lose Miss Crumpets in the custody battle. She deserves better than you."

And then I hung up, pumping breaths in and out of my lungs as my adrenaline skyrocketed. "I can't believe I just did that."

"Yeah." Sunny shook her head, her eyes wide with amaze-ment and a little bit of terror. "That last part was brutal."

I sank against the headboard. "Was it?"

"No, no, but totally deserved," she said, her loyalty unyield-ing. "I mean, that poor dog probably needs to be removed from both of their custody if we're being honest. I just didn't know you had it in you."

I set my mug down a little too hard next to hers, coffee sloshing over the edge.

"You think he really sold you out to the press?" she asked.

I nodded. "He left a threatening voicemail yesterday, and he's still pissed at me for bailing on him."

"I find it baffling that Rebecca's son could be so vicious."

"Rebecca?" I asked. "You mean Jack's mom?"

Her wistful gaze drifted beyond me. "She'll always be Rebecca to me." After a moment, she shook the thought from her head and said, "While you're all hyped up, though, I thought I should show you this before someone else beats me to it."

She pulled up a screenshot on her phone and handed it over for me to see.

PRESS RELEASE

FOR IMMEDIATE RELEASE
CHRISTMAS NOTCH, VT
DECEMBER 25, 2022
INNOVATIONS AGENCY AND MANAGEMENT FIRM
FOR MORE INFORMATION, CONTACT: SDasst@IAGMF.net

NOLAN SHAW HAD NO KNOWLEDGE
OF HIS COSTAR'S PROFESSION

Representatives of Nolan Shaw can confirm that Mr. Shaw wrapped *Duke the Halls* on Christmas Eve. When Mr. Shaw was cast by the Hope Channel to star in this Hopeflix-launching film, he was set to appear opposite Winnie Baker, whom he has known and held in the highest regard for many years.

While Mr. Shaw was happy to work with Ms. Baker's replacement at the last minute, he had no prior knowledge of Ms. Hobbes/von Honey's career as an adult film actress. Mr. Shaw is not associated with pornography nor does he condone the predatory nature of pornography.

Mr. Shaw did attend a team-building outing at a local venue in an effort to support the economy of Christmas Notch, Vermont. As such, Mr. Shaw was unaware of the establishment's more obscene offerings.

Mr. Shaw remains proud of his work on *Duke the Halls* and fully respects and understands the Hope Channel's image and brand as a source of clean holiday entertainment for the whole family.

Sunny's phone slipped from my hands and onto the bed and everything just went . . . numb. My brain began to disconnect from my body, because if I let myself fully feel this pain, I might not leave this bed. Ever.

Sunny pulled me to her and held me, but I barely felt her touch, which would normally be just the kind of comfort that would soothe me.

As if it had needed a minute to catch up after powering on, my phone began to light up with missed texts and calls from Nolan. But what could either of us say right now that would change any of this?

After a few moments, she glanced down at a message on her phone. "Your moms want to grab an early dinner at Frosty's or Kringle's. I really think you need to get out of this room and eat something too."

"Yeah," I said, short gasps beginning to fill my lungs, and even though Sunny had seen my absolute worst, I was desperate for her to leave, because the numbness was starting to fade and at any moment, a sob might rip through my chest. "Just give me like an hour to shower and stuff."

Sunny stood and pressed a kiss to the top of my head. "We'll get through this."

The moment the door shut behind her, I bit down hard on my lower lip—a sign to my body that I could finally, finally let it all out and cry. How could I let myself be so foolish as to buy into this fairy tale?

It was just sex. It was just something we had to get out of our systems.

Until it wasn't.

And now I had feelings. Big, huge feelings that I didn't know how to name. And as if that wasn't confusing enough, Nolan had betrayed me.

Even though I knew I was supposed to get ready to go out, I let myself sink back down into my pillows. I wiped away the tears as they ran down my cheeks and neck until my phone vibrated, and Nolan Shaw sitting in his duke costume next to my director's chair the night of the chili cheese fry scene lit up my screen.

What was there even left to talk about? His statement said it all. He'd disavowed me.

And yet I couldn't stop myself from swiping and answering his call, and I hated myself for it.

He didn't even give me a moment to speak. "Bee," he said, his voice thick with worry. "You answered."

"Against my better judgment."

"What?" he asked. "What do you mean? God, I hate that I can't see you. I should have FaceTimed you. I'm such a grandpa. Let me hang up and—"

"No. Nolan, I don't want—I can't see you right now. I'm just . . . I don't know how it came out, okay? And I'm sorry. I mean, I might know how it came out. But despite everything, I am so, so sorry. I know that this was important to you, and I know you weren't doing this just for you. But I fucked this up for everyone."

"Bee, no, no, no. Listen, this is going to blow over. And maybe the Hope Channel doesn't air the movie. They still have to pay out my contract anyway . . . I think. And even if they don't, there will be other chances. There has to be. Steph is already in damage-control mode."

"Oh, I know."

"So you saw the press release?" he asked quietly.

"Yeah, I saw where you pretty much publicly condemned me." It took everything in me for my voice not to crack.

"Bee, come on," he said frantically. "You know this is all just a game. A show, even. That fucking press release isn't real."

"Maybe not for you, Nolan, but for me it is very real. Have you seen the shit people are saying about me online?"

"None of it matters," he said, like it was the simplest, truest thing in the world.

My blood began to boil. How could he be so out of touch? "None of it matters because none of it is about you!"

"You think I don't know what it's like to be demeaned and reduced to a sound bite on the internet, Bee?"

I didn't know what to say to that. Of course he knew what it felt like, but that didn't change the fact that Nolan was celebrated by the media—even when he was vilified—for his promiscuity and party boy antics. I was just the fat, over-fetishized porn star who deceived her way into one of the few pure and wholesome forms of media left in this world: a Christmas movie. Not only were Nolan and I done for, but so was any post–*Duke the Halls* mainstream career I might have had.

He took a deep breath. "We're arguing. We shouldn't be arguing." Another deep breath. "Bee, I like you so much. I'm not ready to let go of what we have."

And then, because one of us had to say it, I whispered three little words that I had known deep down long before last night. "It's already gone."

"No," he said adamantly. "No. We can be together. Just us. I've wanted you for years, Bee. Ever since the first moment I saw your picture online years ago, you became my fantasy, you became my dream. And then the impossible happened and you became real. Suddenly, you were this actual person, and I felt so lucky to be in your orbit. You were smart and so funny. You quickly became the someone I wanted to share everything with. You were better than any fantasy I could've ever imagined. And now I can't go back to how it was before, when you were just an image on my phone. We can make this work. We can—we can meet up every few months for a little while. And then . . . things will quiet down and we can have our privacy."

"Our privacy? Just us? Nolan, I'm already the dirty little secret of millions of people."

It was the truth. And it was the worst part of my job. Even though most days I was proud of myself and my work, the shame that people so often felt from consuming my content and my films crept up on me sometimes. And if I knew anything, I knew what it felt like to be recognized in a grocery store when a fan was with their whole family or for someone I was dating to keep me around long enough for a good time, but not long enough to meet their parents.

"That's not what I meant," he said defensively.

"No. That's exactly what you're saying. You said it yourself. I was your fantasy. Your dream."

"Bee, I love you," he said desperately, like it was a final attempt to salvage whatever was left between us. It was the first time anyone had ever said those words to me while I was fully clothed and free of liquids or toys or kink of any sort. And yet, it wasn't as sweet and wonderful as I had always hoped it might be, because I didn't imagine my first *I love you* to feel like a last-ditch effort.

Still, his words sank deep into my chest, into a place where I would hold on to them forever, because if all Nolan Shaw could offer me was a broken *I love you*, I would treasure it like a delicate keepsake, even though it could never be enough to keep us afloat.

I inhaled through my nose. I wanted to say it back, but I couldn't. It would hurt too much, because the next thing I was going to say—the next thing I *had* to say—would be something he couldn't live with and something I couldn't live without. "Nolan, I don't need you to love me in private. I need you to love me in public for the whole world to see. And that's not something you're prepared to do."

"Bee." My name broke through the speaker like a cry.

"Merry Christmas, Nolan. Goodbye."

CHAPTER TWENTY-SEVEN

Nolan

I hated the day after Christmas. In fact, the hatred I had for the twenty-sixth was inversely proportional to the love I had for the twenty-fifth, which meant I hated it so much that the mere idea of it made me want to gnaw a hole through the drywall and flee into the frozen suburban wasteland of my hometown. I supposed it was related to the imminent un-cheering of the house, the abrupt drop from that big, cozy, sparkling joy back into the gray cold of a winter that actually didn't care if you were happy or not.

But today was bad even for the twenty-sixth. So bad that before Maddie left for her shift slinging slices at one of Kallum's pizza parlors, she informed me that I was bringing down the vibe of the entire house. Which couldn't possibly have been true because we were dog-sitting Snapple, and Snapple turned any vibe into something between *trapped in line behind a customer who wants to talk to the manager* and that scene in *Return of the Jedi* where Luke Skywalker has to fight a rancor with an old monster bone.

But I had a right to mope today, because last night I'd told Bee I loved her, and she'd told me it wasn't enough.

And she hadn't even said that she loved me back.

I was a few Kahlúa hot cocoas into the evening when my mom found me staring at our Christmas tree as I mentally re-hashed my conversation with Bee for the five-thousandth time.

She just doesn't understand, I kept telling myself. *She doesn't get what's at stake for me, and why I have to play their game.*

But what if she did understand? What if she understood, and it still didn't matter?

"Hey," Mom said softly, sitting on the couch next to me. Horrible Snapple trundled over to Mom's feet and pranced, her way of asking to sit on the couch. Mom scooped up the yorkiepoo and set her down on the cushion next to her, where Snapple turned a circle, glared at me, and then laid down with her head on her paws to glare at me some more. "How are you holding up?"

Mom wasn't on Twitter and very rarely looked at articles that weren't recipe- or craft-related, leaving only one option for how she'd heard the news.

"I'm guessing the scandal has reached Facebook, then?"

"Yeah," she said, rubbing Snapple's ears—which would have cost anyone else a finger and maybe their entire hand. "They're not being very nice about your costar."

I still hadn't told Mom about whatever it was that Bee and I had—or no longer had. I couldn't even imagine trying to explain it to her now. It hurt too much.

"No," I said, my stomach knotted somewhere in my chest. "They're not."

They were saying fatphobic things, shitty slut-shaming things, scary and creepy things about what they'd like to do to her if they found out where she lived—not to mention all the people who believed she wasn't a good feminist or the right kind of bi woman because she had sex for money. And here I was hiding behind Steph's statement, like a fucking coward.

But what was I supposed to do? Let everything burn to the ground? Let my family suffer because my heart was getting in the way of taking care of them? What could possibly be the right answer here?

"Do you really think the Hope Channel will cancel the movie?" Mom asked, lines of worry creasing her forehead. "Just because of her work as Bianca von Honey?"

"Steph thinks they might," I said. "The Hope Channel won't want to risk alienating their audience, not like this. It would be easier to bury the movie and ride out the storm."

"Would that make it harder for you to get other work?" she asked quietly.

I stared down into my cocoa mug before answering. "I don't know yet," I finally answered. "Neither does Steph."

Mom didn't say anything for a moment, and when I looked over at her, her face was bent toward Snapple in a way that told me she was trying to hide her expression from me.

"It's going to be okay," I promised her. "We'll figure it out."

She shook her head, still looking at Snapple. "If I could just work—" she whispered.

"No, Mom," I said. "We don't need that. And anyway, your Social Security disability payments will stop if you start earning money."

"If I start earning *too much* money," she corrected. "It would help, I think. If I made even a little bit."

It would, but the math was more complicated than that. "You know I'll support anything you want to do," I told her. "But your health and happiness are worth something too, even if that something isn't taxable at the end of the year."

"It's just—if I have the energy to volunteer and craft sometimes, then I think I should be ready to do more." Her hand shook as she said it, trembling in Snapple's gray-brown fur, and I put my hand on top of hers.

"The point isn't how far we can push ourselves," I said. "The point is being okay. Being able to live with space and room in our lives *so* we can be okay."

She looked up at me, her eyes watery. "I don't want to be a burden," she said softly. "That's not what a mom is supposed to be."

I squeezed her hand hard. "The best thing that ever happened to me was being your kid," I said. My throat hurt almost too much for me to get the rest out. "You gave me all your love without ever cutting off pieces of yourself to do it. You made sure I could chase any dream I wanted to chase. You believed in my goodness when teachers wouldn't, when the press wouldn't, when the entire world was obsessed with what an asshole I was."

"The press was too hard on you," she insisted loyally. "Those teachers too."

"I deserved them being hard on me and you know it," I said, laughing a little.

"Well, maybe a *bit*," she said. Her smile spread into the full one that put dimples deep into her round cheeks.

"I learned that love was sticking around and believing in someone even when it felt impossible," I told her, my voice turning serious again. "I learned from you that love meant feeling safe and secure even when everything else felt uncertain, and . . . ah, fuck."

Mom tilted her head. "What?"

I pulled her into a big hug and then stood. "Nothing. I just need you to know that you're an amazing mom and you are the opposite of a burden. Every good thing in my life is because you taught me how to earn good things. And on that note, I think I really fucked up, and I need to figure out how to fix it."

"Is this about Bee Hobbes?" Mom asked.

"Yes," I said, surprised. "Man, they're not kidding about a mother's intuition."

"Yes, my motherly intuition. And also you keep forgetting to un-Bluetooth your phone when you let me borrow your car, and I've seen Bianca von Honey's name on the radio display plenty of times. And heard her . . . noises."

"Ah," I said, my cheeks flaming. "Well. Um."

"Go fix things, Nolan," Mom said. "If you think I deserve space and room, then I think you deserve to be with the person who makes you feel like you have those things too." She gave me a smile after taking a deep breath. "And you're right. We'll figure everything else out as it comes. We always have."

Right.

Because that's what love was—more than a word, more than a mountain of the best and noblest intentions in the world. It was saying *I'll be here with you when it feels like nothing else is certain.* It was saying *Let the storm come, because I'll never stop holding your hand.*

And it was the exact opposite of what I'd said to Bee last night.

"Thanks, Mom," I said, and I left her and the demon dog on the couch while I went upstairs.

I had a call to make.

CHAPTER TWENTY-EIGHT

Bee

This morning I woke up to no call sheet under my door but did receive an email to meet Teddy and Gretchen at the production office late this afternoon instead. I spent the morning getting breakfast with my moms and pacing my room while Sunny watched a *Fast and Furious* marathon.

Just as I was about to leave for the production office, my phone rang. Jack Hart's name appeared on the screen.

Sunny stared wide-eyed at the phone.

The biting voicemail I'd left Jack began to replay in my head as I felt myself cowering a little. "Do I answer it?"

She nodded. "Yes, but proceed with caution."

I answered the call and put him on speaker, because I was a good friend and I knew Sunny would just press her ear as close to the phone as she could anyway. Bracing myself, I said, "Hello?"

"I forgive you," Jack said flatly.

Sunny's jaw dropped, and I could see the inner battle unfolding in her head as she tried her best not to say something snarky right back to him.

I held up a finger and gave her a patient but stern look. The last thing I needed or wanted was for the two of them to get into a shouting match. It would quickly devolve. Of that I could be sure.

"Excuse me?" I asked. "*You* forgive *me?*"

"For the voicemail," he explained. "We can pretend like I never even listened to it . . . especially the part about Miss Crumpets."

"Are we just going to skip over the fact that you outed me as a sex worker to mainstream media?"

"Is that what you think?" he asked. "Bee, I'm a lot of things . . . but that's a step too far even for me. You know I only ruin lives tastefully."

"But you called and left that threatening voicemail! You were already pissed I bailed on our scene."

"That wasn't threatening! How could you even perceive that as threatening?"

Sunny bit back a chuckle as she rolled her eyes.

I sank to the edge of the bed, feeling a little silly for jumping to conclusions. "Well, if you weren't threatening me, then what were you doing?"

"I was warning you!" he exclaimed. "That Dominic Diamond sleazeball reached out to me to confirm your identity.

He had that picture of you and Nolan—who by the way, still has it—in that strip club."

"Oh."

A deflated Sunny sat down beside me.

"Maybe next time you're trying to pull one over on the Hope Channel, you should avoid the local strip club."

"So it all started with that picture?" I asked, remembering Nolan's hesitancy and sweet little Prancer's promise to keep the photo to herself.

I could practically hear the bored shrug in his voice. "It's not like your Bianca identity was ever a secret. Only you and Teddy would be stupidly optimistic enough to think this would work."

I looked to Sunny, and she winced a little, which told me she didn't think Jack was entirely wrong. I had been so confident that the Hope Channel stream would never cross the porn stream. I was so sure that those audiences were two totally different people. Maybe they were, but maybe they weren't.

And something about that made me uneasy and hopeful at the same time.

I sighed loudly. "Well, thanks for going to the trouble to warn me, Jack. I appreciate it."

"You're welcome. And you can repay me by getting me a former boy band member to be my postdivorce rebound."

"*Bye*, Jack."

A peppy yip in the background rang through the speaker as we hung up, and I truly hoped it was Miss Crumpets.

TEDDY AND I sat in the production office, staring at each other from across the room like two kids who had been sent to the principal's office—if a principal's office looked like a Victorian parlor with a desk and a decade-old copier shoved inside. And even though it was officially after Christmas now, the old house was still glowing with Christmas trees, fake candles, and fairy lights. It was hard not to feel slightly mocked by all its Balsam Hill cheer.

"You sure you don't know anything?" I asked for the fifth time.

He shook his head. "The Hope Channel has dropped to zero communication with me."

I knew this was coming from the moment Teddy broke the news to me on Christmas Eve, but that didn't stop every muscle in my body from aching with dread. Jack was right. We were foolish to think this could work.

"Are you sure Gretchen and Pearl are coming?" I asked. "Maybe the Hope Channel is going to send in some kind of assassin to finish us off and destroy any evidence of *Duke the Halls*."

He leaned back, tilting his head against the velvet sofa. "I think I might prefer that at this point." His phone buzzed and he looked down, reading a message that made him both grimace and smile. I decided it was better not to know. "I guess I could refinance my condo. For the third time. That might pay for a semester of art school and one run of carbon-neutral nipple clamps."

The door swung open, and Gretchen and Pearl shuffled in

with very expensive, minimalist carry-on luggage. Gretchen wore a sleek down jacket and Pearl a shaggy faux-fur coat.

"Oh, good, you're both here," Gretchen said, her voice neutral.

"Two birds. One stone," Teddy muttered.

My heart jackhammered in my chest. I would do anything for this moment to be over. I stood up abruptly before either of them could even take off their coats and sunglasses and let the word vomit tumble out of my mouth. "I'm so sorry for lying to you both, and I completely understand whatever it is you have to do. And working with you both was such an honor, and I'm sorry I ruined basically everything." I groaned. "I'm just, like, endlessly sorry."

Teddy cleared his throat. "An emphatic ditto."

Gretchen marched directly to me and placed her hands on my shoulders, and I had to force myself not to flinch. I liked and admired her so, so much, and while there were many awful things about the last seventy-two hours, disappointing her felt even worse than I could have imagined.

She opened her mouth to speak, but then Pearl crushed her body into mine with an intense hug. "Oh, Bee, how are you holding up? I can feel the chaotic energy vibrating off you. You must be dying for a sound bath."

Gretchen tugged Pearl's hand, pulling her back. "Are you okay, Bee? The internet can be a violent place, especially for women."

I blinked at the two of them, Pearl curled under Gretchen's arm. Why weren't they yelling at me or making disappointed faces and noises? "W-wait. Neither of you are mad?"

Behind them, Teddy stood up, and I could see the wheels of his brain spinning behind those bushy eyebrows.

Gretchen raised one eyebrow. "At you? No." She looked over her shoulder to Teddy. "This guy's another story."

Teddy shrugged as if to say *fair enough*.

"Let me get this right," I said as I sank back down onto the love seat. "You know I'm a porn star and you're okay with that? Just to be clear, a lot of my stuff isn't like Cinemax soft-core. It's like . . . porn-porn. Like, OB-GYN-exam levels of pornographic."

Gretchen thought for a moment as Pearl plopped down into the armchair next to the fireplace and pulled her knees tight to her chest.

"Yeah," Gretchen finally said. "I mean it would have been nice to know that from the beginning, but, Bee, there's nothing bad or shameful about sex work. The only difference between you and most of Hollywood is that they sell the lie of sex and you're selling the real thing."

"This is actually kind of perfect," Pearl said, as if somewhere in the deep recesses of her subconscious she had planned for this exact scenario. "I mean, I know it's totally beyond the Hope Channel execs' comprehension levels, but *Duke the Halls*—at its core—is about sexual transactions and the disproportionate toll they take on women. So this is sort of perfect, actually. It's the exact social commentary my script needed."

Teddy tilted his head to the side like a confused puppy, and Gretchen and I shared a look. Oh, Pearl. Sweet Pearl.

"Yeah," I said very seriously. "Yeah, I really connected with that aspect of the script."

Pearl shook her finger in the air. "See, Gretch. You knew just from her headshot that she was the perfect fit."

Gretchen sat down in the other armchair, and her brow furrowed for a moment. "You know, this is probably on me for not thinking the topless headshot was a little off." She shook the thought from her head and turned to me. "Look, Bee, you need to know that Pearl and I stand with you." She looked at Teddy. "And with you too, Teddy. But just so we're clear: I don't appreciate being lied to."

"I'm sorry," he said sincerely. "And Bee and I are going to be fine, okay? You two do what you need to do."

She smiled at him, like she'd only now begun to uncover the endearing part of Teddy Ray Fletcher that I'd come to know and love over the last few years. "That's very heroic of you, but I've already spoken with the execs. They're undecided on what they're going to do with the film, but one thing is for certain: it makes the most financial sense for us to finish the movie. There are only a few days of filming left, so we're past the point of no return. It's better for them to have a finished movie on the shelf to air at midnight ten years from now than for them to pull the plug given that the last two days of filming have basically already been paid for."

Finish the movie? There was no point! "What?" I asked, stunned. "You can't be serious. They can't actually be considering releasing this thing?"

Gretchen leaned back and crossed her legs, the toe of her heavy combat boot dangling a few inches above the floor. "Bee,

I'll be honest. I'm really fucking pissed. I'm pissed at the ex-ecs for not immediately standing behind you and for making us all their damn puppets. Their whole brand is the magic of Christmas, and everyone deserves that magic. Not just white Christian people who make their kids dress as Bible characters for Halloween. So, yeah, I'm pissed that they want us to finish this thing just to shelve it for eternity, and if you say no, I'm calling this thing. Time of death: right fucking now."

I looked across the room to Teddy. I was already in violation of the morality clause of my contract. Who knew if they were even going to pay me? Or if they might even consider suing me?

I wanted to play nice with them, but I also felt reckless, like I had nothing to lose.

"It's your call, kid," he said.

I shook my head. "I don't know."

Pearl shot to her feet. "Now, wait a damn minute. You're all looking at this from the wrong angle. We're not Hope Chan-nel pawns if we finish this thing. It's the Hope Channel that's the pawn, because if we wrap this movie and by some divine intervention it's released next Christmas, then we're proving to people all over the world that sex isn't dirty or wrong and just because you're a woman who enjoys sex—and even gets paid for it—doesn't mean you can't live out your own warm and fuzzy happily ever after. The fight isn't won by giving up—oooh! I should write that down." She dropped back into her chair, like the electricity pumping through her body had been shut off and she needed to recharge.

And as much as it surprised me to say so, Pearl was right. Even if the film was never released, there wouldn't even be a chance for it to succeed if I didn't buckle down and make it through the last few days of filming.

Maybe I could never have Nolan for real, but I would never regret what we shared here in Christmas Notch, and even if I'd ruined his chance at a career comeback, I could at least finish this movie for him. Hell, maybe they could CGI someone else's face onto my head like the *Twilight* baby or something.

My chest tightened.

No. Not for him.

For *me*.

Nolan Shaw left me in the rain all those years ago outside of his tour bus when I was just a teenager. He left me again in a snowstorm on Christmas Eve. And for a final time in the midst of a media circus. But I was done apologizing for who I was. If I was going to finish *Duke the Halls*, it would be for me. It would be because I deserved to have it all. I deserved to be the purring girl on your screen whom you fantasized about at night and I deserved to be the rosy-cheeked girl in the wholesome Christmas movie whom your entire family gathered around the television to watch. I was both of those girls, and that was something the Hope Channel and the internet and even Nolan Kowalczk himself could never take away from me.

My gaze bounced from Teddy to Pearl to Gretchen. "Let's make a movie."

CHAPTER TWENTY-NINE

Nolan

Two days, three podcast seasons, and seventeen Clif bars later, I pulled up to Isaac Kelly's gate in Malibu, wired on energy drinks and needing to pee. There was a post next to the driveway with a speaker and a camera. I rolled down my window.

"Um, hi," I said to the camera, feeling stupid. Isaac (predictably) hadn't answered any of my calls on my way here, and the texts I'd sent him had gone unanswered too, so I had no idea if he was expecting me or not.

"Mr. Kelly says he hasn't ordered any pizza," came a no-nonsense voice. A security person's voice.

I looked back at the van I was driving. When I told Kallum my plan, he'd taken one look at my rickety pickup with holes in the floor—and then at the reliable Honda Civic that

I needed to leave at home for Mom and Maddie—and insisted that I take one of his Slice, Slice, Baby vans instead. Which meant that I'd driven a van with a cartoon slice of pizza (with pierced pizza ears, a blond pizza pompadour, and the tagline *Anything less than the best is a pizza felony!*) across Kansas, over the mountains, and through some desert-y bits all the way to the coast.

Ah, that glamorous former boy band life.

"Tell him the pizza's from Slice, Slice, Baby," I said. After a lengthy pause, the gate slid open to reveal a steep, winding drive that was definitely made for sports cars and not for a Dodge Caravan. But somehow I managed to creep up to the house itself and park in front of the glass-and-metal box that Isaac called home.

My former bandmate was waiting for me in front of his open door when I got there. He was wearing a white sweater and drawstring linen pants. His blond hair was tousled over his lightly suntanned forehead and his feet were bare. Even in the fading evening light, I could see the cerulean blue of his eyes, the elegantly angled planes of his cheeks and jaw.

"You look like you're shooting a photo spread for *GQ*," I said as I got out of the van.

"And you look like you drove across half the country to deliver me a pizza I don't want," Isaac said dryly. "Why are you at my house?"

"Well," I said, grabbing my duffel bag and slamming the door closed. "I'm planning on doing something unbearably melodramatic and stupid, and I need a place to stay while I do it. Which you would know if you answered your phone."

Isaac blinked at me, all long eyelashes and haunted pout. "I threw my phone in the ocean," he said finally, in a voice that implied this was a totally normal thing to do. And then he turned back toward his front door. "I guess you'd better come inside."

"I SHOULD HAVE brought pizza," I grumbled as I stared at Isaac's empty refrigerator an hour later. Despite it being one of those giant rich people fridges, there was nothing inside except for a mostly empty jar of relish and some hard-boiled eggs. And half a cantaloupe. I *hated* cantaloupe!

"You know cantaloupe is for funerals and making fruit salads look bigger, right?"

"I've already ordered us something," Isaac said from the balcony, not looking back at me. His house was one of those clifftop mansions that had an entire wall that opened onto a balcony overlooking the sea. It was a little chilly, but the suspended fireplace in the living room and the firepit on the balcony offered some warmth.

"How? You don't have a phone."

"I didn't throw my *iPad* into the ocean," Isaac said. And then he added, "Are you getting us drinks or what?"

With a last unhappy look at the fridge, I went over to the butler's pantry and made us gin and tonics—without limes, because he didn't have those either.

"I could garnish them with hard-boiled eggs, if you like," I offered as I joined him at the railing and handed him his drink. He took it without looking at me, not even reacting to the idea of egg gin.

In front of us, the Pacific was a dark, noisy thing, crashing endlessly on the beach. Around us were mountains and cliffs studded with scores of other too-expensive houses, all of them facing the ocean. It was somehow lonely here, even with other houses nearby and one of the world's busiest cities just a stone's throw away. And I had the depressing vision of Isaac spending night after night like this, staring at the dark ocean alone while he drank gin and thought moody Isaac thoughts.

"So why did you throw your phone into the ocean?" I asked, leaning against the railing. Although it was brisker out here than inside, it was still thirty degrees warmer than Kansas City, so I didn't mind so much.

"People kept calling me," Isaac said, as if that explained everything. Then he asked, "So are you really going to do this?"

"Yeah," I said. "I am."

Earlier I'd told him the entire story of my attempted career relaunch and ClosedDoors and Bianca von Honey and meeting Bee on set. How we accidentally fell into bed and I accidentally fell in love too, and then how I fucked it up.

I'd also told him the plan I'd abruptly hatched after talking to my mother—a plan that involved laying my soul bare and utilizing some unlikely allies.

"And your manager doesn't know about this interview," said Isaac.

"Nope," I replied with a grin. Maybe he could hear it in my voice because he finally turned his head enough to look at me. He gave me the same look he used to give me when I'd clam-

ber onto his tour bus bed with a bottle of Southern Comfort
and an ambitious plan for how we and Kallum should spend
the night in a new city. Like somewhere deep in his unknow-
able Isaac mind, he found me both mildly entertaining and
profoundly puzzling.

Unfortunately for past Nolan, Isaac had always looked extremely hot when he gave me that look. Honestly, it was a
little distracting even now.

"You realize that doing an interview about falling in love
with a porn star while filming a Hope Channel movie is the
opposite of the image you were trying to build by taking that
role in the first place, right?" he asked.

"Yeah," I said simply. I did realize it. But the interview was
all I had to give. I had no social capital, no friends left in the
business other than Isaac—who hardly counted as being in the
business these days, what with being a hot recluse and all.

All I had was the truth. A truth that felt as raw and bloody
as a skinned knee that needed to be kissed better.

"Do you ever think," I said, looking down at the glass cradled in my hands, "that maybe that's what went wrong the
first time? Letting the image mean so much?"

There was a pause, filled up by the suck and roar of the
Pacific.

"Yes."

"We cared more about our given identities than ourselves,"
I went on, my chest hurting for us INK boys then and also us
INK boys now. "Defending a brand that was at best a slice of
us and at worst a shell."

"We did what we were told," said Isaac. "Because it worked out often enough that there was never a reason to question it."

He took a drink, looking at the ocean again after he finished. I wondered if he was thinking of Brooklyn.

"If I'm going to do this being famous thing again, then I think I should do it differently this time around," I said. "I don't think that everyone deserves parts of myself that I don't want to give, but I deserve for the parts of myself that I do choose to give to be honest ones, you know? I just want to be *me*—not the manufactured version of a bad boy or a reformed bad boy. Just me. Nolan. Nolan Shaw, who is in love with Bee Hobbes, full stop."

Isaac looked down at his glass again. "You know, Brooklyn and I were never out of the spotlight. Not for a moment. And there were times when it felt so hard I could scream. But no matter how hard it was"—he dragged in a long breath—"it was never harder than being without her."

I slid along the railing and pressed my shoulder against his. He allowed it, although I could feel the struggle inside him to stay still, as if he wanted to shrink away. I wondered if he'd touched anyone, even a friend or family member, since Brooklyn's funeral.

"I'm sorry," I told him. "Brooklyn was amazing."

"Yes," he said, his voice brittle and splintered, like shards of a glass dropped on the floor. "She was."

A few minutes passed like this, our shoulders warm against each other's and the waves rushing in. Then Isaac drained his drink and pushed away from the railing.

"You're doing the right thing, Nolan," he said. "Even if you fail miserably and look like a giant asshole afterward, at least you'll know that you didn't waste a single second letting her know that you loved her."

And with that, he walked back inside the house, leaving me alone with the inky sky and the restless sea.

CHAPTER THIRTY

Bee

Duke the Halls wrapped on the twenty-ninth of December around eleven at night, and no more than seven hours later, I was on a flight home with my moms to spend New Year's Eve in Texas with them.

Diving back into the movie had been a good insulation from the crushing heartbreak I felt every time I thought of Nolan. The crew had been mostly supportive, especially the handful of people who, like me, were also dirty, porn-making people. But even a lot of the folks hired by the Hope Channel seemed to be unbothered. Of course, there were a few, like Maggie from craft services, who couldn't manage to make eye contact with me. But Gretchen and Pearl went out of their way to make me feel as comfortable as possible. If this single movie was my only experience with mainstream entertainment, then I had no regrets. (Other than the whole hiding-my-true-identity thing.)

Sunny had been my knight in shining armor through it all, never leaving my side. And each night when I came back to the hotel, my moms were there waiting for me so that I was never fully alone beyond the hours I spent in my bed, staring at the ceiling until exhaustion took hold.

Now, on New Year's Eve, I sat alone in my childhood bedroom with my laptop balanced on my knees, FaceTiming with Sunny as she sorted through weeks' worth of our junk mail back at our place in Los Angeles.

"Ooooh, but maybe we should save this one," she said, holding up a coupon from the Greek place around the corner.

I nodded. "Put it in the fridge."

She pointed the coupon at me, then set it off to the side. "Affirmative." We kept coupons for our favorite delivery places *in* the fridge and not on it, which we discovered was the only way to guarantee we'd use them. A fridge full of boring ingredients versus the possibility of takeout: it was no contest.

"Did you see the link I sent you earlier?" she asked.

Sunny had also been keeping a dutiful eye on the internet for me, and it seemed that after the initial shock wore off and the internet had a moment to digest the reality of a sex worker cast in a Hope Channel movie, people had something to say. And so, the think pieces started rolling in, and my text thread with Sunny had turned into a constant stream of essay links— all of which she'd vetted in advance.

What Bianca von Honey and the Hope Channel Can Teach Us About Denying Women as Sexual Beings

A Porn Star, a Christmas Movie, and What We All Really Want for the Holidays

Some Twitter Users Put on the Naughty List for Trollish, Fatphobic Behavior

Why Fat Women Still Can't Have Their Cake and Eat It Too

All I Want for Christmas Is "Duke the Halls"

The Scariest Thing About Sex Work Is How We Treat Sex Workers

Bianca von Honey: What We Know and Why You Should Be Her Biggest Fan

I'd read the headlines. That was as much as I could manage to do. I'd been so easily affected by all the immediate negativity that I didn't trust myself enough not to get caught up in the—what I was sure to be short-lived—positivity. If I'd learned anything from the last few days, it was that living and dying by the court of public opinion was not sustainable.

I smiled. "Some of them look pretty good."

"You don't have to read them. But I just want you to know, it's not all bad. In fact, a lot of it is really good."

I bit down on the corner of my lip. "I did notice a jump in subscribers."

"Get that money, honey."

"Bee?" Mom called from outside my bedroom door. "We're going to order pizza and pop some champagne. Come on down if you want any say in what kind of toppings we get. Mama Pam's on a real mushroom kick."

"Be right down!" I called over my shoulder. "I better go," I said to Sunny, "but hey, I think I'll probably catch a flight to L.A. in a few days."

"Okay, good, because we have some serious roommate discussions to have," she said as she reached over her laptop and held up a huge black cat in front of the camera. The cat was not amused. "Um, please don't be mad."

My eyes turned into saucers. "Is that a cat in our house? In our house that we rent that has a no-pets policy?"

She held him in her arms like a baby, and remarkably, he allowed it. "I got so lonely without you," she said with her lips in a frown. "I hired a cat sitter while I was in Vermont. His name is Mr. Tumnus and he loves cheese puffs."

"Okay, well, welcome to the family, Mr. Tumnus." We'd have to hide him from our landlord, but I wasn't about to orphan our firstborn child-cat.

Sunny beamed. "Mr. Tumnus! Did you hear that! Daddy Bee loves you!"

"All right, all right, I better go," I told her.

"Oh, Bee, uh, maybe while you're home, it might be a good time to redecorate." She pointed at the wall behind me.

I didn't have to turn around to know she was talking about the INK shrine that teenage Bee had carefully curated. I couldn't tell her that I didn't want to take it all down and that falling asleep to Nolan's face was the best sleep I'd had in days. "I know, I know," I finally said. "Okay, I'll call you later. Happy New Year to you and Mr. Tumnus."

I MADE IT downstairs just in time to beg Mom to order half a pizza with pineapple and ham.

After pulling out the stepladder, I helped Mama Pam find the champagne flutes from their wedding. When I was a teenager, they'd tracked down a third glass from the same stemware collection, so I could join them in their midnight toast.

From the living room, I could hear Mom cursing at the television.

"She's trying to get some video on her phone to play on the television," Mama Pam explained.

"You okay in there?" I asked as I stepped down and walked over to Mom.

She wore a paper top hat with HAPPY NEW YEAR in glittering gold letters.

"Here," she said as she handed me a feather headband. "I'm just trying to get this to—"

And then I heard three familiar words as her phone and the television synced. "Well, well, well."

My head swiveled to the television, and I had to fight every instinct in my body to not rip the remote out of Mom's hand and get Dominic Diamond off the screen.

But then I saw him. Nolan. *My Nolan*, sitting in a blank,

totally white studio opposite Dominic. He wore jeans and boots—the kind you worked in—and he had faint circles under his eyes. But his posture wasn't tense. Nothing about him felt defensive.

I sank down into Mom's armchair, unable to tear myself away from the sight of him.

"I'm here with Nolan Shaw of INK and, most recently, *Duke the Halls*." Dominic turned to face him. "Now this is quite the New Year's Eve treat."

Nolan nodded. "They say to end how you intend to begin and to begin as you mean to go on . . . so here I am."

"The boys of INK have really found themselves in the news quite a bit this year: Isaac going all in on his reclusion after Brooklyn's tragic death. Kallum's sex tape. And now you with your new costar and her web of lies."

My stomach clenched at Dominic's mention of me. What was Nolan even doing? How could this possibly end well?

"Make no mistake. Bee never lied about who she was. She planned to do *Duke the Halls* under her real name whereas all of her adult content had been under a stage name. Actors change their names or go by different names all the time. Hell, Shaw isn't even my real last name."

"So you're officially condoning Ms. Hobbes and her ties to pornography?"

My heart felt like it was pounding in my throat.

Nolan sat up straight. "I'm coming out in support of Bee Hobbes and Bianca von Honey and sex workers everywhere." He shook his head, and I could see him trying to rein it in. To stay calm. "Our whole job is to sell the human experience.

Actors, musicians, artists of any kind. But that's not what people really want, is it? They want the idea of humanity, but they don't want the real thing. That would be too messy, too complicated. And, Dominic, you're part of the problem."

"Well, I think we might be getting a little off—"

"No," Nolan said sternly. "You said you wanted this interview, so here it is. You spent years of your life dissecting and picking apart every move I made. Isaac and Kallum too. And even with Bee, you framed that narrative of her. You made her out to be deceptive and manipulative when all she was doing—all any of us are doing—is trying to get by and maybe, just maybe, chase that spark of a dream that got us into this business to begin with."

For the first time since ever, Dominic Diamond was silent.

I wiped at my cheek with the back of my hand, unable to catch all the spilling tears. I felt Nolan's words at the very core of my being. Meeting and falling for him had been the ride of a lifetime, but the thing that brought me to Vermont to begin with was my dream. The dream that I could have it all. That I could be the love interest in a sugary, sweet story and I could also be the object of desire. And Nolan made me realize I could be both of those things and more. I didn't always have to be either-or.

Despite all the pain and hurt I'd weathered over the last few days, I knew that Nolan was stuck in an impossible situation too. And if nothing else ever came of us, I could at least take comfort in knowing that I forgave him, and that, in the end, he'd stood by me.

"Dominic," Nolan said, "I spent all those years in INK

thinking I had to give my fans and the media every part of myself. That the only way to be true and worthy of the attention and adoration was to bare my soul. But even then, that was only a very specific, curated version of myself. If this second shot at my career actually pans out, then I can say I know better now. I don't have to give everything until there's nothing left of me, and I don't have to fit into this very narrow label of who a studio or a manager thinks I ought to be. And I can promise that what I do share will be honest, and that honesty starts now."

"Does it really?" Dominic asked, finally recovered from Nolan's rebuke.

Nolan gripped the arms of his chair and turned to face the camera directly. "I love you, Bee Hobbes. I love you in front of the whole world."

His words knocked the wind right out of me.

Nolan Shaw loved me.

And I loved him too.

This was the very thing I needed, and it was the one thing I thought he would never be able to give me. My eyes began to water all over again as the weight of what he'd just done hit me.

The doorbell rang.

"It must be the pizza," I faintly heard one of my moms say.

"Well, well, well," Dominic said, but I couldn't comprehend anything else. My brain was full of what and how and all the things this could mean for Nolan. Steph would probably drop him. And then he'd be back to barely scraping by. What about his mom and—

"Bee!" Mom said for what didn't sound like the first time. "Bee, it's for you."

I stood, my whole body feeling robotic as both my moms cleared a path for me to the door, where the porch was empty.

I looked to Mama Pam, who squeezed my fingers and nodded.

I stepped outside into the crisp and starry Texas night as Nolan Kowalczk stood there in my driveway in front of a—

"Is that a pizza delivery van?" I asked.

With a snort and a giggle, my moms shut the door behind me.

He tapped the hood of the van with a smile. "Indeed it is. She and I have become quite close over the last four days during our adventure out West."

"Four da—did you drive from Kansas to California to Texas?"

He sauntered toward me. "Yeah, it's my new tour schedule. Not as global as they used to be, but I made sure to hit all the highlights. By the way, did you know that Texas is mostly flat, endless nothing?"

"That's rich coming from the guy from Kansas. We have windmills," I said, helplessly taking a step closer. "And cows."

"And second-tier barbeque."

My mouth opened to fight the fake news coming out of his mouth, and I could already so easily feel us slipping back into how it had been between us. "Did you mean it?" The tears were still wet on my cheeks.

"I wouldn't have driven to L.A. to sit down with Dominic Diamond, whose mere existence makes me want to stick my face in a blender, if I didn't mean it." He took my hands, his fingers sliding up my wrists.

I looked up at him, his lips just a breath from mine. "I love you too, Nolan. I love you in the dark. I love you in the light. I love you everywhere."

He tilted his head up and yelled with all his might. "I love you, Bee Hobbes! I love you loud enough for the world to hear!" And then he turned his face down to me, nuzzling his nose against mine. "I love you so much that when you're not near me, I feel like I'm missing an actual organ," he whispered.

"That sounds like a medical emergency." My voice was breathy and fine as our lips brushed.

"I think the only thing that might save me now is the boob defibrillator."

"Doctor, I think we're losing—"

He crushed his lips to mine, his tongue sliding into my mouth, like he was starving for me. And I felt it too as our bodies clicked together in a familiar way that could only be described as *home*.

We devoured each other there in my moms' driveway until a car pulled up behind us. Nolan held me close as I leaned against his chest.

A lanky kid covered in freckles stepped out of a tiny green car. "Anybody order some pizza?"

CHAPTER THIRTY-ONE

Nolan

Steph (9:01 PM): Call me.

Steph (9:07 PM): Nolan Shaw!!! Call me right now!

Steph (9:08 PM): NOLAN

Steph (9:08 PM): FUCK

Steph (9:08 PM): fuck

Steph (10:03 PM): I'm taking a pill, and I'm calling you in the morning. You'd better pick up, or I swear to God.

I glanced at the notifications on my phone as I walked down the hallway with Bee. I'd known Steph would be apoplectic about the interview, and rightfully so. She was probably going to fire me. She was definitely going to yell at me. But I didn't feel any fear or anxiety as I darkened the phone and watched Bee open the door to her room.

I was exactly where I was supposed to be right now.

"Mama Pam's melatonin should have kicked in by now," Bee whispered as we slipped into her dark bedroom and closed the door.

After ringing in the New Year with us, Bee's moms had promptly turned into pumpkins and disappeared into their bedroom, and then I'd taken a quick shower to wash off the feeling of sitting in a van for two days. Which meant that this was the first time we'd been alone since that night in the church when I'd found her wearing that incredible wedding dress.

Thinking of it now had me straining underneath the towel wrapped around my waist, and Bee managed to turn her laugh into a semiquiet snort when I yanked her into a hug and she felt my erection against her belly.

"You can't be hard already," she whispered.

I walked her backward to her bed, tugging off the towel as she sat down. "It's not my fault," I told her, pulling at the slouchy, off-the-shoulder sweater she was wearing until she was in nothing but pajama shorts and a cute pink bra. "I haven't had time to catch up on my favorite ClosedDoors account lately."

"It's just been recycling old content anyway," she said, working greedy hands up my naked thighs. "For the holidays. But perhaps I could interest you in a private session?"

I climbed onto the bed on my knees, straddling her lap. Her hands slid around my hips and then I felt a curious fingertip press against the sensitive flesh between my cheeks. With a groan, I spread my knees farther apart and nosed her sweet-smelling hair while I unhooked the clasps of her bra.

"Keep doing that and I'm not going to last long enough for a private session," I said as she toyed with my entrance, probing and pushing. I wanted her to finger me there so badly, but I was already having to clench my stomach to keep from erupting as it was.

"We might have to arrange a standing appointment," she said. "If you recall, I have a suitcase of sex things we haven't even touched."

I took off her bra and then pushed her back on the bed so I could pull off her pajama shorts and panties. Once she was naked too, I crawled over her and slanted my lips over hers, licking deep into her mouth until she was arching up into me. I reached down and pushed my hand between her legs, finding her slick and warm.

"I can't believe you had the nerve to tease me about being ready to go when you're this wet," I said, moving my mouth to nibble on her neck.

"Oh, you like it," she shot back, her hand curling around my aching length and squeezing. "There's condoms in my purse."

"None in your end table?"

"This is my childhood bedroom, Nolan. Believe it or not, I don't usually bring people all the way back here to Texas to bump uglies."

I found a condom in the small inner pocket of her purse and

took a minute to look around her room, wanting to take in everything about her, details of all the versions of her that had led to the perfection currently splayed across her bed in a feast of curves and tousled hair.

"Nolan Kowalczk," she said impatiently. "You'll have time to look at my old yearbooks and shit later—"

"Are those posters of me?" I asked as I flicked on the dresser lamp to get a better look. Sure enough, there were INK posters going all the way up the wall and even onto the ceiling. My own face stared back at me from at least thirty different posters, magazine cutouts, and several fan-art prints. Some of them included Isaac and Kallum, but many of them were just me. In cringy clothes and even cringier poses.

But despite the cringiness, I couldn't help the smug swell of pride in my chest. Bee had an entire room covered in me! It was hard not to strut a little. "You still have all these on your walls?"

"Some of them are really high up," she sniffed. "I didn't want to get a ladder out. Are you coming back here or what?"

I gave her my cockiest smirk as I sauntered back to the bed. "You know what I think," I purred, tossing the condom on the duvet and kneeling between her legs. "I think that you liked looking at me. Even when you were mad at me."

She scoffed. "More like I enjoyed looking at your embarrassing clothing choices and thinking about my own fashion superiority."

"Hmm," I said. "Well, in that case, I should probably turn off the light while I go down on you, because I know you'd hate to be looking up at these posters while I've got my tongue in your pussy. It would be a real shame if you finally got to have all your teenage fantasies come true."

She gave me the fierce glare of someone who knew their bluff had been called. "You better not turn off that lamp."

"That's what I thought," I said, and then settled on my stomach between her legs, grinning up at her with my hair flopping over my forehead, mimicking the expression of the poster tacked directly above my head.

"Stop it." She laughed. "You're going to kill me."

"Shh, you don't want your mothers to hear, do you? We don't want them to know that my tour bus broke down outside and you're giving me a place to stay for the night."

"You're ridiculous." She laughed again, but her laugh broke into a groan the moment I ran my tongue up her seam. "But keep going."

"And how will I ever repay your generosity?" I murmured as I searched out her clit and gave it a lingering suck. "I have an idea, but you can't tell Isaac and Kallum. They'll want to join in, and I want you all to myself."

There was no laughing after that. Just her excited little gasps and her fingers tight in my hair and the eventual taste of her coming against my mouth while thirty terribly dressed versions of myself looked on.

"WILL YOUR MOMS mind that we spent the night fucking in your old bedroom?" I asked a few hours—and a few condoms— later. We were lying on top of the duvet because we were too sweaty to be under a blanket, and Bee had her head on my chest, drawing idle circles on my stomach as she answered.

"Nah, they've always been pretty open about that kind of thing. They only care if it disrupts their sleep and therefore their pre-Texas-sunshine morning walk. Also, I mean, they know what I do for a living, so I think some bedroom sex probably ranks pretty low on what would shock them."

"Good. I don't want them to think I corrupted you."

"I think we're probably at equal levels of corruption capability," she murmured. "After all, I've never had an orgy on a circus train before."

"*That* is overrated. Half the people were trainsick and had to take Dramamine partway through, so the beds got filled up with people taking naps. And fucking on train carpet is a recipe for some vicious rug burn." My knees had been raw for weeks.

"Nolan," Bee said after a long pause, her finger getting slower and more deliberate as it drew its circles, "after this . . . do you mind if I continue with ClosedDoors? I don't know what's next, but it might include continuing to do porn with other people."

I thought about it for a moment. Not because I hadn't thought about it before, but because she deserved for me to be utterly certain of the answer. "I don't mind," I told her firmly. "In fact, I wouldn't want you to quit solely because of me. I want you to do what makes you happy, and I know it's complicated, but I'm not bothered by the idea of you having sex with other people."

"Really?"

"For a moment, I thought I might mind," I admitted, "because I had some ambivalent feelings knowing you were with someone else in Christmas Notch. But I grew up and got over it."

She propped herself up on an elbow and looked at me, a line etched between her eyebrows. "With someone else in Christmas Notch?"

I flopped my head back, feeling like a jackass. "You know, in one of your ClosedDoors posts. I could see his shadow, and—"

"Ohhhh," she said, and then playfully twisted my nipple.

"Ow!"

"It was Angel, you cement-head. He took the picture for me because he drunkenly came into my room after a night out with Luca, and I've been in this game too long not to shamelessly solicit a friend's help for pictures when I have the chance."

I really did feel like a cement-head. "Ah, shit."

She twisted my nipple again. Gentler this time. "Now what were you saying?"

I met her eyes, giving her a rueful smile. "I was saying that I realized I wasn't jealous because you might be having sex with someone else, but because you might be *close* with someone else. I don't feel possessive of your body, Bee, or at least, not in a way that precludes you from doing your job. But I do feel possessive of your heart, I guess. I want to have it. I want to keep it. I want you to carry it around just for me while I carry mine around just for you." I took a breath and then decided to go for it. "And if you ever decide you want to wear a wedding dress again, I want it to be for us. For real. You know. If you want that too."

She sucked in a breath, her eyes glassy. "Okay," she breathed after a minute.

"Yeah?"

A nod with a quivering chin. "Yeah. I want all that. For our hearts to be each other's. And maybe the wedding dress thing too. Eventually."

My chest felt like it was ready to crack wide open and spill sunshine everywhere. "Good," I said, my voice hoarse.

"And I honestly don't know what I'm going to do about performing yet," she said. "For a while, I felt like I would never do something as Bee Hobbes again after this, because it was so hard and scary trying something new and then being exposed like that. But I think that maybe I was trying to protect myself. Which is what I did the first time around with acting, you know. I pretended I didn't want it so that it wouldn't hurt when it didn't want me back. And I don't want to do that again."

"So there might be more Hope Channel movies on the horizon?"

There was a laugh that she stifled by pressing her face against my chest. "Oh yes, I can really imagine the Hope Channel wanting me back. Wholesome holiday fun for the whole horny family!"

"You know what I mean," I said as she wedged her chin on my chest and looked back up at me. "Will you try again? Try for more of whatever you wanted when you decided to do *Duke the Halls*?"

She shrugged as best she could while half draped on my chest. "I don't know. But I'm going to give myself the chance to figure it out. And as much as I loved performing in porn, I think I'm ready to take a break while I decide what to do." She seemed to think about it for a moment. "Maybe even a permanent break, because there's so much else I feel ready to try right now. I don't want my exit from this industry to turn into some kind of commentary on rehabilitating porn stars or something. But I also know that it's the kind of career that isn't forever—at least for me. There's no perfect answer to how and when to move on." She sighed, her breath tickling my neck. "What about you?"

"Me? Well, my pornography career is still in its early days, but it's quite promising, I think—"

She slapped my chest. "You asshole. You know what I mean. What if Steph drops you as a client after your interview tonight? What if you're not able to get any more gigs as the wholesome version of Nolan Shaw and you can't support your family?"

I tugged Bee closer and drew up the duvet around us since we were finally starting to cool down. "I guess I also don't know," I said. "But I've decided that it's okay not to know right now. There'd be no guarantee that everything would work out even if I did all the things exactly as Steph wants me to. So why not at least try to do the right thing? And if everything does crash and burn, then I know how to survive it, and so does Mom and so does Maddie. We've been through a lot, and so we know we'll be okay."

"I know you'll be okay too," Bee said. She snuggled against me, using my shoulder as a pillow. "Besides, I'll be around to help any way I can."

"Good."

"You'd make a killing on ClosedDoors, by the way," she said.

"Yeah, but I'd end up spending it all on this other Closed-Doors creator. I hear she's offering private sessions, and I have no self-control when it comes to her."

"You should unsubscribe from that kind of temptation."

"But I'm her number one fan."

Bee yawned a big yawn and nuzzled her face into my chest. "That's so funny because I think she used to be yours."

"Used to be!"

"She might be won back over if you sang her to sleep. Maybe a nice Christmas song? From the *Merry INKmas* album?"

"You drive a hard bargain." I pouted but relented and kissed her forehead.

As Bee slowly drowsed against my chest, her hair everywhere and her legs tangled with mine, I sang "All BeClaus of You" as softly as I could, crooning the cheesy lyrics until she fell asleep. And when she woke up, I'd be right here with her, ready to face all our unknowns together.

Ready to make her every Christmas wish—and beyond—come true.

EPILOGUE

Teddy Ray Fletcher

Seven months later

"The difference is the sauce," Nolan Shaw was explaining to a stoned-looking Tall Ron. "It adds complexity to the flavor, see? Now if you try Bee's brisket, you'll see it's nothing but dry cow slices—"

"I brought fruit salad," Teddy interrupted awkwardly, cradling a big bowl between his hands. When Bee had invited him to her and Nolan's housewarming/Fourth of July party—which also was some sort of Nolan v. Bee barbeque deathmatch—he'd almost said no. Partly because he was scared of seeing Steph D'Arezzo in person again and acting like a buffoon, but mostly because Bee said he had to bring food and Teddy didn't know how to cook.

"I made it," added Angel.

"No cantaloupe!" Nolan exclaimed after examining the salad. "Welcome, welcome. You can put it on the table over there."

Teddy noticed his son hesitate a moment before he stepped out onto the patio of Bee and Nolan's new place, like he was checking to make sure the coast was clear. Weird.

Teddy turned back to Nolan after Angel ventured out to the table. "Congratulations, by the way. On the *Boy Band Bootcamp* thing." Just last week, *Deadline* had announced that Nolan was one of the judges for the *Boy Band Bootcamp* reboot, along with a cranky record producer and deeply eccentric pop starlet from the nineties. It was the kind of gig that meant a steady paycheck—and if Nolan played his cards right and the show struck the right chord, a steady paycheck for several years. Enough years that he and Bee could probably upgrade from this cutesy Los Feliz villa to someplace nicer. Like Bel Air.

Now there was a classy neighborhood.

"Really, I owe you all the thanks," Nolan said, leaving Tall Ron to his plate of meat and guiding Teddy out to the patio, where a bright blue pool shined like a cartoon diamond and a crowd of people milled around it, eating and drinking and listening to a mix of old INK albums and Christmas music. "If it hadn't been for *Duke the Halls* and the giant shitstorm that followed, none of this would have happened."

Teddy Ray Fletcher had been through a lot of shitstorms in his life. His divorce, the time he accidentally joined a cult, a very literal storm of shit on a porn set once that had resulted in the early retirement of one performer (and the destruction of an innocent rug from Wayfair dot com). But never before *Duke the Halls* had he been through a shitstorm that had a *happy* ending.

Except that was exactly what had happened.

After Teddy and Bee were exposed and after the predicted outcry, something strange started. People started . . . *defending* them. Or defending Bee at least, claiming that the outcry had more to do with slut-shaming and fat-shaming than it did with any real concern that the Hope Channel was going to serve up Carolina Reaper–level fare to viewers expecting mild green chilies.

And then something even stranger happened: people started acting excited for the movie. Excited! For their cheaply made movie! There were articles about it, social media hype about it, even something called cosplays about it—which Angel and Astrid had assured Teddy was a very good sign. People couldn't wait to see the Hope Channel film that had made the actors fall in love with each other, and that the actors were a porn star and a pop star only added fuel to the fire. Subscriptions to Hopeflix had skyrocketed, and the Hope Channel had seen an unprecedented influx of sponsors clamoring for ad space ahead of the television premiere a month after its streaming debut.

Basically, Bianca von Honey was good for business, and while the Hope Channel wasn't about to start selling branded enemas or anything, they loved money as much as the next media conglomerate. And they were smart enough to realize that they'd accidentally fallen into a gold mine. They'd begun heavily promoting the movie, had paraded Bee and Nolan everywhere, and already commissioned and announced a sequel—*Duke the Halls 2: A Ducal Wedding*.

Nolan had nabbed the *Boy Band Bootcamp* reboot, and Bee had been cast as the lead in a series called *Nun of Your Business*, a show about a former nun who becomes the personal assistant to her drag queen neighbor. Even though she'd pulled back from doing porn with other people and only sporadically posted photos on ClosedDoors these days, Bee's experience in sex work also made her a very in-demand guest on talk shows, podcasts, and prime-time news slots, and she'd even landed a regular column with some big, smarty-pants website, the kind Teddy's kids were always sending him links from.

And to cap it all off, the Hope Channel was now developing a new content arm tailored for the viewers clamoring for *Duke the Halls*. The people Teddy hadn't thought existed when he'd started this project—people who liked cheerful holiday shit *and* unabashed raunch—were now both clearly visible and clearly ready to spend their money. And the Hope Channel was ready to take it, even if doing so meant adding some spice to their brand.

So Teddy was now contracted to produce the first-ever *Hope After Dark* movie—not that he had a script yet or an idea of who should direct it. Maybe Pearl and Gretchen would be available again . . .

"I'm glad it all worked out," Teddy said to Nolan, and he meant it. Not just for himself and his lowered blood pressure whenever Angel's tuition bills landed in his inbox, but also for

Nolan and Bee and Gretchen and Pearl and for everyone else involved with the movie.

"Me too," Nolan said, huffing out a breath as he scanned the patio. He must have found what he was looking for; his entire face lit up and he looked like he'd just unwrapped a present he'd been waiting for all year. Teddy followed his gaze and saw that Nolan was looking at Bee herself, dressed in a white peasant shirt and jeans, her septum piercing back where it belonged and winking in the sun. She was talking to an older woman and a teenager whom Teddy didn't recognize. Just beyond them, both Bee's mothers stood with Sunny, huddled around her phone as she likely force-fed them videos of her cat, Mr. Tumnus, whom she'd gotten in the habit of bringing on set with her. Sunny had also dubbed Teddy the godfather, a role he had yet to accept, though he had been wrangled into cat-sitting two and a half times.

"I should go make sure everything's okay with the party," Nolan said in the dreamy voice of the newly besotted and wandered over to Bee without even saying a proper goodbye to Teddy.

Ah, young love. Teddy remembered it well, may it rest in peace. At least he had the two best kids in the world to remember it by.

One of those kids came up to him now, a defeated look on his face. "I should have put cantaloupe in the fruit salad," Angel said. "It's gone already."

"Isn't that better than taking home a bowl of soggy fruit?" Teddy asked.

"I guess. Oh, I didn't know Nolan's mom was here," Angel

said, looking over at where Nolan was currently twining his fingers through Bee's and pulling her hand up for a kiss. The older woman was looking on fondly while the teenager made a gagging face. "And that must be his sister. She's starting at Pepperdine this fall."

"How do you know all this?" Teddy asked, genuinely confused.

"I pay attention, Dad. Plus Bee keeps me up to date on everything. Like that Nolan's mom decided she wanted to move out here too, so she's living in the casita behind the pool and is starting a custom wreath-making business. And that Kallum Lieberman now has a rabid sex tape fandom. And that Isaac Kelly won't be here today because he's too sad and broody. And that—*shit.*"

Teddy glanced over at his son, who was now casting desperate glances around the backyard, as if looking for an exit. When Teddy looked around, he didn't see anything, except Luca the costume designer standing in the doorway leading to the patio from the kitchen, slowly putting on his sunglasses and plainly having some kind of main-character moment for himself. Which was standard Luca behavior.

But when Teddy looked back to Angel to ask his son what was wrong, Angel was gone. Teddy thought he caught a glimpse of a thrifted cardigan and cuffed jeans disappearing around a corner but couldn't be sure.

Oh well.

Angel wouldn't Uber home without the fruit salad bowl. He (rightly) believed that Teddy didn't care enough for vintage tableware to take proper care of it and had appointed himself the guardian of all Fletcher serving bowls and platters, candy dishes, taco holders, et cetera.

"So you got roped into this too," came a sharp voice from behind him. Teddy wheeled around to see someone he hadn't spoken to since the day after Christmas.

Steph D'Arezzo had her eyes narrowed as she scanned the backyard. She held a plastic clamshell of grocery-store cookies in one hand, and she wore a tailored pantsuit that made Teddy suck in a breath. It was a mystery to him how Steph's pantsuits could make him weak in the knees when he'd spent the last twenty years watching beautiful people smash, but there it was.

"Hi," Teddy said faintly as Steph deposited the cookies on the seat of a lawn chair with the wary expression of someone releasing a spider they'd captured.

"Let's not play coy," Steph said. "I'm here for you."

Teddy wasn't sure he'd heard correctly. "You are?"

"Well, let's say you're fifty percent of the reason. I had a meeting nearby about my new client, Kallum, and I wasn't ready to fight the traffic to get back downtown yet."

"Kallum? The sex tape guy?" Now Teddy was sure he was hearing things. Steph was famous for turning careers around, and all Kallum had to his name right now was an admittedly impressive sex tape and a regional pizza chain, which was hardly the stuff of a lucrative celebrity career.

"Turns out," Steph said with a sniff, "that there's some money to be made with scandalous celebrities. So I'm now taking on clients who are a little more"—she waved a hand—"sticky."

"Literally in the case of Kallum Lieberman," Teddy said,

but he did so with admiration. Kallum's stickiness was some of the best Teddy had ever seen. "You know, if he ever wants to license that sex tape . . ."

Steph gave him a shrewd look. "I'll talk to him about it. And on that note, if you're on the lookout for more *Hope After Dark* talent, I would be happy to take your call."

Hmm. Teddy hadn't thought about Kallum for his new venture, but it made a certain kind of sense. Another INK member might fuel the fire Nolan had started with *Duke the Halls.* "I haven't really settled on a casting direction for the new movie yet, but that's good to know," he said.

"Well, you better settle soon," Steph told him. "Otherwise the Hope Channel is going to have you cast Winnie Baker or some shit."

They both laughed at that.

"So . . ." Teddy started hopefully. "You mentioned you were here for me? At least fifty percent here for me?"

"Oh yes," Steph replied in a brisk tone. "I have thirty minutes before I have a call. Do you want to have sex?"

Teddy blinked.

"Everyone's outside, and frankly, after all this time bonking on your dime, I think Bee owes you the use of a guest bedroom for half an hour."

"Uh. Yes?"

"Perfect," Steph said, and grabbed his hand to yank him inside.

And the last thing Teddy Ray Fletcher saw before they disappeared through the doorway was Bee giving Teddy a knowing grin while Nolan pulled her into his chest. A bottle rocket streaked into the sky above them, raining down sparks barely visible in the sunlight save for their glitter.

For a moment, it looked like it was snowing in July. Like they were two lovers set inside the sunniest snow globe known to man.

Then the sparks fizzled and faded and the moment was gone. They were just Bee and Nolan in their new backyard, arguing over barbeque and smiling into the bright future waiting for them both, together. Waving back at Bee, Teddy followed Steph inside the empty house.

He thanked God for rogue wooden tusks the entire way.

Acknowledgments

A Merry Little Meet Cute was conceived in the midst of a pie-infused, deadline-driven fever dream, and like many pie-infused fever dreams before it, our idea wouldn't be an actual honest-to-goodness thing without the generosity, expertise, and patience of an entire movie cast's worth of people!

Firstly, we owe a huge debt of gratitude to May Chen, our awesomesauce editor, for taking a chance on us and our un-apologetically raunchy take on a wholesome holiday tradition! Your keen eye for story, pacing, and character was exactly what our wild Christmas Notch fam needed, and we couldn't have asked for a better champion for Bee and Nolan! And thank you to our entire team at Avon: Jeanie Lee, Hope Breeman, Allie Roche, and Alivia Lopez for shepherding the book from its incipient stages to a finished book; DJ DeSmyter, Julie Paulauski, Kelly Rudolph, and Jennifer Hart for spreading the Christmas Notch word; and Erika Tsang and Liate Stehlik for welcoming us into the Avon family with open arms!

Additionally, we are so incredibly grateful to our cover illustrator, Farjana Yasmin, and art director, Jeanne Reina, for gifting us with the world's best cover. (And also with the coolest Christmas trees of all time!) We also owe Diahann Sturge a huge thank-you for our amazing map and for the gorgeous pages inside the book. Thank you to Caitlin Garing and Abigail Nover for creating the fantastic audio version of *A Merry Little Meet Cute*, and a huge thank-you to Joy Nash and Sebastian York for narrating our new favorite audiobook.

Thank you to our doughty agent, John Cusick, for helping us at every stage (and also for not blinking when we told you what we were working on). And thank you to the entire team at Folio Literary Management for your unwavering support! We'd also like to thank Debbie Deuble-Hill for her insight and enthusiasm when it comes to everything movies, romance, and Olympics.

We also owe a big debt of hugs and love to everyone who helped us take the cutest—and maybe silliest—coauthor pictures of all time: Danielle Nicole of Danielle Nicole Portraits, our incomparable photographer; Ash Meredith, our makeup artist, human wind machine, and photoshoot DJ; and Jessica Weckherlin Boyk, who made sure we were coiffed for camera-ready perfection.

Also, this book—and basically all our work in general—wouldn't be possible without our found family of fellow writers and friends! Thank you to Natalie C. Parker, Tess Gratton, Adib

Khorram, and Julian Winters for listening to us chatter and spitball about this book, and a very Balsam Hill-y thank-you to Nisha Sharma, our unofficial Christmas movie librarian, who shared with us her accumulated holiday-movie wisdom (and spreadsheets)! Thank you to Nana Malone, Kenya Goree-Bell, Kennedy Ryan, C. G. Burnette, Jean Siska, Skye Warren, Kayti McGee, Kyla Linde, Adriana Herrera, Joanna Shupe, Eva Leigh, Nicola Davidson, Megan Bannen, Rebecca Coffindaffer, Gretchen Schreiber, John Stickney, Hayley Harris, Deanna Green, Luke Brewer, Jasmine Guillory, Kristin Treviño, Alessandra Balzer, the Pearce and Trevino families, and any other friend who's given us encouragement and virtual and nonvirtual hugs while we worked on this.

Thank you to our dear friend Paul Samples, who helped us create the first iteration of our Christmas Notch map that served as a much-needed guide during the drafting process. We'd also like to thank our book-ly den mothers, Ashley Lindemann, Serena McDonald, Candi Kane, Melissa Gaston, and Lauren Brewer, for fiercely protecting our writing space!

We would also like to take a moment to thank our furry companions, who have yet to understand that we have jobs outside of feeding them, cuddling, and catering to their every whim. Dexter (RIP, sweet prince), Opie, Rufus, Bear, and Max—it's too bad none of you can read. (Though we have it on good authority that books make great chew toys.)

And finally, our nearest and dearest, who cheerfully keep the home fires burning while we are off concocting raunchy little tales! Ian Pearce and Gail and Bob Murphy, and Josh, Noah, and Teagan Taylor, thank you for being funny, supportive, and wonderful. And thank you for letting us take our unscheduled detour in Christmas Notch . . . Turns out the real meaning of Christmas is y'all. <3

—Julie & Sierra